IT STARTED AS A FIGHT FOR FREEDOM, IT WILL END AS A FIGHT FOR HUMANITY.

ALICIA McCOMBS

I0640024

THE INSTITUTE Copyright © 2016 All rights reserved.

ISBN: 978-0-9981434-1-5

Editor:
Tiffany Dawn Munn at Owl Editing
Cover Design:
Mallory Rock
Interior Design:
Mallory Rock & The Illustrated Author

The Institute is a work of fiction. Names, characters, places and incidents are products of the author's imagination, or the author has used them fictitiously.

For those who question their reality, don't ever stop

CHAPTER 1

MEMORIES

THEY came in flashes, fragments of a forgotten life, memories of a happy, peaceful time. A family completely unaware of the destruction awaiting them. A daughter and her mother, Margaret, laughing at the small table sitting next to an open fireplace. The meal sparse, barely enough to calm the demand coming from their bellies. But the company and conversation more than compensated. The smiles and laughter genuine. There was no fear or unknown. Margaret reached over, brushing away a stray hair as she leaned into the caress. She tried holding onto her mother's smile and the sound of her voice, but her memories were fickle things, coming and dispersing as they pleased.

Reliving the bits and pieces of her life that came to her while she slept was the only sense of peace she knew. She could see the smiles and sun kissed skin, hear the laughter in the breeze flowing through their hair. They were free and happy, but then she would wake up. The longer she was awake, the harder it was to remember. A great dream faded into the abyss of the mind the instant the alarm went off.

As it buzzed, the patient kicked the white sheet and blanket off, standing up just in time for the bed to retract into the floor, replaced by a single chair and table for one.

It was Thursday, and Thursdays served up two hard boiled eggs, half a pink grapefruit, and eight ounces of orange juice. No salt; that was unhealthy. The buzz of breakfast arriving was always a good sound. She sat and ate. It was the same every day: after she awoke, she ate breakfast, and after breakfast came the morning shower, followed by a literary session. Every morning was the same in the Institute.

As the patient ate she wondered, *why is it the same every Thursday?* She wondered because she hated pink grapefruit. Shocked that she could ever forget that, she decided not to eat it. The walls surrounding her instantly glowed red; lights came up from the floor accompanied by a different, louder alarm. She instantly knew something was wrong. The sound of the door sliding open brought out her curiosity.

"Prisoner 142/262, you have been marked for restoration. Please come with us." Three men in white uniforms appeared on the east wall of the cubicle.

She stood stepping around her table, glancing back in time to see her breakfast vaporize and the table and chair retract into the floor. She couldn't recall the last time she'd been outside her cubicle, although the goose flesh on her arms said it perhaps was not a good thing.

Following the uniforms down the corridor, her eyes and mind wandered. The walls and floors were white, just like the inside of her cubicle. About every eight steps another corridor leading off to both sides appeared. As she walked she beheld the vast space consisting of the patient floor. The height of the ceiling was tremendous. Along the edges of the room more men in white uniforms were stationed above each row of cubicles. They were spaced evenly among the cubicles, all with their hands at their sides, at attention. The third man in white followed closely. He didn't glance down at her, just kept straight forward.

They took a left and a right, going through a doorway into a wide hallway littered with doors. A flush of adrenaline tingling through her body, her mouth fell open as she thought she saw someone that looked just like her suspiciously moving along the hallway wall. Except she was dressed in a white coat, her head bald and marked by stitches and foreign objects. The vision came too quickly for her to fully process before fading. Blinking her eyes numerous times, her hand absently found the same spot on her head, now covered with shoulder length hair. Her legs weakened as she came across a raised portion of her scalp—a thin jagged circle. Signs of surgery. She left her hand on her head, not trusting herself to be able to keep it from shaking.

The guard placed his hand on her arm and moved her along, down the hallway into a smaller room. The white theme remained constant here as well; a full body support chair loomed in the middle, chrome trays and instruments strategically placed around the edges. This room did not welcome her.

"Prisoner-142/262 reporting for restoration, Doctor," the man on the left announced, his hand still holding her arm just above the elbow. His firm grip, pinky barely brushing the inner part of her arm, created a tingly sensation she did not enjoy crawling over her skin.

"Yes, thank you. You may go," a smooth voice ordered.

Turning, the two men went around her, leaving. The third stepped off to the left, disappearing. She watched them go, the door appearing from the ceiling and sealing the way out. Her pulse raced. A small noise drew her attention to a tall, fit woman, with light blonde hair perched in a bun on the top of her head, wearing a white coat flowing down to her knees. She held a white data pad in her hands. "Sit there," she instructed, pointing to a reclining chair in the middle of the room.

"Why? What's going to happen when I do?" The first time—to the patient's recollection—she spoke. With no interaction, there was no need to speak. The expression on the doctor's face confirmed there was still no need.

"No questions. Sit, now." The doctor was unyielding. The leer on her face changed upon seeing the patient.

Squeezing her eyes shut, understanding she'd receive no other option, she did as she was told. Placed herself on the chair in the middle of the room, which was cold. A shiver made its way up her spine.

"What is restoration?" The question stunned her as much as it made the doctor angry. Quickly pursing her lips together, the patient stared straight at the ceiling—it being the only place to scrutinize once in the chair. Uncertain of what else to expect, or what the doctor would do.

With a slight hiss then a click of success, clamps quickly covered her forehead, wrists, ankles, chest, and waist, holding her in place. She jumped, a squeal escaping her lips as she unsuccessfully struggled, straining to regard the doctor.

"Stay calm; it's just part of the procedure. Precautions meant to keep you from fighting and thrashing too hard while I administer the serum." The doctor wheeled a cart holding a computer screen and keyboard on it close to the patient's head. She placed a suction cup attached to a wire firmly on the patient's right temple, her gaze lingering on the patient's eyes, confusion and fascination in her own. Visibly forcing herself to remove her gaze, she stepped behind the chair and grabbed a tray of needles and vials.

The patient's eyes went wide, the blood draining from her face, beads of sweat appearing on her lip and forehead, cool against the antiseptic air of the room. She pleaded with the doctor, but the woman simply smiled, filling the syringe with liquid from a bottle labeled M-2/194.

She held back a cry as the doctor pushed the tip of the needle into her right arm, gently pushing the plunger. The serum seared its way through her veins. Jumping as much as the chair would allow, she bit down on her tongue to keep from screaming. Pain was not something she was familiar with, or something she wanted to experience ever again. She watched the pea green medicine shoot into her arm and thrashed against the restraints even more, the clamps rubbing against her skin. She could feel it, the serum burning the insides of her veins, forging a path to her heart. Her heart wildly pumping in anticipation—to receive it and pass it on. The further the serum traveled the less she could feel; the pain dissipated. Her body finally in acceptance.

Re-opening her eyes, the patient continued to jerk and squirm, and she noticed a name tag upon the left pocket of the pristine jacket the doctor wore. A picture, accompanied by a title too small to read, but the name was broad enough to make out: Dr. Melvina Heizer.

… Suddenly she was on a transport bus full of people. A woman sitting next to her who, strangely, had hair facial features much like her own—round hazel eyes, light brown hair, and high cheekbones—and Dr. Heizer at the front of the bus giving instructions to the passengers.

"You are here because you failed. I'm in charge of making sure you're able to return to your full citizenship in this great country. After your sentence has been completed, you will be able to return to your life.

"When it is your turn to get off the bus, please find the first letter of your last name and go through the corresponding arch; the arch will determine which doctor and facility you will go to next. There will be a nurse on the other side to give you directions."

The patient lay back in the chair connected to the doctor's machine, the vision gone.

"We saw you, what did you do to us? I remember you on the bus. You did the first restoration?" Her heart beat harder and faster as the memory rushed through her mind, fighting the serum, and a small amount of understanding flashed. A flush of heat overtook her. Her mother rode on the bus with her; they had arrived together. The patient knew this; certainty came with the memory; she did not belong here. Loss snagged her heart, pulling it taut. Tears rolled their way down her temples onto the chair, her mouth and throat tight. "Where is she? Where is my mother? Is she here?" Questions spilled out laced with venom, piercing the doctor's façade.

Dr. Heizer's lips thinned, eyes narrowing as she hit a button on the keyboard. "It really doesn't matter now."

It was the last thing the patient heard before everything went black.

DR. Heizer's thoughts accelerated while she paced in circles around the chair where the patient slept. She'd panicked; she understood that now, but no patient in recent history had ever broken protocol. She knew of only one other possessing eyes like this one. Dr. Heizer lifted one of the patient's eyelids, taking in the hazel iris enclosed with a crystalline light blue circle, alarming and dazzling at the same time. It was unsettling. An unusual sign of medication abuse, or experimentation. Dr. Heizer wasn't sure which one to suspect.

"How is this possible?" She talked more to the patient than herself, not meaning to speak out loud. She racked her memories, trying to place the memory the patient accused her of. She welcomed all buses, hundreds of incoming patients; to pinpoint one individual patient in her recollection of blurred faces was not possible.

Dr. Heizer read Patient 142/262's medical file over and over on her data pad. Her eyes ever so slightly glancing at the patient's face, then back to her data pad as her finger scrolled along the screen. Her eyes fell on the same information occupying every patient's chart. Nothing popped out as unusual. The patient, Astrid Stocklin, and her mother, Margaret Stocklin, arrived three months ago for failure to pay the Life Tax. It was all routine, standard. No problems recorded upon her arrival; none that her file mentioned anyway, not even a small note about her conspicuous eyes. Nothing about Patient 142/262 sparked any specific incident Dr. Heizer could recall.

If I don't figure this out before it hits General Thaxton's desk, I might as well restore myself. She called for the security guards through the internal computer system wired through the entire compound. They took the patient back to her cubicle while Dr. Heizer logged the date and time and why she performed another restoration into the patient's file. Along with the girl's eye anomaly, she added a note to have further testing done wanting to know why she was remembering. She pulled up Margaret Stocklin's file and learned that ten days after their arrival, Margaret was transferred due to 'problems with the restoring process.'

Dr. Heizer read on: *Prisoner 144/262 rejected M-2/19. The patient seems to be oblivious, but it only lasts for 14-16 hours at any given time. She is hereby assigned as Experiment 36/48 and will be sent to the Medical Institution for further analysis. —Dr. Menestas Locati.*

Nothing else. Not where this Medical Institution was located or what took place after the patient arrived or what Experiment 36/48 was or if it worked. A headache formed in Dr. Heizer's frontal lobe. She did not understand. Frustrated, she decided to leave it for another day and left the restoration room to do her rounds. Rounding the corner to the first cubicle on her list for the morning, she came to an abrupt stop, in shock, as she noticed it was open—open and empty.

"What's going on here?" she demanded.

The nearest security guard inspected his surroundings, obviously not wanting to be put on the spot. He finally cleared his throat and stepped forward to answer. "General Thaxton wanted to see a prisoner, ma'am. We delivered him half an hour ago to his office." His eyes darted about under her gaze, searching for an escape.

"Were protocols followed?" Knowing the answer, but enjoying the security guard's clear discomfort, Dr. Heizer held her data pad behind her with both hands, her shoulders set and her eyes focused on him.

"No, ma'am." He shook his head, hunched forward.

"Patients aren't to be taken out of their cubicles without certain protocols being followed. This is procedure, as I'm sure you know. If this happens again, you, sir, will be on the other side of these walls."

Without a second thought to the security guard, Dr. Heizer pushed past him, heading to General Thaxton's office. Her heart raced; the stress of this job ebbed away at her a little at a time. The only reason the general took a personal interest in the patients was if something went wrong. Whatever it was, Dr. Heizer hoped that it did not involve her.

CHAPTER 2
QUESTIONS

WHEN patient 142/262 awoke, it was late afternoon, her screen flashing 1:30 PM. She immediately stood with intense fear, realizing she had slept through the day. This was new. Which caused confusion, an emotion she was not used to experiencing.

In an effort to get back to a sense of normalcy, she moved away from her bed, her head cocked to one side as she watched it retract. A table and chair appeared, topped with food. It felt too late in the day for lunch, but when she saw the sandwich and fruit, her stomach grumbled. Immediately she sat and ate. By the food she knew it was Thursday. Thursdays called for grapefruit, and with that thought, the tangy sour taste let itself be known on the back of her tongue, causing a reaction of revulsion. But she had no memory of eating grapefruit or any breakfast at all.

She searched her mind to see if she could remember any events, but ... nothing came to her. The last thing she remembered was ... still nothing. By lunch she should have showered and attended her literary sessions. She ate as the thought that she couldn't remember intensely forced the food down, the sour taste in her mouth going to her rolling stomach.

Patient 142/262 swallowed her last bite, instinctively standing away from the table and chair, knowing they would retract into the floor. A flash of memory materialized: she was watching her breakfast vaporize on her way out of the cubicle. She jumped, gooseflesh crawling across her body. She'd never been out of her cubicle. This was her station, where she was assigned. Never permitted to leave. She didn't understand how she knew this, only that it was the way things were.

Stepping into the shower, the cold high-pressure water brought prominent goose flesh on her arms and legs. She rubbed her hands over her arms, trying to create warmth while gasping as a full flood of the morning's events flashed before her. A face in her mind's eye belonging to Dr. Heizer.

Quickly she returned her face to a blank gaze, trusting her instincts, trying not to disrupt her schedule and alert whoever watched. Eventually the spray warmed, smoothing her skin. She finished scrubbing, waiting nervously for the stall to turn red with an alarm, but nothing happened. Patient 142/262 relaxed, letting the water rush over her as she examined memory after memory, trying at the same time to force interpretation of what she saw, understanding of what she knew and what she didn't. The more she tried, the less came forth, and the more a pain formed behind her forehead, spreading throughout.

The water ceased, the machine deducing she was clean. Not wanting to face Dr. Heizer again, Patient 142/262 decided she must participate. She knew she didn't belong here; this was not her home. She should have a family, a sense of safety. Memories of a family, a home, and a name …

My name is … my name is …

Nothing.

Anger embedded with the frustration, and the pain grew more intense. She found it strange she could remember Dr. Heizer violating her with serum, but she couldn't recall her own name. Patient 142/262 knew what was considered right and wrong, but not why she was here, or how long she had been here. The stall blew hot air, drying her. She

9

immediately raised her arms, turning in slow circles, schedule and familiarity ingrained in her brain. It came easily to her, methodically, her body responding to her cubicle like a lung knowing it was meant to suck air in only to release it again. She didn't have to think what to do next; her body acted separate from her mind, instinctually.

Stepping out of the stall, she grabbed fresh clothes—which appeared on a shelf to her right—and dressed. On the left breast of her long sleeve shirt was stitched 'P-142/262.' The shirt, pants, and underclothes were white, a basic cotton fabric. Always the same, always white. Patient 142/262 ran her fingers through her light brown shoulder-length hair, brushing it back and behind her ears, out of her face. Clutching her arms to her chest, her mind reeled.

THE closer Dr. Heizer got to the general's office, the more butterflies appeared in her stomach. She had only once spoken with the general, over an intercom. Standard routine dictated that patients' autopsy reports be filed with General Thaxton. Dr. Heizer failed, skipping him entirely. She had received a reprimand from him and dreaded a repeat of the experience. In all her time at the Institute, she'd never heard of General Thaxton examining a patient in his office. If anything he should see patients in the exam rooms on the lower floor, chaperoned, never alone. Protocols and procedures.

Arriving at the end of the corridor on the top floor, she slowed as she noticed General Thaxton's door slightly ajar. A bright blue light seeped around it, pulsing sporadically. Voices made their way out, and Dr. Heizer stopped, chills running over her skin.

"I don't understand," floated an unnerved voice, scratchy and unused. "Who are you? Where am I?"

A second voice full of control and power answered, "You are part of something bigger than you'll ever know. I am a scientist. You, the experiment. Now don't move."

Dr. Heizer recognized it the instant she heard it. General Thaxton.

Instead of knocking, Dr. Heizer lingered for what felt like forever. She wanted to understand what was happening. Was this Experiment 36/48? A flash of bright blue light interrupted her thoughts. Only lasting for a split second but so intense it brought tears to her eyes. She covered her eyes and listened, but she heard no sound. She expected a scream of discomfort or something, anything but the eerie silence.

A third voice, nasal and accompanied by a high-pitched whine, broke the malicious quiet. "What do you do with the soul, sir, once it's left the body?"

"Your job is to make sure I have enough prisoners to perform experiments on and that everybody else knows not to question. Are all the papers in order? Has his cubicle been refilled? These are the only questions you should be asking. Now go, and take this wretched thing with you." The general's response came naturally, more irritation than command and accompanied by the sound of shuffling papers, as if he were unwilling to concern himself with such things.

Dr. Heizer jumped, turning on her heels, and headed straight back down the hallway at a slightly faster pace. *Where does the soul go?* This troubled her to a level she couldn't comprehend. Having never been a religious person, she wasn't sure she even believed in a soul. She believed in things substantial, things she could see and touch, but the idea of having it—her soul or essence, whatever made up what she was—ripped out of her made the bile at the bottom of her gut rise into her throat without consent. She turned the corner, quickly stopping to lean against the wall.

Don't throw up. She repeated this to herself numerous times, working to get her breath and heart rate under control, fighting the threatening panic attack. Behind her approached the owner of the third voice, moving down the hallway at a brisk pace, accompanied by a squeaky wheel on the tiled floor.

Dr. Heizer straightened up and turned to create an appearance of authority, like she hadn't just been about to throw up against the wall. As she turned the corner, so did the gurney with the covered body. She collided with the foot end of the gurney, failing to keep her balance so that she ended up bending over the stretcher. Her hands landed right on the body's thighs, and a heave forced out of her mouth. Instantly the man pushing the gurney pulled back, apologizing for not watching where he was going.

"Hello, Mrs. Heizer, is there anything I can help you with?" He was a short man with fiery red hair and wore a pressed black pin-striped suit with a soft pink dress shirt and a white tie. His voice, coming through his nose and following a whine, scraped razors along her nerves. He seemed to realize that she was confused and introduced himself as Matthew Benson, General Thaxton's assistant.

"Doctor, actually. It's Dr. Heizer. I was on my way to see the general; is he available? Is this a patient of mine?" She tried not to speak too fast and show her nervousness but rather to project a vibe of command.

Matthew Benson did not respond immediately He regarded her with a form of contempt she wasn't sure what to do with. "No, General Thaxton wishes not to be disturbed, and this is a prisoner, but no longer one of yours, Dr. Heizer." He put a bit too much emphasis on the 'doctor' portion of her name.

He must really think himself above me.

The disrespect adding to her growing frustration.

"If you'll excuse me I need to get on with my duties." He pushed the gurney past her, around the corner and out of sight.

With a sigh of relief, she waited, counting to three hundred before returning to her office. After what she'd seen and heard, Dr. Heizer was no longer in the mood to face the general, gladly accepting that he didn't want to see her now.

She traced the same path; going down 111 floors was a long elevator ride, but not nearly long enough to grasp the implications of the knowledge she held. Along the way, the empty cubicle beckoned her.

Only it was no longer empty.

Another patient occupied the cubicle, with the same number as the man before. Dr. Heizer turned to her data pad to pull up P-110/262. She didn't know all the patients' files or names. There was no way to know if the information had updated with the new patient or not. She threw her hands in the air, an exasperated sigh leaving her as she gathered the strength she needed to finish her rounds.

TORO Crow found himself twelve stories below the surface of the Institute. His soft white shoes making no noise as he made his way down a silent corridor. Toro's dark skin and hair were a stark contrast against his starched and pressed to perfection white uniform. He knew he had no reason to be down here, but the questions gnawing at him and constantly churning inside fueled him to go on, forcing his feet step after step. His heart followed along with his instincts, thumping loudly in his ears.

His concerns had bubbled up months prior when he stopped a prisoner from escaping; she had been weak, but burned with a passionate fire. Knowledge pursued him through her eyes, sparking Toro's curiosity and quest for answers. Her eyes, the prisoner's beautiful eyes he would never forget: a light hazel with gold streaks, outlined by a crystal blue fit only for royalty. She had begged and pleaded for mercy, even fought him and demanded an explanation. Toro didn't waiver; he didn't give in. Instead he marched her back to the exam room under force and strapped her to the chair.

Her screams pierced his ears even now, adding fuel to his quest. Her touch still caused his hairs to stand, forcing his hand to absently find his other, helping to calm the nerves, to lessen the want of her touch. The prisoner was not scared or frightened; she was pissed off for what was happening to her. Toro wanted to know why.

His gaze followed the once white walls and floor recently turned a shade of gray from neglect and disuse. He took his time reading the plaques next to the doors, stretching out the inevitable. The first on the left read '2036.' He tilted his head with a serious grin and advanced forward. If all of these rooms were sorted by years, there was a ways to go; this gave him little comfort, but he took what he got. Forty-six doors later he found the one he wanted.

13

Placing his left wrist up to the scanner beside the door, he waited for it to read the clearance chip located just below his skin. His heart palpitated quickly. Would he have access? Would the scan notify his boss of his actions? The lock clicked, and Toro's eyes widened with curiosity, surprised that he was granted clearance. Stepping through the entryway, rows of metal containers, each with labels and handles down the center, greeted him. Entering farther he grasped a handle and pulled gently.

A drawer, full of paper, stared back at him. Tabs stuck out every few inches with indicators. Toro wondered what they could be.

Having been born shortly after the digital age took over, he'd never actually seen paper. This sight filled him with reservations. Paper should no longer exist; it had become a rare item, traded on black markets and at underground shops.

Important information had been recorded digitally and backed up into the Maintained Integrated Sonic Transmission. M.I.S.T. had been set up by the government as a way to control information, and keeping records on paper was expressly forbidden under a penalty of death.

Law breaking scratched against everything Toro stood for. Toro's father and his father before him had both been guards in the Institute; the job passed from generation to generation, along with the morals and ethics. But his father had been killed while on duty years before his retirement, and now Toro was left to decipher what was right on his own. Though he had a feeling his training wouldn't have included what to do in this situation.

Not knowing what he pursued, Toro caressed the tabs lightly, pulling out a random file labeled 'P-98/2031.' Opening the file, he read:

Patient Name: Annalise Lynn Hirsch <P-98/2082>
Date of Birth: 16th day of February, 2076
Date of Death: 21st day of October, 2082
Restoration Date: 23rd day of September, 2082
Restoration Age: 6 years old
Doctor: Menestas Locati
Notes:

Patient restoration process administered at 11:02 AM on 23.9.2031. Patient accepted.

07.10.2031 7:33 AM: Patient was recorded asking for her mother. Blood tests and brain scans show M-2/93 broke down on a cellular level. An antibody was discovered in the patient's blood cells that work as an enzyme to break down the compound and restore patient to normal brain function. Requested bone marrow test.

11.10.2031 9:16 PM: Patient continues to reject restoration processes. Recommended for Experiment 36/48.

21.10.2031 7:41 PM: Patient did not survive Experiment 36/48. Harvested tissue for more research.

A beautiful little girl watched him from her picture placed on the inside of the file. Long black hair, curious eyes, an excited smile, and love pouring from her very soul.

"Experiment? They're experimenting?" Toro muttered.

Gazing around, he began to understand why there were paper records. To keep the information hidden, to keep it secret from the public—more censored truth. Toro believed in the government, in their rules. He had been raised to not question laws or the way of things. Now he burned with doubt and anger. The government did have hostile tendencies, and he was standing in the bowels of its most deranged moment. It disgusted him, and the more Toro learned the harder he gripped the files. His knuckles turning white, the papers shaking furiously in his hands.

He grew frantic, ripping through the storage room with passion, jerking open filing cabinets and pulling out random files to read the same thing. Every one of them sent to an experiment, every one of them dead. Men, women, children, fathers, mothers, sisters, brothers, sons, and daughters. His heart wrenched; his soul ripped. How could they do this?

Whole families destroyed, sending ripples of pain and loss through time, years of death and lies, but what could he do? Who could he tell?

His supervisor was a doctor who administered foreign substances into unwilling prisoners. Other employees—none of whom Toro befriended in his months there—were there simply for the job. Would they be strong enough to keep this secret? Could they join forces and take a stand against their employer? Not likely.

This storage room a black scar, an ugly scar the government was desperately trying to hide, and Toro needed to bring it to light. With determination, he hoped his only option was a better person than she was a doctor, that she possessed more humanity than he thought.

DR. Heizer was recruited not because of her PHD or references, but because of her innate ability to overlook the corporate level breaking of the rules—this didn't mean she agreed with it, but that she could ignore it to do her job. She never much cared for how they made their money, so long as she was on the outside of the cubicles.

She was twenty-eight when she fell behind on her Life Tax and received the notice. She remembered the cold sweat covering her body as she read the notice, the ugly yellow paper taped to her door, dread flowing through her. She was an intern at the only hospital left on the West Coast. People from all over the western region went to that hospital. Her rotations were overwhelming and usually only left a few hours a day to rest and eat. Her student loans were astronomical and demanded over 85 percent of her income. Being a doctor was a terrible career choice, but she wanted to help. So she did. Dr. Heizer beat all odds making it to medical school. And there she stood, being told to turn herself over for not being able to pay the government for the privilege of living in their country.

She was sick, first in the kitchen, again in the bathroom. There were people who depended on her, ones she couldn't leave behind. The dread settling in her stomach would not leave, a heavy stone weighing her down, sending everything she tried to eat right back up. She wasn't sure what she should do. She wouldn't run. Dr. Heizer always played the hand dealt her, and this was just another hand to play. Crappy cards, but still a hand.

Upon registering herself with the Acceptance Agent three days later, she'd been informed that she possessed certain skills they needed. After six meetings and failed negotiations for all of her requests, she was employed by the same government previously trying to imprison her. Now, she imprisoned other citizens unable to pay.

After being employed, she received her doctorate and became Dr. Melvina Heizer, Head of Admissions and Restoration at the L.A. Institute.

Soon after, she decided to do some research on the Life Tax, her initiation like a bad smell in the fridge you just can't find the source of. Much of the history of the country was destroyed during the confusion of the second Civil War, but the story of the Life Tax survived. In the middle of the twenty-third century, the United States government began to implement the Life Tax. It started slowly. There had always been state tax, sales tax, alcohol and marijuana taxes. Next came the pharmaceutical taxes. The percentages rose, and citizens grew desperate. The only ones who could pay the taxes belonged to the upper class, which included Congress and that 1 percent who were the richest citizens.

The announcement of the Life Tax was met with great hostility, which was quickly suppressed by force. About 40 percent of the population was lost to the government takeover only lasting fifty-three days—men, woman, and children armed only with knives and baseball bats shot in mass. It was quick, efficient, and effective.

It came like a cleansing usually does: not needed or wanted, forced on the people. The streets ran with blood. The borders closed. You either agreed, or you died.

Dr. Heizer was in charge of the Western Collection. Any citizens who failed to pay the Life Tax were collected and bused to the West Coast Institution located in Los Angeles. She performed the restoration on all incoming patients, overseeing the intake process. She was also to make sure any problems with the restoration were recorded and corrected. Before this morning, there had never been any problems.

Sitting in her office updating charts, Dr. Heizer replayed that morning's incident.

Curiosity was often the biggest problem. The compound known as M-2/194 could squash love, family, and a will to be free. Curiosity always shone through.

"Excuse me, Dr. Heizer?" Toro, a six-foot-tall guard wearing a military haircut and a scar above his right eyebrow, skidded to a stop inside Dr. Heizer's office, out of breath and sweat on his brow. "Do you have a moment?" His nervousness showed through his hands unwillingly shaking the files of papers clutched in his fists.

Dr. Heizer noticed the papers before showing her irritation with the young guard's disruption. Duty warred with curiosity, and curiosity won.

CHAPTER 3

ANSWERS

THERE'S an enzyme in DNA which defeats the compound, brings back their memories? The patient this morning—this happened before? Under Dr. Locati? Do we know how many failed?" Dr. Heizer's questions emerged faster than Toro could answer.

"Hundreds, thousands, possibly more. I would have to do more research, ma'am. Do we, or you, I mean, have access to the records of Experiment 36/48?"

"No, I arrived after Dr. Locati was assimilated into the program. I didn't even know the experiment existed until this morning. How many rooms did you say are down there?"

"Hundreds, but I'm unsure how many are filled. It's ..." He trailed off.

"It's what?" Dr. Heizer prompted, lifting an eyebrow.

"It's all paper records, ma'am, like the file there. All of them."

"That's impossible. We are a *government* owned and operated establishment," she explained, her hand slapping against her desk. "What you say is treason. Punishable by death, or worse, assimilation."

"I understand, but if that were the case, why do we have security clearance?"

"What do you mean 'we?'" she asked, suddenly appearing calm. "*We* do not have anything. *You* seem to have it. What exactly do you do here, Toro Crow?" Dr. Heizer stayed behind her desk, sitting comfortably, no longer showing any signs of anxiety.

He scrambled to describe his job. "Whatever is needed. It was introduced as a floater job, although technically I'm a security guard. My initiation consisted of a tour and how not to interact with the prisoners; it was a rather hurried process."

"Patients," she corrected. "Interesting, I thought you were just another guard." She fell into deep thought, seeming to be distraught regarding the experiment.

Toro waited in silence, then spoke. "Ma'am, I saw an empty cubicle earlier. What happened to the prisoner?"

The disgust on her face confirmed Toro's fears. He needed to convince her to help him, but before he could speak, the doctor did.

"They are patients." Her voice stern, driving her connection in, forcing Toro to see them as patients—not prisoners. She back, regarding Toro, a decision he hoped was in his favor being made in the silence perched between them.

Toro stepped forward and opened his mouth only to be cut off by a wave of the doctor's hand. He stopped, got comfortable in his stance, and waited.

"How far do you want to take this? Pulling these records alone is treason. Heck, knowledge of these records is a death sentence, so why risk showing them to me?"

Toro had noticed Dr. Heizer's stress as soon as he entered the room. The lines around her mouth never smoothed, and her fingers twitched against each other. Now was his chance; something else had brought her to the edge—he needed to help her get the rest of the way.

"I am by no means just a security guard or someone who is happy just getting by. Something is amiss here, and whether we like it or not, we're a part of it. They're killing people. We can't change the past, but maybe we can help make our future a better place to live—unmarked by fear and control." A breath, a pause to give Dr. Heizer time to process, to realize they could change, they could help. "I can't do this alone. I chose you because I don't believe you are one to hurt or cause unnecessary—"

"Do not presume what I am or am not willing to do. I will do what is necessary for me and mine, and what you're asking is treason."

"I understand." Toro rolled his shoulders, trying to drive the stress out of his neck.

"What exactly are you asking of me?" Her face stern again, she squinted at him, trying to force truth he wasn't sure he had.

"To help me."

"Help you with what? Be specific. I don't have all day." No remorse, no sympathy.

"I don't know exactly what we can do, but we have to do something. Maybe start with getting more information. I heard we're expecting an outside crew soon, so why the reinforcements? And what reason would the general have to remove a patient from his cubicle? What did he do to him?"

"He's dead."

Something broke insider her. The big, deep breath Dr. Heizer took shook her whole body, making a visible change in how she carried herself. She no longer sat ramrod straight in her chair. Her shoulders slumped.

"You need help," she said, "but I can't help you. I have too much at stake here. There's a group who can though." Her eyes grew big, hinting for him to know without her having to say the words.

Toro waited. Was she thinking about the Reformers? People who disowned the government, excommunicated and wanted by the U.S. to every degree. When caught, there was no trial, no judgment of peers. Instant death, public execution, and not just them. Everybody connected to them was instantly hunted down, arrested, and shot on sight.

To endanger himself was one thing, but to knowingly threaten everyone he knew for a chance to say 'you're wrong' was unthinkable. Inconceivable. The people in his life flashed in front of him. His mom. His siblings, aunts, uncles, cousins, friends, coworkers, acquaintances. The old lady who lived in his building and brought fruit to him every day. Did she count? Could he knowingly threaten their lives as well?

"Hello, are you listening?" Dr. Heizer became frustrated with his distraction. Her face was disgusted, worried, and intrigued all at the same time.

"Sorry, I was thinking. Apologies," he replied, shaking his head. "The stakes are raised if I use them. They ask more than I'm willing to give."

Pros and cons listed themselves in his head; Toro weighed his options.

"You raised the stakes going down there, again when you removed this." Dr. Heizer picked up the paper file and let it fall back to her desk with a dull thud. "You made your decision already, Toro. Get out of my office before you take me down with you."

Thoughts of all the ways the government invaded and controlled his life listed themselves in his head, but Toro silently agreed, excusing himself.

Traversing along the main floor through rows and columns of cubicles each housing a single prisoner, Toro's world rested on the edge of an abyss. He knew going forward meant certain death. The government was not to be trifled with. He had been born into this world exactly how it was. He grew up knowing no different, accepting that this was life and it was not going to be anything better. He accepted this at an early age. To always obey, even if he didn't agree or like the situation. Was he destined to live in fear the rest of his life?

A buzz in his ear signaled his presence being requested and pulled him from his thoughts. Rounding a corner, he came across a well-dressed man with bright red hair reciting orders to fifteen guards standing in a semicircle around him, all fully dressed in combat gear.

"I've given you security clearance to access the storage rooms. Remember, nothing survives. Everything must be destroyed. These orders come straight from the president, and we are not to question them. You'll see things you won't understand. Don't read or think, just burn it all. Storage starts on sub-level twelve. The incinerator is on sub-level one. You have a lot of work and aren't to stop until it's completed. Another team is being sent from our sister institution. They'll be briefed and sent down upon arrival." The redhead clasped his hands behind his back, rocking back on his heels, grinning. "All right, off you go."

Toro stood in shock, his blood ice cold. *They know! How do they know?*

"You there! You're Toro Crow, correct?" the man bellowed.

Toro startled, his heart in his throat, but immediately regained enough composure to answer. "Yes, sir."

"You're to help these men clean out old medical records. Clearance has already been granted. The captain will bring you up to speed." He sauntered past him and up a stairwell.

"Captain?" Toro whispered, trying not to show the dots connecting themselves in his head.

"That would be me." A tall, well-built man with a stern expression stepped forward. The company of guards with him wore the same uniform: white and gray combat gear with a loaded side arm. *Be ready for everything* was the motto. This guy took the motto to heart. He could be a poster boy for the Marines. "Captain John Rhodes. You're confused, so I'll clear it up for you. New chain of command in every Institute, effective now. Fifteen men who are highly trained were pulled off the streets to burn paper. One current man from every Institute to join us, show us around. Basically, you're my lap dog." The group of men behind him snickered. "Your name again?"

Toro looked at every man before him, each easily taller than him, each more intimidating. "Toro Crow."

"Well, Mr. Crow, welcome to the ranks. We just arrived and are headed down to storage. Show us the way."

Captain Rhodes didn't move, but he seemed rather larger the closer Toro got. Forced to go around him, he pushed his way through the rest of the unit. Every man was big. Their arms were the size of Toro's neck.

Swallowing, Toro hit the button on the wall for the service elevator. They didn't know, did they? He received clearance because he was assigned to help these guys destroy it, destroy the paper records, the evidence he was trying to collect and save.

They don't know.

Toro watched as these men, his new unit, pulled out file after file throwing them into containers to be burned. All this information, all this proof, gone. He helped reluctantly, although he paid attention to the details of the files going from the drawers to the bins by his hands. Names, facts, birth dates, followed by death dates. Too fast to catch cause of death or the presiding doctor. If he concentrated on the doctor he missed their names. Names were important; names held who these people were as humans; their names proved they existed.

"Well this is bloody boring. Brought from the excitement of the streets to burn papers," one of the men said.

The British accent gave something away. The borders had been closed for close to three hundred years. Europe was at peace, unwilling to fight the Americans over something that didn't affect them. The speaker saw the speculation on Toro's face.

"Yes, British. Recruited by your government to help fight the Reformers. Apparently there's a shortage of loyalty amongst your military branches. Believe me, chap, I'm not the only outside recruit. Name's Logan Jackson. I go by Jackson."

Shaking his hand, Toro introduced himself. "Outside reinforcements? We have sunk to a new low."

"Fascinating, isn't it? The world stood by and watched this once proud country fall to the bitter pits and did absolutely nothing to help, only to wait and send soldiers to aid. After all, you were only hurting yourselves. Trade continued, international relations had never been better, you buggers were going after your own people," Jackson explained, shaking his head, "Personally I think it's out of fear."

"Thanks for the history lesson," Toro snarked, not wanting to elaborate on anything Jackson reported, but what he volunteered was correct. They had gone after their own; tourists were sent home and immigrants sought out and presented an opportunity to leave—but only one. If they chose to stay, they gained citizenship and were treated just like the rest of them. That had just been the beginning.

"Just making conversation. How is it you became a guard for the biggest institute in the country?"

"Luck of the draw. My father was one, and this job is passed down through blood lines. I was born to the right man, educated and trained specifically for this post."

"You sound thrilled. Still, you're luckier than most. You should be grateful," Jackson stated, lifting a handful of files and tossing them in the open bin.

"Maybe. Being lucky, however it comes about, always leaves you with a choice to make sense of the responsibility. Even if you don't agree."

They fell into a comfortable working silence. It did not go unnoticed to Jackson, though, how Toro skimmed the files before tossing them. Toro observed Jackson watching him, hoping he also would read the valuable information he was hired to destroy. Eventually curiosity won over, and Jackson's eyes fell to the files in his own hands.

Hours passed, and Toro's head was on the verge of imploding. Still unable to devise a way to smuggle information out caused frustration to grow in the pit of his stomach. Jackson stuck close by as they moved from drawer to drawer, aisle to aisle. His new captain seemed fair, working just as hard right alongside his men, complaining just as loudly about his current place and orders. Tedious work, but necessary.

"What the hell is Experiment 36/48?" one of the men asked when the captain was out of the room.

"No questions. That was our order," Captain Rhodes interjected as he passed through the doorway.

Their heads snapped to attention, every head but one.

"It has to do with brain function. Try—"

The captain cut off the offending speaker with a reprimand. The soldier jerked unhappily to attention, obviously taking a great force of his own will to turn back to his duty. His eyes were blank as he spoke, glaring at the floor.

"Soldier, do not make me say it again. Our job is to destroy these papers, not read them, and surely not to question our commanders.

Anymore of this talk and I'll assimilate you myself." His loyalties ran deep, no remorse and no question. After his declaration, he grabbed a bin and headed out.

Toro watched as he passed, then searched for the outspoken soldier. He hadn't moved from his spot, still crouched over a lower drawer in the back corner.

"Who is that?" he asked Jackson.

"Red. He came from Vegas before being assigned with us. He doesn't talk much, but when he does it's with such anger his whole face goes, well, red. He hates the institutes more than most. He's seen firsthand what they do," Jackson replied solemnly.

"I need to talk to him."

Jackson chuckled. "Go ahead, man, just don't let the captain see you."

Toro took the current opportunity of the captain's absence to approach Red. It didn't take him long to get Red to finish, the words already formed and fighting to be released.

"—Trying to stamp out freethinking and individuality. If assimilation into the Institute fails, patients are sent to Vegas. The Experimental Institute is strictly for the experiment patients. Zombies, they are. Useless shells of former beings." The horrors he relived were plain on his face, forcing Toro to stay silent, not wanting to push for more.

THE shock was like lightning through the brain. A flash flood of memories, the dam breaking loose, letting the colors of love, family, and life rush forward. Blue was her favorite color. Brown, the color of her mother's hair; green, her eyes. Red, the color of her favorite shirt.

Astrid.

The recognition of her name was instantaneous, and along with it knowledge like she'd never known. She knew herself, and she knew that she didn't belong here.

Anger followed, filling every fiber of her being, causing her vision to go white. But she dared not move from the bed and risk letting them know she remembered. That she remembered everything, including the fact that her mother, the only family she had, was there with her. Tears threatened to fall as the pain of loss and separation replaced the animosity. Her chest grew tight, and her hands fisted as she replayed their parting in her head.

No, she thought. *No!*

Astrid got control of herself just as the first bell went off, surprised her thoughts hadn't yet given her away. Time to wake up.

Yes indeed, time to wake up.

The day was the same as any other; Astrid ate, showered, brushed her teeth. Neurological training, followed by lunch, physical conditioning, reading, fake social interaction, ending with dinner. Day after day, the same boring routine. The hardest part was pretending. Accepting. One step out of place and they would know. The guards would appear, taking her back to that doctor. Heizer. Clever Dr. Heizer. Hatred flowed through her body with her blood. Feeding her need for revenge, or maybe just justice. They came quietly, Astrid and her mother, followed all the rules, only to be betrayed. Their memories wiped, placed in a cell, treated as mice in a lab.

Astrid understood the blame was not hers; the fault lay with the government. The Life Tax was the explanation. Her mother warned her they couldn't pay, and what would follow. Four jobs, rationed food, nothing personal, so that sixty percent of their income could purchase the right to live. It was debilitating. A disease had taken the country, eating away at its good citizens, leaving the corrupt and greedy to take over.

History taught them it had started with the jobless. A way to force every citizen into gainful employment while helping the country pay off its massive debts. The threat of becoming a prisoner should have been enough, and at first, it was. Everybody who could afford to pay, did. Those who could not, found more work. In the first year only 3 percent of the population failed. The following year the fee was doubled. There were riots and refusals by the masses. People were shot in the streets. New laws were created to strip citizens of their weapons, the only way they had to protect themselves. And they were still forced to pay. The cycle continued until the government got what they wanted: the few select rich in control, a government that owed nothing to anyone, and an entire country in fear of the next law.

Citizens lived and worked, their hands and backs broken and bloody. Dreams turned into goals, and the only goal was to survive. The first step citizens took was to refuse to give the government any more people to control by refusing to procreate. They would rather die than bring children into this world, children who would just become slaves. But as always in the past, the government was prepared with a solution. For every child birthed, the mother would be exempt from the Life Tax for the next five years. What a brilliant plan: have children and the government left you alone. The announcement that the Life Tax was for everyone was announced within a year after. Yes, the mom was exempt, but the children were not, the father still not. Population had spiked. Morale and hope were beaten back down, and the government won again.

Fear of the government was engrained in every citizen. To do as they were told, keep their heads down, work, and pay. A vicious cycle for years. Until a certain man decided to run instead of turn himself in. He disappeared, and soon after were attacks; resistance rose. Hope was alive after all. The Reformers were established, proving a sharp thorn in the government's side, unreachable. Digging deeper with every opportunity.

Astrid had heard of the Reformers. They represented freedom, peace. To be a part of the resistance fighting for more than survival.

Astrid wanted that; she wanted to live, not just survive.

MINUTES turned into hours, hours into a blur of days running together. Astrid still had not been discovered, but that left little room for peace. She thought it odd but didn't dwell on it for too long. Since her last visit to Dr. Heizer, she had not been out of her confined space. All social contact was through a screen appearing on her wall: social and mind games played with other patients in cells mirroring hers.

Her frustration and boredom grew. Bored of the same schedule. Frustrated with the lack of human contact. Worried about her mother. She lost what little patience she possessed, making the smallest of tasks arduous. Lunch appeared in time to keep her from screaming out every curse word she knew. Astrid sat down, grabbing her tuna sandwich, ripping off a bite.

The ground beneath her feet shook, following a rumbling sound growing with the physical disturbance, forcing the walls surrounding her to wobble back and forth. Glass shattered in the distance, and Astrid's world filled with dust and smoke. She stood to better stabilize herself, her heart beating faster, palms sweating. She could hear the confusion enclosing her with thick smoke, noise from other prisoners filling in the spaces surrounding her.

One wall slid away, giving her a way out. She wanted to bolt immediately, but she hesitated. She could barely see or breathe enough to bolt into the fray. The dust penetrated her nose, throat, down to her lungs. The pain of trying to breathe engulfed all she was. Shock and confusion had quickly replaced her anger and boredom.

She stumbled forward, reaching for the frame of the wall. Coughing, she peeked down the corridor. Both ways prisoners emerged, screaming with fear as they weakly stumbled, trying to get away from the debris and smoke filling the corridor.

Gaining nerve and strength, Astrid took a tentative step outside the threshold. The smoke was thicker to the right causing less visibility, giving her no way to determine which way would be better. She picked a direction and took her first step into the chaos. The only ones daring enough to take on the Institute would be the Reformers; she wanted to find them. Glassy eyed prisoners poking through the smoke as she passed them; confusion only one of the ailments they battled. At the end of the corridor she took a left, following her instincts. Picking up speed, holding her sleeve over her nose and mouth, she ran. The adrenaline kicking up made her heart beat in time with her feet.

A coughing fit overtook her, forcing her to slow. She fell to her knees. Her vision blurry with tears overflowing, trying to clear stinging smoke from her eyes. Closer to the floor breathing became easier, the air a little clearer. Stretching out, she laid her cheek flat on the floor. A shard of glass made its way into her cheek, causing a new, warm wetness. Catching her breath, she tried to ease the pain overtaking her body. She searched her surroundings, attempting to recognize something, anything. Staring back at her from a far corner crouched a little boy. Blond hair, green eyes, and tears streaking his chubby cheeks, his pale skin glowing with a few freckles. He wore a white outfit identical to Astrid's.

The fear emanating from his unblinking eyes imitated her own. Without thinking, Astrid crawled to him. She grabbed his hand, standing in a low crouch, his tiny hand warm and so small within hers, giving no resistance to her comfort and guidance. His hand held tight, aching for contact, an unspoken bond of trust desperately needing companionship, and it fed Astrid with new determination to get out. She jogged, dragging the boy behind her.

Running along a corridor, she slowed to step over debris once belonging to the surrounding cubicles. Guards and prisoners alike were scattered amongst the rubble. Long pieces of steel contorted and sticking out at odd angles around them. Stepping around bodies and climbing over destroyed materials, moving forward to what she assumed was the outside wall. Having no way of knowing other than the air whirlwinds picking up speed around them. The gray, dirty smoke turned into swirls and moved toward the outer wall with slight patterns and an unfriendly beauty. Marking their passage to clear skies. Both coughed, constantly rubbing the tears from their eyes.

"There," Astrid called, pointing. "Come on, we're almost out." She hurried, moving faster. The closer they got the faster she moved. Her legs shaking, her body protesting at the sudden increase in activity, but she pushed on. "Almost, keep moving. We're almost there." She talked to encourage herself more than the boy behind her who was trying desperately to keep with her pace in his drug-induced confusion.

Upon reaching a gaping hole in the wall, Astrid slowed, uncertain of what lay ahead. Her instincts silent, letting fear creep its way up her spine. They snaked along the wall holding hands, holding back coughs and sneezes, climbing up the now destroyed side of the building. Coming upon a giant crevice in the wall, she peeked outside, lifting just the top of her eyes above the jagged mount of concrete. There were people everywhere, some in white like her and the boy, and others in black; scattered dark spots within the sea of white spilling onto the pavement. Beyond the throng of confused people buses were stationed accepting the people in white.

"They're taking prisoners!" Astrid exclaimed as fear left her entirely and was replaced by hope, which in her current position could be argued as a much harsher feeling. Stopping at the top after lowering the little boy to the ground on the other side, she paused. A tingling on the back of her neck forced the hairs to stand up on end. At first she tried to ignore it, the feeling of being watched, of eyes on her backside.

Peeking down at the boy with a smile of assurance, she glanced over her left shoulder and observed the scene behind her. Smoke was clearing, the dust settling on every available surface, and just above the vast space holding a maze of cubicles perched two men. Each with their eyes directly on Astrid. The one on the right, tall and bulky, a military type, nodded slightly, giving her the extra courage she needed to move forward; the other man, his dark skin offsetting his white uniform in an admirable way and his dark hair vivid in the contrast of the surrounding lack of color, stood with his hands held together by metal. His head cocked slightly to the right in wonderment. He was curious, Astrid could tell; he wondered what she was going to do.

She decided not to disappoint.

She moved, carefully stepping over the rubble and avoiding landing on the boy. Moving swiftly down the outside edge of the building, she retrieved the boy's hand. The mass of people overwhelmed Astrid as they drew closer to the blue and white buses. She started moving at a slower pace, and people closed in around them, obviously taking comfort in the newly found open air.

The boy jerked Astrid's hand mumbling something, but she was distracted with the many new forms of contact. It had been such a long while since she was this close to so many people. The noises and smells assaulted her senses. The constant intrusion from elbows, hands, and feet set fire to her every nerve. They fell in line behind an older gentleman with graying hair, waiting to board the nearest bus and trying hard to watch their own elbows and feet.

A man in black coursed through the mass of prisoners with a megaphone up to his mouth giving directions. "I know you're confused. Please stay calm. We're with the Reformers, and we're here to help. Anybody dressed in black with a red band around their right bicep can be trusted. Please line up to get on a bus. We will take you to safety. We have shelter, clothes, and food. Please stay calm. You're going to be okay."

The man moved along the lines, patting prisoners reassuringly. The prisoners in white streaming from the building lined up in a serene way, facing forward. A drugged stupor floated around them. The scene was unnerving. Reformers in black placed everywhere, all armed, helpful, and seemingly trustworthy. Astrid followed instructions, moving in the same direction as the sea of bodies encompassing her,; they traveled at a snail's pace toward a bus.

As Astrid took her final steps to board, the small boy clutching her hand, a string of gun fire erupted, sending everyone to the ground. She shakily glanced behind her and saw security from the Institute attempting to regain control. They pushed against the line of Reformers that formed to protect the prisoners. Security and the Reformers were falling; black and white both fighting for what they thought was right. Stray bullets flew in every direction striking innocent bystanders, crushing them to the ground with a last breath.

Astrid collected the boy to the ground, covering him with her body, willing to take a stray bullet for this child who so innocently captured her heart. Wanting to put him in a safer position, she clutched him to her and crawled up the steps of the bus, forced to clamber over prisoners cowering in fear who blocked the way. Windows shattered above them, forcing screams and gasps from their lips, and glass flew all around them. Astrid continued to use her body as a shield, the boy beneath in the fetal position with his hands over his ears, his eyes squeezed shut as he mumbled to himself.

The spray of bullets failed to cease, and panicked prisoners rushed to find cover while the Reformers tried their best to protect them. The bus came to life with a giant shake and a roar from the engine. Relief fought Astrid's fear and adrenaline—they were leaving; soon the bus would be moving, moving away from the prison and the fight.

"Come on! We can't hold them. Let's take what we got and scram!" a deep voice yelled, piercing the air with knifelike precision.

The bus shook with every running, stomping step that boarded. Astrid listened to the sounds of the bullets fade as the bus picked up speed and left the terror behind. Lifting her head carefully, she saw everyone surrounding them scrunched up in seats or on the floor, sitting on glass and torn fabric. Some cried openly and loudly; others were silent with wide eyes full of fear. Three Reformers occupied the bus, including the driver. One at the back, braced against the seats holding his gun through the broken window on the emergency exit door located to the left. The bus was old; the brown fake-leather seats lining both sides were filled with rips and tears. The smell was worse than what it portrayed.

Movement forced the reminder of the fragile body underneath her. Peeking toward the front of the bus over her shoulder, she spotted two other Reformers. The bus driver concentrated on the road, frantically checking his mirrors. The last reformer, a female, stood at the front.

The boy underneath her squirmed, harsher this time, pushing his frail body against hers. Turning her full attention downward, Astrid loosened her grip on his violently shaking body. His face was covered with dust and dirt striped with lines of clean skin created by the tears streaming down his face. Putting her attention on him helped her calm herself, pushed her own fear away.

"Hey, no crying. It's okay. We're safe now, we're with the good guys." Astrid wiped his tears, succeeding in only smearing the dirt on his face. Although trying to calm him, she could see it wasn't working; if anything, he became more hysterical. She removed her weight from him, making shushing noises and rubbing his back. She picked him up and sat him in the nearest seat, staying crouched in the aisle next to him, her body swaying with the motion of the vehicle. Made calming noises along with telling him it was okay. He pulled his knees to his chest and retreated into himself. His crying soon faded to a shallow whine, a muffled moan.

Astrid pulled back. Glancing forward, she watched the lights of the bus pierce the darkness ahead, illuminating a path to a destination she knew nothing of.

CHAPTER 4
TIME TO LEAVE

TORO sipped at his steaming coffee, taking a much-deserved break between storage rooms. Red's words played on a continuous loop on a marquee in his head. The ground shook beneath him, and the shock sent his cup to the floor, spilling coffee all over his well-shined boots. His pant legs and socks were riddled with dark blotches. Running out the door and down the hallway to the catwalk lining the patients' floor below, he rushed to see the commotion. Floor security closest to the blast zone motionless in odd angles on the floor. Doctors and nurses lined up on their knees, noses to the wall. Soldiers in black holding guns at the staff's heads. Smoke, dust, and debris everywhere, impairing his vision.

He squinted and watched patients timidly making their way out of cubicles where the smoke had broken and cleared away. They were clearly confused, gazing around with perplexed eyes.

"What the *hell* is going on?" Captain Rhodes snapped, appearing behind Toro, closely followed by Jackson and the rest of the unit crowding along the railing.

"Reformers," Toro muttered under his breath. "It's a breakout, they're after the prisoners."

"How do you know?" Rhodes asked, showing rage wanting to be released and startling Toro.

Did I say that out loud? he thought.

"Well," he said, clearing his throat, "they're ushering them out the doors, holding back the nurses and doctors, keeping casualties to a minimum. It's a nice plan, something I would have done if I—" Toro stopped.

"Jackson, watch him. The rest of you with me," Captain Rhodes barked the orders and left the catwalk, heading to the first level His men followed, guns drawn, pulling fabric masks from underneath their uniforms and placing them over their noses. Gunshots followed in their wake.

"Sorry, bloke." Jackson slapped manacles around Toro's wrists and turned to the crevice in the wall, his eyes searching.

Toro attempted asking why he thought restraints were necessary, but Jackson's response, if he could call it a response, was simply more focus. He slightly nodded, and Toro followed his gaze and saw a prisoner with a vivid ring of blue in her eyes staring back at him. She perched at the top of a concrete mountain, sitting on a makeshift fence between freedom and the Institute. The same prisoner he'd stopped from escaping a couple months before. A slight cock of his head and she was gone. His attention returned to his shackled wrists, his heart lighter. Knowing the wrong he committed was now corrected.

"Didn't peg you as a traitor," Jackson said.

Toro laughed, and Jackson stared with disbelief in his eyes. "Honestly, I don't think I am, but when I came across what the government ... all those people." He shook his head. "It's a disgrace. I don't ... I won't be a part of it."

"Aren't you a special kind of stupid? What exactly do you think the government is? An optional book club?" Jackson leaned against the rail, his face showing disappointment.

Toro's chest tightened, the manacles hanging heavy on his arms.

"It doesn't matter. I assume I'll either be restored or put to the firing squad. All for thinking out loud. Illusion of freedom at its best."

His soul was oddly calm about the situation. Knowing he would rather die than work for the government put him at ease. His mind and heart slowed, clearing unnecessary thoughts.

"Well, those are options. Not superb ones. Have you thought about joining the Reformers? You'd do better with them than on your own."

The shock on Toro's face surprised even himself. Did this man really talk about the Reformers openly in a government Institution to a security guard?

"Seriously? And you call me stupid. I'm surprised they make as big of an impact as they do. I'll take my chances with the government."

"We all do what we must to survive." Jackson's body shifted, his weight firmly on both feet, his hands clasped and resting on the bannister as he observed the scene below.

Toro watched him, going over the information Jackson had slowly released. Jackson, who seemed indifferent to either side of the war, doing what he must. "Wait … are you … a Reformer?" he asked hesitantly under his breath, leaning forward in anticipation of the answer.

Jackson shrugged, his gaze on the chaos below them. "Maybe, kid, maybe."

With barely anybody left on the patients' floor, there wasn't much to look at. A few patients being funneled out the doors. Jackson's crew had broken the hold on the Reformers and was now sweeping the rest of the area. Security had finally arrived, pushing back; the Reformers had retreated toward the crevice in the wall.

They watched together as security and the rest of the unit went through the hole in the exterior wall and fought the Reformers. The first floor was left in disarray, debris mixed with scattered bodies. Dust was finally settling, and bullets were flying as the final men marched for the doors.

During the commotion, Matthew appeared at the railing next to Jackson. "Oh my. Wh-what is going on? Who are those people? Wh-why are they … this is not good. Oh my."

"'Those people' are the Reformers. Security and the rest of my unit have them on the run. It'll be over soon," Jackson explained calmly.

Matthew blabbered in distracted shock. Finally getting a hold of his senses, his attention turned to Toro's cuffs. "What are those for?"

His voice, high-pitched and whiney, made his way around Jackson and drifted to Toro's ears.

"Security measures," Jackson insisted. "Searching for a rat. Although I don't think he is it."

"Un-cuff him, he has work to do."

This caught Jackson's attention, finally getting him off the railing and standing up straighter. He took a deep breath and gave a forced release. "Can't. Waiting on the captain."

"I am in charge here!" Matthew's voice rose, the color of his skin scarlet. His hands shook, and he tried to hide them by fisting them at his sides. "You will do what you are told," he ordered a bit more calmly.

"Okay, you're the boss." Jackson reached forward and undid the manacles on Toro's wrists. Rubbing the slightly reddened skin, Toro thanked him.

"Sir, what is it you want me to do?" Toro pointed the question at Matthew, but his gaze stayed fixed on Jackson, impressed by his calm nature and confident attitude.

"The head doctor … that tall, blonde lady who thinks she's in charge."

"Dr. Heizer," Toro prompted.

"Yes, her. Find her. We need to know exactly who we lost. Coordinate with head of security and Captain Rhodes to see what direction they went. I want to know everything; how they got in, which guns they used, even if one of them stopped to blow their nose. I want to know what they were after."

"The prisoners. That's all they took," Jackson inserted.

"Hmm." Matthew regarded Jackson, thoughts flashing across his face. "You help him. Keep me posted." Spinning on his heels, he took two steps, but a thought brought him back. He pointed at both of them in turn. "Oh, do keep this out of the reports. Last thing we need is the President on us. She's not keen on failure."

"He's a short spitfire, isn't he?" Jackson stated, watching Benson march away.

"Looks that way." Toro brought his wrist up to his mouth and paged Dr. Heizer. "Dr. Heizer, come in. This is Toro Crow. Over."

"Dr. Heizer, good or bad?"

"I'm honestly not sure."

DR. Heizer stood in awe while the building was decimated around her. Dust and debris flying around, disorientation sweeping over its residents. The Institute was a fortress, steel beams and mesh underneath sheet rock and paint. The building itself constructed in the middle of twenty-five hundred acres, all dedicated to labs and military camps. The compound was surrounded by a thirty-foot wall topped with barbed wire. Security measures were top of the line—cameras, infrared lights, automatic guns. Just to get to work Dr. Heizer had three check points and a bag search to arrive and again to leave. To attack such a place was either madness or brilliance.

It was glorious. The black suits spilling in from openings on all sides of the building, fluid motions like liquid driven by an unseen force. She watched as soldiers burst through the front doors, leading employees in front by gunpoint. A target in their sights, mission orders driving their feet. They worked in unison, a well-trained team. Some heading straight to the center of the patients' floor, releasing and opening doors as they went, others to the giant hole in the wall to help those who required the extra convincing.

Dr. Heizer stood vigilant from her second story perch on the catwalk as these men and women removed from her the passion and work that had consumed her for so long. It marked a critical moment in her life, creating a unique choice: she could fight the change or accept it. A moment that would change the ripples in the timeline. No going back. She knew the moment when it arrived, a window opening wide, showing her a way out.

She acknowledged just how unhappy she was.

These saviors in black with their guns and bombs unrelenting in their rampage on the Institute. Dr. Heizer watched as her patients went for cover before being told to leave. They slowly rose and obeyed. The plague of indecision crossed everybody she saw.

"Run! Go!" she trembled. *Run*. It took her a minute to accept she talked to herself. *Run*. Such a small word holding such power. She pushed herself away from the wall and headed for the stairs.

Reaching the ground floor, her chest rose and fell with exhilaration. Excitement a drug all on its own, mixing in her blood stream with adrenaline. One patient stood between her and escape, someone she needed to make sure got out before allowing herself to leave. Disoriented from the dust and gunfire, she made her way down an aisle, taking turns from memory without having to glimpse at the corners of the cubicles for bearings. She often visited this particular cell—not to read charts or play doctor, but to just see, to watch, to be a part of.

She took the final turn and stopped short. A few cells ahead, the girl she had re-assimilated earlier that month ran, and trailing behind her being led by her hand was Dr. Heizer's favorite patient.

Her son.

His attention never wavered; nor did she call out. He ran, running away with conviction and purpose toward a safe place she could never give him. Being on the run would prove difficult on her own; it would not be a safe place for her boy. Dr. Heizer did the hardest thing she could do in the moment. She let him go. Tears spilled down her cheeks, the imminent separation spearing her heart, leaving her soul ragged; a pain threatening to knock her to the ground and take her very life.

A crunch behind her snatched her attention and made her spin around. A man clad in black with a gun pointed at her stood tall and firm, a sneer in his eyes, a smirk on his lips. His features blurred through her tears.

"Are you in charge here? You look important enough." His voice was deep with a light scratch to it.

His mission was her, and she knew it.

Without hesitation or a crack in her voice, she simply answered, "Yes, I am Dr. Heizer, the head physician and head of research here. And you are?" She wiped her face clean of tears, standing a bit taller.

He grinned, lowered his gun, getting closer. His breath was rancid; teeth being eaten away by an unseen parasite. "Your collector," he whispered.

The movement was quick, too efficient for her to follow. Before she quite understood, a needle had breached her neck, and the plunger went down.

"Night, night" all she heard as everything went dark.

AWAKENED by a jolt to her senses, the fog lifted from Melvina's head, allowing her to view her surroundings. She was on a bus, the bumps of the road sending her side to side as she lay on a seat. She tried to move, to sit up, but soon discovered her hands were confined behind her back. A major headache claimed turf on her frontal lobe, making movement harder than normal, so she didn't fight it. Whatever he gave her left one heck of a hangover.

"Hello? Anybody?" She winced with pain.

Speaking, bad idea.

"She's awake," came a voice, piercing its way through the discomfort. "I thought for a moment that I may have over done it." The rancid breath man again; his helmet and gloves removed now. He sat down opposite her, helping her sit up.

"Where are you taking me?" she asked, wrestling the wave of nausea coming up her throat from the sudden vertical position. She rested her head on the seat in front of her, which served as comfort to her swaying brain. "To our hideout. You being a valuable person and all, we had to take you. Of course you understand."

"Are these necessary?" She indicated her manacles. "I'm a doctor, not a threat."

"They're more for your protection than ours, Doc. Wouldn't want you making bad decisions and getting hurt."

"And who are you with exactly?" *Stay strong, stay confident.* She turned her head, her forehead still in contact with the back of the seat in front of her.

41

"The Reformers. Mitch at your service." His five o'clock shadow outlined his strong chin.

"Mitch, I'd say it's a pleasure, but considering the circumstances …" Trailing off, she carefully lifted her head and scanned around. The bus was old and small. Just Mitch, the driver, and herself. She didn't sense imminent danger—after all, if they wanted her dead she would already be dead. Instead, she was handcuffed and taking a ride; her circumstances could be worse.

"Aw, believe me, love, pleasure is all mine. *Melvina*." her name was drawn out with emphasis.

"Doctor Melvina, if you must. My credentials are the same, captive or not."

"Doctor Melvina. Just sit tight, love, we'll be arriving shortly." With that he got up, making off to the front of the bus.

Chatter on the radios rose above the tires eating the road, voicing something about an attack. Melvina strained her ears, catching bits over the rattle of the bus. Mitch and the driver conversed back and forth, before finally deciding to stay on the current path. Melvina's chest swelled. Her life held few privileges, and to sacrifice other officers and patients under attack to get her to safety made her feel special. But then a thought occurred to her; her son was on one of those buses. Her son could be attacked and taken back without her. Her own pride diminished as worry took over.

THE ride was horrid, everybody jumpy and jostling around, trying to find comfort. Across from Astrid, the boy sat, still sobbing, his body shaking and tears flowing over his face.

"Not supposed to be out! She'll punish me! Need to go back." At first incomprehensible, his words, escaping between gasps, finally began to make sense as he became more aware and his breathing cleared.

"Hey, it's okay. Nobody's going to hurt you; we're going to be just fine." Astrid tried to calm him down.

"Not supposed to be out."

The fear radiating from his eyes shot straight into her heart. Astrid reached over and pulled him into her lap, holding him tight against her. His whole body shook with the effort just to breathe.

"Shhh, it's going to be okay. I've got you. I promise, I won't let you go." She continued whispering calming words while holding tight.

The ride smoothed out as they pulled onto a highway. Whispers around them hushed as the tension evaporated. The man and woman strode the aisle handing out water, fruit, and reassurance to the confused and frightened.

"Where are you taking us?" Astrid asked the woman, taking an apple and biting into it. The juicy sweet crunch helped stop her from screaming with frustration as the woman stared at her, uneasiness in her eyes. She chewed and chewed until no taste left existed in the mush between her teeth, waiting on an answer.

"Out of the city, where you will be safe. We have every provision you will need." The woman tried to show compassion, except Astrid could still see the pity rolling off her in tides.

The questions lining up in Astrid's head came to a complete halt. At that moment she believed. She believed in safety; she believed in a life that meant something, full of love and meaning, because she wanted it. She wanted it more than she wanted anything else.

"Okay." She responded with no 'thank you for sacrificing your safety for me,' just 'okay.

Really? she asked herself.

The woman smiled, taking one last review of Astrid, slightly shaking her head before she left. The boy in her lap stirred. Glancing down at the peacefulness on his sleeping face, knowing it was the only thing holding him together, she didn't loosen her grip.

Following the boy's example, she let her head fall back, closing her eyes, enjoying the fresh wind coming in through the space left behind from shattered windows. As she found her blissfulness, the space between reality and the dream world, the bus jerked to the side.

The force sent Astrid to one side. Scrambling to hold on to the boy, she re-centered her equilibrium. Something had sideswiped them with enough force to send them off the road. The bumps worse than before, out of control; bodies thrown, screams rising. White knuckles gripped the seats, trying not to slam into one another as they spun with incredible force and velocity. The bus spiraled violently, continuing to toss its riders, sending dirt and grass into the air around them—closing off any chance to see what hit them. Vertigo and dizziness settled in like a close friend, hanging around well after the bus halted. The man and woman in black picked their guns up off the floor and slowly got to their feet.

Helicopter blades cut through the air, thumping loudly, pulling more cries from the passengers. Astrid attempted to stand, the little boy on her lap making it difficult. His eyes were wide as he stared up at her.

"She's going to punish us. I don't want to go back now. Please don't let them take me to her! You'll protect me, you won't let me go?" The fear, the shivers and shakes in his soul, coursed through his body.

Astrid intended to answer; it was on the tip of her tongue—she meant to tell him it was okay, that the Reformers would protect them—but gunfire bound every unstrapped thought and word.

The man shot at the circling helicopter from the back of the bus. The woman yelled at the driver to shut the bus down, and the engine shuttered to silence. The gunfire was loud and piercing within the small space. The helicopter pitched sideways, spinning out of control, the tail spitting fire and sending spiraling light through the windows. It crashed not far from the wrecked bus, lighting up the field. The explosions sent strong vibrations that rocked the bus. Astrid held the boy tight, turning her back to the open windows.

"How did they find us? It was a clean break." The female Reformer was obviously panicked, losing control. Her weight shifting from foot to foot, her hands unable to find anything constructive to do.

"It doesn't matter; we need to get back on the road!" the man shouted.

The woman forcefully calmed herself and rushed to the front.

An unfamiliar blinding light appeared, filling every nook and cranny of the bus. It came out of nowhere, along with a voice. Every eye had been covered with hands, leaving their ears open to the assault. The

44

voice penetrated to the bone marrow. It manifested power, anger, and hunger, coming from nowhere and everywhere at once.

"You have broken the rules. The punishment for rule breaking is death. You know this. It's in your programming. So please tell me, why'd you choose to break the rules?"

Astrid held her breath as the voice sent piercing pain in her head. Her immediate response was to flee. Her feet tap dancing underneath her, ready to carry her body along with them, while the boy stood stock still in her arms.

A gray-haired man toward the front of the bus moved. Old but strong, once full of life. His hands shook as he made his way to the door and shoved it open. Stepping down, he took two steps before falling to his knees.

"I beg your forgiveness," the old man yelled into the harsh light. "Please, I'll go back. Those men and women they took me from my cubicle. I … I was coerced. I want to go back. Please, please take me."

A chuckle, then, "If you insist."

The light changed, manifesting from the ground, illuminating the immediate area even more. Slimming into a soft, warm welcoming shade of blue, washing over the old man on his knees—the brightness no longer invading.

Then came a sound Astrid would never forget.

They watched as the man held his hands up to the light, his body shaking violently. His mouth opened, letting out a bloodcurdling sound. His pain evident, written all over his rigid body. A soft white light gathered at his chest. It was pulled from him with such force and violence that his body jerked forward, landing face first in the dirt. The string of light floated into the blue mist, evaporating, absorbed into the menacing light that gathered it.

"What was that? What just happened?" somebody asked, bringing everybody's attention back to the bus. "I'm not going out there."

Questions and statements tripped over each other, each trying to be heard. The noise level rising to an unbearable level. A little voice penetrated the wall of sound, shattering the confusion with two syllables.

"His soul," the little boy wrapped in Astrid's arms whispered.

"What?" she asked, turning the boy around to see him. "What did you say?" Her hands gripped his arms tightly, forcing him to look at her. The bus fell quiet, every set of eyes on the boy.

"His soul. The general, he eats them." He still whispered, and everybody strained to catch the words.

"Now that that's taken care of and out of the way …" the voice boomed. "You have three minutes to turn over these men and women who forced you out. Or you'll receive the same fate as your comrade."

Screaming started again, the passengers in white fighting for purchase, trying to grab hold of an arm or shoulder of one dressed in black, all wanting to throw them off the bus. The Reformers waved their guns, shrieking loud instructions, attempting to regain control, and obviously not wanting to resort to violence.

The blue light penetrated the bus, the steel and paint giving no protection. This time taking a teenage girl, screeching in a higher pitch than the old man. Everybody froze, searching for the source. Her body slumped to the floor, cold and gray, her once vibrant blonde hair laid over her blank face, the life stripped from her.

With no time to process the situation, Astrid let her instincts tell her to flee, to get away from the evil threatening her life.

"Run!" the woman in black yelled. "Everybody off the bus and scatter!"

Everybody moved, elbows and knees jamming against other bodies to reach the door. Window frames popping out as emergency exits were discovered. Bodies spilled from the bus. Astrid tossed the boy through a window, watched as he landed, then followed him out. Finding her feet, she grabbed the boy's hand. Panic engulfed the field; people ran and screamed in all different directions. The pillar of blue light moved, emanating from the ground and going straight to the sky without an ending, attempting to pin a body down.

"Come on," Astrid whispered to the boy.

They headed for the trees in the distance near the fallen helicopter, searching for cover. A phantom of a man appeared in front of them, forcing them to skid to a stop in the dirt, their breathing labored. The boy's face pressed against her leg, holding tight to her pants. She could feel his hot breath on her skin. The eerie blue light cut the man's features as he smiled. He stood tall, his hands clasped behind his back, the light featuring more a ghost than a real person. He was prestige, a man in charge and used to being obeyed, to being feared. His suit and well-groomed hair emanating power.

"You will not succeed. I need you all, and I will have you." His voice hurt her ears. She lifted her free hand, touching a finger to the ear, feeling something warm and wet, pulling it away red.

Blood.

With new determination, Astrid gripped the boy's hand firmer. "Go to hell!" She pushed forward, and the blue figure dissipated around them, leaving a cold sensation making its way down her arms and back.

CHAPTER 5
THE JOURNEY

WITH no response from Dr. Heizer, Toro worried. "Do you think she was in on it?"

Jackson shrugged his shoulders, and they moved down the catwalk, heading to the other end of the building toward Dr. Heizer's office.

"She's not here." Toro entered the office, circling the desk, heading back out the door and down the stairs. The patients' floor crawled with security and medical staff. Making their way through the rubble, Toro paged over the intercom with no answer. "Security …"

"What?" Jackson probed.

"Security. There's a room full of monitors storing the feed to all the cameras in the building. There's a camera in every corner, cubicle, and hallway. Third floor." He turned on his heel, bypassing Jackson, heading to the stairway. Frantic people occupied every available space. The air still thick with surprised confusion.

The monitor room was manned by only one employee, who was currently overtaking the colossal task of going over all the feed. The room was massive, the epicenter of the nervous system to the building. Everything ran through the computers in this room, flashing on the screens lining every inch of the walls.

"There are over twenty thousand cameras in this building and an additional five thousand throughout the grounds. We just have to narrow it down." As Toro explained, they took up positions in front of keyboards.

"Officer," the technician greeted him.

"We need access. Benson sent me to find Dr. Heizer," Toro countered, his gaze never tearing away from his monitor.

"Taken in the chaos."

"What?"

"She was taken, shortly after the first of the buses left with the patients. I have it here." He turned back to his monitor, typing. The screens on the front wall came together in one image—a camera outside of Dr. Heizer's office. There she was, against the wall right outside her door.

"What is she doing?"

"She's in shock. When she finally comes to, she heads down the hall to the stairs leading to the patients' floor; she comes out here." The monitor changed, Dr. Heizer appearing at the south end of the patients' floor. Following a corridor, she disappeared out of the side of the screen. "She makes it halfway down the corridor, stops briefly. She saw a couple prisoners leaving the building, then this guy comes up behind her. There's a short exchange of words, the man sticks her with something, and Dr. Heizer passes out. Here." They watched in silence as the guy tossed Dr. Heizer over his shoulder and scurried out the door with her.

"She was kidnapped," Jackson stated.

Toro didn't answer, deep in thought. He turned, leaving the monitor room.

"Thanks, man. I guess we're done here." Jackson hurried his thanks, following Toro out the door. "Crow, what's up? This is good, right?"

"For who? Good for who? We need to go back down to storage and find a couple files before we leave."

"What? We? No, *we* need to check in with the captain. I cannot blow this." Jackson grabbed Toro's shoulder, spinning him around. "Calm down. I must keep hold of you until the captain sees you again. If we do this, we do it right, we do this my way. I have to get you back down to the catwalk." They stood close, battling for the higher ground.

"What do we do?"

"Our jobs. Check in with the fiery redhead, give him an update. Then we go to Rhodes."

"Benson, this is Crow. Come in." Toro lifted his hand and paged Benson, not releasing Jackson's eyes, not willing to admit defeat.

"On the prisoners' floor, Crow. You find her?" came an answer.

"No, sir, she was taken by the Reformers during the break-in, sir. She's gone." They waited for a response, but none came forth.

Jackson let out a slight moan, his head falling back. Toro showed similar signs of frustration.

They made their way three floors down the stairs, coming out on the prisoners' floor. Captain Rhodes, a statue in the corridor barking orders. Everybody skittering around him, mice on hot plates. His face scarlet, muscles bulging. He paused when he spotted Jackson and Toro. His jerking movement sent the storm straight at them.

"Why is he wandering free?" he demanded, stepping toe-to-toe, nose-to-nose with Jackson.

"Benson, sir. He ordered me to free him and help him find the doctor. I don't think he's a traitor, sir, just wrong place wrong time." Jackson didn't seem to be afraid of Rhodes; he stood his ground, his voice calm and forceful. His opinions clearly mattered to Rhodes, and after Rhodes continued to consider Jackson's point, he finally relented.

"Fascinating. Well, I guess we'll see. Did you find this doctor?"

"Taken by the Reformers, drugged and carried out the front door."

He hung his head. "We know which direction they went. They got 80 percent of the patients, about two hundred. Four bus loads worth of drugged up tax evaders."

"Sir, why would they come for the prisoners? What could possibly come of that? They have no memories. If anything, they would burden them."

Toro witnessed the exchange, curious to know why Jackson risked speaking freely to the captain. Rhodes didn't seem like the person to stray too far from the rule book.

"They had a target, and the rest of the prisoners were a cover up. Now we find out if it was the doctor or a prisoner they were after. You," he said, turning his attention back to Toro. "Did you work the prisoners' floor?"

"Yes, I'm part of the guard force." Rhodes cocked his head, waiting. "Sir," Toro added quickly.

"Jackson, take wrong place wrong time here up to security headquarters and go over the tapes. I want to know who their target was."

MELVINA rode along silently, watching the Pacific Ocean roll by out of the dirty window. They headed south, and knowing what lay south of Los Angeles left her jittery. The excitement of being taken captive was trying to spill out, her muscles twitchy, hands in a constant state of movement. Mitch left her to herself, giving her water occasionally, not conversing further. She attempted once to ask about the bus that had been attacked. But then decided Mitch would have no way of knowing which bus her son had gotten on.

South of Los Angeles the maintained roads came to an end. Abandoned roads and potholes hindered their progress, and the bus slowed to a crawl to weave through the twisted metal and broken glass. They passed by the border patrol north of San Diego, the structure dark and ghost-like. Cars sat in line, perpetually waiting to get through, to get their owners to safety, forever in wait.

Melvina watched with interest, never having been out of Los Angeles. The closer they got to San Diego the straighter she sat in her seat. The buildings were run down, highway exit signs off their poles in the ditch on the side of the roads. The spectacle intrigued her. Where else would be a perfect spot for the Reformers but in a ghost town that the entire country thought completely abandoned and left to Mother Nature?

"San Diego?" she asked, curiosity getting the best of her. She repeated herself to be heard over the engine, and Mitch's sly grin appeared at the sound of her voice.

"Who suggested we were stopping in San Diego?" His response coming from the front.

"No one. I just assumed, as we can't go any farther south due to the Mexicans shooting anybody on sight the instant you get too close."

"Interesting. So, you do know what's going on outside of your Institute."

"It's not 'my' Institute. The Institute is my place of employment, nothing more."

"You don't believe that. That was your life, you trained to be a doctor, and the Institute played as your saving grace. Be honest, if not with me, at least with yourself, love." He worked his way back to her, taking residence in the seat opposite hers.

"Yes, you're right, it did save me." Melvina hung her head. "Maybe not for the better, but I did survive. Where in San Diego?"

Grinning slightly, Mitch sighed, "A piece of history that speaks to us all. We're almost there." He stood up and returned to the front.

They drove along, taking a right exit off the highway, merging onto a side access road. A path previously forged, used often; cars were pushed onto the curbs. It occurred to Melvina that this was a giveaway, a trail that would lead anybody inspecting straight to their front door. The bus took a right as the front of a building slid off to the side, revealing a hidden tunnel. *Well,* she thought, *I did not see that coming.*

The only light came from the headlights, illuminating the man-made tunnel. Shovel marks were clear along the sides. The momentum tilting sent Melvina forward unintentionally. She pushed herself back into her seat. Only for gravity to pull her forward again. Her head snapped up as she braced her feet against the floor, holding her back into the seat. They were headed underground at a slightly steep angle. She had to push herself into her seat or risk face planting into the seat in front of her. About the time she felt her legs giving out on her, the bus leveled, pulling into a concrete circular room.

"Come on, love. Up you go." Mitch gently put his hand on her bicep, pulling her up and placing her in front of him in the aisle.

Stepping off the bus, a strong rotting smell slammed into her. Hitting her with such force she scrunched up her face in a sad attempt to stop the assault.

"What is that?" she asked through a breath of her mouth.

"Salt water and fish. Nice combo. You'll get used to it. It fades the longer you stay here."

Melvina didn't agree; the smell was horrid. Unable to plug her nose, she cursed Mitch under her breath.

"It's not quite that bad."

"So you say. To me it's rank." She strode alongside Mitch, being led by a slight touch to her elbow when they needed to change direction. The round room was thirty feet high, and to the left was a tall wide window. "What was this place?"

"It was a holding tank for orcas. A theme park, rides, and shows all for paying customers, even petting areas to interact with the animals."

"Sea World? We're standing in a holding tank from Sea World?" The disbelief was clear in her voice.

He laughed, nodding his head. "See, you do know your history. I'm honored." The sarcasm was not lost on her.

"Thanks, I aspire to make you proud. I like to read about the world destroyed. How did you cover the tanks?"

"Don't know, it was done before I got here. The Reformers have called this fish hole our home since its inception. You'd think the smell would go away, but it seems it's seeped into the concrete and grounds never to leave."

"It smells because the animals were left to fend for themselves. They starved to death in unclean tanks. I would assume that the original Reformers were forced to clean the place out, whale carcasses and all to turn it into your hidey hole." She did like to read in her downtime, and the history of forgotten places was her favorite subject.

Mitch laughed. "Glad we now have a historian in our ranks. Come on, you're expected." He went through a door on the other side of the tank.

Now on her own, freely, Melvina followed Mitch through the hallways, soon lost within the maze of unmarked turns. The compound was decrepit in its appearance—clean, but at the same time not well taken care of. The farther in they went, the smell dissipated, much to her relief.

Numerous Reformers, dressed in black with the red band on their arms, filed out an open door down the hallway on the left. Mitch held her back, stopping her momentum.

"Benji should be out soon. We wait here, love." Pulling his keys free, he relieved Melvina of her manacles.

"Benji?" she huffed. A strange sensation in her toes curled and crawled its way up to her chest, stopping her breath and the beating of her heart. But it couldn't be, this meant … She knew as soon as she heard the footsteps coming out of the room. The smell of his aftershave—forcing the last of the fish from her senses—confirmed it.

"Mel, I'm so glad you could join us. I admit, though, I didn't honestly think that Mitch would be able to get to you. Come on in, we have a lot to discuss."

Mitch pushed her forward. Her body had quit working on its own accord.

"Oh no," was all she managed before her feet betrayed her and stepped forward.

THE boy shook violently. A silent sob wracking his body. Astrid's concern for him rose, but they ran until unable to go any farther. Coming to rest alongside the road against a tree, she held the boy. Overfilled with questions, a slight chill caressed her as her thoughts replayed the blue outline. His eyes, the screams. The prisoners scattered, and in the chaos Astrid had slipped away through some trees down the road. The sun set made the temperature drop, creating a new set of worries for her.

"Are they going to find us?" He pulled her away from her thoughts.

"Who?"

"The good guys, in black?"

"I hope so."

"The bad guy, in blue?"

"You don't know who he is, the guy in blue?"

"No, the only person I knew was the doctor." A pause. "The guards are scared of him, they think about it. I could hear them."

At first she wasn't sure she heard him correctly. *He could hear them thinking about it? No, he must still be confused.*

"You're awfully smart for one so small. How old are you?"

The stream of tears gliding down his cheeks were unceasing. "I don't want to go back. Don't let them take me."

"I won't, kiddo. I promise." She coddled him. Her hand absently stroking his blond curls. "Do you have a name? Something you want me to call you?"

"The doctor, she used to whisper something. Ben? Maybe, Ben. I think." The boy stilled, but the tears flowed freely.

"Ben, I like it. A tough name. My name is Astrid."

"That's a strange name." Ben's eyes turned a bit brighter.

Astrid laughed; he was right. She was named after her grandmother on her father's side. The only thing she owned of her father. A name passed down the female line. A grandmother she never met as her father left when she was a baby. Astrid didn't even know the meaning of her own name.

A sound startled them. Coming from down the road; opposite of the crash. Holding hands, backs against the tree, they waited. A soft light moved toward them, matching the sound. Growing louder, rumbling up the road, the light emerged brighter.

"A vehicle." Astrid beamed.

"Good guys?"

She didn't answer right away as she didn't know for sure. They waited in the bushes out of sight until the bus passed by, glancing at the driver in black with passengers also wearing dark clothes and holding weapons.

Good guys.

She jumped instantly, yelling and waving her hands, Ben behind her moving quickly to stay close.

Trying her hardest to get the passengers' or driver's attention wore her out, but before long the bus's brake lights illuminated, and the bus slowed its momentum. Astrid let out the fear she didn't know she held, releasing the tightness in her shoulders and back.

"Yes, good guys," she assured Ben.

After the bus made its way back, a tall man in black stepped off and trekked around the bus, his gun raised to their level, his eyes glancing at their tattered dirty uniforms. He was the epitome of military protocol. "Were you on the bus that was attacked?"

"Yes, are you with the Reformers?" Astrid's hand held tight to Ben, trying to keep them both still.

"Yeah, we are. We came as soon as we could. Had to drop off the load of patients we picked up first. Are you the only ones left? Where's the bus?" As his questions spilled out, the aim of the gun went to the ground, his hand guiding its way back onto his shoulder via a strap.

"We ran. The attack happened back there through the trees in a clearing. Down the road a bit, there's a field." Astrid's nerves were strung thin, her words jumbling up between her brain and mouth.

"Can we get on the bus?" Ben spoke up.

"Yes, of course. I'm sorry." He motioned them forward.

Stopping at the door, Astrid and Ben glanced at one another. After the last bus ride, she was a bit apprehensive to get on another one so soon. And surprised that Ben seemed anxious to go aboard.

"Astrid, I'm cold." He pushed past her, letting go of her hand, embarking.

"Uh, yeah. Me too." She followed him on, forcing her nerves to still, the hairs on the back of her neck erect.

The clearing wasn't far. Coming upon the scarred space, they saw the other bus sitting in the middle. A mess of burnt metal sat not far off, smoke still billowing from the burned wreckage of the helicopter. Bodies were scattered all over the fields, dressed in white. Gasps escaped the Reformer's mouths in unison with Astrid's. Tears came along with the gasp, and she didn't bother hiding them. She could no longer mask her emotions; they remained plain on her face. As the bus came to a stop three forms came out from the other side of the field: the man, the woman, and the bus driver who escorted them from the Institute.

Stepping onto the bus, the woman stopped at the sight of Astrid and Ben. "You made it? Where did you go?" Her eyes were wide and her voice shaky as she boarded. The men following her on let out a gasp at seeing them.

"We ran, up the road through the trees. Did he kill everybody?" Astrid tried hard not to count the bodies scattered about the field. Her chest tightening around her heart, her fingers absently ticked off body after body as she took a pause on each lifeless form.

"No survivors except us. Instead, we stood by helpless, watching as he killed everybody. All the training couldn't prepare us for that. Useless, we were useless. All those people."

"It's not your fault, Sibella. There was nothing either of us could do." The man was calm, collected, and sharing it with the woman. Both were clearly shaken, frightened a bit. "I'm glad you guys were able to get away. Why is your head so clear? All the others seemed clouded still from the medication."

"My memories came back a while ago. Dr. Heizer seemed quite irritated." Astrid talked, not wanting to untangle the confusion, the unclear. Not wanting to do anything. Not wanting to even sleep, too scared to move, to dream.

"You didn't set off any of the alarms? I don't understand," he asked. They were interested. Trying to understand.

Fine, she thought.

"At first, they reissued medication. I don't know how long it lasted, but soon enough I remembered everything. If I played my part, the alarms never went off again. It was weird. The first alarm went off because I remembered I didn't like grapefruit. They knew, read my mind, knew I remembered. It was instantaneous. The next time, nothing. As though the monitor had been turned off. Or the person monitoring me let it slip. However it worked, I was able to get by," she explained, wringing her hands together until they hurt. She still wasn't sure herself how it worked, just that she was out. The bus moved; headed south again. Hopefully this time, their journey would not be interrupted.

57

"Your eyes? They a side effect of the medication or experiments?" The blunt question caught Astrid by surprise.

"What do you mean? What's wrong with my eyes?" Her hands shot up to her face, tips of her fingers searching for a defect.

"The ring of color around your irises? He has it, too. Don't you see it?" The man motioned toward Ben, for Astrid to see for herself. Ben's eyes, bright green and crystal clear, were wide and full of the unknown. "We thought it was from your time at the Institute."

"I don't see anything. What are you talking about? His eyes are fine, there's nothing wrong with them." She tried to keep the panic away. On the verge of exhaustion, of not caring any more. She just couldn't take any more today.

"The orange ring around his iris, you don't see it? Yours is blue, bright against the hazel of your eyes. It's pretty, but unnatural." He slowed, seeing how uncomfortable the situation was making her.

Ben shot questioning glances between both the Reformer and Astrid, filled with curiosity and worry, his head tilted to one side. She inspected his eyes again, trying hard to see the orange.

"Was it as bad as the rumors?" Sibella spoke up, changing the subject. Her eyes rimmed with red.

"It's a tight schedule, a lot of isolation. They draw fluids once a day. The needle hurts. We get an education." Astrid knew she was trying to talk it up. In truth, she had been miserable. Only because she understood. Was it not so bad for those who didn't know? "Horrible, after I remembered. I knew that it was unfair."

"Fluids?"

"Blood and spinal fluid mostly." She never thought much about it. "But it was for research, right? What else could they do with it?"

"Cloning, we think. That's why your eyes are so strange," he explained. "What's your name?"

"Astrid." She held out her hand for introduction. "As far as I can tell I'm not a clone, and there's nothing wrong with my eyes."

"Reider. I'm glad you survived, Astrid. You and Ben here will be a lot of help to us. And no, I figured you weren't, but I haven't met one. I'm not sure if I could tell the difference."

Astrid recoiled, she didn't remember telling them Ben's name. She had not escaped just to become subject to another group who would trick her, lie to her. She refused to be used that way.

"How did you know his name?" She asked carefully, showing curiosity.

He seemed confused, trying to remember if she had stated the boy's name. "You mentioned it, earlier on the bus, before the attack." He sat back in his seat, trying to relax, his eyes twitching.

Astrid didn't contradict him, but wondering how much she could trust them clouded her mind with doubt. She would have to be more careful from now on. She viewed her own reflection in a window over Ben's head, watching, confirming her suspicions—her eyes were unmarked, normal.

CHAPTER 6

ARRIVAL

HOW could you?" Melvina screamed. They had been 'talking' for a while now, and she'd found herself fed up. Her temper not improving with the new information Benji, or Benjamin Heizer, her late husband provided. "We thought you were dead. I buried you! You just left us?"

"Please, try to calm down. As I was attempting to explain before, it's convoluted. It was not easy leaving you. It needed to be done. For your safety as well as my own. Have a seat, Mel. I'll have some hot tea and broth brought in for you, and we'll talk about everything, I promise."

He could always stay calm no matter the situation. It royally pissed her off. She wanted to scream, to throw things, to cause him just as much pain as he ever caused her.

"I'd have gone with you. Why didn't you take us with you?" She stopped screaming, but her anger lingered. Hands fisted at her sides, she refused to take the seat and olive branch offered.

"I couldn't. Your Life Tax was paid up for five years, mine was not. It was either run, or turn myself in. I couldn't do it! I could not turn myself in to those life-sucking, law-abiding monsters who turn people into robots. So yes, I left. I knew you were safe, so I left." He relaxed in an old beaten up office chair covered in ripped, worn fabric showing thinning foam, behind a white fold-up table, hands crossed in his lap.

Still as handsome as she remembered. Salt and pepper hair, and his facial hair, how she loved it. Not as well-groomed as in the past, but Benji remained sophisticated as always. Forevermore going for the bad boy look. Didn't matter how old he'd gotten, not even when the gray started to appear. If anything it helped. His skin was a bit darker and rougher. Laugh lines and stress strong on his face along with some new scarring.

The fight abandoned her; she sat, bowed her head, letting the tears fall. "Yes, my Life Tax was paid, but not the baby's. They came when he was two, telling me that if I couldn't pay they would take him. I ended up working for the same people you ran from only to save my own hide. They took him anyways! They took him and put him in a cubicle, told me to stay away. Told me if I didn't want to join him that I should just do as I was told." Hatred boiled in her gut. She wanted to destroy something, or someone.

"I know, Mel ..." Somber, calm—too calm.

Her head shot up. "You knew? You knew and you didn't rescue us, you didn't come back to help me? You still just stayed away?" Her heart was held hostage by a crushing force she could not stop.

"You know the laws, just as well as I do. If I'd shown back up after my death was already recorded, they would have killed me, you, and our son. What good could have come from that? This was hard, on all of us, but we survived it. We can be a family again, here."

"You have him? He's here?" She was back on her feet, excitement replacing the anger and fear. The idea of holding her son again overfilling her with giddiness. "Take me to him. Now."

"He isn't here, sit back down please. We're not done." Seriousness taking over, he shuffled forward in his seat, moving papers on his makeshift desk.

She didn't sit. She crossed her arms, a stubborn look on her face. What was more important than her son?

Benji regarded her, taking a deep breath, and began again. "We need to talk about the Institute. About what's been going on. Are you aware of what they're doing?"

"Wha—yes, of course I know. I work there. What are you getting at? They come in, they serve their time. Later they're released."

"No, Melvina. That's not what happens. Nobody gets out. Nobody is ever released. If the government finds a prisoner useful in some way, anything they can harvest—skin cells, body fluids, hair follicles—they are kept alive, used up, dispersed. If not, proper paperwork is filed to keep the family happy, and they mysteriously die from unknown causes. Body released, ceremonies given. Nobody ever gets out!" His Adam's apple bobbed with a gulp, and Benji struggled to keep his composure.

"No, that's not true. I handle the paperwork for discharge myself. After their time is up, they go home to their family, back to work, back to their lives." Her legs gave out, dread filling her. Benji's information did not seem correct. It stuffed her head with doubt. Doubt was a ten ton elephant, heavy.

"Melvina, think about it. Did you ever see a patient leave the facility? Did you see them leave their cubicle alive?"

"Well, no. The patient numbers would pop up on my screen for discharge. I filed the proper forms, passing it on. I'm a doctor, why would I show patients to the door?" Right? But the more he made her think, the more she felt he knew something she did not. The government would not kill its citizens; a government ran with murder and harm was not a government, but a dictatorship. They did not live in a dictatorship.

"Did you have any dealings with the patients? Face-to-face I mean? Anything other than filling out forms?" he continued, pushing, prodding. Forcing unwanted thoughts and misinterpretations.

"Only when the alarms were triggered. If they remembered, or questioned anything, they were brought to me for restoration. I was to re-administer the—" She remembered now, the young woman she saw a while ago. The one who hastened out with her son. She had been lucid, the patient had received her memories back even after Melvina re-administered the compound. That patient, the girl, remembered.

"The compound that we introduced to the patients, it's a memory wipe; we were told it was to keep them compliant, easier to deal with. Quieter, I think, was the term used. We're not allowed to have dealings with patients after they were wiped and assigned a cubicle. There was no need. The cubicle provided everything for them. I strolled the corridors to listen, to make sure everybody was happy and quiet. There were never any reasons to pull a patient from their cubicle."

"They used you. I thought maybe you were in a higher position, closer to the big man in charge."

"You mean the general?"

"Do you know him?" Benji straighter in his seat. Obviously this was his interest.

"Not really. I was 'spoken' to once for failure to file a report. He was stern, in charge. Likes things run a certain way. But nothing seemed off about him. That is until …"

"Until what?"

She didn't answer but replayed in her head what she heard between the general and Matthew. Shivers crawled up her back, making the hairs on her neck stand at attention.

"Melvina? Until what?" Benji prompted again.

"Until …" Could she explain this without incriminating herself? "You have to understand, I didn't know. I didn't realize what was going on."

"It's okay. Just tell me."

She hesitated, but then the story spilled out of her. It was a relief to share it with someone else, to tell the truth. She stopped, closing her eyes, listening to the scream again before describing the awful sound from the patient. "After the bright light … nothing. I was so startled that I ran. I was almost sick. The patient was dead, Benji, gone. What was I supposed to do?" The tears returned with the recollection; a slight panic in her voice.

"Mel, there was nothing you could do. We're just trying to figure out what's going on. We have so many reports, we're not sure which to believe. ·

"One of our buses was attacked on the way here. The bus Ben was on, but he's okay. He's on his way. The survivors say the general could talk to them, but that he wasn't physically present. That he took the souls of the patients by the way of a blue light. Melvina, I don't know what to do any more."

Melvina could see his fear. He never used her real name unless angry, upset, or dead serious. Benji was out of his depth, and she almost felt bad for him. Remembering what she went through after he abandoned them, her sympathy deserted her.

"I don't know what to tell you, Benji. If he can do what you say, we're all as good as dead. Now, where's my son?"

HOURS later, Toro and Jackson sat in front of mind numbing screens going over what was declared as the most successful break-in in recent history. The fact that the Reformers proved the government was not as strong and smart as they portrayed hurt the government. Security measures would be reevaluated and upgraded, no penny spared. The attack had been quick, clean, and precise. But not without costs. Jackson kept muttering swear words every time he watched a new video of a Reformer being shot. The aftermath was still being cleaned up. The security team moving bodies of the dead Reformers into a trench on the south side of the property line next to a fence. Any employees or patients who did not survive cleaned up to be returned to their family. The Institute in complete chaos.

The general came down off his high perch to yell at everybody. His voice beamed over the intercom system with force and disdain. Jackson rolled his eyes, continuing his work.

Toro was going over it all in his head. He'd been a slave, ignorant to it all. A minion to a government entity whom he knew nothing of. And who would take his life without a thought if it meant getting closer to its goals.

He turned. "I'm in."

"In?"

"With you." Dropping his voice to a whisper, he leaned closer. "You know, the Reformers. I want in."

"Shh. Bloke, are you crazy? You can't talk like that here," Jackson whispered, his head spinning around, making sure they were not overheard.

"I'm serious."

"Uh-huh, yeah okay. I'll jump right on signing you up." Chuckling, he turned back to his monitor.

"Come on, tell me."

Jackson sat back, glancing sideways at Toro. He took a deep breath, his chin dropping to his chest.

"I'll put it in, and you'll be contacted and given instructions if they accept." He eased back to his monitor.

"Wait, that's it? To be put on a contact list? Do they interview?" Jackson scrutinized Toro with a raised eyebrow, making him regret his hasty words. "What about those who just run away and join? Do they have to wait for a call? What the hell, man, help me out." This did not make sense; wanting to join was proving hard enough; waiting to be a turncoat harder still.

Jackson chuckled, shook his head. "The Reformers are vast, underground. We've infiltrated the government. We each know our part, which usually doesn't include everybody else's jobs. They'll call."

"Thanks," he asserted with sarcasm, but the excitement and nervousness flushing through his system told a different story. They remained quiet for a while, going over the feed. Knowing there was nothing new; everything they saw was for the third or fourth time.

"Jackson, return to patients' floor. Over." The order came suddenly, unexpected.

Jackson replied, rising and stretching. He strode out, leaving Toro behind.

Toro was stretching his back and neck behind his chair when he noticed something interesting: Matthew Benson on the bottom right screen of the display. Positioned in a hallway on the top floor against a wall, a tall, distinguished man in a gray suit stood over him, bearing down.

Toro quickly brought the correct live feed to his monitor, turning up the volume.

"… find out all my work is gone. Do not fall victim to them as well, Mr. Benson. I'd hate to add you to my list." With that the man in gray left.

Visibly taking a deep breath, Matthew straightened his suit and tie, going the opposite direction.

Toro's understanding of the Institute was minimal at best; he knew operations and chain of command. Business men ignoring paperwork and employees, expressways to the government offices. Any research or 'work' completed by scientists and doctors on different levels.

Interesting. He wasn't one to eavesdrop, but this just happened to spike his curiosity. Lost in his own thoughts he failed to notice the entrance of somebody behind him.

"Find anything good? Something we can use against them?" It was Benson, his voice scratchy, nose pointed up.

Toro visibly jumped. Heart racing and palms sweaty, he fumbled over his words to find an answer. "No, sir," he finally managed.

"Dammit, we're screwed. The president herself is on her way to review the situation. If we don't have answers … well, let's just say she doesn't have mercy for those who fail." Matthew shook, visibly scared. Maybe Toro wasn't the only slave—they all were, even the men he worked for. "Find me something, Crow, or it's you who will be put in as a replacement."

"Replacement for what?" Toro forgot himself. The gaze he received quickly reminded him. "Sir."

"The patients of course."

Toro's previous decision was now set in stone; he needed to leave. He knew danger; he knew that if he stayed it would get worse, but he didn't have anywhere to go. If he left his post, he would be labeled a traitor, charged with treason. Upon being found they would shoot him on the spot. Finding Jackson and gluing himself to his side seemed a safe option for now.

Toro found Jackson on the monitors. He was on the ground floor withstanding a barrage from Captain Rhodes, whose arms flailed around dramatically.

The patients' floor was without microphones—too many people and too much noise to discern a certain conversation. Toro just watched.

Jackson would nod occasionally, continuing to listen. Just before Toro switched to a recorded feed to go over, bored with Jackson being scolded, Jackson seared a look straight at the camera. A mischievous grin spread across his face. Pulling his side arm, he shot Captain Rhodes in the chest.

Toro stared in disbelief as Rhodes' body fell backwards, bouncing on the floor, blood pooling underneath him.

He froze to his chair. He had been assigned to Captain Rhodes. His own loyalties jerked and twisted to an unrecognizable moral. Toro always took pride in knowing exactly who he was, and what he was supposed to do. At this moment, he had no clue.

He cursed out loud, focusing again on the monitor. Jackson loomed over Rhodes' dead corpse, seemingly transfixed. Joined by Red who secured Jackson's attention and got him to move. They moved at a slight jog out of the frame, weapons at the ready.

Bolting from the security room, Toro intended to track down Jackson. He needed to confirm, needed guidance on what to do now. Finding Jackson and Red waiting in a running Jeep backed up to the front door, he dashed up to the passenger side.

"What are you doing?" he asked.

"You coming? You mentioned you wanted in. This is your call." Jackson didn't even cast a look his way.

"I-I, uh. I thought I could help from here, be a mole, an informant."
No, not this soon.

Toro wanted time to adjust. Time to be informed, make sure he made the right decision. Prep his family. Not just leave, not just become a traitor.

But in the end, this was what he wanted, right?

"Fine." Jackson's hand shot out, punching him right in the nose.

Toro fell to the ground with blood pouring from his face like a burst pipe. The pain immense; his eyes teared up, a headache instantly overcoming him.

"Bastard," he mumbled. Jackson moved quickly, placing a black cloth over Toro's head, tying his hands behind his back. "What the hell, man? Let me go." His words were jumbled from a stuffed up septum and blood in his mouth.

"Nope, I'm kidnapping you. Now you're not a traitor. You're a prisoner of war." Jackson picked Toro up and tossed him in the backseat, helped him stay vertical, and buckled his belt for him. "Safety first, hmm?"

"Jerk" was all that came to Toro's mind. The cloth over his face soaked with blood, and the coppery smell made him nauseous.

"A simple thank you would have sufficed, bloke. I just saved your life. It's on video."

Toro heard a car door shut; movement followed. Shots could soon be heard, bullets chasing the racing Jeep off the compound. A strong jolt, lots of metal twisting and shouts.

"What was that?" Toro inquired.

"The front fence they were trying to fix. Don't worry, they hadn't gotten far. Now, time for you to sleep. I don't want to be answering questions the whole way."

Something stuck Toro in his upper thigh. The pain was sharp but short. Soon he drifted off, slumped in the backseat.

ASTRID rode in silence, mostly reminiscing. Sibella and the other soldiers had quit talking a while ago, some of them nodding off with the motion of the bus. Ben curled up, falling asleep as well.

Her mother was at the forefront of her thoughts; not knowing whether she was at the Institute or on another bus. Was she waiting for her at the Reformers' Compound? After she had turned eighteen and refused to leave her mother alone, their relationship went from mother/daughter to best friends. She wouldn't have wanted it any other way. Their late afternoon hikes were her favorite; her mom would take her down to 'the happiest place on earth.' Astrid loved the broken-down rides. The castle in the middle of the park was their talking spot. The overgrown brush and ivy growing over the castle made it easy to climb. They would sit and talk for hours, moving to stay with the setting sun. Sometimes, if they could get packable rations, they would eat. The park loomed hazardous; still they did it. Just about every day. Her mother told her that before the hostile takeover, citizens would pay hundreds of dollars just to spend the day roaming around the park, riding rides and interacting with special characters that moved around. The word she liked to use the most was *magical.* Astrid could picture how it could be 'the happiest place;' she felt that if they were together she would be happy.

The notification had lain in wait at their living quarters after such a walk. A fierce piece of yellow paper taped on their front door. The dread was instantaneous following the sighting of the abrasive yellow. Her mother tried to hide it, hurrying ahead faster and grabbing the paper, holding it behind her. Turning it into the only argument between them.

"What was that?" Astrid asked, trying to keep calm.

"Nothing, dear, just a note about my job. They're reclassifying it." Her mom wouldn't even lay a glance her way.

"Mom, don't, please. What is it? You can tell me."

"We uh … we weren't able to make the last payment, with the shortage of shifts. I'm sorry." Margaret fell onto the front step, becoming hysterical. "I tried, I tried picking up more shifts. They kept telling me that I wasn't their 'type.' What does that even mean?" She continued to blubber on about how all jobs were assigned, that it made no sense that suddenly after thirty years she was not their 'type.' Somebody younger, able to work more for less, was taking her position.

"It's okay, we'll figure it out. We always have. I can pick up more shifts in the fields. Work nights if we must. We can do this." Astrid joined her mom.

Her mom's frail frame fell easily into the protective embrace Astrid offered. In truth, she didn't know what they were going to do. This fear always loitered over their heads. Constant slaves to this thought, that someday this yellow note would appear. They'd seen it on their neighbors' doors, on doors of people they knew nothing about. But they knew about the tears and angry conversations that would flow through those closed homes. Angry wives blaming husbands for not working enough—for not saving their family.

"It won't work, we owe too much. I'm so sorry, sweetie. I'm supposed to protect you and keep you safe." She sobbed, her body in shock.

"Come on, let's go inside and have some tea." She helped her mother up, ushering her inside, the yellow corrosive note dripping from her mother's tight grip. After sitting her mom at their unstable table, she built a fire, heating up some water.

Her mom rambled on about how she had failed Astrid. Nothing she countered with helped, so she sat a hot cup of tea in front of her mom, sat next to her with her own steaming cup, and listened.

"Mom, I'm an adult. This is my fault, too. I am just as responsible for these fees as you are. We will do what we need to. Even if it means cooperating. So we spend some time in the confinement with the government. When we get released we'll have a clean slate. We start over. It's okay. Besides, we could use a few really good meals." Astrid had never thought that she would end up instituting herself. Always the dreamer, she assumed she would fight it. Being brave came easily, up until the moment she thought would never come, breaking down the door of her peaceful home.

They spent the night cuddled together, unable to sleep and unable to discuss what would happen. The notice gave them four days until they were to turn themselves in.

Jobs were forfeited once the yellow note was delivered, giving you insufficient time to either pay the fee or turn yourself in. Astrid believed they possessed enough food to get them through. What little money they did have was confiscated with the arrival of the notice, another aspect of their lives in which they had no control. With nothing to do they spent four days in tears, shaking with fear as the moment creeped closer. Margaret finally calming down enough to try to be a parent, only to understand Astrid didn't need that; she needed a friend. They found solace in each other's fear and denial of what was to come.

Now Astrid found herself in the same state of denial and fear. On a bus coming to a city covered by time and disuse. San Diego, once beautiful, full of diversity and culture.

She missed when they had turned off the highway. The tunnel was interesting, but she was unable to ask any questions. Silence probably boded better for her and Ben at this point. Finally, the bus came to a stop, jostling everybody awake; stretches and yawns broke through the tense air previously filling the bus.

Astrid woke the reluctant Ben, stood him up, and guided him to the front. The soldiers waited to get off behind them. Once disembarked, Astrid took in her surroundings, and her gaze latched onto the austere Dr. Heizer.

"Are we in the right spot? I thought we were rescued from the Institute." Astrid tried hard to keep her calm, her hands fisting themselves, her breath catching in her chest. "Yet it seems to have followed me here." She tried to turn around to leave, only to face the soldiers filed behind her. Ben's hand in her grasp quaked as he finally saw the doctor and froze in mid step.

Dr. Heizer moved forward but was stopped by the tall man standing behind her. Dark strips of dirt streaked her white coat here and there, but she still emanated the poise of authority.

"What's going on?" Astrid, losing her calm, demanded answers.

"Welcome to the Reformers." The man next to Dr. Heizer addressed them, his eyes bright brown, with the widest and brightest white Astrid had ever seen. "We apologize for any confusion. We're pleased you're here. Dr. Heizer was taken from the Institute just after you left. She means you no harm. My name is Benji, I am the head of the Reformers."

His presence immediately added tension to the air, forcing Astrid to retreat.

"Okay, can you tell me why she's here?"

"Her being here has nothing to do with you. Sibella, can you show our guest to her room? I'm sure she would like to get some rest." Benji held his hand out in a calming way, no doubt trying to keep the situation from escalating.

Sibella, who had made her way off the bus but stood by to watch, jumped to attention. "Uh, yes of course."

Astrid could see structure was not their forte. Deciding unconsciously to take Ben with her, she glanced down at him, seeing him staring straight at Dr. Heizer, frightened.

"Oh, he needs to stay here with us."

Benji's demand jolted Astrid. Ben stepped back out of Benji's reach and screamed, answering Benji for her. The high-pitched sound filled the ears of those in the vicinity, making everybody lunge to stop the noise. Astrid, being the closest, turned Ben around and crushed him into her chest.

"It's okay, Ben, I'm still here. You're still safe. Please, Ben."

Too late; she had already lost him. In the fit of an attack she knew nothing about. Ben shook violently, his hands covering his own ears. With a firm hold on Ben, Astrid glared at Benji, snapping, "I'm not leaving him with you. He's been through enough." Picking up Ben, she turned and followed Sibella out of the parking garage.

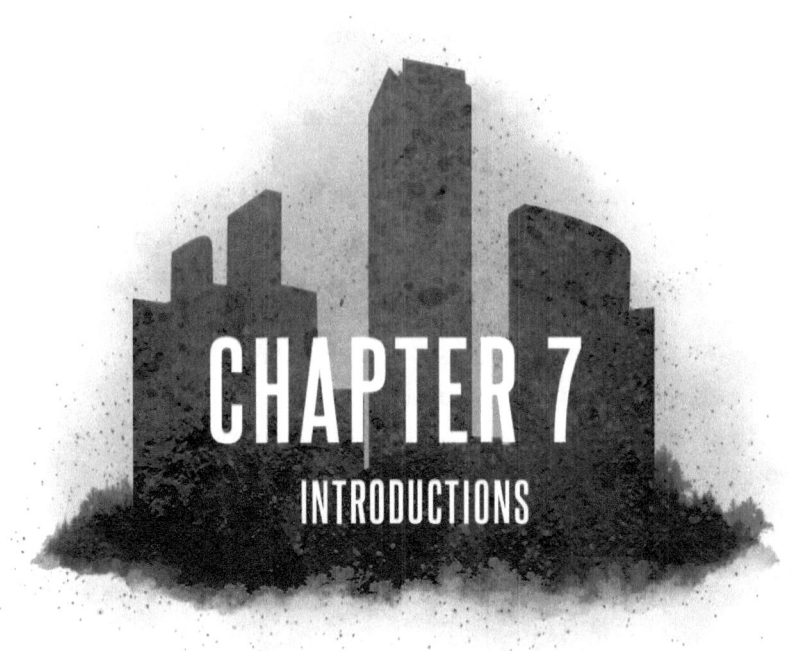

CHAPTER 7
INTRODUCTIONS

NO. No!" Becoming hysterical at the thought of being so close, yet not being able to hold her son again overwhelmed her. "Benni, it's me, Mom! Benni, I love you, I'm sorry!" Melvina's hysterics grew with each inch Ben moved away from her, his head buried in that woman's shoulder with his hands over his ears. She attempted to follow, but Benji held her back. Anger filled her—arms and hands making contact anywhere she could reach, with the intent to cause as much physical pain on Benji as she currently experienced inside.

Benji didn't move; he was an unyielding brick wall. He tried to speak while trying to keep her from bolting after her son. Losing control was not something that Melvina ever did. She was logical, an intellect. Emotions a thick tar she loathed. The less, the better. Lately, they'd been forcing themselves upon her. And she felt like she was drowning. Energy draining out of her, she held a fistful of Benji's shirt, her forehead on his chest. Heaving, she tried to catch her breath and her sanity.

Ben's rejection shredded her heart and soul. Dizziness and pain invaded her head, and her knees buckled. She soon found herself sobbing on the cold concrete floor as it sucked the last of the warmth she retained as her soul began to shatter and spread. Benji stood over her, shaking his head.

"You don't know! You don't know what it was like," she explained between breaths. "You weren't there when they took him from me. They pried his arms from around my neck and carried him away as he screamed for me. I was helpless. I cried for him as I listened to his screams fade. The next time I saw him, he had no idea who I was. No idea. I gave birth to him, cared for him every day, and he didn't know me. I thought that because he was without his last injection, his memory would be returning."

"He'll come around. It's been a long night. Come on, I'll show you to your room."

"I hate you." Melvina squared off with Benji. Turning around, she stormed back the way they'd come, not caring if she headed in the right direction or not.

"Love! Doctor," Mitch called to her. "You need to go this way to get to your room. Come on, I'll lead you." He unnerved her, but not having many choices forced her to turn and follow.

Her room was small and bare. Only the necessities provided—a bed with a pillow and a threadbare blanket. A sink to the side with a scratched up mirror above it. No facilities. "How quaint." Her living quarters at home were modest and clean, but with a few comforts: a comforter, air conditioning, and her books. She missed her home. Always quiet and safe, providing a level of comfort she now knew she took for granted. Of course all this was given due to her job status. She sat down on the bed, which squeaked with her weight, and let her head fall into her hands.

Melvina awoke hours later, in the fetal position facing the wall. Her face swollen and sore. Exhaustion filled her; her grumbling belly protested every move. Moving slowly, stretching each limb, each digit one by one, she threw her legs over the edge. After rinsing her face and hands in cold water, she made her way to the entrance, wondering if she should leave, wondering if she could leave.

She got lost, ended up wandering around, refusing to ask help of those who asked her if she needed anything, until stumbling upon the mess hall. Which was lit, empty, and peaceful. She found fruit and oatmeal, the food satisfying her in a way she didn't know possible. After the stress and adrenaline over the past few days she wasn't sure how much more she could handle. Winning her son back would take time and energy she felt she just did not have. She had betrayed him in the worst of ways, and it ate her up inside.

"Can't sleep?" Benji, his voice making her jerk and move away. "He's fine. He's grown attached to Astrid and is unwilling to leave her side. He goes into a panic every time we try. She's even unable to visit a bathroom without him." He smiled; the same smile that made her originally swoon for him, now threatening the food she'd just consumed.

"Is that supposed to make me feel better? That he found another mother figure and screams at the thought of seeing me?"

"He doesn't know who you are. According to Astrid, he knew you watched him. And that you would whisper his name. He associates you with a scary figure who will punish him at the lightest of transgressions. You need to give him time until his full memory returns. We have started flushing their systems, to get all the toxins out that you injected them with. Hopefully by tomorrow he will be our boy again."

"'Our' boy? Since when was he ever 'our' boy? He is *my* boy, and only *my* boy. He was only ever my boy!" She cleared her dishes more harshly than necessary, accidentally banging them together as she tried to get away from him.

"Are you in any way the least bit curious as to why we brought you here?"

"So you could have your happy little family?"

"No, I knew you were safe and doing the only thing you could for Ben. I need your help." He stopped, waiting for a response. "We are on the verge of overthrowing the Institute in California. We plan to hit Nevada after that. Those are two of the biggest institutes in the country. The government's weak spots. I'm fighting to get everybody's happy little families back. Not just ours. Not ever just ours. This world is full of heartbreaking stories, most worse than ours. I need your help."

"Why not ask? Why did you have to keep secrets, drug and kidnap me?" Her thoughts spun; he'd betrayed all over again. Almost as bad as being told your husband was dead. Having to plan a funeral with no body. He didn't need her; he needed what she had access to. The tears threatened to return. She grasped her middle, trying—no—forcing her food to stay.

"So you were not marked as a traitor. We need your clearance. We knew that if you were to leave on your own accord, you'd have been marked for death, all your records and clearance destroyed."

Without answering or conversing further, Melvina left the room. Benji appeared behind her at a brisk pace matching her own.

"I'm sorry, Mel, I truly am. I never meant to hurt you. I just did what I felt was right at the time. I'm trying to do that again. We don't have much time. Six months at the most, if we are lucky. The latest attack may have bought us more time."

"I don't understand, Benji. More time for what?"

"They ... they are picking off our families. Most of the Reformers were born here, born into this way of life, generations after generations, taught our lessons, morals, and reasoning. Trained in battle and war. But recently we have received an influx of new trainees. New recruits wanting to join the cause. Their mothers, cousins, brothers, wives, and parents targeted to flush them out. And it's working." His eyes serious, searching for something in her she wasn't sure she still possessed. "These young soldiers are returning, right into the government's paws to be tortured and to answer questions. They don't know much but could very well give up our location. We're going to respond, and quickly.

"We've done everything we can to assure safety, but truth is unless their family came with them we can't do a thing."

"Sad." She would not pity a bunch of strangers. She did not choose to join the Reformers; she was a target, pulled from her life and thrown in this. She was a prisoner of war. They took her freedom, just as much as the government.

"Mel, come on, a little empathy goes a long way. We can't pay you what you were getting, but I can reunite you with our son, and you can

76

work. You can show us what they were doing and why … help us reverse the damage. You have an opportunity to help people, the right way."

That was it, the last of it. The truth of what Benji wanted from her, leaking out as if the plumbing had gone bad. By accident or on purpose she did not care. Frustration appeared in her, pushing the rest of her patience aside.

"Interesting. I took a job to keep myself from being a patient, and I'm being indicted with the rest of the government. I was following orders, Benji, I did what I had to do. You admitted it yourself. You, of all people, do not get to judge me."

"I'm not judging, just giving you a chance at redemption."

They had arrived at her room. She stepped through the open doorway, turning around.

"I don't need redemption from you. Leave me alone. If I'm going to be a prisoner I want to be left alone." She didn't give him a chance to respond, just shut the door. It took everything in her not to slam it in his smug face.

Redemption? Is he delusional? She hadn't done anything wrong. She became a doctor, not necessarily in the way she thought, or the facility she wanted to be in, but still, she met her goals. Melvina succeeded. She was a doctor. And nobody, especially him, would make her doubt it.

THE drive is only an hour and a half. But whenever you guys bring in newbies they're asleep, why?" The voice was high-pitched, undeveloped, and annoying.

Toro rolled his head, stretching his neck, lifting it slowly, trying to open his eyes. He was lying on a gurney in a gray room, strapped down. His nose still hurt, but nothing compared to his head.

"Ugh" was all he managed.

The lights were too bright; every time he tried opening his eyes, nails shot through his retinas straight into his brain.

"Hey, he insisted we kidnap him. He kept going on about loyalties and traitors. Had to make it convincing. Have to admit, though, drugging him was totally unnecessary." Jackson laughed, his hand on Toro's left shin. "You'll be all right, they've got you hooked up to the right stuff. Get some rest."

"Why?" Toro got out.

"Why what?"

"Why am I tied down?"

"In case you wanted to return the broken nose. Just protecting myself."

"Jerk." Toro kept his eyes closed, listening to their voices as they continued their conversation. Overall the mission had been a success until Jackson shot Rhodes.

At this point, Toro forced himself to pay attention.

"He was sharp, resourceful, on to us. He'd linked the doctor and her son. He would've been the end of us; you'll understand soon enough." Jackson sounded hurt, but at the same time relieved. "I'm going to go update Benji, maybe get some rest. Take care of him. He'll be useful to us. Just needs to be trained up a bit."

Finding it too hard to think any further, Toro fell back asleep.

The next day he found himself being shuffled about, shown the ropes. Being told different ways he could assist. He seemed to have come into the folds of the Reformers without question or initiation. He still hadn't met Benji, but over lunch saw the woman and boy Jackson referred to, the prisoner he had stopped from escaping. Her shoulders tight, huge bags under her eyes, short-tempered with everybody except the little boy, stress covering her entire form. After the shock of seeing her again, Toro became excited. He decided that no matter what it took, it was vital to help her. Help her with whatever she needed. He was at her mercy.

"Hey." Jackson sat down next to him and started attacking his food. With a mouthful, he announced, "There's somebody here who's asking for you. You game?"

"Who?"

"The doctor from the Institute." He finished his meal. Draining a cup of water, he stood up, disposed of his dishes. "You coming?"

"Yeah, I guess I'm done here." Toro took care of his unfinished lunch by wolfing it down and followed Jackson out.

The massive compound had proved hard to master; he kept getting lost, having to ask for directions when he wasn't being escorted. Then there was the addition of the horrendous fish smell.

"I see they fixed you up. Nose isn't abnormally defected. Your headache ever go away?" This was Jackson's idea of small talk, apparently.

"Yeah, thanks for that, I guess." Toro accepted his current position; he knew he might as well make the best of it. "I start training with the new recruits soon."

"So I heard. You'll do well, man. You deserve to be here; you need to be here. She's through there."

They came to a stop in a hallway housing personal rooms. The door Jackson referred to was open, and he could see Dr. Heizer's head on a pillow, her blond hair a stark contrast to the blanket pulled up to her chin. "She's expecting you. Try to cheer her up a bit, will you? She's been a real pain to everybody."

Dr. Heizer's skin had a gray tone to it; her face was sunken. Toro cleared his throat gently. Since arriving, there hadn't been a structure given to him on how to address people, but calling her ma'am in this condition didn't seem right.

Her eyes popped open, finding him with haste. "So it's true, you deserted."

"I was taken against my will, like you. Just not having as formidable a time with it."

"So it would seem." She moved, leaning against the wall and patting the bed next to her for Toro to take a seat. "Tell me."

He explained everything, from the storage rooms to being hit in the face, to waking up strapped to a gurney.

"Well, I guess you're the only friend I have here." She still hadn't fully focused on him since she'd sat.

"I don't understand, Doctor. You have a chance to do good, to help get our world back. Why are you fighting this?"

"They have my son and are refusing to let me see him."

"The boy? The one who arrived with the patient from the Institute?"

"Yes, him. You must think I'm a horrible person. Who would let the government take their child to save their own skin?" Her head fell, her hands working the blanket. "Well, you really don't know what you are capable of until it happens to you. I didn't have a choice; I only thought I did. I did what I had to do, and would do it again." She paused, getting control of herself. "I have this opportunity, you say? What opportunity? Fixing up people who choose to get shot at? People who choose to fight against the one form of structure still standing? This country will fall into anarchy if our government falls. Don't they see that? We can't let them succeed." Her eyes were wide, and her hands stilled.

Toro's thoughts started to twist; he tried to make sense of what she had suggested. If the country needed to die to be reborn, then so be it. He knew then, what she was asking of him. The thought opening itself to him, like a flower in spring. She needed him. Melvina felt he owed allegiance to her in some odd way. To lead her on would be wrong. He owned no intention of ever going back.

"There's that word again, 'we.' You knew I was in storage searching through old dusty records to get proof. You told me to keep you out of it, as to not indict you as well. But now we're a 'we'?"

"Overlooking secrets is easier to do when you don't have to deal with them every day. And yes, we. I am still your superior. Just in a different location. Toro, they plan on blowing up the institutes, both here in California and in Nevada. They're psychos, the lot of them."

Since arriving his view of the government and the institutes had changed dramatically. He learned a lot, and for once finally felt included. He now knew a cause, and he was enjoying every minute. His family needed to be freed of the suppression they were under. He needed to find a way to get to them. That didn't include helping to save the institutes.

"I don't think so, ma'am."

"What?" Shock and malevolence overtook her face. "You work for me. We, yes, *we*, are prisoners of war. You don't get to trade sides whenever you feel like it. You will do what you are told, or you will be marked."

"Then I will be marked." Toro stayed calm. He knew the decision was correct. Jackson was right; this was where he needed to be. "I hope you decide to help; you could do a lot of good here." He stood, the bed groaning with relief. Closing the door behind him, he stepped out.

Jackson stood at the end of the hallway, waiting. "Benji would like a word as well, if you're up to it?"

"Benji? The guy who oversees all this? Okay."

Toro followed Jackson, again losing his way with all the turns and intersecting hallways. He wanted to meet this guy; was interested in knowing the plan and what his part in it would be.

The patient and the little boy from the Institute rounded a corner in front of them. The patient froze, pulled the boy closer, moving to the side of the hallway. Jackson nodded at her and continued on. Kindness, getting the best of Toro, caused him to stop, to try.

Her eyes were what caught him. Full of love. It practically poured from her. The color transfixed him—deep brown with golden depth, encircled by a bright crystal blue. It was fascinating as it was beautiful.

"I'm glad you got out, and that you're okay." He smiled at her. Her eyes captured him, the golden threads reaching out and pulling at him.

"You're from the Institute, too, aren't you? Which side are you playing on? White or black?" She was pissed; her anger overtook him. He felt she was too pure to have such a dark passion as anger coming from her.

Stepping back, he dropped his head. "Recently? New convert, as of yesterday, black." He heeded her again, and she was still standing there. "I'm sorry." He apologized for more than she knew. Toro understood she may not remember him stopping her that fateful day from escaping, and he understood she needed to find herself again.

Whatever she needs, he reminded himself, continuing on his way, giving her a wide berth. Not wanting to give her any more reason to dislike him.

"What changed your mind?" she called after him.

His spirits lifted. He considered conversing in any way with her positive.

"The truth seems to be hidden in the most unlikely spots. Wouldn't you say?" he called over his shoulder.

ASTRID spent days reassuring Ben that Dr. Heizer wasn't going to kidnap him in the middle of the night. He refused to leave her—they ate together, slept in the same bed. In fact, Ben would even sit outside the shower stall waiting on her. She hummed and talked to him, reassuring him that she would not leave, a compromise to leaving her foot where he could see it.

She didn't mind. Having to constantly worry and take care of a child kept her from obsessing over what the Reformers' plans were and what they planned on doing with Dr. Heizer. Which bothered Astrid. What reasoning could there be for Dr. Heizer to be here? They were supposed to destroy the evil, not bring it with them.

Other than Ben, she only really interacted with Sibella, who stayed close and made sure she knew her way around, and Jackson, who made sure they received everything they needed. Tall and dark, the mysterious, bad boy type. Conversations with him always made her happy. He had recently asked if she planned to join training—all the new recruits went through a rigorous program to weed out those who couldn't cut it in the field. This intrigued Astrid.

There were many other things she could do: cleaning crew, the cooks, the nursery, the infirmary. She could go into training for anything. But being able to help level the playing field against the government was an attractive option. She needed to decide if she had what it took. Could she fight? Could she take a life if necessary? Could she do what would be asked of her to free her mom?

"Uh, Jackson? Do you have a few minutes?" Astrid had spotted him coming out of the shower room. She and Ben had been out for a walk, exercising, getting to know their surrounding area. She pulled him along at a hurried pace to talk with Jackson.

"Yeah, of course. What's up?" He stopped, leaning against the wall with his shoulder, hands on his belt.

Wow, he's cute.

"I, uh, I …" *Geez, get it out already. He's not that cute.* "I want to join the training program with the new trainees. I want to be able to help get my mom back."

He smiled that gorgeous smile of his, showing off dimples. "Perfect, you'll do well. I'll make sure you're on the list and that Sibella knows to get you to the right place."

"Do you know if my mom, Margaret, was in the L.A. Institute? If she got out?"

"No, the only person who would know that would be Benji. Sorry. Good luck in training, and finding your mom." He pushed off the wall, continuing down the hall. Her stomach fluttered, her palms sweaty.

I have no time for this, she thought.

Ben tugged on her arm. With a smile, she looked down at him. His green eyes were bright. She was concerned that he would never talk to anybody but her; it was selfish of her to enjoy that so much. They continued down to the mess hall for lunch, Ben trailing behind her with a death grip hold on her pinky.

"There you are," Sibella fretted. When she wasn't in her black Reformers gear, she was quite pretty. Her face softened a lot toward Astrid. After greetings and an attempt to get Ben to acknowledge her, she turned her attention back to Astrid. "We have some news we need to share. Benji has requested an audience with you."

With a quizzical look Astrid gestured at Sibella in acknowledgment and for her to lead the way.

"What are you going to do about Ben?"

"What do you mean?" They continued navigating a hallway. Taking a left turn and heading down a hallway Astrid hadn't traversed before.

"You do know who his father is, right? Benji is short for Benjamin."

"I had an inkling. It doesn't seem Benji has much interest, so it should be okay."

Ben hadn't reacted to Benji on the day they arrived, only to Dr. Heizer.

Sibella moved aside, her arm outstretched, pointing the way and letting Astrid and Ben pass. The lights of the small makeshift office pushed darkness away. The earthy smell she'd grown used to was even stronger here. Benji stopped what he was doing as they entered. He glanced quickly at Ben and then concentrated on Astrid.

"Come in, have a seat. We have much to discuss."

Astrid placed herself in front of Benji's desk, as comfortable as she could be with a child on her lap before speaking. "Benji, is it? You run the Reformers?"

"Yes, I see you've been filled in. Good, it'll shorten this meeting. Upon your arrival we drew blood, do you remember?"

"Yes, I was told you took everybody's blood."

"We do. But yours has something special in it. I have a feeling it has something to do with your eyes. Ben has it as well. Something we might be able to use it in our war."

"Your," she corrected.

"Excuse me?" He seemed confused for a second before comprehending what she was saying.

"It's your war, not ours. I'm being drug into it, by what everybody else sees in our eyes." Astrid had promised herself not to get caught up and used again by somebody else. She sat with her back straight, feet on the floor. Ben balanced on her lap, his head resting against her chest, calm, waiting patiently.

"No, this war is everybody's … everybody who is a part of this country. This is *our* war." He placed great emphasis when he asserted *our*, and his eyes darkened. Trying callously to convince her. This war was obviously his life; this war meant everything to him. A quizzical expression covered his face, creasing lines around his eyes she hadn't noticed before. Glancing at his papers, he shook his head, finally returning to the conversation. "Back to you. You have a unique enzyme in your blood that is unknown. You two are the only ones in this compound who possess it. Maybe that's the cause for your eyes. Proof of experimentation."

"What is it?" She wasn't startled by the news, and she'd didn't show any response, having become comfortable with different reactions to others seeing her and Ben's eyes. And she still no idea what they were seeing; when she looked in the mirror, her eyes were brown. Just brown, no blue, no proof.

"It makes you immune to all the drugs and antidotes the government uses. After initial testing we weren't surprised at this. That's why you beat the M-124. That's why you have your memories and most of the other patients are still trying to find theirs. Some may never succeed." His hands clasped in front of him in his lap, he sat back in his chair and stared at her.

"Okay, what does that mean?" Astrid's calm slipped as information she did not want forced itself inside her head. Gaping black holes existed in her memory, where anything could have transpired.

An experiment.

"It means you're special. It means that because you're special you were experimented on. You may have an ability you don't know about. We have you, and we plan on using you. I hear you want to start the training program?"

"An ability? I was housed in L.A., right? No memor—use me how?" She decided it best to keep what little information she owned to herself. This journey was becoming something she didn't want to be a part of. She no longer wanted to be used by anybody. Choosing to be a Reformer was a choice, but along with it, was she signing up to be used again?

Astrid concentrated on those holes in her memory. Her mom lived there, her mom's location hidden inside her head. Going along with Benji's plan might be the only way.

"The Institute in Vegas is the only place you would have gone through this and have been given that anomaly." He nodded his head, gesturing to her eyes.

"Why do you want the Experimental Institute?"

"Because of what's inside. It needs to be destroyed. We need to stop them from taking the last bit of humanity." Stopping, he took a deep breath, his knuckles now white from the grip he held on his hands.

"Melvina is proving to be difficult, and she was our ticket in. Now we need to be creative. I hear this is where your mom is."

She had asked, searched, focused on every incoming patient's face. Her mother hadn't been rescued. She was not here. In her lap Ben started shaking his head side to side, mumbling again. Astrid placed her hand on his head to soothe him.

"How do you know that?"

Hope was a dangerous foe she did not have the energy to fight. She needed more information, one thing at a time. If Benji spoke the truth she needed skills, abilities to help and protect her mom. Not idly standing by watching someone else do it for her.

"I make it my business to know everything about anybody we purposely bring in, especially if that particular person is caring for my son." He gestured to Ben. Astrid was now extremely anxious about the situation and fidgeted along with Ben. "We need your help. As you're an escapee, if we were to release you on the streets, you would be sent straight to Vegas for tests. We would shortly follow."

"If I am an experiment, and Ben is as well, why were we in the L.A. Institute in the first place?"

"I don't know. We stumbled upon you by chance. I knew Ben was there, only because I was watching Melvina."

Ben's head shook more, side to side. A small whimper.

"Who is Melvina?" Astrid shushed Ben and thought about what Benji had said previously. He'd told her he purposefully brought her in, which meant he knew she was there. He hadn't stumbled upon her by chance. She held more leverage than she originally thought.

"Dr. Melvina Heizer. His mother."

"She's refusing to help?" Astrid's mind spun. Dr. Heizer—a mom? Ben's mom? Why would Ben react the way he did? Why was he scared of his own mother? What had she done to him?

"Not quite refusing, just not cooperating in a way we need her to. She's not content about the reunion she had with Ben."

She didn't answer, didn't respond in any way. Just watched him. He seemed concerned with Dr. Heizer's reunion with Ben but didn't seem to be trying towards Ben himself.

"Other than Las Vegas, we don't know where this institute is located. We would have to place a locater chip in you. Follow it." He switched back to his focus, no concern given or emotion shown.

"And none of your other soldiers are willing to do this?" Her uneasiness grew. The quicker she could get out to process, the better. If she were a patient in Vegas she wouldn't be able to go after her mom; she would have to trust them to do it for her.

"No, none of my other soldiers have ever been in an institute before. Since you've already been through the process, you know what to expect. You know how to act. And you're guaranteed to remember the experience. I want you to think about it. Attend the meeting we're having tomorrow. It might enlighten you into helping us."

"If I decide to do this, I need a guarantee from you that my mother makes it out alive with me." Her sternness shocked her. She demanded from Benji something nobody in their right mind would promise.

"If she is still alive, yes. We already planned on emptying the place before we destroyed it. We are not heartless."

"I'm not so sure." Astrid stood, putting Ben on his feet, who mumbled to himself, moving away from her and backing toward the door. Interested to see what he would do, she let go of his hand. Watching for the first time as Ben did anything on his own.

Benji stood abruptly, his legs hitting the table, knocking contents over and creating calamity and distraction. Ben jumped, rushing back into Astrid's embrace and protection. Now he pulled her along with him.

They left without another word, Ben leading the charge. His grip tighter than normal. Her heart pounding, dizziness pulling her side to side, feeling that no matter what she decided to do, Benji would find a way to use her, even without her consent.

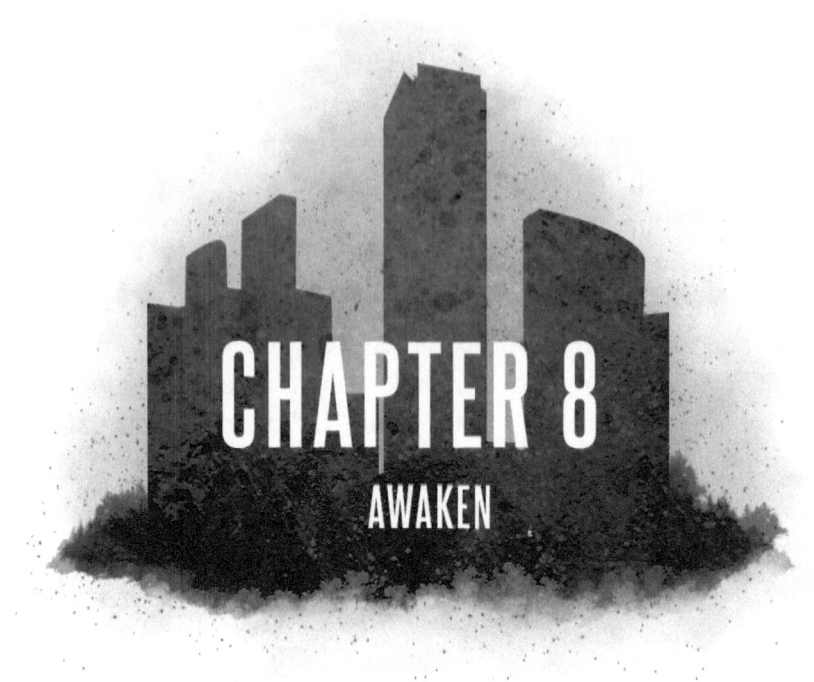

CHAPTER 8

AWAKEN

TORO wasn't sure about Benji. They'd talked and talked, Benji wanting to know Toro's decision on joining training or not. Toro fired questions about operations, plans, training, the fate of Captain Rhodes. Anything and everything he felt the need to know. Only to be answered with a smirk or a sidelong glance at Jackson.

"We're going to hold a meeting. We have some new information that I think everybody will want to know. Maybe even answer some of your questions," Benji said. Toro felt he liked being in charge just a little too much. "Did you have any luck with Melvina?"

"Melvina?"

"Dr. Heizer."

"No, she's troubled. Thinks you're barbaric."

"She's refusing to eat, won't leave her room. Won't speak to anybody. And is refusing to believe anything we tell her."

"What are you telling her?"

"That she's a patient. Her blood tests show the memory drug in her system. We tried offering saline to help flush it out. But if she's not eating or engaging it won't do any good."

Toro blanched at that information, thinking back at his employment at the Institute. If the government did it to their own employees, they were not safe ... nobody was. Dr. Heizer performed her duties with educated precision. If she was indeed a patient, how did her memories about her husband and son stay intact? Questions forced themselves to the front of Toro's mind. She was programmed to do exactly what they wanted her to.

"Wait? No, that's not right. She's the head doctor for the Los Angeles Institute. She oversaw everything and everybody. How could she have been a patient?"

"Don't know. If she's remembering anything she's not sharing. I was hoping seeing you would help."

"Why do you need her?"

"Clearance. She can get us back in."

"No she can't."

"Excuse me?"

Toro stopped, having to force himself from boasting too much. Was there something he knew that Benji did not?

"Do you honestly think that the security clearance of a kidnapped doctor and guard are going to be left active? Our key chip codes are frozen. It would notify security and the general the moment we scan in."

"Our intelligence inside security says different."

He was all-knowing. How annoying. Benji didn't even have the decency to notice anything other than the papers he continued to shuffle on his table. And if he did, it was Jackson.

"Uh ... if you say so. I'm not going to argue with you. But I'm telling you, this will not work."

"We'll see you at the meeting tomorrow? We're happy to have you and excited you've decided to stay and help. We can use a guy like you. Don't miss the training sessions. Jack doesn't react well to tardiness or absences." He didn't miss a beat. Didn't bother acknowledging his previous comment or take it at all.

"Jack, got it. Thanks." Toro got up and shook hands with both Benji and Jackson before heading out.

He stood outside for a few minutes, going over the conversation regarding Melvina. It was disconcerting. The head doctor, who oversaw everybody else. What Benji said did not make sense, in any way.

Toro spent the rest of the day meandering aimlessly, his thoughts bouncing between old information and new.

He found the compound impressive, a mini hidden version of a self-sustained village. The Reformers had created their own underground ecosystem that supported everything they needed to grow all kinds of vegetables, fruit, and herbs, and to hold and keep livestock. Electricity used from old solar panels collected from surrounding buildings and homes in the area. Toro's fascination grew the more he learned how these people escaped the government for so long. With all the technological advances that took place, it was nothing short of a miracle. The Reformers were living proof that it was possible. That hope survived, that the government could fall.

During his tour of the compound he came across an open room. Entering, he found bookshelves covered in dust and single bulbs hanging from the ceiling in intervals dangling by exposed wire. The light blared with a flick of the knob instantly astonishing him. The room was small, but filled, every nook and cranny loaded with books, and slim plastic cases with happy people on the front and a synopsis on the back. The side labeled them as DVDs. A movie? Toro had heard about these. After the downfall, they ceased being made, along with everything else that was found unnecessary. This room was treated as forgotten history, left to the touch of time.

The books grabbed his attention. Digital copies served the story, but lost something in the process. A physical book provided a connection. A constant reminder of other worlds, other people; all screaming for visitation, never forgotten. Pulling a leather bound gently off a shelf, Toro turned the book over in his hands. The motion made him deliriously happy. The smell and brittle pages in his hands bringing euphoria like he'd never known before. So much lost when the government violated every right. Down to their right to escape the world that was currently forcing humanity out.

"Ah, I see you have found our little bit of history."

The voice startled him into dropping the book. He bent to gather it back, glancing behind him to see Red.

"I thought you didn't like to talk?"

"I don't, much. But I've been told to talk to you, so here I am." Red stayed near the door.

Trying not to make the situation more uncomfortable than it already was, Toro tried to keep his focus on anything other than Red.

"You've been told? By who?" He enjoyed being left to his own devices, only called upon when necessary. Being left alone to adjust.

"Find anything interesting?" Red gestured to the book in his hand. Sweat breaking out on his forehead, his hands shaking. Ready to bolt. Toro noticed Red's obvious distress and chose to try to alleviate the situation.

"I love to read. My tablet was connected to the Digital Approved Library, and I find myself missing it. I read all the time."

"This room is for our use, take what you want, just return it when you're done. The movies are my favorite. I find myself a fan of *Batman*. The masked crusader appeals to me. I relate to putting a mask on and pretending to be somebody else. We only have one of the DVDs, but I have a feeling there was more to it." He wasn't quite babbling, but the nerves were still showing themselves.

"Where did this all come from?"

"Old libraries, houses nearby. Anywhere we could get it really. They stopped adding to the collection due to lack of storage. It's sad; it's not trivial information. It was part of who we once were. Now everything is digitized, censored, and controlled. If it's not approved, you don't get to see it."

"A much simpler time. These books, I've never heard of some of these titles."

"Help yourself."

"I will, thank you. Was there something specific you were supposed to talk to me about?" He tried again, knowing Red knew something he did not.

"No, just talk." He shook his head, and, his task completed, exited, leaving Toro alone.

"That was awkward. Why would they 'order' somebody to come talk to you?" another voice asked.

Toro moved slowly, scanning the rest of the room. Seeing what he missed before. A dark-skinned reader with black hair cuddled in a corner surrounded by a cocoon of books. Holding one in his lap, he stared up at Toro.

"Seto," he introduced himself with a smile.

"Yeah, it was a bit awkward. I'm Toro. You been here long?" He moved closer, scanning the rest of the floor space, searching for others he may have missed. Satisfied they were alone, he joined Seto on the floor. Somebody to share concerns and thoughts with would ease his mind.

"Weeks, I think. With nothing to keep busy day after day they all blur together." Seto shuffled, making room. Scooting stacks of books closer to himself.

"I know what you mean. Will you be training?"

"Yes, you?"

"Yea, I need something to do. I'll go stir crazy otherwise."

"True."

"Were you reading in the dark? I thought I had to turn the lights on when I walked in? Did I disturb you?"

Seto smiled. "I was sleeping. This room's unoccupied most of the time. It's peaceful, no noise. You didn't disturb me."

"Well, I'll leave you to it then. Nice meeting you. See you around."

Seto answered with similar niceties as Toro stood with his hardback in hand.

THE voice hadn't stopped. Ever since Benji spat those noxious lies to her, it just wouldn't cease. Different than her inner voice, it startled her at first. Was she going crazy? Was this the abyss finally swallowing her? She listened; she did not have any other choice. Benji was out to use her, out to get her back for doing well after he deserted them. To punish her for what happened to Ben. She was, after all, a prisoner. The food was poison; the voice convinced her of it, and unable to know exactly what information they were after, she stopped talking to everybody, including that traitorous Toro. How could he? Melvina ordinarily was strong, smart, assertive, but since her departure from the Institute her thoughts became strange. New information jumbled her knowledge, made her wonder, question things she would not have before.

Benji came in daily. Insistently offering food, trying to assure her she was safe, that nobody would hurt her. She would sit in the fetal position with her back in the corner at the head of this despicable bed they had her on, glaring at him over her knees. He was hurting her. Telling her the M-124 coursed through her system, that the general was using her, using her son to keep her compliant.

But Benji didn't need to know he was right. The special gene found in Ben's blood had earned him a one-way ticket to experimentation. No matter what she did, who she begged, the general would not release him. Melvina chose instead to do her job, but she checked on him every day. Although, since leaving the Institute the motherly bond in her strengthened with every passing minute. She found herself dreaming of holding him, smelling his washed hair and the nape of his neck— the pure, innocent smell everybody wished they could hold on to. She missed him, and her heart hurt beyond anything she could explain, the pain making her dry heave and sob until finally she passed out from exhaustion.

Her hatred grew, developing into a monster out of her control. She had to fight the urge to lash out at Benji each time he came in.

The voice spoke up again. Repeating the danger she was in, that the only way out was to bolt through the door when it opened. Standing in the corner near the foot of her bed, head against the wall, the motion began with a simple lift, contractions of her neck muscles pulling her head from the wall. Subconsciously, she let it fall without interference.

Bang.

Again, to sense the physical connection.

Bang.

The pain feral, calling for help. An outward cry.

Bang.

Nobody ever answered. The sound made her grind her teeth.

Melvina is safe. Melvina is in danger. Rescue is coming. It never ended.

Ben. She wanted to see Ben, but she was told he didn't want to see her. They were trying to keep him happy. She was his mother!

"I will keep him happy!" she screamed to an empty room. "He's mine." Her voice cracked, the tears hot against her cheeks. She detested being weak. Being weak made people pity you. Pity made you rely on somebody, anybody else.

How many days have you been locked up? the voice continued.

Bang.

Please stop.

You'll never survive this. You're weak.

Bang.

Please.

Weak and filthy.

Bang.

How dare you sink so low?

"Melvina."

Was that the voice? Her conscious?

"Melvina, stop." There it was again.

She held her head inches from the wall, turning gradually. She could see Benji through the dirty strands of her hair covering her face. How long had he been there?

"Melvina, you need to eat." He held a tray, and she cocked her head to the side, leaning gently against the wall, sliding down to the floor. "I have broth, soup. Not sure which kind. It's good."

He crouched down in front of her with the tray, holding a bowl accompanied by a spoon. He was careful, like he was trying to calm a rabid dog, not wanting to be bitten. The smell made her stomach turn in knots and threaten to spew what limited amount it held.

"I'm worried about you. It's been almost a week. You haven't eaten. Are you even sleeping? You can't survive like this. Ben needs you to be healthy, he needs you to take care of yourself."

Sympathy. It was there in his eyes pouring toward her in a comforting blanket. She blinked, and he was gone. The soup on the foot of the bed.

It's poison, don't eat it. But she chose to ignore the voice. There was one thing Benji was right about: Ben needed her.

She crawled hand over hand to the foot of the bed, picking up the bowl, taking a sip. The voice screamed at her. *It will kill you.*

Melvina shook her head, taking another sip. The taste euphoric; her stomach growled. The soup was cold, but she finished it anyways. Slow and steady, not wanting her stomach to expel it. When the bowl was empty she placed it in front of the door on the floor and curled up on her bed with the threadbare blanket on her shoulders, falling into a fitful dream-filled sleep.

When she awoke—not knowing how long she'd slept, not sure if it was day or night—she felt a bit better. She had regained some strength, but she was hungry, dehydrated, and in desperate need of clean water. Sitting up carefully, the blanket falling on the floor, she noticed the bowl was gone, replaced by a pitcher of water and a single slice of bread. She quickly devoured it, wanting to get it in before the voice told her not to, not wanting to give it a chance to talk her out of it. The water so cool and clean crossing her lips, moistening her dry tongue and burning throat. It was not enough.

The door's locked; you've joined them now. The voice quieter than before; the sudden company made her jerk, searching, praying for there to be someone in the room. She was still alone.

The voice repeated its toxin, pushing doubt into her mind again. Melvina stood, stepping toward the door. *Benji locked you in; you're dangerous to him.* She timidly grasped the handle, the knob cracked and cold. It turned, opened. The light on the other side brighter than the one in her room, sticking needles into her eyes, blasting through the voice and doubt in her head.

"Well hello there, love." A familiar voice, to the right. She glanced, blinking the needles away that left her eyes watery. "Do you need something?"

"Water," she answered. "And a shower." The little water she had managed to get down did nothing for her voice. Her words came out rough, jagged.

"Of course, the showers are across the hall there." He pointed. "I'll go get some fresh water for your room."

He left her standing there, blinking. Mitch, it was Mitch. The one who took her, now guarding her.

She went to the room he directed her to. The hot water over her body felt divine, washing away the pity and self-destruction the recent path had forced upon her. At this moment the shower was incomparable to anything she experienced before.

"Glad to see you up." Benji's voice came approvingly from beyond the sheet that divided her from the rest of the room.

She'd lost track of how long she stood there. His voice brought her back to herself.

"Go away." Her voice cracked, still weak. She cursed herself.

"And she speaks." He was too enthused. Triggering a quiver in her stomach that sent bile to the base of her throat.

"Go. Away," she countered more firmly, her commanding voice slowly returning to her.

"There's more food and water in your room per your request. You're not confined there though. You're free to roam around, see the compound. Get some exercise, maybe even see Ben."

At this she shot her head out from behind the sheet. "I can see him now?" Water droplets followed paths made previously down her face, dripping into her eyes and mouth.

"You could always see him, but the one thing we can't control is his reaction to you. He has a deep fear of you. He shuts down and has anxiety attacks whenever you're mentioned. To him, you are not his mother, you are the doctor that caused him pain."

"No! No, this isn't right." She shut the water off, wrapped a thin piece of cloth around her midsection, and stepped out to face off with Benji. "I never hurt him. I tried to save him. I couldn't ..."

"Well, whatever you remember may not be what he remembers. Please try not to push him past a point he can't handle." He turned and left, the door shutting slightly behind him.

The judgment, the audacity. Benji held no right.

Melvina let loose a scream full of built-up frustration, bending over to expel every ounce of anger out. She ended up on the floor, again.

No tears this time, Melvina. Time to get up, time to fix this. Time to show the Reformers exactly who you are and what you're capable of.

TORO found a seat in the mess hall, waiting for the meeting to commence. Astrid sat across from him, the little boy next to her with a piece of fruit in front of him. Toro's heart had skipped a bit when she sat down. Her hair was silk, and he so desperately wanted to touch it.

"How are you holding up in here?" he asked, his hands fidgeting under the table, hoping she would answer. Hoping she hadn't taken the seat just because it was one of the last few available.

"Okay." He didn't expect her to be so kind toward him after their last run in. Her eyes never met his, and her hands searched for something to do. "You joining the training?"

"I planned to, yes." They were conversing, though Astrid's attention never failed to leave Ben.

"Me too. I'm not quite sure what to do with Ben though."

He never pictured her timid, always imagined her enduring, dedicated to any cause she chose to pick up.

"Isn't there a school, or maybe somebody who could take him?" Toro's thoughts instantly went to the boy's parents, Benji perhaps.

"Maybe." Astrid patted Ben's head, flattening his hair on his head. Toro could tell this separation would be hard on them both.

Benji and his band of followers arrived, talking amongst themselves. Their presence changed the air in the room, causing everybody to settle in. Toro's attention was now torn; he wanted to continue the conversation with Astrid. Talking with her brought with it a calming effect, but Benji's meeting also important. Jackson and Red stopped to stand near the door, leaning against the wall. Sibella and Reider took seats along with the rest of the red banded Reformers. They were a bit intimidating. Toro found himself admiring them, wanting to be like them. Wanting now to listen.

"Hello." Benji took a stand up toward the front of the room, his hands in his pockets. "Glad everybody could join us. I see we have quite a turn out ... new recruits, current trainees, and of course those who scare away the new recruits and current trainees."

Laughter filled the room. Not sure if it was worth a full laugh out loud or not, the girls covered their mouths, and guys smiled with a huff.

"Now to get on with it. We have decided to move up our timeline. As you know we were lucrative in the breakout. We were successful in reaching our targets. And we're making progress with information regarding Las Vegas."

Warranted cheers rose up from those who already belonged within the Reformers, fists pumping into the air matching their loud hoorays.

"All the new recruits start training in two days. Brace yourselves, it is not an easy program. Jack is crude and harsh, but he is the best we have. He happens to be the best knife thrower in the country. Put your heart into it and you'll join the best of us soon.

"It has been brought to my attention that there are rumors regarding my family." Everybody went quiet, backs and shoulders straightened to attention. "Yes, my wife and son were rescued from the L.A. Institute. They are here. My wife was under the assumption that I was dead. She's having a hard time accepting this new information. That's all you need to know. I politely ask that the talking and whispering behind my back come to a halt, now."

Benji took a deep breath. Toro felt that he forced himself to share that bit of personal information at the push of somebody else, to stop the inquiries into his private life.

"Red, who has been with us for a while, who's been through more than most, has a story to share. This is important for everybody to understand why we are doing what we do. This story just recently came to my attention, and I feel it's necessary that everybody is aware. Red needs everybody's attention and respect, and no interruptions please. I will explain further after he is done. Red?"

Red came forward, wearing a somber expression. This was difficult for him; it was all over his posture. He was physically struggling to form the words he needed to tell his story.

"In the early twenty-first century, the Arvilla enzyme was discovered, named after the founding scientist, Cahn Arvilla. A happenstance discovery during routine cloning DNA research. The mere existence of this enzyme paved the way to the world as we now know it, opening a doorway to the unexpected, the unbelievable, and at the time what was impossible. The democracy at the time ordered research on the Arvilla enzyme; they wanted to know exactly what it was, even down to the molecular level. They wanted to know its properties, its capabilities, and it's potential. Would it help or hinder their progress? So, Dr. Cahn opened a testing program, one that would entice lower income citizens to his doors without questions as they weren't sure what would come from it.

"His research found that the enzyme protected its host from blood and mind-altering drugs. They were developing what we now know as the M-124. A drug to censor its hosts, make them more compliant and controllable. The Arvilla enzyme broke the compound down, eliminating it all together. As you can imagine, the government did not like the report presented by Dr. Cahn. It was problematic to the government's goal. They ordered the research to continue with a goal of eradicating the enzyme from its host. Many, many people died from this, teaching Dr. Cahn that it could not be separated by will or even force. They spent two years failing before the General Surgeon ordered testing of the entire population, searching for the answer to the question: How many were affected?

"The answer was 35 percent. Ranging across race, religious beliefs, income, and geographic location. Nothing creating a common link between those infected. They announced an outbreak, causing mass panic. Those testing positive were marked with the contagious symbol on a red band they wore on their arms, a bright warning for others to keep a safe distance." Red absentmindedly touched his own band, which now held more meaning for everybody in the room.

"Hatred and prejudice bred within the society, creating one common thought fueled by propaganda and lies. The infected people were considered a virus, a walking, talking disease threatening the population. This enzyme was not contagious; it's something people were born with, in the blood of its host. It was not viral or air born, and it could not be caught from a hand shake or a sneeze. But the fear spread hand in hand with the rapid growth of the Arvilla enzyme.

"As time passed the enzyme spread to babies with two clean parents. Thirty-five quickly became 38 percent within a decade. As it continued to spread, fear seeped into those who did not have it, mainly those in control. The red arm bands slowly disappeared along with those who wore them."

A collective breath was taken as thoughts were reorganized thoughts. This was history they only thought they knew brought to light.

A movement towards the back of the room rustled the somber air. Somebody raised their hand, a question bubbling to be asked. Red stopped, nodding at the new incomer.

"How do you know this? The histories of that time were lost during the civil war." The question sparked everybody's curiosity. The kid had a point. Nobody really knew for sure what happened back then.

"As you know, everybody calls me Red," As he spoke he wriggled his arm out of his red band, spreading it into a wider circular cloth in his hand. "They call me Red because when I'm angry I turn red. Truth be told …" He wasn't looking at anybody. His hands turned the red cloth over and over on itself, his eyes fixed on the dark color. "I am Dr. Cahn Arvilla's descendent. My name is Oryx Arvilla."

A collective intake of breath spread unspoken judgement through the space, but before anybody could counter or react further to Red's admission he continued. "This story, this history is a black stain on my family name. A story told generation to generation to ensure its survival. Dr. Cahn's own grandson tested positive and died during an experiment." His hands stopped spreading the red armband out, allowing everybody to see a symbol that nobody knew centered on it.

"This was his arm band. We use them now as a sign of freedom and resistance, but its history has more meaning."

The round, fading ink was hard to see, but its implications were clear. He refolded the band, returning it to his right bicep outside of his uniform, continuing his history lesson.

"This particular moment marks the downfall yet to correct itself. After what was a cleansing act, the bodies were destroyed, houses removed and replaced with condos and shopping centers; life was grand." His sarcasm was thick, and he owned everyone's full attention. "You see, they couldn't control the enzyme, and it greatly affected their plans of controlling the citizens. The only other option was to eliminate it. For a while everybody was happy. It wasn't until the Life Tax was introduced that everybody saw the mistake they made. You all know that story. But here's another one you may not know.

"The government has not stopped. They are now successfully experimenting and cloning humans, and in doing this they are unlocking certain parts of the brain that are dormant. Gaining ground and getting closer and closer to their goal. And until a few days ago, we had no idea of the extent of what they were doing. That there were side effects to the experiments and, most important, that people were surviving."

Toro noticed that Astrid dipped her head at this, her eyes darting around; she had been exposed. His head spun, connecting the color of Astrid's eyes to the words Red was saying.

"We know from history that some are immune to the drugs the government is using against us. The M-124, for example. It censors its host, blocks memories, feelings, and individuality. Basically, everything that makes us ... well, us.

"The government built a specific Experimental Institute just for those who are resilient to the M-124. They recently learned that those who have the Arvilla enzyme are indeed those who are resilient. There are only a handful of these people, and fewer still who survive. At this institute ..." He paused, took a deep breath, closed his eyes, and forced the rest out. "At this institute experiments are conducted—experiments to clone, experiments to suppress or eradicate whatever is giving these people a fighting chance. Experiments to create faster healing times, to create people without feelings or thoughts, but who obey every command." Another deep breath, eyes still closed. Something horrid playing for him behind his eyes, something he did not want to watch but was forced to relive. He fought, trying to escape.

Benji stepped forward, and without making contact, he whispered into Red's ear. Red calmed himself, turned, and left the room.

ASTRID watched Red leave, Jackson following. Her heart had skipped a beat when Jackson first entered; she was positive that her face flushed. Being able to hide behind a toddler was helpful and much appreciated. Benji talked about the upcoming mission, something about destroying the L.A. facility. She didn't see the point. They got the patients out who wanted to leave, and Benji received what he wanted, right? Why sacrifice more lives?

"At this point, we have weakened their security. We know how to get past the outlining fence and the check points. This should be easy and quick. After re-enter—"

"Excuse me," Astrid spoke up. Everybody in the room shuffled their attention to her.

Benji cleared his throat. "This is Astrid. She was one of the rescued patients from the L.A. Institute. Go ahead, Astrid." He was flustered, thrown off topic, his stance moving from foot to foot.

Astrid glanced around, surveying the room. The tables were filled with happy and tired Reformers and newcomers alike.

She hated to burst the safety bubble everybody found themselves in. but they deserved the truth; they needed to know what they were facing. If what Red said was true, this wasn't just a fight for freedom. This was a fight for their humanity.

"Are we going to discuss the general at all, and his ability to kill people without being physically present?" The question was needed, honest, to the point.

The atmosphere changed, going from serious to fearful. Whispers got louder; panic quickly settled in.

Toro leaned across the table, tapping her hand. "Are you serious?" he inquired.

Since panic had overtaken the room, Benji stumbled to formulate an answer while regaining control. Before Astrid gained an opportunity to answer Toro, Benji quieted the room with a loud, ear-piercing whistle. Everybody hushed, shifting back toward their leader.

"What Astrid says is untrue. As we have no surviving witnesses to the attack we are unsure what exactly took place."

Astrid's reaction was swift, almost knocking Ben off his seat. "I was there. I am a surviving witness!" With every word, she became more upset. "I saw it. I saw a blue light come from the ground like a beacon, and the instant it touched a person, they ... they screamed in horrible pain, dying on the spot. You could see their life force being gathered toward the center of their torso and ripped from them. They were left, cold and distorted on the ground. On the side of the highway! You two, Sibella, Reider! You were there. Tell them!"

She motioned toward them, who were both wide eyed and angry. Sibella's head fell toward her chest. Reider simply shook his head, saying, "No, Astrid. You're not remembering it correctly. It's okay, though. You're still fighting off the effects."

She snapped her attention straight at Benji. "You said that I possess the Arvilla enzyme. That I can fight the M-whatever. Which makes me immune to these effects you're talking about. No—"

"Jackson!" Benji ordered over her.

She continued rambling on to make her point, but it was clear nobody believed her. Everyone started throwing questions at both her and Benji, not one making it through. She was on her own. Jackson came into the room in such a way that suggested he was waiting for the call.

"Could you please escort Astrid to her room?" Benji gestured to Astrid, who still stood in the center of the room, now screaming that she witnessed it and Benji was lying, that they were just falling for more propaganda and lies.

Jackson stepped up next to her, grabbing her arm. His grip forceful and tight.

"Let me go." Astrid tried jerking out of his grip, quickly learning she was no match for his tight, well-toned muscles. "Sibella!" Trying a different tactic, twisting towards the woman. "Sibella, please, you were there. You saw it. Help me!"

Sibella never considered her.

"Come on, Astrid, don't make this worse." Jackson pulled, and she let him push her out, using little force against him. At this point, Ben noticed Astrid leaving and he froze. Panic seeped into his darting eyes. Toro attempted to comfort him to no avail.

"Ben! Come on, come with me, sweetie." Astrid stopped, twisting around before they reached the door. Her arm bent at a bad angle, causing pain to shoot through her shoulder, but still she fought. Ben stayed on his seat—his eyes closed, hands over his ears, his body rigid. "Ben!" she yelled a little louder.

"Sibella, get Ben. It's time they're separated. Take him to Ms. Laura. She will handle him." Benji gave the order as a last thought before returning to his papers. His orders correcting the chaos Astrid created.

"*No!*" she screamed at him, forcing her words to make sense. "He needs me! Benji, please. I'm sorry, don't take him."

Jackson pinned her back against the wall near the door, his hands over her biceps. Massive, capable muscles adhering her to the wall. Now she was forced to watch as Sibella obeyed, wrestling Ben over her shoulder because he would not let her touch him any other way. He jerked his hands and arms out of her soft grip as she marched him past Astrid. Her inability to help him or calm him ate at her every fiber. He was in a full panic, the screams bouncing off the walls and metal furniture in the room, never fading, even as Sibella moved farther into the compound. The screams stopping only long enough for Ben to breathe, then starting back up. Soon being muffled, by a door, Astrid figured.

They had taken him to a new room with new people and locked him in.

"How dare you! You're his father! Why would you treat him this way?" Astrid continued, screaming so hard it seared her throat with fire.

104

She called him names, kicking at Jackson, happy at every purchase she gained.

Benji stood tall at the front of the room, glaring at her. With a nod from Benji, Jackson pulled her off the wall, shoving her out.

"You're in on it? You know he's lying!"

"Astrid, come on." Jackson grabbed her hand and led her down the hallway.

"No, take me to Ben. He needs me." She was being dragged along—her small frame nothing compared to his big bulk. She fought his grip, trying to pull her hand out of his, embarrassed that she ever liked him.

"I can't."

"Jackson, you need to believe me. Please," she pleaded. Anything to be understood, to be believed.

"I need to do what I'm told. You keep this up and he'll lock you away. Keep your head down, and do what you're told. Make it through training. Ben is young; he'll bounce back."

"No, he won't. Don't you think he's been through enough? Please, Jackson, forget me. Don't do this to him."

They'd arrived at her and Ben's room. She didn't want to enter without Ben next to her. They'd spent every moment together, waking and asleep, since their first contact at the Institute. Ben needed the constant confidence her presence fed him. Not once she'd begged for a break; not once did she wish anything other than to help him.

"I. Can't," he emphasized. He stopped and spun around. Obviously physically uncomfortable. His eyes darted past her, watching the hallway. "Be careful here."

He reached out, grabbed the handle, pushed open the door, and shoved her in. Closing it behind her, a click following the movement. Sealing her in.

"*No!*"

Ben's screams resonated inside of her. She was a prisoner once more. Her head against the closed door, her hands placed next to her, she stood quietly. Banging and screaming, she was sure, would do no good.

Astrid no longer felt safe. She no longer felt her own. At the mercy of another organization who followed their own agenda, for what they thought best. No matter who they hurt in the process.

CHAPTER 9
DISCOVERIES

TORO watched Sibella haul Ben out and Jackson man-handle Astrid into the hall. Unsure what to do, his anger ran high, knowing he'd once treated Astrid the same way. He sat frozen to his seat, his mouth hanging open.

Benji moved to shut the door behind them. "I apologize for the disruption."

"What was she saying? About the general?" A new trainee spoke up; young with jet black, greasy hair.

"She went through a traumatic transfer here. I believe it's having some lingering effects on her. Don't worry, she'll be attended to and back to normal in no time." Benji forced his smile, not letting it reach his eyes.

Toro's anger conflicted with his desire to be a Reformer. To prove his ability and usefulness in the war. But he owed Astrid; he needed to help her. But to help her would hamper Benji's view of him. He was aware something was wrong.

Benji, realizing that his explanations were not fully accepted, continued. "Her transfer bus was attacked by a helicopter. Security from the Institute ran the bus off the road, killing everybody onboard. The only ones who survived were Astrid and Ben, along with three of our own. My soldiers have told me what happened. Astrid's recollection does not match. As our people haven't received mind-altering medications, and proof that her mind has been messed with are in her eyes, their story is the one I chose to believe."

Toro sat quietly through the rest of the meeting, listening to questions and responses, letting the information slide over him unheeded. Instead apprehension turned his thoughts over themselves, creating mass confusion with the information that he already knew.

After dismissal, he stayed in the mess hall, grabbing a snack, eager to read some more, wanting to settle his thoughts.

Carefully opening his hardback, he returned to the imaginary world where the troubles and concerns were not his to worry about. Toro let the words wash over him, pulling him from the mess hall. Relaxing, letting the stress pour out of his neck and shoulders.

Soon a voice broke through the dream-like movie the book had created.

"Reider, we need to do something. This isn't right." Sibella sat close to Reider at another table, the distress clear on her. Both unaware of Toro's presence, who stayed still as a statue.

"Sibella, we've been over this. Benji told us which story to tell. We made our peace. Let it go." Reider sounded irritated, like it wasn't the first time he was having this conversation.

"I know, but it's not sitting well with me. I'm physically ill, unable to sleep. Every time I close my eyes I see them. All those people, and Astrid is right. How are we supposed to fight something that can kill us in an instant? Benji knows about it and doesn't want the rest of us knowing." There was panic in her tone.

"Easy, keep your voice down."

Over his book, Toro could see through his peripheral vision that Reider had spotted him.

"No, Reider. You can't sit there and tell me you're okay with all this. He's using us, and he plans on using them. Why should we just sit by and help?" Her voice rose another octave. Toro, trying not to be noticed eavesdropping, stayed still, absently turning a page in his book. Taking another sip of tea, running his eyes over the words he wasn't reading.

"Out, now." Reider stood, dragging Sibella behind him.

Toro set his book down next to his tea, ambiguity rumbling in his gut. An inception of thought in his head. The Reformers were not as truthful and free as he formally believed. Questions bubbled to the surface of his mind. Questions that would not quiet down and let him continue reading.

"Great," he mumbled, dropping his tea cup in the dish bin, and headed toward the sleeping quarters. "Down the hole I go." He didn't run into anybody on his way, which he felt was unusual. And for once he found that he had not gotten lost. Ben's screams were muffled in the distance, but still present. Toro needed confirmation, and for that he needed Astrid.

Mitch, who'd been standing outside Dr. Heizer's door, was the mark Toro went for. "Did you see Jackson and Astrid come through here?"

"She was taken to her room."

Toro acknowledged some thanks, moving on.

He banged numerous times on Astrid's door, calling out to her, only to be answered with silence. "Astrid, please, I need to speak with you." Still nothing, no response, no trust. He didn't blame her. "I believe you. I have some theories. We should talk."

"Go away," Astrid's voice sneaked its way from underneath the door.

Not wanting to keep bugging her, he whispered an apology before leaving, heading down to his own bed.

Maybe some rest would help de-muddle his mind.

A banging on his door roused him from his fitful rest a few hours later. His dreams had been plagued with blue pillars of lights chasing him, burning him where they made contact on his skin. The disruption was welcomed.

"Yeah?" he greeted, jerking the door open to stop the incessant noise. Dr. Heizer stood there. "Oh."

"Nice to see you too. Can I come in?" She was weak on her feet, with dark circles under her eyes, her steps slow and calculated.

"Yeah … yes, of course. Come in." He stepped back, giving her room. She fell onto his makeshift bed, out of breath. "Feeling better?"

"No, but I'm working on it. Food and sleep helps. How long have we been here?" She sat ramrod straight, her hands together between her thighs and her eyes straight forward. Always the presence of authority.

"Five days, maybe a week." Toro timidly sat down on the foot of the bed as far from her as he could get. The situation was uncomfortable. "Dr. Heizer, what changed your mind?"

"I haven't changed my mind. I am not helping these people." She practically spit the last word out. "I am going to get my son back. They still won't let me see him. Even with him screaming like that they won't let me in. Nothing I say works, and Benji won't even talk to me. Something about having a mission to plan. His lackey told me he'd come to me upon his liking." Her hands flailed around as she spoke.

"I see. Anything I can help with? I'm not quite positive why you're here." Gently, easing into it; he needed to break it to her that he was no longer on her side, and he needed to be quick about it.

"What was the meeting about?" This time she turned her head. Her stare so intense he felt the need to lean back.

"About the mission, training schedule, welcome to the Reformers, stuff like that. Red told a bit of history. They know about the enzyme, that some people are able to fight the compound." He dropped her gaze.

A quizzical expression covered her dark, tired face.

"The one that breaks down the serum allowing the priso—umm … patient." He took a break and cleared his throat. "Allowing the patient to fight back and keep their memories and free will."

"They have a name for it? The Institute doesn't even know what it is, and they have knowledge of it?" Now she was angry; she was scowling and her hands balled up into fists in her lap.

"But the Institute does know. That's why there are institutes, and the one in Vegas? It's called the Experimental Institute. Red said anybody who tested positive for this enzyme was automatically sent to

Vegas." Now Toro was just as confused. Dr. Heizer oversaw all the entry tests and distribution; how could she not know this?

"No, there is no enzyme test upon entry. There's no medical way to search for that without doing a full gene test and blood work up. It would take too long. That one patient's mother …"

He'd lost her; she followed a trail in her mind that he failed to see.

"Doctor, whose mother?" he prompted, trying to pull her back.

"That woman, the patient, the one who was brought here with my son."

"Astrid?"

"Is that her name, Astrid?" She scoffed, shaking her head. "Anyway, her mother failed the assimilation and was sent off, assigned to an experiment. But her chart didn't say where. Could she have been sent to Vegas?"

"We could assume so. Red reported that's where they're taken if they possess the enzyme. Why would the Reformers care about this? They have no medical facilities or training; how does this help them?"

"They want it. Think about it. This is their way of getting back. The government wouldn't have any way of stopping them, or controlling them. The more of them they recruit who are able to block the effects of the drugs, the more dangerous they become."

Toro didn't reply because he didn't fully agree with the doctor. If the government found out, they would all end up dead. What else would the government do to a bunch of people they couldn't control? *Same thing they did in the past, just more violently.* This thought unsettled him. Reading about the civil unrest and death of its citizens was enough even before he had intentions of fighting in such a war. "No, controlling them has always been an issue. I don't think the Reformers want to administer it to their people. It seems to me that they're after knowledge. Knowledge is formidable, more useful.

"I'm joining the Reformers," he blurted out, surprised at his decision. Before, it was just a thought, words that held no meaning; even signing up for the training hadn't made it real. But telling the doctor he wouldn't help her … this made it real.

"I know. I saw it in your eyes that last time you came to see me. It didn't surprise me. You do what you must. Just promise to answer any inquiries I may have in the future." She'd gone soft. This woman was extreme, one end to the next in just a few minutes.

Toro shook his head trying to keep up with her. "No, I'm not promising that. I would like to help, but not at the cost of their trust in me."

"We will see. Good luck." She stood, wobbled a bit, heading for the door. When she reached the knob she stopped. "Be careful who you put your trust in. Knowledge is powerful, and you have more than you think."

And she was gone, leaving Toro on the foot of his bed, bewildered.

WHETHER he wanted to or not, Toro would always give Melvina the information she desired. She just needed to get him to talk. Having lots of experience with employees, this was an easy task for her. Her next stop was Ben's door again. She sat down in front of it and just listened. Her poor boy was traumatized and in pain. No words ever formed, just high-pitched screams, and they got louder anytime somebody tried to engage with him. It broke her heart, but she must try. He was hers. Her son.

With her forehead and palms placed on the door, she hummed a song she used to sing to him when he was a baby. Tears found their way onto her cheeks. Weakness … tears were weakness. She continued with the song. It was a few minutes before she noticed that he had stopped screaming. Not wanting to jinx it, she continued, just a little louder. Minutes passed, and the door creaked open.

The head of an elderly woman with a hard face appeared. "Oh, it's you. You put him to sleep. Thank you."

She promptly shut the door, leaving Melvina in the hallway with her grief and sense of loss. She cried, her whole body racked by the sobs. She wasn't positive how long she sat like that or when she ended up on the floor. A brush on her shoulder brought her back from the brink. Benji. She blinked, wiped her face with the back of her hands, and stood, sniffling.

Instead of talking, Melvina forced herself around him toward her room. Without a word, he followed, leaving enough space between them to not be overbearing. Still weak from not eating or sleeping, she didn't want him to see her like this. It was embarrassing.

"Mel." He stopped, trying to get her attention as she continued.

"No" her curt reply.

"Mel, it's going to take time. You know this." He continued to follow, defeated.

"No." Again. *Don't talk to him, he's the poison.* "It wouldn't take that much time if you let me in the same room as him. You told me I could see him, which was another lie, I suppose. I had to sing his song through a locked door with strangers listening, strangers watching him. I should be watching him. It's sickening. You're sick."

"I understand, but it's not possible. We just separated him from Astrid."

"You really are a true idiot. Go be stupid someplace else, please." Melvina reached her sleeping quarters, but before she could shut the door he was there, his big black boot blocking her from solitude.

"Do *not* talk to me that way. I am the leader here. You'll do what you're told. And you'll be respectful." He was upset, not quite pissed off, but well on his way.

"Or what?" She was spiteful. Unnecessary maybe, but it felt good. All the grief being trumped down with good red-hot anger.

"There is no 'or what.' Be. Nice." He removed his boot, backing into the hallway. Without missing a beat, Melvina slammed the door in his face.

"I'm done being nice," she revealed to the closed door. Seething with rage, nowhere to go, she lay down on the dirt floor, working on her breathing and trying to calm herself down. This rage was no good to Ben.

For some time, she lay there, the cool of the dirt beneath her pulling the toxins and bitterness from her body. It helped her think.

She was being controlled, instead of being the one in charge. It had never been this way; she'd always been the authority. She still thought about Ben, more than before, but different thoughts this time. She didn't register when Ben's screaming returned in the background, bouncing off the insides of her skull.

This is ridiculous.

She thought of her boy, of how they curled up together under every blanket she owned when it got cold outside. How the food was scarce and Ben would unknowingly eat all they had. It never bothered her; it would never bother her. She would sacrifice her life for him.

She thought of the days in the Institute, when she would watch him. He always ate with care, would watch the approved programming. Sometimes she'd stand there for hours, before noticing she'd been spotted and coming back to reality. The memory of when she first noticed his eye anomaly raced through her, bringing back the pain and misery it originally caused. Proof of betrayal. He had been experimented on. And in turn, she had let it happen to him. She was supposed to keep him safe, and she failed. The betrayals continued to the ultimate one, when she accepted what they did and was thankful he survived, that he lived.

The voice returned, coming out of the scream in the background. Telling her how dumb she was for being taken. Telling her she was being used, that they were going to use her to get what they wanted and then dispose of her. It made Melvina sick, but she was unable to stop it; she emptied what little occupied her stomach on the floor. The voice retained a distinct tinge to it that made her want to scream. So, she did.

She screamed until her voice gave out, until her hair and the ground below her head was wet with her tears and saliva. Her body racked with sobs. She was angry … with herself, with the world, with her lot in life. It was horrid. What did she ever do to deserve this treatment? To be separated from her son, to be forced to listen to his anguished screams?

"He needs me," she whispered to the empty room.

He needed her; he just didn't know it. She had showed him that she was there, that she would take care of him. She must continue to show him until he no longer questioned it.

Melvina stood, dizziness flooding her head and forcing her back down. On her knees with her head in her hands, she planned.

TORO never got a chance to speak alone with Astrid. Trying to drop signals of his understanding and belief in her was turning out to be messy and confusing. He would sit next to her at meals only for her to scoot away, or even get up and leave. Not wanting to push the issue, he left it alone.

Toro trained with ease. Since the other trainees came from the alleys or a drug-induced state from the Institute, he found himself ahead of the curve. The first day was an initiation of sorts, getting to know everybody. Jack had yet to show his face. A few trainees were whiners, others silent. There were only two who seemed like they could give Toro a challenge. His goal to come out at the top of his class became brighter to him, within reach. They all arrived on time, to a poorly lit room with no instructions. Instead of working together or waiting, they each fanned out to their own interest and started in on equipment.

The training facility was well-kept, even with the dirt floor. Punching bags, free weights, and a sparring mat, all beat up and well used. Holes showed through, duct tape trying to keep them together.

When Jack finally strolled in, it was a shock to them all. A ginormous man, at least seven feet tall, huge shoulders, his arms the size of Toro's legs, and a black eye patch with a jolly roger over his right eye, a scar peeking out from underneath it.

"Holy …" Toro breathed, being the first to see him. "Jack?"

"No, not Holy Jack. Big Jack will do just fine." His voice was light, not at all what Toro felt it should be. It didn't match his body or the force that emanated off him. Jack pinned Toro with his eyes, wanting him or somebody to react.

Startled, Toro took a step back, treading on another trainee's toes. Apologizing without taking his eyes off Jack, unwilling to risk the spotlight on him again.

"Now," Jack continued, eye still on Toro. "I'm Big Jack. I'm here to get ya ready to go outside without getting killed. This is no picnic. Ya will get hurt, and there will be pain. A day of training is not successful unless somebody gets sent to the infirmary. We'll begin with hand-to-hand. Everybody pair off so I can see what ya filthy rats got." He flailed his arms about and continued bellowing instructions as Toro tried to grab a partner comparable to his size and weight without getting too close to Big Jack.

Astrid, he saw, paired off with another female about twice her size. Toro shook his head, finally seeing Seto.

Seto held his elbows, his gaze someplace else. A shyness about him.

"I guess we're it. We should start." Toro loitered over, but Seto didn't acknowledge him. Toro leaned over, waving in front of Seto's face. "Hey?"

"Sorry!" Seto jumped and stood ramrod straight, hauling off and punching Toro square in the nose.

"Son o—" Blood poured out everywhere, an open fountain with overflow.

"Oh my! Sorry, I'm so sorry! I thought we were sparring? Were you not ready?" Seto knelt next to him, his hand hovering.

Toro continued blowing snot and blood out of his nose onto the dirt floor. It hurt. It really hurt. Tears popped out unwanted. He was positive his nose was broken. Without a second thought he reached up, placed his hands on both sides, and popped it back into place, letting out a sound comparable to a dying animal. Blowing his nose again on the floor and standing, his head swimming with pain.

"You're right, we are. Nice shot." Toro flung blood and bodily fluid off his hands, standing ready for the next hit. Rolling his shoulders and pulling his arms up in a sparring stance.

Seto smiled, nodded, and prepped. They spared, each having some sort of training before. Toro had received hand-to-hand training from the Institute. He noted that the guy was good, quick with firm reactions. They continued, unable to get the hand up on the other. Jumping, kicking, and blocking, forearms made contact, legs missing entirely. The focus of the fight cleared his head, pushing the broken nose out of his mind.

"All right, enough showing off," came Big Jack's voice, busting through their concentration, forcing a reboot. The two stopped and turned—the whole class surrounding them in a semi-circle watching. Sweat dripped off Toro's nose, his shirt soaked through. "What's ya names?"

"Toro."

"Seto." He was breathing hard and just as sweaty.

"Ya both need work." Jack nodded his head in their general direction, turning back to the rest of the class. Toro's ego deflated.

They continued this way for the first half of the day. Big Jack swaggered around critiquing and judging, changing partners as he broke them up based on skill. Toro noticed that Astrid had a good size bruise on her cheek and she was cradling her shoulder. He wanted to see if she was okay or needed anything, but not wanting her to think he saw her as distressed, he stood his ground.

During lunch, nobody spoke, everybody nursing injuries or too sore to move, no energy to waste. It was the first time since breakfast they rested—that was without being knocked down. Everybody was relieved; even a few heads relaxed on the tables. Toro tried sitting next to Astrid, expecting her to move away, flooding with relief when she stayed.

"You doing okay? I see you received a good hit," he inquired, finding energy between bites.

Astrid turned. He couldn't tell if she was going to answer or hit him. He waited, trying to urge her on with his eyes, wanting to be friendly. Not wanting her to dart away and ignore him again. She watched him, squinted with pure focus and something else Toro recognized, but was unwilling to acknowledge.

"My skin crawls when I see you, I try—hard. I try hard to stay away from you, pretend you don't exist. When I let my guard down or am not paying attention, I end up right next to you." She stopped, took a breath, dropping her gaze. This was not what he ever thought she'd say. "Like there's an outside force pulling me to you. I have other things to fight for now. There's no energy left to hate you."

Toro wasn't sure how to respond, so he did what his grandfather taught him: apologize or at least take responsibility. His grandfather,

Clyde, had ingrained himself in his grandchildren's upbringing. Passing on lessons and morals to leave better people in an unpredictable world. Toro knew he needed to make it right. "I'm sorry. I know you see me as responsible, and I can and will do everything to make it right. No excuses."

Astrid's head popped back up, her eyes searching him as he spoke. "Why?"

"My papa once suggested that we don't get to decide if we've wronged someone, that we can only make it right. You've decided I wronged you, now I need to make it right." He smiled; his grandfather would be proud. If he could only see him now.

"Most people would argue they haven't done any wrong." A slow smile lifted the corners of her mouth.

"I know. I am sorry." Toro knew he was apologizing for putting her back in the chair. For stopping Astrid from escaping the Institute. He knew why she felt this way, even if she didn't.

"Okay, let's try that question again. I'll—uh, I'll try again." Her radiant eyes lightened as she spoke, the air cheerful around them. A wall previously erected between them rumbled, disintegrating, enabling the beginning of a friendship much desired.

Toro smiled in return, repeating his question, glad to be making progress.

"Yeah, a lucky shot, and I'm sure it's not the only bruise." A smile with a small laugh followed. "I'll survive; I've survived everything else. I keep reminding myself I wanted this, right? I signed up for this, crazy." Another laugh.

Toro laughed with her, in agreement. But she was only partly right. He was unsure if this was really what he wanted. He was happy, and now, here he was going through another boot camp trying to impress a trainer who frightened everybody in the building.

"We did the right thing?" he asked, unsure who he was really asking, himself or Astrid.

"Depends on why you're doing it," she answered. She finished her lunch, placing her hands in her lap, trying desperately to keep her head off the table.

"Do you know why? Why you … um …"

"To find my mom, to fight back. I have to try."

"Where is she, your mom?"

"I-I'm not entirely sure. We arrived at the Institute together, but …"

"But she's not here," he finished for her.

She was heartbroken; it was written all over her. Whatever she had with her mom engulfed her being. It was everything to her. Toro watched as Astrid got lost in her memories, her head dipping. He fought with himself about discussing this further; he wanted to help. But training had just started, and he didn't want to upset the Reformers right after arriving. Having already turned on the government, he was not ready to make more enemies.

"You'll find her" was all he could manage.

Astrid nodded without lifting her head. He felt horrible, his heart and soul shrinking inside while his mind repeated that he was doing the right thing.

After lunch, they filed out, back down the hall to the training facility. Nobody excited and everybody hardly able to move. How they were supposed to finish the day, Toro wasn't sure.

ASTRID'S head stayed low—she had just finished her lunch and was lost in memories about her mom. The morning session had been rough; bruises and sore muscles she hadn't even known existed throbbed. She constantly reminded herself that she wanted this, wanted and needed the skills to find her mom. To fight back, to protect herself.

Everybody left without her realizing it, heading back to the training hall. She jumped, hurrying after them, only to end up at the back of the group behind the girl who had delivered the wicked right hook to her cheek this morning. Jazmin—she was short and well built, with dark rich skin and hair in little braids all the way to her waist. Astrid had tried to make a friend, be nice, all that good stuff that she was taught. Jazmin had other plans. When they had squared off, Astrid really had no idea what she was doing, so she essentially became Jazmin's punching bag. Every hit forced a mystical blue haze to beat in and out of her vision. Instantly making her think about the ring everybody insisted they saw in her eyes. She didn't want to believe it.

But there had been no time to worry about it because Jazmin had shown no mercy, even when the blood started to flow. Astrid never gave in to the pain, the fear, or the tears. She never let Jazmin know that she was winning, never showed the weakness flooding through her with the strong sensation to give up. Standing, she had squared back off with Jazmin, forcing her reasoning to the front of her thoughts, forcing herself to remember why she was doing this—her mom.

Focused on her mother, Astrid swung at Jazmin and made contact, a lucky shot in her favor, snapping Jazmin's head back. Blood, scarlet and pissed, spilled from a gash on Jazmin's left jaw line. Astrid stopped bouncing on the balls of her feet in response to Jazmin's glare, slowly studying her knuckles now red with irritation.

"Watch it," Jazmin stated.

"Uh, I—" Astrid had tried hard not to laugh, succeeding by letting a smile crack across her face. Big Jack had stomped between them, saving Astrid from an epic retort she was sure would cause a bit of pain.

Astrid was brought back to the present as Big Jack shoved her aside to enter the training room. The memories faded as fast as the pain from the beating. He continued shoving people out of his way as he made it to the center of the room. "Now that we have had ya beat each other to wheezing, limping excuses for trainees, we get to teach ya how to throw a blade."

He palmed an eight-inch throwing knife, tossing it back at the class. It spun point over hilt between hairs, ears, shoulders, and heads to hit the center of the closed door right above Astrid's head. The entire class stared hard at the blade inches above her head. Big Jack's face was the epitome of excitement and giddiness, his eyes dilated and skin flushed.

"Come on!" Astrid exclaimed, trying hard to insert humor into the tense room. Reaching above her, she tried to pull the knife out of the wood but was unable to. "Dang, Big Jack, nice throw."

"Thanks, little lady." He laughed, a deep contagious belly laugh. Grins and laughs spread through the trainees with glee. "All right, let's get on with it," he bellowed now, his face returning to serious after showing a different side.

Astrid still grinned; she now knew that she would make it. If Big Jack could be happy, mean, scary, and a big teddy bear all at the same time, she could find her mom without losing herself in the process.

"Yes, let's do," she whispered with a grin. The rest of the day progressed quickly. Without having to pair off, there was little to be frightened of. The trainees lined up to the right of the room, facing targets placed at intervals along the other side. Each person needed to take a turn, first at ten feet, fifteen feet, and so on at five feet intervals. Each trainee throwing in front of everybody else. Numerous knives hit hilt first if they hit the target at all.

Toro's knife hit point first and toward the center of the target every time. Astrid was able to hit the target, but her strength was not enough to make the knife stay. It always wobbled, falling flat on the floor, and every time Big Jack would yell, "Fifty push-ups to build arm strength."

By the end of class nobody but Toro and Seto could lift their arms.

"All right, I think that's enough torture today, and we were successful. Three trainees in the infirmary." Big Jack grinned ear-to-ear. The thought of blood and pain obviously made him happy. The class groaned with the memory. "We begin tomorrow just after breakfast, and we start conditioning along with what we did today." He was still laughing as he left. The whole room of trainees instantly fell to the floor.

"He's gonna kill us," somebody declared.

"No, he's going to make us kill each other," somebody else remarked. Slight laughter followed.

"What the hell is Big Jack, his accent, the eye patch?" Astrid spoke up. She'd collapsed with the rest and lay on the floor taking inventory of her body. The aches and pains were sharp, her shoulders on fire, and chest muscles pulsing.

"Big Jack, he's a pirate, and will make us walk the plank. We should rise with a mutiny against him. How long do you think we will last?" Toro, who was just one trainee over to her left, answered.

She wanted to survey the room but was unable to gather the strength to turn her head. The thought of a shower and bed fascinated her; at the same time she had no idea how she would accomplish it.

"Long enough to know we made the wrong decision." Another trainee decided to move first. "I'm famished, come on. I know you are, too." He started helping trainees, moving them toward the door.

Astrid rolled over, pushing herself up, making her muscles scream with the effort. Limping out, she stopped to stare at the knife hole in the door. Chuckling, she shook her head. She was braver than she originally thought—she could and would finish this.

CHAPTER 10

CHOICES

THE next day proved to be a challenge. Toro arrived with the rest of the group as instructed right after breakfast and observed that the training facility had been rearranged: a makeshift track ran around the outside of the room. Big Jack stood just inside the door on the other side of a rope, standing tall, arms crossed over his chest with a tooth pick sticking out of his mouth that moved methodically with the motion of his jaw.

"Get moving! Last one still running gets to sit out of one training session of their choice." His right arm opened, pointing down the track. Everybody stared at him, processing the task put before them, and eventually the trainee who helped them up last night moved toward the front of the pack, gently shifting people out of his way.

"Okay, let's do it. Come on, guys, no need to stand there gawping." He was tall, with blond hair flowing down into his eyes. He jumped a few times and took off at a leisurely jog. One by one they followed his example. Being spread out gave them lots of elbow room to move. Toro paced somewhere in the middle with Astrid behind him. They ran with slight talking. Sometime into their run somebody stopped, breathing hard with her hand on her side and leaning against the wall.

"You there, come on, off the track." Big Jack toured along the inside of the training hall watching. Occasionally he'd nod his head as they passed by.

The trainee, a girl with a pixie cut, dyed hair, and more holes in her face than was supposed to be, made her way to the rope, ducking under it. She timidly approached Big Jack as he squared off with her. He threw a punch. She ducked, tripped over her own feet, and landed on her butt, scooting away from him as fast as she could.

"Are you frickin' insane? I'm not fighting you!" she practically screamed at him.

"Ya don't have a choice, darling. Ya were the first one to stop. After the run is hand-to-hand. Until somebody else is done running, ya practice with me. Now get up." He circled her small form on the floor, his hands at the ready.

She swallowed visibly, getting to her feet. Toro watched from the track, overjoyed he was still running. Big Jack intimidated on a good day with the right light and holding a teddy bear. This was insane. He shook his head as he ran, watching Big Jack and the small girl continue hand-to-hand. She got hit numerous times, ending up spread out on the floor and spitting blood. Big Jack barked instructions at her, helped her with her stance, then started again.

After the fourth time of her getting knocked down another girl ceased running. "Stop," she announced. "I'm done. I'll practice with her."

"Good, maybe ya can teach her something. Her head's rather hard." He stepped back, motioning for the second girl—who was dark-skinned and heavyset—to join them.

One by one they dropped off the track. All odd numbers were forced to face off with Big Jack until somebody else quit running. Only once did two try dropping off at the same time, but instead of letting them pair off together, Big Jack fought them both at the same time. Both earning bloody, fat lips and black eyes before somebody else collapsed on the track. Soon the tall blond who started running first, Toro, Astrid, and a couple kids from the streets were the only ones left. Toro was rather impressed with Astrid. She kept a brisk pace and didn't get distracted by anyone passing her. Her concentration fearless.

But then she stopped in the middle of the track, hunched over, breathing hard while rubbing sweat off. She hobbled over to Big Jack. "I guess it's my turn to be knocked around. It's been a while as it is. I'm starting to miss it."

Big Jack chuckled, squaring off.

Crazy. She was crazy. *She's a fraction of his size! She could have lasted longer. What is she thinking?* Toro panicked, and trying to run while panicking was not easy. He quickly lost control of his breathing, almost tripping. But not wanting to face off with Big Jack himself, he left Astrid to her choice. She tried and failed to duck in time as Big Jack's hand came cracking down on her. She did manage to block a few, but she would be black and blue by the end of the day.

It didn't last long—somebody else finally collapsed on the track. Big Jack stopped his advance on Astrid to drag the trainee by the foot off the track. He dumped the trainee at Astrid's feet. "Get him awake in thirty seconds or we continue."

Toro shook his head. *Talk about impossible tasks.*

This training session proved intensely violent. The government's training easy was in comparison. They took your measurements for the uniform, assigned weapons and job posting. Three days of conditioning, two of hand-to-hand, and one of weapon training. Out to sink or swim.

Nothing like this. These people were monsters who enjoyed the sight and smell of blood. Laughing along with the thought, Toro evened his breathing and continued. He almost missed it—the blond in front of him tripped, rolling head over feet numerous times until finally coming to a skidded stop. Even though he was a good distance behind the guy, Toro still couldn't move around him quickly enough. He was forced to jump over the dirty form through the dust cloud he had kicked up with his fall. The kid moaned while trying to return to his feet.

Watching Astrid, Toro smiled again. She had somehow woke the kid and was now training with somebody closer to her size, even managing to get a few hits in. *Good girl.*

His sides and lungs burned, in desperate need for water, and his feet felt ready to fall off. He enjoyed running; it had been part of his morning routine before all hell broke loose in his life. The freedom of running always calmed him, kept him in shape and ready; he felt and slept better on days he ran. It was a part of who he was. He kept his thoughts focused on this instead of the dehydration taking over his body.

"Hey!" a voice boomed.

Toro startled, his attention shifting. He was the last one. Everybody else stood together grasping aluminum bottles of water, watching him.

Big Jack yelled, "Come on, showoff. Ya did good. Come get some water."

Toro was more than happy to obey.

ASTRID'S lip bled, her head screaming with pain. Yet still she continued. The run was easy until her body won over her mind. Even knowing what she was about to face she couldn't go on. So she faced Big Jack with everything she had left, and still got knocked to the ground over and over. The next kid to drop literally passed out. Was he really that scared?

With thirty seconds to wake the kid, she snatched an aluminum bottle, tossing water up the kid's nose. He quickly came to, sputtering and blowing to expel the water from his sinuses. With a grin of satisfaction, she stood, glaring up at Big Jack. Huffing, he trotted away.

Not an easy guy to please that one.

You could make him laugh, but to get him to say you did well … well, there would probably be another war before that happened.

Hand-to-hand proved to be just as difficult as the day before. Standing up after every hit, trying again. One girl asked for water, and Big Jack chuckled, denying the request. No water until everybody was done with the run. Great; not only were they all dying from exhaustion, they were dehydrated as well. The guy Astrid sparred against was firm with a good swing. Her forearms were bruised from the previous day, and this guy added new bruises on top.

She learned quickly to protect her head. With every hit, the blue ring pulsing with her heartbeat appeared. She wasn't sure what it was, or what they would do if she shared this information. But it was eating at her. She wasn't sure what it would do if it succeeded in taking over. Every time her head received a hit, it pulsed. The harder she got hit, the faster and thicker it would pulse. At one point, instead of keeping her head down, her gaze on the floor, Astrid looked around her. Chie—a street orphan who happened to stumble upon the compound—startled at what she saw with a gasp of surprise or fear escaping her mouth.

Astrid kept her gaze on Chie as she gained control of her breathing along with the blue haze trying to take over her vision. Once clear, a couple blinks later, Astrid watched Chie take a gulp, swallowing fear, her disbelief clear. Chie shook her head, continuing to train. She was quiet and the shy one of the bunch, of East Asian descent with short shiny black hair.

Astrid tried to work out her decision as the other trainee continued playing with her like she was a rag doll. Her thighs burned and her ribs, she was sure, were cracked from his constant kicking.

He never encouraged her, nor did he help after knocking her down—he just stood there, bored without a challenge. Astrid got a few good hits, but he was faster and much stronger. The push-ups from the day before did little for her arm strength. Frustrated, she stood against him again, determination already set it. She must get her mom back.

I'm coming, Mom. I'm coming.

Big Jack's voice boomed. When he motioned to the water, everybody rushed forward, grabbing as many bottles as they could hold while pouring liquid down their throats. Amazing how cool and good it felt. Her tongue and throat were a desert. Big Jack's voice boomed again, and the class gathered in the center to watch the lone runner on the track.

Toro ... of course. Trained by the government, probably as intense as this if not more so. *Traitor.* As much as she wanted to like him and be friends, she couldn't forget that he worked for the Institute.

And at the same time, remembering she told him she would start fresh, Astrid swallowed her pride and doubt as if it was a sharp oversized bite.

Toro left the track, glancing at them before proceeding over, ducking under the rope, and downing water as fast as the rest of them. His body glistened with sweat, the odor coming off him proving his run a good one. He stopped close to Astrid, still pouring water down his throat. She could hear him gulping between deep intakes of air. She nodded at his achievement.

"All right, we have some time left for hand-to-hand. Toro, ya finish off with Seto here. Let me know what ya want to sit out of. Yar choice. The rest of ya back to work with a different partner this time." Big Jack was back to giving orders, brushing past and Toro slapping him on the back as he pushed him toward Seto. The rest of the class shuffled, grabbing new partners, and continued to hit one another with instructions inserted at appropriate points to improve their timing and power.

Soaked in sweat, barely able to move, they made it to the mess hall for lunch. They ate in silence, all of them in too much pain to want to talk.

Benji came in and spoke with Big Jack. "Sounds like everything is in order and going well. We have anybody you would recommend going into a different training program?"

At this, every head popped up.

"Not now, their determination hasn't died. Give me a couple more days will ya, boss?" Big Jack replied, his fork halfway to his mouth, shaking his head at the question. After he answered he continued eating.

"I need to borrow one. We have an issue to take care of." Benji, who had leaned over close to Big Jack, straightened, pinpointing Astrid with his gaze.

Uh oh, only two days in and already an issue. Astrid stilled, unable to move.

She stared in disbelief, fork still in her noodles. She had watched the interaction with detached amusement. Now her palms sweated as her gut rolled. Toro elbowed her to get her back to the present. Shaking her head, she took a bite.

"Astrid," Benji requested, taking a step to the door. "We need you. Please come with me." It wasn't a question, more of a demand, and Benji was now upset. Without waiting to see if she followed, he strode out.

"Okay then." Astrid left her uneaten portion, chasing after Benji.

"Push-ups and pull-ups wait for those who are late," Big Jack grumbled.

She stopped. "I'm being asked to leave, not leaving by choice."

"Not my problem." He shoveled his lunch in his mouth, portions dripping out the corners.

"Great."

Benji was already down the hall and turning a corner, forcing her to jog to catch up to him. "What issue do you have that involves pulling me out of training?" she asked.

"Easy, trainee, wouldn't want you to get in trouble so soon." He kept his impossibly fast pace. "I'm sure you would like an update on Ben. To be honest, I'm surprised you haven't inquired about him sooner."

"Are you serious? You pried him off me and took him away. I've listened to his screams. I know how he's doing. I don't have to ask. The whole compound knows how he's doing." Her anger with Benji flared; there was something about him she didn't like or trust.

He suddenly halted, bearing down on her. "You've few chances left. I am in charge here, so either you watch your tongue or I'm going to cut it out. Understand?" Nose to nose, the back of her head against the wall, she nodded slightly. He backed up. "Ben is doing better. He's stopped the screaming, but we still can't get him to talk to anybody. We need to draw blood, but he won't let us. So instead of traumatizing him further, we promised him a visit with you."

"Why do you need more blood?"

"To see what Thaxton has done to him."

"Who's Thaxton?"

"The general of the Institute."

"This general, is it the same general you told everybody I imagined?" She knew she was toeing the line, she didn't care.

"You did imagine it. With nobody to collaborate your story what else were we to believe?" They arrived at an open door, and Benji stopped, turning to face her. "You have five minutes with the kid. Don't be late back to training ... push-ups and pull-ups the way Big Jack makes you do them could make your arms fall off." He turned on his heel and strode down the hallway, his chuckle echoing off the walls behind him.

"I didn't imagine it," Astrid muttered under her breath. She could picture the blue outline of the general in front of her as she held Ben's hand; she could feel his voice in her veins as he spoke. It was real; it did happen; she just needed to prove it.

Astrid stepped into the dull and dark room. A couple chairs and tables were situated against the makeshift walls. Battered old toys littered the floor with no one to play with them. Once her eyes adjusted to the lack of light she saw Ben. Curled up in the fetal position under one of the tables, his head hidden in his arms. She gracefully hastened over to him, crouching down. Her legs burned and screamed, so she sat, grunting. Ben's arms broke apart enough for his eyes to get a peek. Instantly registering who she was, he bolted to her, his head buried in her neck, arms and legs wrapped around tight.

"Hey," she managed. She didn't know how much she missed the little kid; even only after being with him for a week it was hard to let go. Having his small arms around her and his smell flooding her system brought tears. She hugged him back fiercely, fighting back the lump in her throat.

"They wouldn't let me see you," Ben coughed out. He loosened his grip a bit, pulling back in her lap, his gaze on her face. His voice hoarse and scratchy.

"I know, I'm sorry."

"You told me these were good guys. Why can't I see you?"

Exceptional question.

"They think ..." She paused, not sure how to explain it, not sure if she believed it. "They think they're helping you, that being with me all the time is not good for you, especially because you weren't talking to anybody else and because of your reaction to Dr. Heizer."

"Don't say her name. I don't like her. I don't want to see her again."

"I know, but what about the girl taking care of you here? Is she nice?"

"She stuck me in the arm to make me sleep. Said I scream too much. That I'm an annoying brat. She hates me. And her thoughts are the same. She's telling the truth. She doesn't say her feelings, but I can hear them." His shoulders slumped as he spoke. "My throat hurts."

He can hear thoughts? Astrid tried to keep her composure. She didn't really know Ben that well. How could she know whether he was being truthful or telling a lie to get her attention? Thinking back on the bus ride helped her decide. He had confided hearing thoughts of the guards; that's how he knew they feared the general. He heard his mom watching him outside his cubicle. Maybe he could really hear thoughts. But could he hear Astrid's? He seemed to accept her, bond with her even.

Deciding to hone in on one problem at a time, she concentrated on what Ben could tell her.

"It's from all your screaming. It'll heal, but you need to eat, sleep, and not scream."

"But I miss you. They make my head hurt. The extra voices hurt, but you block them. You stop them."

Astrid didn't answer. Ben was unique; she knew that. She also concluded he knew things he couldn't possibly know. She smiled, asking, "What voices, Ben?"

"What they think, what they know," he whispered now. "I can hear them.

The doctor ... it's not real. Her thoughts are ... made up. Her thoughts are not like everybody else's. They're different." He pulled into himself, his fingers toying with her shirt, shaking slightly.

Astrid knew she had probably missed the beginning of the afternoon training. She was worried about Ben, pissed off at Benji, and at the same time wanted to get back to training.

"Ben, we will figure this out, but I have one more question for you." He relaxed a bit, nodding. "What color are my eyes?"

Ben contemplated Astrid like she asked a silly question. She nodded in encouragement, and he gave her an honest answer as only an innocent child could do. "They're pretty. Brown, like sand with sparkles in them." He stopped to get her approval which she gave with a huge sigh of relief. As she was about to initiate her goodbye he added on to his description, causing Astrid's heart to jump into her throat.

"And the blue ring, better than the sky. Why do we have them and nobody else?"

"You can see yours too?"

"Can't you?" Ben cocked his head.

"No, Ben, I can't." Not wanting to discourage him or make him feel bad, she quickly added, "I'm glad you can though. I'm proud of you, but listen, I must go. I don't get to stay." Ben panicked, wrapping himself around her tightly. "Easy, bud. I'll come back and visit you, but I can only visit if you behave. Did you give blood to the doctors?" He just shook his head from side to side, his body starting to shake. "Easy, it's okay."

Astrid rubbed his back while rocking back and forth with him. There was no time; she couldn't deal with this right now. She felt for him but reminded herself that he was not her responsibility. She remembered grabbing and dragging him out of his cubicle. He'd chosen to stay, and she forced him out; maybe he had become her responsibility.

"Time's up." Benji, standing at the door, his disinterest clear.

"I know, but he's panicking again."

"Then we take him, again."

"Because that worked the first time," she argued softly, more into Ben's ear than to Benji. "Ben, listen." She pried his arms from around her neck. Placing his hands in his lap and grabbing his face, she spoke delicately. "I will come back. I am not going to leave you. But these people, good or bad, we need to do what they say. I need you to be a good boy. Can you do that for me? If you're good, and if you let them get some of your blood, I can come back and see you. We can talk about what you hear, what you know."

He still shook, but he nodded his head.

"Okay, I'll be good." He took a deep breath, letting it rattle out slowly. "I can block them if I squint my eyes and try hard."

An instinct had woken up in Astrid since meeting Ben, one she couldn't quite explain to herself or anybody else. She wanted to help. Now knowing she could block his pain, she wanted to; she wanted him by her side if only to help him have pain free days. To be a child. But she couldn't. This—like so much else—was out of her control.

"Thank you!" Astrid wrapped herself around him, once more sitting him in front of her. Ben pushed himself back under the table. "I'll be back." She tapped the top of the table and headed toward Benji and the door.

He put his hand out to stop her. "You really shouldn't make promises you can't keep. He needs structure, not to be babied."

"He is a baby, and if you want him to continue to behave maybe you should change your tactic."

"Hmm. You have a thing against authority."

"The last authority I obeyed threw me in a box and erased my memories, so forgive me if I'm a little skeptical. Regardless, you don't believe a word I say. Excuse me, I don't want to be late." She pushed past him, keeping what Ben had told her to herself. Benji didn't need any more excuses to hurt him.

HAVING nothing to do besides watch her surroundings, Melvina gained strength—she ate, hydrated, and slept on a schedule of her own desires. She watched the trainees, the agriculture hall, and the infirmary. Her favorite place to sit was the mess hall, in the corner with little light, animating shadows over her, giving her peace and safety. From there she felt she found the pulse of the place. Everybody who lived, worked, and trained here eventually came into the mess hall. It played as the epicenter for socializing. The stainless-steel garden of tables and cabinets were hardware for new and old friendships alike. One of the biggest rooms in the compound, it held everybody comfortably. Families in whole, orphans, runaways, traitors and sophisticated alike. Together.

Melvina saw new and old faces … faces she wished she'd never seen and faces she wished to never forget. Benji came in numerous times a day; he would contemplate and leave again. If he noticed her he didn't show it, which was probably for the best. Her anger and fury boiled over at the sight of him, hard to contain. She found as long as he didn't come near her, she could restrain it.

She spent a lot of time thinking about the past, thinking about Ben, her days in school, her time at the Institute. How she had let things get so out of her control, she was unsure. She wanted things to go back to before. Before the Life Tax, before the Institute, but not so far back she would lose Ben. The hardest thing. Remembering themselves as happy, even though Benji left, forcing her to think him dead.

Shock from his betrayal still surprised her. At times, she wanted to shout the hurt and pain he caused, to cause him just as much—to throw anything she could get her hands on, scratch his face, burn his hopes and dreams to the ground. She knew she couldn't; she knew who he really was. He would move on, rebuilding his life again without her as though she had never been a part of it.

The more she watched, she concluded that the only way to hurt him was to keep denying him what he wanted. To not help. Melvina decided that she wasn't going to turn; she would not become a Reformer, a traitor. She would not be marked. When the government came in, she would be a prisoner of war, and the government would take her back. Congratulate her on a job well done, give her Ben, and let them return to their lives. Maybe even exempt them from future taxes. She just needed to wait it out.

Toro seemed to be fitting in well. He was fitter, bigger, and taller somehow. The training treated him with grace and gifts. He no longer spoke to her, even if she started the conversation. She would ask how he was doing, if he liked it, but he never answered. He responded like she was invisible. His eyes were only for the girl, Astrid, the patient who spirited Ben from her, the patient who Melvina let take Ben out of the Institute. That woman. The one Ben talked too. Everybody loved this Astrid, but there was nothing special about her. She failed in the same way everybody else did. She ended up in the Institute just like everybody else. Her eyes did not make Astrid special; they made her different, unacceptable.

Irritation swarmed Melvina, making her back teeth grind. She was better than this girl, higher. She was a doctor, an employee of the government that helped people like Astrid. It infuriated her, so she tried to not think about it. She would get up and leave just before the training class came in for each meal and not return until after they left. It was obvious Astrid felt the same way; anger and fury rolled off her every time they saw each other. She recognized it, because it matched what was burrowed down into her own soul as well.

Benji still would not allow her to see Ben. She waited outside his room, trying to get a peek when they opened the door. Just one peek. His soft baby blond hair, his scent. Anything would do, but most of all, she needed to know what they were doing to him. Those that watched him—they knew she was there, so it never worked. He stopped screaming a few days after she sang to him. The longing and pain was too much at times. The grief would roll over her as a wave would the beach. Sometimes it was bearable; other times it drowned her, sent her back to her room to cry in shame and disgrace, shaking until there was no more energy to feel sad.

CHAPTER 11
DECISIONS

TORO'S curiosity peaked when Astrid received her summons. What issue could they possibly have that would merit calling a trainee out? Not to mention a former patient, not a guard or security, just a patient.

He checked himself. If it didn't involve him, he needed to make sure he didn't inject himself. He tried to concentrate on the rest of his lunch, but his mind kept wandering back to the interaction between Big Jack and Benji. If Benji was in charge, why would Big Jack treat his commander that way? He was dismissive and standoffish, almost afraid of contact.

Unfortunately, Toro didn't have much more time to dwell on it. Having not finished his lunch in the allotted time, he was forced to dump the extras in the recycling bin. Astrid still hadn't joined their group.

They made it through the rest of the hand-to-hand. Chie—one of the girls who first battled it out with Big Jack after their run—was stuck without a partner and again pinned with Big Jack. Hard to watch the first time … the second even worse. He slapped her around, blood flying about. After Chie had picked herself up off the floor about the tenth time, Astrid finally scrambled in.

"I told ya not to be late. Look what ya did. Punishing others for your mistake is not tolerated well here. Help her up, take her to the infirmary. When ya return we start yar push-ups and chin-ups." Big Jack's eyes lit up, and he watched carefully as Astrid helped Chie out the door. "Back to work, ya lazy slods," he bellowed, and everybody who had stopped to watch the interaction all jumped to attention and started wailing on one another.

Continuation in knife throwing showed nobody improved overnight. Toro managed to get a few in and would smile only long enough to have Big Jack pull it out and tell him to do it better. He was too far to the right, to the left, his throw all wrong. Always something.

"Ya will always have room to improve. Ya will never be perfect here." Big Jack repeated it to anybody who showed complete devastation.

Toro finished a set of push-ups after watching his throwing knife embed itself into the dirt floor below his intended target. He wiped the sweat off his brow and face, seeing Astrid in the corner. Also in the push-up stance except with weights on her shoulders and hips. Her arms shaking, about to collapse. Toro shook his head, retrieving his knives for another turn. A few more tries resulted in more push-ups, sore arms, and miraculously, a change in schedule.

"Now that ya wussies somewhat know how to hold a knife, we move on to the next step: how to fight with one. Knife fighting is hard and painful. Ya think yar arms hurt now, just wait. The sting of a well-honed blade is worse than anything yar poor, wimpy muscles have been through." Again, the excitement of pain and blood. A twinkle in his eyes, like a child with a new toy.

Toro's heart picked up speed. The thought of metal slicing through his flesh did not entice. If there ever was a time to quit, it would be now. But he didn't. He swallowed the lump of fear and forced himself to pay attention.

The trainees gathered in a semi-circle around Big Jack. Astrid was still in the corner, this time doing pull-ups with weights strapped to her ankles.

"How many more does she have?" Toro asked, gesturing toward her.

"Until I tell her to stop." Big Jack eyed him. "Ya need a lesson as well?" He advanced on Toro. "Cause I love teaching 'em."

"No, I'm good." Toro stepped back without realizing it, not wanting to fear Big Jack, but it sure was hard not to be intimidated by him.

"Of course ya are, but since ya think it's okay to interrupt me, why don't ya help me demonstrate." This time he took a couple giant steps back, arming himself with two well shined and sharpened silver knives.

Toro took a deep breath. Having been sucked into what Astrid was doing, he hadn't known Big Jack was still yammering on. Still cussing himself, he picked up his knives and prowled toward Big Jack.

Big Jack grinned, his face low, full of expectation. Toro had always felt tall, but Big Jack dwarfed him, made him feel tiny, insignificant. Googling up at Big Jack's eye, he set his stance. He made the first move, lunging forward on his right leg, shooting his arm out with the knife securely in his hand—or at least he thought it was secure.

"First lesson is grip," Big Jack stated after he easily smacked Toro's knife out of his hand, sending it flying across the floor. "If ya can't hold on to it, ya can't stick it in."

That grin. He enjoyed this. Toro was usually a fast learner, just not this fast.

Big Jack continued to let Toro set up just so he would fail; he would only instruct after the lesson was taught. After fifteen such lessons—which included grip, lunges, soft spots, and blocking—Big Jack finally cut everybody loose to practice on each other. Everybody assigned a goal … unfortunately, it wasn't to avoid being cut but to cut their opponent.

Toro received an epic number of cuts. His arms, chest, back, and thighs all covered in blood from shallow slashes. Seto ended with just as many. Chie, after she returned from the infirmary, turned out to be the best with a knife. Fighting with Big Jack had taught her a few things. They ended up in a circle around Chie and Jazmin at the end of the day.

Jazmin was frustrated and angry; she couldn't get past Chie's defenses to get a strike in. Every time she tried she pulled back, fresh blood spewing from a new cut.

Big Jack finally stepped in. "All right, time to calm it down now."

But Jazmin wouldn't stop. Big Jack constantly tried to stay between them, and Jazmin would just circle around to try to get back at Chie.

He landed Jazmin on her back on the floor and stood over her. "I said to calm it down!" he bellowed.

Giving them some room, unsure how Jazmin would react, the trainees watched. Her face was red with a mixture of exertion and blood. After a few breaths from everybody, she dropped her head to the ground, releasing her knives, still shiny and clean. The only sound was her ragged, jittery breaths. Toro tried not to chuckle, but the sight of Big Jack body-slamming Jazmin to the ground was just too funny. He swore to himself he would never make Big Jack tell him something twice.

ASTRID, dripping blood down her torso and all four of her limbs, performed the best as she was able in the knife fight training. Her pinky on her right hand hanging by mere centimeters of throbbing red skin; the knife had nearly cut all the way through. Still she switched hands and continued to fight.

"All right, everybody make a trip to the infirmary. I'll bring a cleaning crew in for the equipment. We pick up again tomorrow morning." Big Jack huffed the dismissal. The trainees one-by-one put their blood-covered knives back on the metal magnet strips on one of the displays. They limped, all of them sore essentially dead on their feet, to the infirmary to get patched up.

The doctor on duty was a tall, skinny, dark man with a bad sense of humor. He told jokes as he pushed the needles through their cut skin after brutally cleaning their wounds. Moans and groans persisted as they ate dinner.

"Why were you so late?" Toro asked, shoveling the first bite in from an overfilled bowl.

"Wow, straight to the point, aren't we?" Astrid answered.

"Curious, is all." He continued eating.

"Ben, the little boy I came in with. They need his cooperation; he needed me. Took a little longer than they allotted." Astrid put her fork down, carefully placing her bandaged hands in her lap. Talking about Ben reminded her about his current state. "He's so scared. He says they drug him every night so that he will sleep. He says—I don't know what to do for him. Benji won't let me take him back, says it's not good for him. That he needs to grow up and be stronger, and some other BS I wasn't really listening to."

Commotion in one of the back corners of the mess hall called for attention. A figure dressed in black baggy clothes, a hood covering its head, jumped up so fast and rushed by, bumping the table they sat at, rattling their trays. All conversation stopped as every head turned toward the noise. The person didn't stop to acknowledge their audience; just stormed out, head low, only a strand of blonde hair trailing behind.

Dr. Heizer?

MELVINA abandoned her lunch and raced through hallways pushing past people, finally busting into his office. *Drugged? They're drugging my baby so that he slept all night?*

"You're drugging him? I thought you were trying to flush his system, so that he'd remember me!" Her level of anger was beyond anything she'd felt in the past, with herself more than Benji. She'd let this happen, and it was unacceptable.

After Benji observed the pain on her face, he dismissed everybody before answering her. "Calm down, Mel. He doesn't sleep at all if we don't give him something to help, and nothing has helped with his memories. We've tried everything we have. I'm sorry." Returning to his seat, he started turning papers over on his table.

"He doesn't sleep because he needs his mother. He needs me. How do you expect him to remember me if he's not allowed to see me? Benji, come on, have a little mercy," she begged.

"No, he doesn't sleep because he's scared, terrified actually. His nightmares plague everybody around him. It's the only time he screams now though. His daily visits with Astrid have improved his behavior. I think seeing you would dampen his progress, push him back. You don't want that, do you?"

"Don't you dare. Don't you play that against me. Why is Astrid seeing him? She has nothing to do with him! She is not his mother! I am!" Anger boiled into furiousness, about to run over. Her head hot, hands sweaty and shaky.

"Mel, sit down. Ben fears you. You are what his nightmares are about. You can't see him. Maybe when he's older and can understand why."

She stood up again, tears threatening. Her heart shredding all over again. "That's not true. He loves me, and even if you don't believe it, he needs me, he needs me to fix him. I will see him." Her words choked her as she spoke; hot tears overflowed, falling down her thin face.

Benji played with a pen, shaking his head. "Not going to happen. I heard you sat outside his room. He's been moved. And he doesn't need to be fixed; he needs to grow up."

No sympathy, no understanding. *How could he be so cold?*

"He's your son, too." Speaking through tears, Melvina tried to get through to him. Tried to get him to see the pain he continued to cause.

"You should go lie down. You need the rest." Benji escorted her out. Once in the hallway he turned, closing her out.

WHO was that?" Chie asked as the woman Astrid was pretty sure was Dr. Heizer stormed out of the mess hall.

Astrid shook her head, not wanting to deal with any thoughts of the doctor.

"She does speak," Toro exclaimed, turning back to his food.

"Shut up," came her curt reply.

"Who cares? How do you guys have energy to talk?" Seto, from behind Chie, joined them.

Astrid liked them; it was hard not to.

"Sheer will," Toro replied. "Chie, you doing okay? That was quite the beating you took today."

"I'm good. Learned not to be a target and that I may have picked the wrong partner." She smiled. "I'll learn more this way, become stronger."

Her positive attitude uplifted Astrid's spirits. Maybe this would help her mood, get her mind off Ben. Friends—she'd never really made friends before. The change of pace might be favorable to being alone.

"Those push-ups were bad." Chie's gaze stuttered between her food and hands. Astrid could see she pushed herself hard to make conversation with them.

"Yea, don't be late. I don't recommend it. He made me continue until I couldn't even push myself up off the floor to sit up. Simply told me to grab knives. I needed to 'catch up' to the rest of the class. The narcissistic, torturous—"

"Easy there, wouldn't want somebody to overhear ya." Big Jack happened to be moving behind them with his tray. "Ya survived, and yar stronger 'cause of it. Don't complain."

Stifled laughs from the surrounding tables rose. Astrid's eyes widened along with her mouth, a fork suspended in air. Toro trying to not choke, Chie just as terrified as Astrid, and Seto burying his face in his hands to cover his laugh.

"He's gone, but you really should watch what you say." Jackson sat down on the other side of Toro.

"Thanks." Astrid put her fork down, letting out a light laugh, shaking her head at herself. Butterflies no longer made an appearance for Jackson after he managed to man-handle her out of the meeting. Now he was just another authority figure, somebody there to bark orders.

"You're all doing well in your training. Just a note, though … when we start weeding out the weak, it's a whole new game. Best prepare yourselves as much as you can."

"How do you do that?" Seto regained control of his laughter long enough to ask.

"We choose a different method for each candidate, something tailored to you specifically. If you succeed, you continue training. If you fail, we pull you and find something else inside the compound for you." He made direct eye contact with each of them in turn as he explained.

Seto stopped laughing altogether, seriousness falling on the table like a cloth. Those chewing finished swallowing hard along with the lump that formed in their throats.

"Nothing you guys do is simple or easy, is it?" Toro asked. The lines of his face turned hard. "I'm all for training, but it's like you're out to cause us as much pain as we can handle."

"Yes."

"Why?"

"To see what you're capable of. If we know you can handle it here, we know what you can handle out there. You think we're cruel?"

"In a way."

"What the government has done is worse. We're just preparing you for the fight of your life. Any man who causes harm upon another human being, even if they believe they are doing the right thing, are not doing their best. They are at their worst. We are simply trying to teach them a lesson they are in desperate need of. You can help, or you can be left behind." Jackson patted the table, ending the conversation.

Nobody regarded Toro—they all knew where he came from— this shed a light on his feelings and thoughts toward the government.

"How can you stand up for them? After all they've done, to you, to us." Chie glared at Toro.

"They did what they felt was necessary for the situation they were dealt." His jaw was tight, eyes unblinking. Nobody challenged him; just took a collected breath as he removed himself.

"Ho—" Seto tried, immediately jumping up and chasing after Toro.

Astrid shook her head. "He won't change his mind. Like many government employees, he was born into a privilege we can't imagine. Maybe seeing things from our point of view will help, and maybe it won't."

"You knew him before here, didn't you?" Chie asked, placing her fork down.

"He was a guard at the Institute where I was a prisoner." She played with the food on her plate, pushing it back and forth with her fork, having lost her appetite.

"And your eyes? Did that come from the Institute as well?" This time Chie's gaze locked on Astrid's, unwavering.

"Do you … can you see a blue ring around my irises?"

"Yea, it's all anybody talked about after you arrived. What's it from?" Chie struggled to keep it casual, but Astrid could see the curiousness and questions getting ready to burst forth and take over the conversation.

"I can't see it."

Chie startled at her admission and did not have an immediate reply. Instead she worried her lips against her teeth, unsure what to do.

"I can't see Ben's either, but today in training … I don't know how to explain it."

At this, Astrid knew Chie understood. She'd seen Astrid; more importantly, she'd seen her eyes. "Chie, what happened to my eyes today?"

Chie took her time to answer. "The blue ring spread, and at first I thought it was a trick of the light, but, your eyes, they went black, even the whites. All except the ring of blue. It spread—little tendrils reaching out, taking over. Your entire eyes went from black to blue." She grew physically uncomfortable the more she shared.

Chie's words sunk in, Astrid's breath getting harder and harder the more she thought. If this happened every time she hit her head, she'd be the local freak. The science experiment—she stopped, staring blankly at Chie. "An experiment." The admission caused more pain than anything Big Jack could dish out.

"They experimented on you?" Toro's voice pierced through her thoughts, startling her at his return.

Astrid glared up at him. Seto was nowhere to be seen. Toro was not invited. He should not be a part of this conversation, this information that would bare her inner fears, leaving her raw.

"Toro—you should leave."

Chie's suggestion was not received lightly. His mouth opened to retort, but then he shut it. After Toro's rough departure, Astrid finally turned her attention back to Chie.

"Thanks. I don't think I'm ready to face this subject with many people."

"He hates them too, you know. Maybe he just hasn't realized it yet. It's obvious he really cares for you. On some level I think he feels responsible for what you've been through, what ... what they've done to you." Chie dropped her head, her voice going soft.

"Toro was one of the guards keeping me locked up. He should feel responsible. Logically, I know he was doing his job. The face to go with my pain, the loss—its Dr. Heizer's, but he was there too. I can't explain it. It's just a feeling I have."

She was shocked by the concern Chie showed for Toro, and she shut her eyes, letting her breath slow, her anger disappearing. "Chie, I can't see the blue in my reflection, but I could see the blue when it tried to take over, when I hit my head. I ... I think they experimented on me."

"Why do you think that? Do you remember ... anything?"

"No, but I do know I wasn't born like this. What happens when it takes over? What happens if I stop fighting it?"

"Don't do that, don't ever give up. We need you, and you don't know what it does. You could be taken over by a computer or go into a coma." Chie's desperation showed in her voice, getting higher as she pleaded with Astrid. "Maybe you should tell Benji. Maybe he could help."

Astrid shook her head at the idea. "I'm not sure I can trust Benji. I have a feeling he may already know."

"What about Ben's mom?"

"I think I'm ready for bed, but thanks for your help."

Chie nodded as Astrid excused herself and returned to her room.

Exhausted, she immediately fell into bed. Her body screamed when she moved, but a dull thud of her pulse through her veins reminded her she was still alive.

Another day was on its way—another day closer to her mother, another day to do what was needed.

MELVINA came to in the corner of her room on her bed. Her head against the wall, face wet and swollen. She felt weak and lost. Never before had she felt this unsure and shaken. She needed Benji to understand that she needed Ben. His coldness toward her shocked her to her soul. Unable to force his understanding, she was left on her own ... again. Locked in this filthy compound these savages called their home. Disgraced, that's what they were. Fallen so far from society they lived underground with the stink of dead fish, trying to force their way of life upon others, along with their views and inhumane ways of dealing with things.

She gradually let loose her muscles as she stretched herself from the fetal position. Her were muscles tight from being in the same position so long. Little needles of pain stabbed her feet and lower legs. She cried out in pain as her body came back to life. When she wiped her face, a spot of black on the back of one of her hands caught her attention. She pulled back and inspected them. They had always been her livelihood, her way of communication with her world, her son, and her job. Now they were cut, bruised, and filthy. Dirt caked them, her nails chipped and broken. Black little moons formed under her nails.

Panic overcame her mind first, slowly forcing its way into her body. Tears again, trying to scrub the dirt and bruises off her hands, shaking wildly as she screamed. Standing in the middle of her room, she spun, frantically searching for water and a rag. As she moved, she tripped, smacking her head on the metal bed frame. Opening her eyes she noticed a pair of boots, which she followed to the upside-down form of Mitch standing in the doorway and gawking down on her.

"You okay, love?" He stretched a hand out, an offer of help.

Melvina gently rolled her body over, pushing herself up on her knees. "No, does anything about me seem okay? I'm in rags, on a dirt floor, and unable to see my son. My e—"

"Whoa, easy. I meant physically. I heard you hit the bed. Is your head okay?"

"Oh, just another bruise and scratch added." She immediately became shy; sharing her personal details with strangers was not something she would normally do. He continued to stand, one hand on his side holster, the other still held out to her. She reached with her left, noticed the amount of dirt she'd added to her already dirty hand, and pulled it back. "I'll be fine. Thank you for asking. And again, it's doctor." She dropped her gaze to her hands in her lap, slowly wrapping themselves up in the oversized shirt they gave her.

"Okay, I'm outside if you need anything, Dr. Love."

He's outside. There was a guard on her, always. Betrayal was always a hard thing to swallow, and Benji forced it down her throat over and over, unwanted and unneeded. Where was she going to go? The ocean? *Who is he kidding with this?*

Rising, she tiptoed toward the door, and as quietly as she could she opened it, peeping through the slit. There he was, standing to the side of her door, leaning up against the wall. His head turned in her direction, so she quickly closed it.

"Love, you need something?" came his voice from the other side of the wood.

"Doctor! I'm a doctor!"

"Sorry, Dr. Love."

She kicked the door with the flat of her foot. The pain woke her up a bit, but not nearly enough. As she stood there her tummy growled. She held her stomach, remembering she hadn't finished dinner the night before. After hearing Astrid's declaration about Ben's condition, she had cleared out straight to Benji's office then later to her room.

"Great," she muttered. Reopening the door, she glared at Mitch. "I need a shower, and dinner." She quickly shut it again.

"You'll have to come out to shower, Doctor." The emphasis on the word *doctor* was not lost on her.

"Right." She opened the door for the third time and took a step into the hallway. Luckily, he backed up a bit to give her room. He followed her to the showers and waited outside the door. She scrubbed

147

so hard her skin hurt and became red with irritation. The water and soap felt good though. She felt more like herself, a problem solver, a higher breed for society, a doctor, and a mother.

After she dried off and got dressed with semi-clean clothes, she inspected her hands—they were still bruised and cut, but clean, which calmed her, mind and soul. It helped reset her focus and sharpen her mind. A step in the right direction. Big plans called for little victories and even smaller steps.

Mitch, still in the hallway, gave her half a grin while heading toward the mess hall. Melvina gradually followed behind him, careful not to get too close.

"When did the screaming finally stop?" The question had spent time rolling around in her head and finally burst forth so hard it caught her off guard. She cursed herself, glancing up to see him watching her over his shoulder.

"Yours? A little after three in the morning."

"Mine?" *What?* Shaking her head, deciding to dwell on that later, she corrected herself. "No. Ben's? My boy?"

"Oh, your son? Yes, he's been fine. No screaming since Astrid has been allowed to see him again. He's doing well."

So casual, as if the weight of a little boy's life didn't haunt her every thought. When it came to Mitch, she was just a chore.

"Why are you guarding me?" She made the last bit as sarcastic as she could muster.

"Scared of what you might do, yes. I'm yours until he states otherwise. Doctor."

She ate in silence, thinking about her boy. Mitch departed to stand outside the mess hall against a wall. She needed to first build an acquaintance with him, a foundation for a heavier conversation, so she didn't try to pry more information out of him for now.

With more purpose than she'd felt in days, she finished her meal in a peace she basked in.

CHAPTER 12

ACTIONS

AFTER returning to her room from Benji's office, Melvina's decision was made for her. Not only was she apparently screaming in her sleep, Ben was accepting his situation, and that just would not do. As long as Ben fought everybody she was okay staying there, just to see what Benji's plan was. But with Ben in acceptance, the seriousness of her situation dawned on her. If Ben stopped fighting, she would have to start.

She paced the corridors for hours, her bodyguard following a few paces behind her, until she knew them as well as the Institute. She could traverse them with her eyes closed to get to her destination now. Next she would need to find where Benji had moved Ben to. And find out when Astrid was seeing him. Showing up to kidnap her own kid while Astrid visited him was a no-go. Melvina knew that Astrid fed Ben ideas, feeding his fears of her. Seeing them together and Ben happy proved something she was not ready to face, ever.

During a review of the map she created in her head, while Mitch slowly sauntered absentmindedly behind, she somehow managed to slip away. She walked along a small corridor in the back of the compound and came upon a sweet little voice coming from a vent above her head. Immediately coming to a halt, she leaned against the makeshift wall, pushing herself up on her toes, trying to get her ear as close to the vent as possible. It was Ben! Was he ... giggling?

No! No, Ben, don't be happy, don't accept!

She scanned the walls on both sides of the vent to see if she could find where it led. So close. A door to her left about ten feet away grabbed her attention, begging to be opened.

In a rush to discovery, Melvina burst through the door before any thought that her actions would hurt her progress entered her head. The room was dark, the only light shining in from behind her. After letting her eyes adjust she found white tables side-by-side in the middle surrounded by chairs. The table held maps laid out with blue ink marking arrows and lines. The walls held even more plans tacked up against the wood. Spying around for a light, she closed the door slightly behind her to keep from drawing attention to herself. She gently tugged on a pull string connected to a single bulb above the table, flooding the dark room with low wattage yellow tinted light.

Her breath was stolen away at the sight. The L.A. Institute and the Reformer's strategy to bring it to the ground was laid bare before her. Benji planned to use the entire force of the Reformers, including the new trainees and incoming patients. Melvina took a seat in the nearest chair, pulling a map closer to herself labeled 'ground's security and fence.' Little red X's marked spots along the outside of the wall, with four arrows marking their way through the front gate, which she knew was in disarray from the last attack. If Benji burst through those gates with the number of guns and explosives the Reformers owned, the Institute would fall. She knew they were still reeling from the past attack, probably having to call in reinforcements to fill the gaps left in the security.

"Oh no," she whispered. They were going to blow up and level the L.A. Institute. Schematics, plans, electrical grids, guard shifts, weapon inventory ... Benji had everything. Most likely someone fed him the information. This was terrifying. Putting her head in her hands, she sat back down, overwhelmed. She knew she was unable to stop this from inside the compound. One against hundreds was not feasible.

Ben's voice busted her concentration, snapping her head up. Standing, she listened, trying to determine where it originated from. Glancing around the room, trying to overlook the papers and maps, she saw no other exits besides the door she came in. The room was makeshift, created with wood and paneling. Following the voice, she found herself in the back corner with her hands against the wall. Leaning closer in, pushing more pressure onto the wall, she was surprised when it shifted beneath her hands. Not wanting to show anybody what she discovered, she opened the panel just far enough to peek in.

A light room, spacious compared to the other rooms she had come across in the compound. In the center on the floor playing was Ben. He giggled, happy, light emanating from his eyes. She needed to get him away from this place. Only when he stopped, his face falling and his head turning in her direction did she pull back, out of view.

Closing the panel, placing her forehead against the now secured wall, she whispered, "I'm coming, Ben. Just hang on for a few more hours."

She returned to her room to wait and found Mitch frantically running up a corridor in search of her.

"Where have you been?" he demanded.

"Walking. Where did you run off to?" she countered.

"I was right behind you. Keep your pace slow and make sure I can see you, Doctor." His stern voice was a frantic surprise. No 'Dr. Love' or flirtatious advance. Just orders.

"Not my problem. Maybe you should pay more attention." With that she entered her room, leaving him in the hallway. Not wanting to worry him too much, she didn't slam it but closed her door rather softly, trying to yawn and show how tired she was.

A few hours after lights out when she was sure the rest of the compound would be sound asleep in their fake sense of safety, Melvina snuck out of her room. Managing to time it when Mitch—against orders—napped against the wall. Shaking her head, she stepped over his outstretched legs. Without making a sound she made her way to the map room, finding the secret panel and Ben. He was sound asleep, underneath an old table covered in dusty, worn down toys, covered with a thin blanket. His caretaker asleep on a bed on the opposite side of the room.

Finding it too easy, but not letting her mind sit on it long enough to talk herself out of it, she lifted the sleeping Ben out from underneath the table. She wrapped him in the threadbare blanket and carried him out of the room, careful to close the panel behind her.

Without stopping, she made her way into the circular garage past the buses. It was black, dirty, and smelled of fish. The smell—much like the first time it hit her nostrils—made her want to expel the contents of her thinning stomach. She held it in without coughing or throwing up, managing to make it to the top of the ramp in the tunnel, her lungs burning, her arms about to give up and drop Ben to the ground. But she dared not cause any more physical pain to her boy. She held fast, making it to the end of the tunnel without being seen.

Putting Ben down, she stretched her arms and lower back before searching for a way to exit the tunnel without using the automatic door. The whole wall was fitted to a device that extracted the wall upon command. Without having the opener, Melvina was forced to find a simpler way of escape. She took several deep breaths, spinning in circles to get her bearings. The low light spewing in through dirt-covered windows illuminated a door to her right. Hoping for the good luck of an unlocked door, she gently stepped toward it.

Tonight, a good night, she happened to be in luck. Pushing the door open to an alleyway between two tight buildings, she had her escape. After going back for Ben she exited the tunnel. Not wanting to give her pursuers any help, she closed the door tightly behind her, securing the lock.

A few buildings later, after zigzagging her way through alleys and side streets, Melvina found herself in a corner on the floor with Ben in her lap still covered by the thin blanket. Through a window on the far wall covered in dust she could see more daylight. The sun was fully risen. They would know. They would come. She couldn't lose him. Not again.

ASTRID found herself on a schedule set by somebody else. She got up, ate breakfast, attended training, lunch, back to training, saw Ben, ate dinner. Slept. Repeat. With no days off, no rest and no recovery. Exactly like the Institute. She had to constantly remind herself that here at the Reformer's compound she was being trained. It was for her betterment. This was good.

Her body became a machine, able to keep up with hand-to-hand and run fifteen miles at a brisk pace without stopping. Her knife throwing abilities improved, down to only one to two sets of push-ups a training session, and her knife fighting skills flourished. Once they learned how to hold the knife and where the weakest parts of their opponents were, it was easy for all of them to end up in the infirmary day after day.

The wounds and bruises just built up on one another; ribs cracked, blood oozed. They would wipe themselves off, spit blood out, pick themselves up, and carry on.

"The better ya get, the less you get hit, the more ya heal," Big Jack would bellow during training.

It was exhausting, trying to keep up with all the rules, all the lessons. Every few days they would catch Jackson and Red near the door, taking notes, nodding their heads at the trainees. Benji was only ever seen once; he pulled Big Jack aside, asking him to point out numerous trainees while discussing amongst themselves. They found it distracting, wanting to know how they were doing, and at the same time not being told. Frustration led them to harsher training sessions. They quickly learned to keep any expressions other than pain and victory to themselves.

At first it was only one or two not coming to sessions. Discussions of the missing trainees were shut down quickly, those still in attendance told to not worry about it. After that it escalated: two to four trainees a day no longer in training, and now they were down to half the number they started with. Some of the remaining trainees mentioned seeing the others in various parts of the compound, planting crops, working in the kitchens, or cleaning the shower stalls.

During breakfast one morning, Benji came storming into the mess hall.

"Astrid, you see Ben last night?" He was obviously in a hurry, his breath heavy and sweat on his brow.

"Yes, why? What's wrong? Is he okay?" Pain crept into her thoughts and heart, fear overloading her senses. She pushed up from the table, making her way toward him.

"He's gone." Without further explanation he left the mess hall. Astrid hopped over the bench, her hands placed on backs and shoulders to propel her to the door, jogging to catch and keep up with his long strides.

"What do you mean he's gone? Where could he go? I thought he was constantly being watched?" Questions spilled out; frustration, worry, and anger forged a path toward panic.

Benji shook his head, slicing his hand through the air in front of him. "Don't know. Mrs. Laura woke up this morning to find Ben gone, not in the room. We're trying to narrow down a timeframe now." He picked up his pace.

Astrid came to a full stop in the corridor. "Benji? What about his mother?"

She gazed at the floor as she thought. His mother was here in the compound, upset that she was unable to see him. Would she take him? Would she kidnap him in the middle of the night? Forcing her attention back up she saw Benji hadn't heard her, or chose not to. He stood down at the end talking to Jackson. She ran fast to hear what they discussed.

"Do a full sweep. He's small. Call out to him. Find him!" Benji gave instructions, and people ran all over the place. Astrid could hear his name being called, echoing through the compound.

"Benji!" she called again.

"What?!" He turned on her, seething mad.

"His mother, do you know where she is?" she asked calmly, trying not to feed his anger, but his mind instead.

"Mel," he cursed to himself. A new thought process seeming to emerge, he took off at full speed. Astrid followed as fast as she could, falling short at being able to keep up with him. All the training worth nothing compared to his pace which was much greater than her own. She turned the final corner as he came to a skidding stop outside the doctor's door. A guard perched outside it against the wall, reading. "Where is she?"

"Hi, boss. She's inside. Haven't seen her since dinner last night." He pushed himself off the wall, slowly backing away.

Astrid approached as though she was coming up on a dog fight, silently and aware. Not intruding, just witnessing the exchange.

Benji stepped forward, kicking the door in. The crack of the wood followed by the crash upon landing, sending dirt and dust into the air. Rushing in, they found an empty room. "You've been here all night?" Benji demanded of the guard.

He stuttered, glaring at the empty space on the bed.

"Yes, she entered the room after dinner. I haven't left," he exclaimed.

"Well she did." Benji spun around, grabbing the guard by his jacket, slamming him up against the wall, getting close to his face. "You were supposed to watch her, Mitch! Where is she?" he screamed, his voice getting louder with every interrogating question.

"I was watching her. I di—I don't know, Benji! I didn't leave!" Mitch scrambled for an explanation, for an answer.

Benji dropped him, storming out, taking off at a run.

Astrid watched the bewildered expression spread upon the guard's face. "I was here," he repeated to himself, inspecting the room, lifting the blankets and checking under the bed. "What did you do, love?"

Astrid turned, trying to find which direction Benji had gone. She attempted to track him down, running past the mess hall, the showers, the garage. Everybody was circling around searching for Ben. As she ran past the training room she heard her name. Coming to a halt, she backed up.

"Come on, you're going to be late again." Toro stepped toward the doorway, reaching to pull her in.

"He's gone, Toro. I have to help find him. She took him." She fought against his grip, trying to twist free.

"What? Astrid, you're not making any sense. Who's gone? Who took him?" Concern etched the corners of his face.

"*Ben!*" she screamed. "Ben is gone and she took him!" Trying to gather the information to explain it to Toro proved to be a bigger task than she was willing to take on at the moment; she really just wanted to find Ben. When she fought to get past Toro and move down the corridor again, he reached out, grabbing her arm, stopping her.

"Astrid. Stop, Astrid!"

She struggled against him. "Let me go!"

"No! Astrid, listen! Listen." She stopped. "Listen." It registered; everybody was calling Ben's name, everybody tending to the problem. "They'll find him, but you'll be punished if you do not get in that room right now. You thought last time was bad? You think it will be the same with your body stronger? Think about it. Put your worry and your anger into the training."

He was right. She knew he was right. They would find him. With a heavy heart, she nodded, letting Toro guide her into the training room.

"Right on time." Big Jack was waiting on them. "Ya two pair up and start hand-to-hand."

Astrid could barely keep her thoughts and eyes on his fast-moving hands and feet. He constantly made contact with her body, her face. Helping her off the ground more than once as she forced the blue circle into the corners of her vision. It grew thicker the harder he hit.

"Focus, Astrid. Come on," he would say as they squared off again.

"Better get yar head in the game, little lady," Big Jack stated, shuffling by. "At least get one hit on him. Ya shouldn't let a guy beat on ya like that."

Toro helped her up again with a grin on his face.

They kept at it, moving on to conditioning, knives, strength training, more knives, gun safety, target practice. Astrid hadn't been this off since they started many weeks ago. Her frustration building, anger getting the best of her. The butt of her knives hit the target and bounced to the ground. Spinning around, ready to give up, she ran right into Benji.

"You're throwing it with anger instead of precision and calm."

"Did you find him?"

"Aw, you're distracted. That will do it, too. No, he's gone and so is she. The best we can piece together is she snuck out when her guard went to the bathroom and got into Ben's room while Ms. Laura was asleep." He was strangely calm. It irritated her.

"How?"

"What?"

"How was she able to just leave with him? He wouldn't have let her—you were drugging him still?" she asked accusingly.

"Yes, but if we didn't he didn't sleep. I've sent out a crew to canvas the surrounding area. Due to the dense buildings it will take them a while, and having no idea when she actually left, she may be a good ways away."

"You're serious? She's on foot! Right?"

Benji didn't bother gracing her with a dignified response, instead turning on his heel with an angered look in his eyes.

Astrid watched, infuriated, as he stalked away. The knife in her hand passed his head hilt over point and embedded in the door jamb to his right. He didn't flinch, just stopped, glancing at the knife before pulling it out with a swift tug.

"Precision and purpose. Nice throw." He was gone.

Astrid calmed herself. The other trainees had stopped to watch the interaction. Big Jack glared at her from the other side of the room.

"The one person who could end yar life in this compound with a thought and ya throw a knife at his head." He shook his head. "That was a nice throw. Back to work!"

"I missed," Astrid claimed, picking up her knives to begin again.

TORO tried to keep Astrid focused, but handing her a high-powered weapon was not something he felt would benefit anybody at the moment. They set up their targets at the end of the room, opened the vents, put on their safety goggles and ear plugs. The problem with target practice underground was ... well, there were numerous problems. One, they could only get up to a certain distance before they literally ran out of room. Two, the ear plugs barely protected their ear drums from being ruptured at the sonic bombs that echoed off the walls. And three, if a bullet missed the intended target, the chances of it bouncing off a concrete wall and flying at their heads was higher than they wanted to admit.

They lay down flat with their Harriet M107 long-range sniper rifles on stands stretched in front of them. Little wooden tiles—each with a letter and a number—were placed randomly on the targets at the other end of the room. The newest way to see how their sniper skills progressed was to spell words; the higher the score the better you did. Big Jack and Red set up behind them with binoculars. Having done this numerous times, Toro looked forward to it.

"To make things a bit more interesting this time, we have fitted yar weapons with night vision scopes, the tiles have already been heated and will disappear as they cool. Red, if ya would."

The lights went out. Pitch black. Big Jack's booming laughter filled the dark space around them.

"Challenge accepted." Seto, who perched on the left side of Toro, showed just as much excitement as Toro felt. They each set up, putting their eyes against their scopes, pointer fingers on the trigger. Calling out a guess of numbers to see who would go first. Jazmin choose wisely; lucky number seven was in Big Jack's head today. She called out a *G* hitting it square on, punching a hole through her target, making the tile disappear entirely.

"A *G* for the Arabian princess. Work ya way down the line. I'll keep score. Ya know how I like it."

It was the same since they learned how to shoot. One of the only exercises that didn't cause them extreme physical pain or humiliation. Rules were absolute. They needed to spell a word in order, and once the word was completed, the total score was calculated and compared to the rest of the class. Each board held the full alphabet with extra vowels.

They could spell any word they wanted, and with only seven shots, no easy words with high numbers. Top score was awarded with a pass; they didn't have to clean their gun or tear down. It didn't seem like a lot, but after a hard day being the first one under the hot spray without having to share was euphoric.

They each took their turn, taking a shot at the board one hundred feet from them. Seto started with *M*, and Toro chose *J*, trying hard to remember the word he'd recently read and the correct way to spell it. Red was there for a reason; well read, his vocabulary was superb. They all chalked it up to his lack of liking to talk, that he kept his words locked up. Astrid started with an *E*.

"Seriously, Astrid? An *E*? Where's your head?"

"On the board, Toro, where yours should be."

The trainees heckled each other, attempting to break each other's concentration and focus, while trying to keep their own. The words began to build, each adding one letter per shot, excitement filling the room with anticipation of cutting out early. The thought of a hot shower always brought out the best in them.

Seto so far had *mania*, and Jazmin, not being too original and showing she really didn't know that many seven letter words, was spelling *ghostly* again. Astrid was at an *M* which gave her *exhum*. Chie's word was something to do with guns, which always made Big Jack smile. Toro finally remembered his word and had *jauki*. With only two shots each left, the jeering and cackling picked up. They watched the tiles fade into the background, coming to room temperature.

"Chie, way to brown-nose. You know how to get Big Jack to show his yellow teeth." Seto could always bring out the blush in Chie's cheeks.

Laughter filled the room between the big booms of the shots.

"Astrid, where you going with this?" Toro was out to beat her. He'd won every shooting contest they competed in, even if it wasn't a contest. His training from the Institute gave him an edge, although he did admit they were catching up to him.

"Just helping them bring out the light." She shot another *E*, re-cocking her gun. Toro added *N* to his word, Seto a *C*.

"All right, you maniac, nice word play," Toro said.

Seto laughed at him so hard he almost toppled his gun over. Toro tried hard not to join him. Red still hadn't breathed a word, only allowing a slow smile to spread across his face. They made their rounds back to Astrid, who finished with a *D*, just as the tiles blinked out one-by-one.

She put her gun on safety and laid it down, sitting on her heels. "And that's the game. The rest of you don't have what it takes. Sorry, ladies."

She was cocky, but right. Her use of the *X* pushed her over the top. Chie shot the last booming shot with a *T*, finishing her word of *gunfight*. Red nodded toward Astrid and left.

"Astrid, twenty points. The rest of ya fall short. Have fun cleaning up."

The lights came back on, forcing the trainees to blink at the sudden change. Red stood by the door with his slender fingers on the knob. Big Jack moved to follow him out.

"Exhumed? Astrid, where do you come up with these?" Seto packed his gun over to its case.

"My mom always insisted I read. Didn't matter what I read, just that I did. If I wasn't, she was reading to me. Thanks for the hot shower, boys."

Toro watched her limp out while massaging her right shoulder. She headed around the corner.

"Dang, I thought I had it with *jauking*, thinking the *K* would get me there."

"Don't complain, Toro. She earned it. She's learning quick. Even with the setback of that toddler hanging on her, she's kicking our butts. Hey, what do you think of her story about the general and the bus attack?" Seto stopped in the middle of wiping his gun down.

The change in subject took Toro a second to catch on. The pause did not deter Seto.

"I worked there, Seto." He stopped, remembering Reider and Sibella's conversation. Sibella saw something that day. It was crazy, what they said happened, but how could all of them be wrong? "I don't know, man. I don't know." He paused, for effect or to catch his own thoughts; he wasn't sure. "Since coming here I've learned things about the Institute that shock me."

His thoughts turned back to Astrid's story. Having never seen General Thaxton, it was hard to imagine the scene she'd described. He knew the government performed experiments, but what Astrid said meant the general was stealing lives, trapping souls. It seemed so fantastical to him. Like a book he would read, not something he would ever have to face himself.

"I don't know, man, she seems pretty convinced. She knows what she saw. Makes me wonder what the government is actually up to, if they are doing what they say they are."

"You believe her?"

"Absolutely. I will believe every word she utters. Somebody has to." The grin on his face betrayed him. Toro had just enough energy to feel jealous.

THEY were lost. In the middle of an abandoned building in a city Melvina knew nothing about. The gravity of the situation astonished her. No food, no water, and a child who despised her minutes from waking up. This was not good. What was she thinking? Unsure of what to do next, she rested with Ben's head in her lap.

She absently caressed Ben's beautiful silky blond hair, grown out enough to trail between her fingers, sending shivers up her arm. She watched him slumber, love outpouring from her as his eyes swiveled behind his lids. She wondered what he dreamt of: super heroes, space adventures, a deep-sea diver in the depths of the ocean hunting creatures undiscovered. The options were limitless. His dreams protected him, giving him the safety of a world entirely his own. She envied him, his innocent, carefree life. If only she could return to that, if only she knew which moment in her life marked the loss, if only to just hold on to it, if only for a minute longer.

CHAPTER 13
REACTIONS

IT wasn't long before Ben stirred in her lap. She wasn't not ready. Having no idea how to handle the situation, she wished she knew of a way to make him sleep longer. Not wanting to scare him any more than she was already going to, Melvina lowered his head onto a makeshift pillow and moved to the other side of the empty room. It didn't take him long; he soon stretched his little body, cracking his eyes open.

She watched the panic overtake his face, the confusion of not knowing where he was taking form. Ben shot to his knees, and gradually, as his eyes focused, he scanned the room. When his gaze fell upon Melvina, the panic took a deeper grip, and he pushed himself back against the nearest wall. To his credit he didn't scream as she thought he would.

"Hello Ben. Good morning." She kept her voice soft and her body close to the ground in as non-threatening a way as she could possibly keep it. She didn't want him to start making a bunch of noise she couldn't control, which in turn would lead the Reformers straight to them. "I'm sorry you woke up here. I wasn't completely prepared. I … you probably don't need to know all the details," she mumbled. After taking several deep breaths she continued. "I, I'm sorry. I know you think me a horrible person, but in truth I only did what I thought was best. I love you." She paused, going for the big question. "Do you know who I am?"

She found it hard to stare into his eyes, his once beautiful, bright green eyes now hindered with a circle of orange.

He nodded. He pushed himself farther against the wall, curling up into the fetal position, with just his eyes peeking out from behind his knees. She could see the orange growing, trying to take over his baby green irises.

"Oh good, I was scared you didn't remember me." She let out a sigh of relief, sitting in a more comfortable position to continue the conversation.

"You're the lady in the white coat from the white building." Ben spoke in such a soft voice Melvina struggled to hear him.

"Yes, you're right." Her heart dropped. Ben remembered her, but not as she wanted him to. "I am the doctor from the Institute. But I'm also your mom."

"No," he whispered.

"Yes, Ben, I am. You were young when they took you. I'm sorry, I know you don't remember me, but that's not my fault." She continued to explain, watching him. He needed to understand that she didn't have a choice in letting him go. In letting them reform him to their purpose and science. It was not her fault. He must see that.

Ben didn't want to believe her. She could see that he was barely holding it together. "Where's Astrid?" he interrupted to ask.

As she was babbling on, she asked him to repeat it. When he did, her anger spiked immediately.

"She's not here." Closing her eyes, she forced deep breaths through her lungs. She opened her eyes again to see the tears forging a path down his face. "She couldn't come. Ben, please don't cry. I'm here for you."

"You were mean to me. I want Astrid." He became hysterical, being trapped in a vise-like grip of panic she was unable to loosen for him. Melvina was helpless as she sat there watching. His eyes got bigger, his hands shaking, the tears heavier, creating puddles on his clothes.

"Ben, breathe. Please? Close your eyes and breathe. You're safe. I'm not going to hurt you." She talked in a soothing voice without moving, repeating her affections over and over, hoping her voice would break through his episode. He'd never before had panic attacks. This was something as a mom she was unsure how to handle, but as a doctor, she had a slight understanding of what the body needed to calm itself.

They continued this back and forth, Melvina talking to him and Ben trying to get control of himself. She knew they needed to move; they couldn't stay here much longer, but Ben needed to want to move. He needed to want to go with her. She knew if she forced him that the scene he would create would draw Benji straight to them.

Once he exhausted himself he lay his head on his knees with his face to one side, concentrating on his breathing. Melvina stood calmly as to not startle him.

"Ben, we need to go. We can't stay here. The bad guys will find us. We need to make our way back to the city."

He didn't move. She took a step closer; this snapped his head up and his hands to the ground beside him as he pushed himself even farther into the wall behind him.

"No," he simply disagreed, his eyes going wide, the orange ring becoming brighter and more vibrant.

"Please, I won't hurt you. I promise. I love you. I wouldn't hurt you ever. Please, come with me?" She wished she could help. Or at least she should have stolen some medication to keep him asleep until they arrived back at the Institute. "Please."

"What will happen to me?" he asked. Ben did not take his eyes off her as she crept toward him.

What an odd question.

"Nothing bad. I want to get you fixed. I want you to get your real memory back. I want my little boy back. So we can be a family again."

"Fixed? What's broken?" His eyes darted back and forth.

Uh oh. She'd disclosed the wrong plan, incorrect information.

"No, there's nothing broken. Your memory is … it's just locked up, so we need to unlock it and free it." She hurried the explanation out to calm him, choosing not to explain the meaning of his eyes. As the words registered, his gaze steadied and focused on her again. She was only about three feet from his toes now, still advancing at a snail's pace. Moving inch by inch, kneeling in front of him, gently placing her palm on his calf. "There is and never was anything wrong with you, baby. Please, we need to go. Let me help."

He stopped moving as he watched her, battling an internal war she could only give him weapons for. His eyes moved slowly back and forth between her eyes and her hand upon his leg. Finally, after what seemed an eternity, he nodded and relaxed, moving to a standing position in front of her. His eyes, fully engulfed with orange, now receded back to the beautiful green she'd fallen in love with.

Melvina fought the urge to throw her arms around him and squeeze him tight. She stayed where she was until he passed her. He stopped, turning to see if she was following. That simple act of inviting swelled her heart. She stood, reached out for his hand, and they shambled out of the dark, dank building hand in hand.

ASTRID searched for Ben an entire day and night, unable to accept that Melvina simply tiptoed out with a sleeping child unnoticed. The entire situation was unacceptable. They were supposed to be safe; she promised Ben that nobody would hurt him here.

As she strolled the corridors she passed numerous staff members who still wouldn't meet her eyes, due to her speaking out about the general or her abnormality; she wasn't sure. She did know that what they saw made them uncomfortable, uneasy.

Toro, Seto, and Chie set out in search with her as well, skipping a meal to help. When they could be taking time to rest. Tomorrow all the trainees headed for the final test outside of the compound.

The idea of Ben being out there unprotected with that witch of his mother set Astrid on edge. She tried hard not to snap, not to kill everybody who came near her. When Toro, Seto, and Chie had offered to help, the massive weight of worry lifted a bit off her shoulders to be shared amongst the four of them.

Camaraderie was new to Astrid as the only friend she ever had was her mother. When it came to sharing secrets, problems, triumph, or joy amongst fellow trainees, she found herself to be inadequate. Everybody else seemed to fall into their own cliques and friendships with ease and little discomfort. The joking and picking at one another commenced at every meal and training session. Since they ate and trained together there was little time left in the days they were alone.

Astrid found herself unable to keep from being snatched by the net that was friendship. Toro pushed himself in, Seto creeping in behind him, and then Chie's with her timidity, making it hard to leave them be. While she was unsure what their purpose was, she found herself thankful for their presence.

She spotted Jackson and Red ahead, close to one another and engaged in a conversation.

Astrid marched straight up to them. Locking eyes with Jackson she demanded, "Do you know where they are?"

He didn't have to ask what or who she was talking about. She knew that he was toward the top of the chain. He knew the answers; the real question was whether he was willing to share them with her.

Toro came up behind her, at a slightly slower, less aggressive pace to await the answer.

"No," Jackson answered without elaborating. He stepped back on his heel to not be so close to her. Red leaned against the wall, pulling a knife out of a side sheath to clean his nails while watching the interaction, clearly not wanting to be a part of it.

Astrid was taken aback by his lack of reaction. She forced herself to calm the anger flaming up in her heart. "Do you think she will hurt him?"

"No."

"Do you know where she is taking him?"

"No."

"Do you know how she was able to leave with him?"

"No."

"Do you know anything about this situation?" She'd come to the end of her patience; dealing with him was worse than dealing with a child.

He grinned in response, leaned down to get closer to her, and countered, "No." Snickering, he turned.

Astrid stepped in front of Red, blocking him in hopes that Jackson would turn back around to address her. She was wrong. Red simply pushed past her to follow him.

"If we don't hurry back, we'll all be late. I'm not sure about you, but that is not something I'm willing to put myself through the day before our test." Toro had a point.

They turned, jogging back toward the training hall to start the day.

They were no longer sore; their skills had been honed into a sharp knife to be used against their enemies. Astrid would never have thought it possible in such a short amount of time, but they did it. Big Jack screamed, spit, hit, and demanded until they were the precise weapons he wanted. Weapons which were needed for a war she still wasn't sure she wanted to be in.

But she knew that the instant she finished her training she would have the ability to find Ben. The skills set into her soul and bones would be able to help her free him, and free her mother. She was ashamed; so much worry for Ben left little thought dedicated to her mother.

Her thoughts now swarmed to her mom, wondering if she was still alive. If she remembered her own daughter. Suddenly, the fear of what would happen if her mom didn't recognize or remember plagued her. Astrid didn't have the ability to flush her mother's system and refresh her mind.

Training flew by. After dinner they shot at lettered tiles again. This time she didn't come out on top which meant she needed to help with the equipment. When they finished cleaning and were putting away their guns, Jazmin came up next to her at the gun rack. She shouldered her way through Astrid to put her gun away, sneering down at her.

"What?" Astrid demanded. "I don't have patience for you today." She shook her head, trying to step around her, but Jazmin had a different idea. She grabbed ahold of Astrid's shirt, pulling her up to face level until her toes scraped the dirt floor.

"Do not talk to me that way. I am more than you will ever be. You, a freak, should not be here. You and your eyes belong in a lab."

It made no sense. Why was everybody insistent on letting her know how low she was on the food chain? It was exhausting.

"Fine, put me down." Not wanting to fight with Jazmin outside of training, she tried to placate her. "Let me go."

Instead of satisfying Jazmin it seemed to have lit a fire of hatred in her. She lifted Astrid even higher, sending her sailing across the room into a padded beam. The impact pushed the air from her lungs and made the room spin around her head, forcing the blue circle to get closer to the center of her vision than ever before, bringing in a sense of panic along with the pain.

Everybody converged on Jazmin at once. It took four of them to stop her as she screamed her hatred toward Astrid. Toro and Chie ran over to help her up. "Okay?" they asked in unison, concern and anger clear on their faces. Chie reached up, gently placing a hand on Astrid's pounding head. Her fingers covered her eyes. Astrid took the hint, keeping her eyes closed.

She tried to answer, still heaving and trying to breathe. Pain rattled in her ribs when she did manage to expand her lungs. She fought the circle of blue in her vision threatening to take over, the pulsing matching the beat of her racing heart.

"Come on, I'll help you to the infirmary." Toro picked her up with ease, carrying her out of the room. "Will they let her test in this condition?"

"I don't know that she should. If it's a concussion she won't be lucid enough to understand." Chie's voice, full of concern and fear. Concentrating on their words helped keep her in the present, helped keep Astrid conscious.

Breathing was hard, and talking while breathing with Toro's steps jostling her in his arms was impossible, so she didn't bother trying.

She let her head fall upon his shoulder, making it more of a rocking sensation. Her mind replayed the blue circle expanding and nearly closing. She was still trying to fight it back.

TORO watched Astrid lose consciousness in his arms. He hurried to the infirmary, Chie right on his heels, busting through the swinging doors. Gently laying her down on a bed, he pulled his hands away from her and discovered blood on his fingers.

"No," he whispered, searching for the people in charge who could help.

"I'll get help." Chie, who seemed to have read his thoughts, took off.

Her breathing seemed to be fine, but the blood in her hair worried him.

The healers finally arrived, taking over. Toro stood back—Chie having to pull him aside—so there was room to work. Astrid wouldn't be able to test tomorrow.

If you don't test with the class you train with, you don't pass and you don't get a second chance. They'll reassign her to another division within the compound.

He couldn't let this happen. It was unacceptable, and Astrid would despise and fight against it. It would cause an uproar. She seemed to have an ability to call out the best fight in anybody who disagreed with her, as she was now suffering the consequences for.

Toro worried—worried about Astrid, worried about the government, and worried that he was on the wrong side. Astrid made it known there were other things to fight for. He'd never thought about this before, never been poor, never forced to suffer through poverty. He didn't understand her struggle. His parents worked as they were told, passing their jobs and status on to him. The government never showed him any harm or discomfort.

The Reformers offered something he knew nothing of: freedom, and not just the illusion but true freedom. Once a man got a taste of freedom it was hard not to go after more. The freedom to think and act as one wanted, instead of being censored, instead of being told what to think, what to do, what to read, what to watch. It was enticing. Family, something else one should always fight for. Freedom and family. Toro was lost in thought when the door next to him flew open, letting Benji and Jackson through.

"What's going on?" Benji demanded.

"Three broken ribs and a mild concussion, but she'll be fine. Just needs to rest and let her body heal," one of the healers announced to Benji, his attention still on Astrid.

"Will she be able to participate tomorrow?" Benji asked.

"It's not a good idea."

Benji stepped closer to the healer at this declaration. "She will be released for training no later than 0600 hours tomorrow," he stated, staring straight into the healer's face.

"Yes, sir. She will be medically released at 0600 hours tomorrow," he replied almost mechanically, robotically.

Satisfied, Benji left the infirmary without noticing Toro and Chie behind the door.

"What the hell was that?" Toro asked.

The healer spun around with a surprised expression on his face. "What?" he questioned, shaking his head.

"Why would you change your mind about releasing her for the testing?"

"I didn't change my mind. She'll be fine by tomorrow morning." His face was clouded with confusion.

"You did." Toro stepped closer, putting his hands on the bed next to Astrid. Chie grabbed his arm with a huffed warning. "At first you told Benji it wasn't a good idea to let her participate, then you agreed with him to release her tomorrow morning. Why?"

"I ... You shouldn't be in here. Please leave unless you need tending to." His back straightened as his voice grew firmer, more authoritative.

Questions flew through Toro's head, but not wanting to start a fight he couldn't win, while simultaneously messing up his chances for tomorrow, he left, losing Chie somewhere along the way. He headed back to the training hall wanting to exact revenge on Jazmin only to find it empty and set fresh for the next day.

"She'll be okay tomorrow," came Red's voice from behind him. Toro spun and saw him against the wall on the inside of the door.

"She has a concussion and cracked ribs. How will she be able to test to her full ability?" Toro countered, his emotions running high.

"She'll be okay. Even if she's not at her best, she'll pass. She's needed. You shouldn't worry so much." Red took his knife out, picking at his nails.

"Maybe you should worry a bit more. Why are you talkative to me but no one else? What makes me so special?" He was angry now, stepping up to Red in a challenging stance.

"Easy, boy." Red lowered his knife, standing straighter in acceptance mixed with a little reluctance. "No, you're not special. But we can't have you running around here trying to get some from the little woman. No, she's the special one. Get through tomorrow without losing your head to your privates." He chuckled, pushed Toro away from him, and left.

More riddles, more questions, more issues to sort out. "Great," he muttered, heading to the showers.

"Hey. How is she?" Seto was wrapped in a towel, coming out from the shower heads in the back of the room, water still beaded on his skin.

"A mild concussion and three cracked ribs, but apparently she's special and will pass tomorrow's test even though she's unsuited to take it," he answered as he undressed, lining his words with sarcasm.

"What?" Seto shook his head, processing the words. "They're going to release her to participate with a concussion and cracked ribs? On whose authority?"

As Seto got worked up, Toro's jealousy spiked again, and he concluded it was a mistake to tell him anything further.

"It's what Astrid would want. You know if she misses this chance she'd hate everybody forever. We need to let her try."

This calmed Seto down a bit. Toro felt that between himself, Seto, and Chie, they could help her through it; his goal was to make sure they survived. Rumors flew through the trainees that if you came out the other side of the test breathing and not in last place you passed.

Toro was confident in himself, Seto, and Chie for sure. There were a few others who he knew he would need to watch, some who would find their path easier if he were dead. Adding the complication of helping Astrid through the test would make the trial that much more difficult.

CHAPTER 14
TESTING

ASTRID awoke and immediately leaned over the side of her bed, vomiting all over the floor. A hammer and nail worked its way through her cranium side to side, the blue encasing her vision still pulsing with her heart, but no longer trying to overtake her. After spitting again, she gently rolled back on to her bed, trying to open her eyes. The lights assaulted her retinas, turning them to fire. She cried out, covering her face. The motion made her head spin even more.

Hands fell upon her. "Easy, don't move. Take slow, small, short breaths," the kind voice instructed. Breaking through the pain with a lace of love and smoothness that calmed the raging storm inside.

Astrid forced her hands away from her face, relaxed every muscle, and concentrated on her breathing. It helped enough to ease the pain to a dull thud and spin in her head, which happened to remove the blue around her eye sight … but brought out the pain in her chest. The short breaths seemed to be aggravating her ribs, so she tried harder to smooth and shorten them even more.

"There you go. I'm going to give you some pain medicine. It will help with the queasiness and light sensitivity." A sharp pain in her arm followed the voice. Soon after, the pain receded and a fogginess took over. She found the ability to open her eyes, only to find her vision blurry, but she was flooded with relief as she noticed the crystal blue ring was now completely gone. "That's it. Better, no?"

"Thank you. What happened?" She managed a whisper out of her acid-filled throat.

"You suffered a mild concussion along with three cracked ribs. We've fixed you up a bit, just waiting it out now."

"What time is it?"

"Just before four in the morning. I'm glad you're awake. I was afraid I'd have to wake you."

"The testing day." More of a confirmation than a question— she knew which day it was. She also knew she was in no condition to participate and survive.

"Yes, you have a bit before you need to check in. Just try to rest your head. Hopefully you'll come around and be ready." The healer stood to the side of her. Not wanting to anger her head any further, she refrained from turning.

"Thanks." She closed her eyes, concentrating every cell on healing her injuries.

Before she knew it, Toro's voice broke through the haze settled in her head. "Astrid? Astrid, I need you to wake up. It's almost time."

She gently tested her ribs; the sharp pain reminded her they would need a moment. Slitting her eyes open to test the lighting, she found it wasn't nearly as bad as earlier, the pain medicine apparently still coursing through her system. Toro stood where the healer was earlier, with bright eyes and concern etched on his facial features. It was kind of him. Astrid smiled a bit, starting to test her muscles and energy level.

Her head was sore; the more she moved the more her stomach protested. She stopped, adjusting to a new position after every move. First goal was to sit in bed with her feet off to the side. She barely made it. Having to heave over the bed again once halfway vertical was not her idea of reaching the goal.

Toro took a step back, his hands hovering. When he leaned in to help her sit up, she waved him away. "What time is it?"

"Almost five. Breakfast is about to start. The healer dismissed you." He stopped, took a breath and a deep swallow. "He said you were good to go."

"I don't feel good to go. I think maybe the healer has lost his edge. Maybe he should go through the training program, see if he still finds me fit." Her humor had deserted her, going dry. She didn't understand herself or why she babbled on about the stupid healer.

Toro chuckled at her words. She felt good at being understood even if it was somebody other than herself. Pushing herself up off the table, she landed on her feet hastily. She had moved too fast, and her legs crumpled beneath her, unable to hold her own weight. She would have landed in her recent pile of vomit had Toro not reached out and caught her. When she leaned against him for support, his smell invaded her nose, clean and fresh.

He mumbled something as he held her. Astrid heaved again, expelling the last of her stomach on to the floor. "What?"

"This is not right! You are in no state to be tested. Ma—"

"No, I can do this. There are no second chances here. I have to try." She forced herself straight, closing her eyes as her head spun against her wishes. With Toro's help she headed to the mess hall to see if she could hold any food down.

She ate sparingly, accompanied with a few sips of water. Anything in her stomach would be better than nothing, but the more she moved and ate the worse it became. The whispers and thickness of emotions in the room closed in on her. She knew she was missing chunks of time. Not remembering how or when they got to the mess hall, the journey a blank slate in her mind, as was how the food appeared in front of her or where half of it disappeared to. Finishing it with the last of her water, she witnessed the rest of the trainees stand in anticipation to get to the training hall.

Astrid put her cup down, hesitantly standing, waiting to see if the food and liquid in her stomach was going to make an introduction to the room. She moved slowly, happily on her own, to the training room.

The last to arrive, but still early. The room stood empty. All the training equipment that had appeared as needed was cleared out. Midway through the room tables were set up, end to end in one single row, with chairs perched behind them.

The trainees stood huddled together just inside the door, not knowing what to do. Toro and Seto arrived just ahead of Astrid, waiting for her to join them. Chie moved to be slightly behind her, a hand out just in case. She limped in, holding her stomach and her head. The room no longer spun, but the pain wasn't abating much. She scuffed up behind Toro, laying her head against the back of his right arm to catch her breath. The stroll had been overwhelming; she should have let him help.

She began to question if she was going to make it through this day, if it was even worth the try. She was regaining strength, a little at a time, but not near enough of what she would need to get high marks, to come out on top, or even to survive.

HAVING Astrid so close behind him messed with Toro's senses, and knowing she shouldn't be forced through this just to prove herself confused him even more. Seto promised to help as much as he could without hindering his own progress. Chie nodded in agreement, commenting that they were in this together. For whatever reason, Astrid needed to pass; she needed to get her arm wrap and be inducted into the Reformers. They would make sure that she did.

She swayed a bit, her forehead going side to side on his arm, her cold sweat being left behind only to be smeared as she moved again. He adjusted to better support her. Big Jack, Benji, Red, and Jackson filed in, skirting the group and taking seats behind the tables in the center of the room. The trainees' anxiety soared. Everybody shuffled between their own feet, backs straightening tighter, and breaths being taken deep into their lungs.

"I know you're anxious to get this over with. Just a few notes before we start." Jackson stood, putting his hands on the table in front of him, leaning over it. "You will all likely not survive this. I do not say this lightly. There has only ever been one class where everybody survived. The risks are high, the challenges even higher. Try your best. Cover yourself and don't worry about anybody else and you'll do fine. We are under no circumstances allowed to intervene. Once you are released, you are on your own." He took a seat, along with letting out his breath.

Red studied the class, his gaze slowing slightly as it landed on Toro, then quickly moving on.

Big Jack spoke next, but he didn't bother standing. His voiced filled the room without him having to put too much energy into it. "Ya have several challenges to complete. They are ranked by difficulty, though they are not laid out that way. Ya all will be separated, dropped off at a different course before the start. All the tests are tailored to the individual trainee. Every one of ya will experience something different. We will be watching individual skills, how ya work as a team and which of ya bilge rats would make good leaders. If ya make it to the middle, what ya choose to do at that point is up to ya. Ya can either continue alone or team up. If ya die we will take care of what remains after the test has been concluded. The only advice I have for ya is to know who yar enemies are. Good luck, ya will need it."

Benji stood, taking the floor. "You will be watched; you will be judged. You don't just have to survive this to pass. You have to not come in last. The final person to complete the test will not become a soldier, but will have an opportunity to repeat the training. As there is only one chance of repeating, do not use this as an escape or an easy way out." Toro watched Benji's eyes stop on a trainee and followed his gaze over to Jazmin. "If you fail the second time, you go to farming."

Benji hadn't been nice; there were no words of comfort on what to expect. Just don't die and don't come in last. Toro had disliked him from day one, his dislike quickly turning into loathing and hatred. Benji carried on, his gaze stopping at each of them as he continued to speak.

"You will not get medical treatment on the field. You will start with a pack of essentials. Each one has enough supplies to last one person one week, in case you take longer than planned. How you ration and use these supplies will help you either live or die. There are currently forty-five of you. You will be dropped off in stages to decrease the chances of help during the first round. It would be nice if all forty-five of you survived. We are trying to up our ranks. Any questions?"

A few shifting feet and hands before finally someone spoke up. "Will we be required or put in a position to kill each other?"

"No. And if you do, the killer will be disqualified and banned from the Reformers," Jackson answered the question directly to the trainee who asked.

The kid nodded, dropping his head. Jazmin, to the right of Toro, huffed in response, shaking her head. Toro noted an enemy, not for himself, but for Astrid. There were a few more questions regarding the challenges, but nobody was able to get any specific information regarding what they were being released into.

"If you're trying to increase your numbers, why would you put us through a test that would possibly kill us?" Toro spoke up. There was a lot not making sense to him.

"This test was initiated by our founders; it is made to thi-."

"Thin out the weak, we know that, but those who don't pass could be used elsewhere. You know right now which ones of us are going to make good soldiers, so why put us through this?" Seto backed him up. Smiling at Toro.

The rest of the trainees nodding in agreement now, some even vocal.

Jackson, not used to being interrupted, regained his composure and answered their worried and raising voices. "You're right, but this is the way it is, and we're not going to change it now. You each have what it takes to make it through. Use what you have been taught. Each of you can survive this, so go do it."

Nobody responded to him. Jackson was right; they could disagree and ask every question they could think of, but the only thing to stop the test would be themselves.

Big Jack asked them to spread out and line up to check in and receive their packs. Toro gently shuffled Astrid to the side to let everybody bustle around them without running in to her, unsuccessfully though. Jazmin shouldered into Astrid on her way to the front of the line, mumbling something under her breath. Toro, choosing not to mumble, lifted his voice and spit an insult towards Jazmin's back. He helped Astrid up off the floor and into a line in front of him so that he could keep an eye on her. Her eyes clouded over—the blue circle a bit thicker and brighter than usual—with sweat on her brow and upper lip.

She could hardly open her eyes, nevertheless move, communicate, or pass a challenge specifically programmed to kill her. A slight shiver racked its way through her body ever so often. Her balance gained strength but only if she didn't move around too much. A loud noise behind them made her jump and try to spin around to see what it was. Toro caught her as the dizziness overwhelmed her and sent her to the ground. They reached the front of the line where Red sat behind the table. Toro had positioned them this way on purpose; Red seemed to think she could do this. He wanted to show him different.

Red motioned Astrid forward. A data pad was placed on the table in front of him, and they required everybody to give a drop of blood and a fingerprint as part of the check-in process. Instead of Astrid being able to understand what was required of her, Red reached across the table, took her hand, and did it for her. She hardly jumped as the needle punctured her skin to let a droplet of blood escape. Red handed an essentials pack across the table, but not to Astrid. Toro reached up, taking her pack from Red and shuffling her aside a foot to do his own check-in.

"She can't do this," he whispered under his breath, the data pad scanning his finger.

Red didn't respond, just took a blood sample and handed over another pack. Toro shouldered it along with Astrid's, moving to the side of the room to examine their supplies. The trainees tore through the contents of their essentials packs all secretly, trying not to let anybody see what each of them received. Toro found it all childish. He opened his pack and glanced inside, shuffling the contents aside by shaking the pack and repeating the process with Astrid's. He noticed she did not have any weapons, while his gear consisted of both throwing knives and a hand gun, neither his strong suite. He chose Astrid's best skill out of the two, making an addition to her pack quickly and secretly, followed by zipping them up and placing both beside him.

Astrid slid down to the floor, leaning her head against the wall with her eyes closed. Toro's anger had simmered with the knowledge of what was to come, but now that he knew more of what they headed into, he became livid. How was Astrid supposed to get through the first challenge alone? And if their entrances were staggered there was no telling when or how far apart they were to be released. He would have to find her. He leaned against the wall, slid down next to Astrid, took her hand, and dared a silent prayer to anybody who would listen.

"How is she?" Chie inquired, crouching in front of Astrid with a hand outreached to gently make contact.

"Not good," Seto mentioned as he joined Toro on the floor. "I can't believe they released her for this. She's in no condition. She's going to get killed."

"Positive thoughts, she can hear you," Chie shot towards him, her hand still gently rubbing back and forth on one of Astrid's knees. "Jazmin should pay for this."

"I agree, but who's going to do that? Best we can hope for is she dies in the test." Toro decided what he wanted to share with them, how far he could trust them. "Any of you find something odd about all this? The data pads, Benji, testing off the compound?"

His thoughts about the government had always been restricted, but since arriving at the compound they'd been able to develop. The government had access to advanced technology that could pinpoint any data pad with power down to its exact location. They should know exactly where they were; still they didn't show up with black helicopters or bombs. Instead, they were left alone to train. Train incoming recruits on how to hate the government.

Seto leaned forward, his hands toying with a strap of his backpack, thoughts dancing in his eyes. "There's talk, about a mutiny. Sibella and Reider were sent away on a mission late last night. I overheard them in a hallway." Chie's questionable stare forced an answer. "I couldn't sleep; I like to pace. Anyways," he said and took a breath. "Sibella was talking about lost time, doing things she would never do. Waking up to a new reality with Benji in charge. Something is not right here."

"Where did they get the data pads? Aren't all the pads connected through the MIST? Wouldn't they just give the government our position?" Chie's thoughts were in line with Toro's.

"Benji told the doctor to release Astrid. It was weird. At first the doctor admitted she couldn't test, and the next minute he pointed out she would be fine. We need to be careful. I'm not sure we chose the right side." They sat in silence, each toying with the facts the others divulged, unwilling to talk about it any further.

THE room spun, and resisting the urge to throw up was a constant battle. Astrid's thumb on her right hand stung and bled. She didn't understand why. She found peace when she slid to the floor for a break as she waited for the next wave of dizziness to take over. Her head still felt like a rolling bowling ball, but the good news was the line of blue around the edges of her vision had not made a reappearance. All she really wanted to do was curl up and sleep until the pain went away. Every time she found peace someone nudged her to move again.

She knew Toro was nearby—she could sense him, smell him. She found comfort in his presence; he seemed to be the one watching out for her. She needed to remember to thank him when the haze lifted. Soft voices wafted around her, lulling her further away from the room.

She also knew that the test was today; she remembered Toro telling her. Although when or what was going to happen she had no idea. Surely they would be telling them. They wouldn't just cut them loose in the testing area without telling them, right?

Soon a hand found hers, not gripping too hard, but enough to let her know it was a friend. She tried to grip back but couldn't.

She found herself in a clearing suddenly and, glancing around, discovered there were bodies scattered everywhere on the grass. Confused and frightened she moved slowly; she knew that if she made it to the woods she would survive. A blue, soft, inviting pillar of light appeared in front of her. Astrid stopped to inspect it. A form of recognition tickled her mind, but not quite giving her enough to remember fully what it was or what it meant.

"Join me," the pillar announced. The voice just as soft, just as inviting. She took a step closer to the light, curiosity getting the best of her. "Join me," it repeated.

"Astrid?" A smaller voice behind her cut through the trance.

She had reached out to the light about to make contact, but instead turned, pulling her hand away. A little boy. She knew this boy. What was his name?

"Astrid, don't. You know it'll hurt you. Please, don't leave me. You promised you would protect me. That I was safe. Why did you let me go? Why did you let her hurt me?"

More confusion. "I don't know what you're talking about. I don't know you," she replied to the boy. She crawled over to him, kneeling in front of him to be at his height. "You shouldn't be here."

"Join me," the voice repeated from the light. The trance began once more as she glanced back to it. As Astrid stood a hand caught hers, pulling her to a stop. She blinked again, shaking her head.

The hand gripped tighter, and when she opened her eyes she was in the training hall. Toro stood over her holding her hand, trying to get her to stand. Seto and Chie with stood behind him with confusion on their faces. Gazing up at Toro with the light behind him sent a sharp pain into her eyes and head. Her other hand shot up, covering her eyes.

"Toro, what the hell?" she snapped. She didn't want to stand. She wanted to sleep.

"Well, at least she's almost lucid again."

Seto. She knew that voice. He seemed irritated.

"What happened?"

"You have a concussion. We're being bussed to the testing spot. You and Seto are in the first wave to be released. You need to get up, now."

She could tell Toro tried to stay calm and keep his relief out of his voice. Bits and pieces of the night before and that morning came back to her—the run in with Jazmin, throwing up, and Toro waking her, smelling clean and fresh. Her skin hot with a fever; she knew that if she moved the floor might pitch her to the side and she would have to empty her stomach again.

Squinting her eyes, she placed her feet beneath her, slowly standing. She placed all her weight in her heels to keep her head from moving in any direction but up, closing her eyes and fighting off the dizziness and the blue ring that came with it. "Okay."

As they proceeded, Toro kept talking to her, giving her instructions and trying to explain what was about to happen. He finished with a big breath just as they reached the parking area. He pulled Seto aside, whispering something to him. Seto nodded, patted Toro's shoulders in assurance, and got in line.

"Here, it's your essentials pack." He helped her put it on and stood back as Astrid said a heartfelt and quick "thank you" before joining Seto. She smiled to try to reassure him—grateful that he was helping so much, but the idea of being somebody's damsel in distress put a bad taste in her mouth. She needed to prove, not only to him but to herself, that she could do this. There were people depending on her, waiting on her success and help.

She leaned forward to Seto, getting his attention. "Where are we going, and what the hell is going on?" she asked slowly, having to form each word carefully before she spoke.

Seto just huffed out a laugh, shaking his head in disbelief. Her anxiety level rose and with it the bile in her stomach. She turned to show Toro and Chie a smile, waving at them. She did feel better ... not at the top of where she should be but better.

Once on the bus Seto explained the evening and morning events. The ride was bumpy and long; it was midday, right before lunch, when they finally came to a stop. As the windows were covered nobody knew where they were.

Astrid watched as one by one each stop meant another trainee exited. Jackson would stand up, call out a name, and escort the nervous trainee off the bus. They would continue. A few minutes would go by before he would climb back on, taking his seat, and off they would go. Before long Astrid heard Seto's name, sending a jolt through her in recognition of what this meant.

"Seto." She didn't want to sound desperate, needy, or scared. It seemed to come out that way of its own accord.

Seto simply smiled, placing his hand on her shoulder, told her she would be fine, to just stay alive, and exited the bus. Astrid slumped back down into her seat with her head in her hands, trying to keep control.

"Astrid." Jackson's voice boomed at her from over her head. He stood over her, glaring down. Since Seto's departure she hadn't been paying attention. Irritation in his eyes made her wonder how many times he had repeated her name. "You're up."

"Jackson," she acknowledged, standing with her pack on her shoulders and following him to the front of the bus. She placed her hands on the seats to help minimize the dizziness from taking full effect. "If I don't survive this, when you find my mo—"

"Easy, girl, you're going to do fine. Just keep your head up and stay alive."

"Yeah, that seems to be the advice of the day: 'stay alive.' I think it's easier said than done. Was Benji right? Will there be death?"

"Yes. Out of the seventy-four in my trainee class only fifty-two of us survived. It's meant to filter out those who are not strong enough … those who'd cause issues in the war or who aren't loyal to the cause."

"The cause. A war that started long before we arrived, but here we stand. Ready to die for it."

They came to a complete stop after stepping off the bus. Astrid noticed a giant wall that continued forever with no end in sight in both directions and a door about twenty feet in front of her. The ground hard and dead, no vegetation to be seen. The dry wind whipped sand across her face, blowing her jacket up off her body. They were in a desert. This was her test. On the other side of the wall was her life or death. The fog completely cleared from her head, but she was still nauseous, and with each breath pain pricked her side.

Jackson stepped away from her. Reaching the door, his strong hands reached out, pushing against it. The door popped open, creating a ledge, which Jackson's fingers could just barely grasp to pull it out. No door handles or buttons, the edge was barely visible even if you knew it was there. He motioned Astrid to come forward as he pulled the door open, granting her passage.

"Thank you," Astrid said, unsure what exactly she should be thanking him for as she pushed past him through the open doorway.

"You're welcome," he replied, quickly and efficiently closing the door behind her.

CHAPTER 15
TRUTH

DOCTOR, I'm hungry."

Melvina knew he wasn't trying to be whiny, but his voice scratched her brain, causing unimaginable thoughts—thoughts a mother should never have toward their own offspring. Not to mention the incessant need to continually call her 'Doctor' after giving him numerous other options. Of course 'Mom' being the top one, more for her than him.

"I am too, but look around, Ben. Where do you see food?"

They trudged along every waking minute. Three days and nights, stopping at any shelter found so Ben could rest and sleep. Melvina rested but never fully slept. She waited, awake night after night, for a sound to break through the night to capture them, but he never came.

Benji should know by now they were gone, so why hadn't he come after them? Did he really not love them at all? She began to understand that she really was just a tool ... a means to an end for Benji.

"How much farther?"

That scratch again. Closing her eyes, Melvina took a deep breath. Her nerves were fried, and Ben wore on her last one.

"I don't know. I've never been out of the city before this. We will continue until we can't anymore."

Trying to comfort a hungry five-year-old proved to be impossible. If he wasn't complaining about his stomach being empty, his stomach did it for him.

"My feet hurt. I don't want to move my feet anymore. Doctor, can we stop? Please?"

"Don't call me doctor!" She lost it. She stopped, spinning on the child. Ben shrank into himself; she could see she'd set him off. "No, it's okay, I'm sorry."

Too late. She watched helplessly as Ben retreated into a panic attack. He eventually would find his way out, calm himself down and they could continue.

After shrugging her shoulders, she searched the surrounding area to see if she could get them out of the stinging sun rays prickling their skin, sucking away what little moisture they had left.

"Come on, you can continue your panic attack in the shade." She reached toward Ben only for him to jerk away, letting out a blood-curdling scream. *Great. Just great.* "Okay, stand there."

Leaving him, she drug her feet, pushing herself to a patch of trees.

Ben screamed. Not as bad as when he screamed in the compound of the Reformers. There it ricocheted off the walls and empty tanks to make the sound cause more pain. Out here it fanned out, hardly noticeable. As this was not the first panic attack since they'd left, she gotten used to just waiting it out. He eventually would calm down, dry his tears, take a nap, and be ready to continue. She tried hard not to think of how much distance this was costing them, how much closer Benji was to finding them the longer they sat.

Melvina watched, shaking her head. "We don't have any water, Ben. Remember how much your throat hurt last time you screamed? You need to stop. I understand you're upset. I know it's my fault, bu—"

There it was, the loud noise she'd constantly hoped to hear while dreading it just the same. Although it wasn't the buses or jeeps she'd seen in the garage on their way out. This burst through the sky with rotating blades cutting air and sending it every which way. This was something and somebody else.

"The Institute," she whispered to herself. Jumping up, Melvina sprinted to Ben. He stopped screaming to cover his ears and watch. "Ben, it's the good guys!" Her excitement overflowed her system, her irritation and second-guessing her decisions gone. Placing her hands around his shoulders, she slouching her head to help keep the wind and noise from assaulting him. She could feel his body shaking; the arrival of the helicopter hadn't helped his panic.

It landed thirty feet from where they stood, and men and women in white flooded out, all armed, with the muzzles of their weapons pointing straight at them.

"Name?" one of them demanded.

"Doctor Melvina Heizer, I work for the Los Angeles Institute. We were kidnapped by the Reformers during the break in months ago. This is Ben, a patient of ours."

"Verification codes, ma'am?"

"Echo-6-Alpha-9-3-5."

The man repeated her code into his com and waited on verification, all the while keeping them inside their circle, every gun still aimed true. The guard's focus changed suddenly. "Good to see you survived, Doctor." They dropped their arms and rushed forward to guide them into the helicopter.

Relief flooded Melvina; she was safe again. Back where they belonged. Ben attached himself to her side after being seated. She watched his eyes dart around, taking in the new development and surroundings as they lifted off, the orange circle in his eyes pulsing in and out. The ecstasy of safety, of knowing what was going to occur, was more than she could bear. Tears streamed down her cheeks.

These are allowed. These are happy tears. Not tears born from weakness.

Ben mumbled beside her, his body still shaking violently.

At least he stopped screaming.

After landing on the roof of the Institute, Melvina tried to listen in on what was being said between her rescuers but found herself unsuccessful.

Wanting to help ease the traumatic transfer for Ben, she gently pried his hands apart on her waist, mumbling sweet nothings to him. One of the orderlies in white reached into the helicopter, picking him up by his back and holding him to his chest, hauling him to the doorway. She reached out in instinct for him, crawling out herself, upset that the orderly felt the need to move Ben aggressively and without permission. Ben's limbs were hostile, outstretched and flailing wildly.

"Well, well. Back from the grave. Do you know what your mistake cost this company?" Matthew Benson patiently stood in the elevator, standing as tall as his small frame allowed, shoulders straight and an ugly smirk on his face. Melvina tentatively entered the elevator with worry and surprise, the orderly entering just before her and placing Ben on his feet, who quickly scrambled to her side, gripping tightly.

"My mistake? You think that was my fault?"

"Yes, we do." His confidence shattered her own.

Her safety net disintegrated out from underneath her as the conversation unfolded; she could feel it. She had come back to where she belonged. To where her loyalties lay. Now, she was being condemned for something she did not have anything to do with, something that reached out and dragged her in and along for a ride she did not want to be on.

"The boy is to be re-assimilated, and you're to be seen by the general to be debriefed, and hopefully released."

The elevator came to a stop, and Matthew stepped past her, exiting, expecting from her the blind obedience that before she would have given freely.

"He's not to be harmed, or re-assimilated, as you put it. This is my son. He comes with me, or I don't go." Her own conviction scared her. She always just went along, did her duty, held her loyalties in place to keep them happy. Living in fear of what they were capable of. Ben stood on her right side, his small hands encircling her leg with all his strength. She could feel his body shaking, his head going back and forth.

Matthew stopped, slowly turned, and slightly nodded.

Melvina realized too late that he wasn't nodding in acceptance to her demand.

The prick in her neck was a harsh sting of betrayal. She was supposed to be safe. They were supposed to protect them, take care of them. The Institute her home, the government her family. Too late to know that this was not safe, that the government was the enemy.

WATCHING Seto and Astrid board the bus challenged every ounce of self-control Toro owned. He twitched, caught himself numerous times heading toward her, only to turn around to see Chie shake her head at him. Having other things to think about was slightly helpful. He was currently scheduled to be released with the third set of trainees two hours after the second. Each set designed to be released after the previous was already well within the test. Problem with that was Astrid could be dead by the time he got through his first test and was able to find her. So he paced; he paced and he worried. Back and forth between the garage, the training hall, the mess hall, and his room. Four hours until he joined the others. Four lengthy hours. Chie, being scheduled to leave after him, followed him, so they paced together in silence.

It lasted forever; he lost count of how many times he entered the garage only to be turned around again to start over by a Reformer standing watch. Other trainees huddled together eating in the mess hall, some in the training hall still with their sack awaiting their turn. Toro couldn't sit still. He tried once, got some lunch, taking a seat in the mess hall, but after failing a few times to put food in his stomach he stood, leaving his tray, and Chie, to pace again.

"Second set," Mitch announced as Toro rushed forward seeing trainees boarding.

He slumped with disappointment. Unsure how much more of this he could handle. The anticipation, the worry, but most of all the not knowing.

"Hey, haven't seen Reider or Sibella lately, they doing okay?" The question came out as concern, genuine concern for fellow Reformers.

"They're out on a mission." Mitch's answer was short, letting Toro know he wouldn't be saying more. Instead of prying further, he kept his mouth shut.

"Seriously, Toro?" Chie, gaining on his fast pace down a silent hallway, grabbed ahold of his arm swinging him around. "You okay?"

"It just popped out. Seto stated they were both assigned to a mission. And if something is wrong I want to be friends with those who have been here and are questioning Benji—" He stopped, his hand up in the middle of a gesture. It was Benji's fault she was testing; he had convinced the doctor to release her.

With new determination, Toro turned on his heel, heading for Benji's office. Jackson left with the first set, and Red was scheduled to leave with the second. This meant that Benji would be alone. Toro didn't bother knocking on the door. Instead he pushed it open and stepped in, leaving an open-mouthed Chie in the hallway.

"Why?" he demanded.

Benji stood behind his table reading some papers. "What are you doing here, trainee?" He didn't even bother a glance.

"Why did you send her out there? Why did you push her release?" He took another step into the office.

"Because she needs to be tested." Benji set the papers down, prowling around the table to face off. He got close, scrutinizing Toro, and offered, "She will be fine. You're going to find her and make sure that she passes, alive."

"I know that. I want to know why you released her from medical care when she obviously was not well enough to move," he demanded again, taking a small step back.

He didn't want to admit defeat, but something did not feel right. Benji was intimidating, sure. But this was something else. He didn't seem to care. Normal people in charge would be upset that someone busted into their office. Normal people in charge would be pissed if their decisions were questioned.

"Have you found them? She'll ask," he said.

"No. You should go. You load soon."

"Second set just loaded, and I'm in the third."

"Which loads in twenty. You should go."

Without a second thought Toro turned, leaving Benji's office. No, this wasn't right. The second set just began loading as he left the garage, which gave him two more hours. Chie should be waiting for him in the hallway. He had only been in there a few minutes. The hallway stood empty, and Chie was nowhere to be seen. Toro took up a sprint, and upon arriving at the garage he found Benji was right. The second set was gone, the bus from the first set had returned, and Jackson stood at the head with a list, taking attendance of trainees already lined up.

"Third set. That's you, right? Where you been? You've been pacing all morning." The Reformer motioned for Toro to join the line for the third set of trainees.

Chie popped up from a wall with a questionable look, mouthing 'where've you been?' Her hands out, waiting to receive his answer.

"Wha— How?" Toro racked his brain. He somehow lost close to two hours of his time. He retraced his timeline, his actions, his thoughts. Each time coming up blank.

"Dude, just line up."

Toro lined up with his fellow trainees, his pack on his back, waving a confused hand to Chie with an apologetic flash on his face. Dropping the issue and worry for another day. Finally, it was time. Jackson nodded at him, checking something off on his clipboard, moving aside. One by one the final set of trainees boarded the bus. Toro took the seat in the front, hoping Jackson would sit across from him in the last empty seat.

"Toro, you ready?" Jackson asked, taking the seat, instructing the driver that they were good to go.

"Yes, do you have anything on Astrid and Seto? If they're alive or …?"

"No, I don't get updates until all the trainees are within the testing center. She seemed okay. She was my last discharge. Lucid, able to stand straight. I think she'll make it."

"She still wasn't top notch."

"You're right, and that's why she started with the easiest test. Which means she'll be fine when you get there to pull her out of her distressed situation."

"I went and saw Benji, to ask some questions. I somehow lost two hours of my day standing in his office, having a conversation that lasted maybe three minutes. I've racked my brain, gone over it step by step, word by word. I don't understand what happened."

Jackson watched Toro slightly with wide eyes, shook his head, and sat forward, indicating the end of the conversation.

Okay, I guess we won't talk. Toro followed suit, trying to take what Jackson mentioned about Astrid as a comfort to ease his mind, even if he hadn't talked to him about the missing time. If Jackson indeed put Astrid in the easiest test to begin with, he was on their side. Out to make sure she survived. Maybe this wasn't going to be as bad as he originally thought.

The ride wasn't long. When the bus started to slow, Toro learned he would be the first one off to start his testing. Excitement getting the best of him, he jumped up, stepping into the aisle before the bus came to a full stop. When it did, it lurched Toro forward so much Jackson had to stick his arm out and catch Toro's backpack, keeping his face from planting in the dash.

"Easy," Jackson advised, straightening Toro upright and patting his shoulder.

"Thanks." Embarrassment flooded his face. He cleared his throat, fixed his pack, and followed Jackson off the bus.

They were in a tropical setting, trees everywhere. He could hear the ocean nearby, and the salty breeze on his face felt amazing after being cooped up underground for so long. The sun stung his eyes, but Toro refused to list that as a con. Through the palm trees a tall wall went on forever in both directions, and just ahead was a door. Jackson sauntered off toward the wall without motioning for Toro to follow.

"Do me a favor, Toro, stay away from Benji. If you're on his radar you'll find nothing but trouble, he's a fierce … leader." Jackson stood stock still, his clipboard in one hand at his side, his face forward. "You'll find that this portion of the test has no easing into it. It will start the instant the door is closed with you on the other side. Keep your head down, your mouth shut, and don't stop moving. Ready?"

"Yea." Revelations of Benji helped confirm his suspicions. Putting them to the back of his mind, Toro got ready.

"Not so anxious to start now, huh?"

"Just nervous is all, not knowing what to expect. You can't tell me anything?"

"No, I can't. Good luck." Jackson opened an unseen door, and Toro stepped inside.

ASTRID stepped into a frozen desert. A desert normally meant hot, dry weather, so to see Old Man Winter taking over and creating a new scene was something confounding. Having lived on the West Coast her whole life, the sight and the bitter bite of cold assaulted her senses. Frozen cacti, brittle to the point of cracking, surrounded her, and the hard sand beneath her combat boots voiced a crackle with every step she took. The sky, still warm and inviting, made the scene confusing. All her senses fought each other to understand the intake of information.

"How are they doing this?" She knew snow and winter existed, up in the mountains, farther north. But here? Not a chance. This was fabricated, right? She strode forward with a light skip in her step. It was exhilarating. The cold air on her cheeks and the bite in her lungs. She never felt anything like it. It swept the nauseous feeling from her stomach with every breath. She turned around slowly, taking in the sight, enjoying the newfound freedom and feelings that came with it. Being on her own for the first time felt amazing. It took everything she had in her to remind herself she was being tested. That every reaction, word, twitch of her face was being watched.

She stopped, remembering her situation. Her feelings didn't ebb away, just pulled back to be hidden, to be by themselves where nobody could bear witness. After gathering her wits, she re-adjusted her pack, taking in her surroundings as a testing facility. Which meant there was only one way to go, in the opposite direction. With new determination and a happiness she hadn't experienced since home, Astrid set forward.

After hours of repetitive step after step, her feet ached. Her pack, if possible, was heavier, and it dawned on her that she was clueless as to what it contained. The landscape was still the same as when she started, except the door and wall behind her were now so small she could block it out of sight with her thumb. With nowhere to sit she crouched down with her pack in front of her and inventoried her items.

Her pack empty, the contents spread before her, she sat on her rear in the cold sand with her legs crossed in front of her. Two water bottles, empty. Twenty-one silver packets of what Astrid assumed was food of some sort. A set of heavy silver throwing knives and a thermal blanket. She did the math with the help of her fingers, concluding she had enough food for about one week. But the two water bottles balked at her, empty. Astrid wasn't a genius, but she knew that frozen desert—in which she could currently see her breath every time it exited her lungs—would not hold fresh water in a state in which she could put it in the bottles.

With her head hung, heavy with a new problem to solve, she slowly repacked her bag to continue forward, keeping the throwing knives out for quick access. As it was still early in the test she wasn't dehydrated or starving, so she felt there was plenty of time to make it through this test and find water. Reaching for the first bottle, Astrid saw the inside covered in moisture. The little droplets of water clinging to the inside of the bottle moving and colliding with the forced movement of her hand.

With haste, she unscrewed the top; the cap was thick and heavier than the aluminum ones used in the compound. Little ridges rounded the entire thing, and the top was smooth to the touch. A suction created and a *pop* lifted the lid as Astrid beheld the inside. Running her index finger along the bottle to feel the water, she brought it to her tongue. Fresh with a slight chill. She shook her head, closing her eyes and letting out a sigh; she would have water as the bottle made its own. Deciding not to worry too much about the science, she recapped the bottle, put it on top of her pack, zipped it up, and moved on her way.

Later she forced herself to take a longer break that included some water and food. Her stomach had finally settled, and she was indeed hungry. Her stomach wailed in protest of the constant movement with no nourishment. She saw no place to 'be comfortable,' and with no real path to follow there was no reason to leave it. Pulling out her thermal blanket and spreading it out, Astrid took a seat.

Opening a small silver package sent a wretched smell up to fill her nose. "Whoa!"

The rancid odor assaulted on her nose and eyes. Without thinking she threw the pack as far as it would fly from her, the contents swirling out in a green spiral as the package soared through the air. Gagging, she grabbed the water bottle and took a swig of water. After the smell left her nose, her appetite returned, and she tried another silver package.

Twenty-one packages later, Astrid was without food. Every single package rotten. Her head swam with panicked thoughts about what to do. She would have to eat eventually.

A sound among the wind snapped her head up, bringing her ears to attention. Nothing. She swore she had heard her name. Who else could possibly be here? Was she moving so slow to not make any progress? Seto? Chie? Toro? Her mind spun; the hairs on the back of her neck stood to attention along with those on her arm. A slow chill worked its way through her nervous system. She stood slowly, pulling the thermal blanket into her pack and zipping it up, her eyes scanning her surroundings for movement.

Again, faint on the wind, her name. Spinning in circles quickly, attempting to determine which direction it originated from made her head spin. She stopped, closed her eyes, forcing her ears to listen to every sound surrounding her. The sand pebbles beneath her boots crunched with her shifting weight. Her breathing hitched and uneven. Panic seeped in, showing through her strength. She worked her hands on the hem of her jacket, waiting. She knew it would repeat itself. Eventually it would happen again. She just needed to wait, to be utterly silent.

Having no idea how long she stood there she made a subconscious choice to listen to the wind as she moved. She took a deep breath, letting it out as she opened her eyes. Her surroundings had changed. She was back in the clearing with the bus, trees, and dead bodies; everything the same as she remembered.

Confused, Astrid absorbed every detail. It was all there. She even knelt to the nearest body, her trembling fingers feeling the flesh, still warm. Another test? How did they move her? A ringing in her ears brought with it a sharp pain that went to her brain. Grabbing her head as the pain intensified, she fell to her knees, clutching her head in her hands.

"Astrid?" That voice again.

This time, she knew it wasn't the wind. Slowly opening her eyes, she startled, finding herself surrounded by the frozen desert.

"Ben?" He sat cross-legged in front of her, calm and collected. "Ho—why are you here?" She jerked suddenly, her head swimming with the effort and movement.

"Are you okay, Astrid? Are you hurt?" Having been kidnapped, Ben wouldn't just sit there asking questions about her well-being. He wouldn't have thought to ask that. "Astrid? Why?"

"Why what, Ben?" She cocked her head, lifting an eyebrow to this impostor, not wanting to get close and endanger herself.

"Why did you hurt me? Why did you give me to her? Why? *Why?*" His voice louder with each word until he screamed at her, his face going red with the effort. He continued his 'whys' until they combined into one stride of screams.

Astrid's heart shattered. She had lost him; she had failed him. Now here he accused her, throwing it at her and forcing her to face it. She tried numerous times to get him to stop, to get him to understand that he wasn't her responsibility—that she thought he was safe. How was she supposed to explain it to him? As he screamed, tears slid down her cheeks.

CHAPTER 16

LIES

TORO stepped through the door to pitch-black. His equilibrium instantly going sideways, he stepped to the right to catch it, putting it back into place. He stopped himself before peering around. Remembering Jackson's instructions, he put his head down, gripped his jacket, pulling his hands close to his body, and moved forward with his lips sealed.

There were little brushes against his shoulders, his hair, arms, cheeks, every part of him, and he had to fight to move. After much effort, Toro leaned forward, pushing against an oil slick of resistance that choked him. He never stopped, never lifted his head or opened his mouth. He refused. If the only advice he received was destined to get him through his first test, his determination would see him through it.

The resistance gained strength, causing Toro to falter. *No!* He shook his head; he would not lose. The pitch-black darkness and absence of sound wore on him. *Does it ever end?* His mind spun, his confidence being chipped away by the contents of the test sliding down his skin and jacket.

Toro was now almost horizontal as he pushed against the resistance—step after step after step, not sure if he had moved from the spot he started in. *Keep moving. Don't stop,* he repeated to himself.

His right foot slipped, placing his weight on his knee. His hands shot out to help keep himself off the ground, but they fell into … water? Which gave way with his pressure, and the surprise plunged him forward headfirst with the rest of his body following.

His mind reeled while his body remained frozen with shock and surprise. His eyes opened to dirty black water, and his arms flailed around, searching for something to help, his legs kicking in search of a step but finding none. The cold filling his boots found every inch of his skin, exposed or not. Goose flesh creeped up, following the flood. His lungs straining from the lack of oxygen, his mind fighting itself to make sense of the situation. Death by drowning, and before he could see Astrid. Toro needed help.

He tripped … well, by definition a trip was an accident, not on purpose, not his fault. Yet here he was, head butting the consequences of his actions. He'd asked to join the Reformers.

As stars started to form in his vision his feet met a hard surface. With no restraint, Toro crouched, pushing against the ground with every bit of consciousness left in him. His face burst forth from the surface of the water, and he took a deep breath of life-giving oxygen. He floated in the fast-moving water, breathing and letting panic leave his pores. He wiped the water from his eyes to see his new surroundings.

It was beautiful. Trees and rocks lined both sides, going by as he continued down river. The wind brushed through the green trees and grass blades. The blue in the sky so pure it was hard to observe anything else; the sun bright and high in the sky. The air was pure and clean, the black water now crystal clear, a rock bottom visible.

Toro kicked his way to the shoreline, pulling himself up out of the river and lying on the bank as the water washed over his lower legs and boots. The warmth of the sun pulled the wetness out of his clothes and pushed the goose flesh away.

I survived. A smile broke across his face, unrelenting and surprising.

A gun shot rang through the air, the sound bursting through his head, causing him to snap up in a crouched position in a silent well-rehearsed motion. Quickly pulling his pistol from his pack, he stepped forward over the wet rocks, onto dry rocks followed by solid ground covered in grass, weeds, and multi-colored wild flowers. The wind played with them as it did his half-dry hair.

Another shot cut off any thought. He ducked his head instinctively, trying to gauge where it was coming from. Just through the trees he saw movement. A security guard, dressed in white, the emblem of the Institute on his breast pocket. He carried a standard sidearm in one hand, lifting it every ten feet or so and letting off a shot.

"I know you're here. You traitor. You gave them our secrets, didn't you? You turned against your own kind who protected you, who gave you a job and a safe life. You turned to *them*? Those traitorous dogs who sabotage everything they can. Who steal our subjects to do God knows what? You deserve to die." The security guard spoke, not yelling at all, just talking in such a way as to suggest somebody was right beside him hanging on every word uttered. He continued to spit out the poison-steeped ideals.

Toro kept his head low, his pistol ready to fire. Was he ready to kill a man? Sure, he trained for this, mentally and physically, so that when the time came he could take a life with no hesitation, no remorse, no guilt. But now, having flesh and blood on the other side of his gun pulled at morals he thought he'd suppressed.

The security guard continued forward, ever so often shooting another bullet, releasing a boom that shook the leaves. All along, he talked of Toro's betrayal and his imminent death. He wasn't someone Toro recognized.

"Then again, if we take you alive, we could turn you into a double agent. You could tell us everything, especially where to drop the bomb. Where's their base? That protected, coveted compound that nobody can find. You know, don't you? That's where they took you. You can tell me, you know. It could be our little secret. You could return to work, return to the life that was gifted to you."

This seemed cruel. This testing that all the trainees were forced to go through to prove they were prepared, that they were fully trained. Nonsense. The stories the Reformers gave them about the government, the stories the government told about the Reformers, the propaganda to remind the citizens what their fate would be if they failed, if they left, if they claimed to be a Reformer. No quarter would be given. No mercy asked for. Who was he to believe? Astrid? Benji? Jackson? The general? The President?

He sat crouched behind a bush, watching the security guard make his way closer to him, and Toro made a decision. A snap decision that would change the fiber of his being. A gunshot rang out, the smell of gunpowder filling the air, and a body hit the ground.

Time passed. Once more, Astrid's head pounded, but without the intense blue circle appearing, she found it easier to bear. Nothing worked with the imposter Ben. He continued screaming at her, calling her names that should not be coming out of his young mouth. She tried yelling back, telling him everything in her heart. He screamed.

"I'm sorry, I'm so sorry. You're right." Her head fell into her hands, shoulders shaking. Curling into herself, she hid from the scream, the test, the Reformers. Enough was enough. She just wanted her mom. Why couldn't they just help? Why did she have to prove herself worthy first?

Wiping her face, she cleaned snot and tears from her hands onto her pants and took a deep breath. She needed to move on. She wasn't sure exactly what this test was supposed to prove, and she no longer cared.

Astrid stood, palming her throwing knives in her hand. She knew the grip, the hold, even the force she would have to use to guarantee the blade found its mark. A breath, a decision. Her actions would follow her, haunt her if she stabbed him. Remind her on an hourly basis.

Instead, her gaze surveying the landscape, she stepped around the impostor Ben and continued on her way. After about twenty steps the screaming behind her stopped. She turned and saw that Ben was gone. Another deep breath, a shake of her head, and she continued counting her steps.

Soon enough a wall came into view. Astrid sped up her pace, excitement filling her. It was a replica of the door and wall she entered through. Doubt started filling her, but she forced it out with a shake of her head. No, she never turned around. She always faced the same direction, keeping the sun on her left. Checking now that she was correct, she noticed behind her the footsteps she'd made. They ran in a straight line, disappearing in the distance. She had gone in the same direction; it was not the same wall.

Bringing her attention back, she noticed a thin line in the shape of a door, so she ran her cold fingers up and down the hard, cold material. Her fingertips skimmed for a notch, an edge to get a grip on, something to open it. There was nothing. No doorknob, no rope or secret button. Utter exhaustion filled her from head to toe, and it rammed her faster than anything before. Having no idea how much time passed, she wasn't sure how long it'd been since she'd eaten. Turning around and leaning against the wall, she slid to a sitting position, pulling her pack off and searching for water. When she placed her throwing knives next to her, an idea pushed its way in past the tiredness and pain in her head. She slowly pulled one of the throwing knives from the cold sand, turning over on her knees and facing the fingernail-width seam marking the door.

She worked the knife into the small space sliding it top to bottom to find a ledge, something, anything. A click sounded. Then another. A whoosh of air escaped the door as it sprang open, knocking Astrid back over her pack and landing her on her rear end.

"Who do you think it is?"

"Which wave were you a part of?"

Voices wafted out from the other side of the door. Astrid stood quickly, brushing the frost and sand off her. She moved through the now open doorway and found herself in a pleasant circular courtyard full of warm air. The concrete wall encircled green grass and tables topped with food and fresh water. Closed doors, most likely sealed like the one she'd come through, were situated along it every ten feet.

"Astrid? Oh thank God!" Seto rushed forward, pushing other testers out of his way to get to her.

"Hi," she rejoiced with a smile.

"Glad to see the special whelp survived." Jazmin of course, spitting insults.

"Back off, Jazmin." Seto stepped forward.

"Why? Afraid I'll kill her this time?"

"If you do you're out," Astrid shot at her, the challenge there, wanting to be taken.

Jazmin stood for a few seconds. Finally shaking her head, she said, "You're not worth it." She strode off to the other side of the confinement.

"This is what we have determined as the center circle. The food and refreshments were here, and as you can see there are fifteen distinct doors which all lead to different tests. We can't get them open once we've come through. You okay?" Seto led her away from the wall, and they were now making their way through the audience. The expression on his face made it clear he'd noticed the strain on hers.

"I think so, just a little shaken. Toro? Chie?"

In response Seto shook his head, leading Astrid to the center tables for food.

"The food packets, they were rotten," she said.

"All of them were … well, everyone here reported the same. This is nothing like we thought it would be. The way they described the test, participation, death. I don't understand."

"Maybe that was part of it." Astrid picked up fresh fruit and shredded chicken, stuffing her mouth full. She was ravenous. The smell of fresh food filled her nose, making her stomach growl in anticipation, her mouth watering at the known tastes. "What was yours like?"

"I-I don't want to talk about it. Nobody has shared actually. Nobody is willing or strong enough, take your pick. Point is that we survived." Seto dropped his head, working his hands together, showing his nerves. Something had happened to him, something bad.

"That bad? I saw Ben. Blaming me for everything that happened to him. In a frozen desert with no food. Not cold enough to freeze to death or get sick, but enough to be uncomfortable if I stopped moving for a period. Other than the mental issues they pushed on me, it wasn't too bad. I just continued to move."

Seto stopped, gawking at her with wide surprise. "You talk as though it was just another training day. That was it? That's all you did?"

"Yeah, why?"

"You got off easy ..." Seto didn't finish, just strolled away toward a space between two doors on the outer circle, taking a seat, his head shaking.

Astrid began to wonder what Seto's test consisted of to make him act this way. He seemed always to be a 'whatever' kind of guy, go with the flow, not letting anything bother him. What happened in his test to break him?

She moved over, sitting next to him, placing her hand on his knee, her other hand still shoving food bits into her mouth. "Seto, I'm sorry. I didn't mean to pry or brag. I don't know why mine was 'easy' as you put it. But we're here, we survived. Let's concentrate on that and move on. What do you think is next? How long have you been here?"

Seto lifted his head, leaning it on the wall behind him. She watched as he took a deep breath.

"Yeah, uh, I don't know how long. Jazmin was here before me. I was followed slowly by the others. We've tried all the doors, unable to continue the testing. This can't be it. All that training? Months and months of conditioning us body, soul, and mind for a few hours in a locked room where they fed us hallucinogens? I don't believe it."

"Hallucinogens? You think they drugged us?"

Seto closed his eyes again. "How else do you explain Ben?" He opened his eyes, turning his head away from her.

"A ruse, a set-up. Do you think they would fake his kidnapping to do this? Put that boy through this?"

"No. Benji wouldn't have been able to keep the doctor hidden long enough for it to work. You saw what they wanted you to see. It was meant to mess with you, to force you to believe it was your fault. They wanted to see your reaction."

"Seto, did you see something? Someone? To make you believe this?"

"I told Toro that I believed you. What you saw? When your bus was attacked. That somebody needed to believe you. My question now is, if the government is capable of mass murder, genocide even, what exactly do you think the Reformers will be capable of to rectify the wrong? To fix the hurt that was caused?"

Seto's thought pattern forced Astrid to think. What would they do, to make sure they won? A cause they desperately wanted to fight for, but now she felt she was going about it wrong. And they were fighting to be included. She doubted now she had joined the right side.

THE ringing in his ears lingered. The gun backfired, knocking Toro on his back. When he came to his senses, pushing himself off the damp ground, the security guard was gone. No body, no blood.

"Seriously? Just wanted to make sure I would pull the trigger, huh? Thanks for the broken gun. Nice touch." His anger level shot up. Unable to control his sarcasm, he found himself talking to the sky, knowing they watched him. "Did I pass? Huh? You guys having fun?"

He shook himself off, walking along the forest, having no idea where he was supposed to go. Anywhere but here would be better. He stepped over bushes, downed trees, roots, and puddles, picking his way through the foliage and trees. Toro thought this meaningless; they could see perfectly well how they were doing in training, so why not pitch themselves against one another and pull out the bottom half of the class as failures or those simply not good enough? Or whatever they felt like saying? He forced the negative from his mind, only allowing the positive to push him onwards.

After what seemed like hours later, Toro burst through the edge of the forest into a field. The smell and feel of the air changed; the sun dropped low in the sky, and clouds came in, bringing moisture and unwanted rain. A drizzle upon the leaves and grass, forcing Toro to move on, his face upward, shaking his head at the weather choice. The rain droplets left the strands of his hair slick as they were forced to the ground. Stepping farther forward into the tall grass, he came upon a bus, overgrown with weeds and overtaken by dirt, sand, and blown leaves.

Curiosity getting the best of him, he jogged to get closer for inspection. His toe caught on something, pitching him forward to the ground.

With his balance regained, he turned to see what set him off. A shoe, once white, now tarnished from the elements battering at it over time.

"Stupid sho—"Toro stopped, his glance following the shoe.

The position was not right. A shoe by itself could not balance on the side of its heel like this one did. His eyes found what was attached, the shoe to a foot, the foot to the leg, which led to a dead, partially decomposed body. A skeleton with only shards of skin left scattered over bones, nicks and teeth marks left by wandering animals. The femur broken, bone marrow gone. At closer inspection, he saw the uniform stripped and tossed aside, white, with a number on the breast pocket. Toro picked it up with the tip of his broken pistol.

This was a patient from the Institute. How could this be? Where was he? He dropped the piece of rag and stood. He took count—six decomposed bodies, and those were just the ones he could see. With the grass being knee-high he would have to comb the field to determine the exact number of bodies. Deciding he didn't really want to know, he went for the bus, making sure not to disturb any more of the dead with his clumsy feet and ignorance.

He forced the door open with his hands, the rust cloud making him cough as it dissipated around him. The inside was empty, dirty, and stale. Proceeding a little farther, shapes and faces appeared, an apparition ... ghost-like forms of faces he recognized from both the Institute and the Reformers compound. There toward the back sat Astrid with Ben in her lap. He watched with amazement and disbelief as the story she told during the meeting took place with sharp accuracy before his eyes.

He watched the pillars of pale blue light appear, the fear filling the occupants' eyes as they searched for guidance and direction from both Sibella and Reider. The old man who gave himself up only to be used as an example. The panic, the death.

Toro followed the ghost Astrid off the bus to witness an encounter with the general that she hadn't mentioned. The sound turned up, he witnessed the general's hatred and control, and his confidence in their ability to defeat the Institute wavered.

Astrid led Ben away. Instead of following, Toro watched and listened as the blue lights sucked away life, flashing through the field. The Reformers were paralyzed by disbelief and horror at being caught in the middle. They turned in circles, pointing their guns at something they couldn't shoot and kill. Tears appeared. They were helpless.

At the end of the massacre, Toro witnessed pure helplessness, hatred, and finally acceptance cover their faces. They checked bodies for pulses, finding none. No survivors but them. They circled the field searching, Reider stopping suddenly. "You! You did this!" He focused on something past Toro, his feet pushing him forward. Toro turned, not seeing anything, returning his attention in time to catch Reider's right fist with his cheek. The pounding continued, and not just from Reider. Sibella, Jackson, and Red soon joined in.

The kicks causing more harm than hands after Toro fell to the ground, holding his arms above his head. "This was your fault." "Their blood is on your hands." "She can do this without you." The accusations being slung without care or thought of pain. The swings of steel toed boots bursting ribs and blood vessels.

The pistol in Toro's hand cocked—without a second thought of right or wrong—he pulled the trigger, over and over and over. The pain stopped; no more insistence that everything was Toro's fault. Slowly he uncurled, glancing through the tight space between his forearms to see the clear sky. The breeze blew through the tall grass in the field and trees surrounding. No Reformers. No bodies. Just silence.

Taking his time, Toro inventoried his injuries. Every part of him hurt. Blood dripped from his nose, and small cuts stung all over his exposed skin. Once on his feet, he headed back to the bus to rest. He needed to think. Astrid was telling the truth, and Reider and Sibella had witnessed it. Yet why did they not come forth when Astrid told her story? Did the general really have these powers? How did he not know anything about it? Granted, he was only in security; he never even met the general, just seen him. Was the government capable of treating its citizens like this? All the fighting for equality, civil wars,

Democrat and Republican debates. All for nothing. They now lived under a dictatorship—you gave them a reason to keep you alive and use you, or … or what?

The pain reminded him that he needed to move slowly. He would help Astrid; that was what he started this test doing, and that was what he would finish it with. He creeped to the back of the bus, opening up the emergency hatch, stepping down. Instead of his body going down, he tripped over a flat surface.

He found himself in a courtyard with the other trainees, tables with food and water standing a short distance away. Astrid and Seto made their way across the enclosed space to him. He turned, watching the bus disappear behind the closing door.

He did it. He made the right choices and decisions and beat the first part of the test. He made it to Astrid.

He ran to her, grabbing and hugging her as tight as she would let him. They both started talking at once, asking questions while nodding. A frantic, happy reunion.

Seto's voice finally busted through the euphoria that fogged up Toro's head. "*Hey!*" he yelled.

Stopping, Toro laughed, pulling Seto into an unwanted hug. He resisted, pushing Toro away with a laughable force. "Thanks, thanks for helping her," Toro said.

"She didn't need my help. Glad you made it. You okay? You look awful."

Seto didn't ask for more, and it didn't make sense to Toro to explain. They came to a quiet understanding that something had transpired, and the details would be discussed later.

"Nothing I couldn't handle. It'll be fine. I'm just a little sore. You?" He nodded at Seto, who nodded in return, his smile wavering in answer.

Astrid led him to the tables, explaining where they were as well as their assumption that they'd been drugged, while she wet napkins and helped clean the blood off his hands and face.

"None of the doors open from this side?" he asked.

"Seto thinks it's all a joke, a way to work us up, play with us. Break us down enough to do everything they say." Astrid picked her way through shredded chicken and pineapple chunks.

"Hmm." The government did a satisfying job censoring its citizens, trying to break them down to shells, to retrain them to what they thought was useful. "I think this test was the Reformers' way of making sure we are still ourselves, that we understand we have rights. That our minds are still our own."

"What?" she questioned. Toro could see the confusion in her eyes.

"Just a thought. Glad you're okay. Jackson told me he put you into the easiest test. How was it?"

"I don't know. Seto said it was easy too. I didn't love it, but I made it through okay."

"How's your head?"

"Fine, just needs some rest. I hope Chie is doing okay." She continued eating small amounts of chicken, alternating it with sips of water. Her color had returned, and her eyes were clear. Tension in his shoulders abated.

"Do you remember anything? From last night or this morning?" It came out serious, though he hadn't wanted it to. But he needed Astrid to understand the danger she was put in.

"I remember the fight, throwing up. Nothing until we were in the training hall and you were pulling me up. The bus ride with Seto. I've lost everything in between, but Seto helped me figure it out. He told me Benji ordered my medical release so that I could participate?"

"He forced your release, reasoned you had to pass. To pass you needed to take the test. With all the authority he has, you'd think he could just pass you on a private test, instead of forcing all this on you."

"Not wanting to play favorites maybe?"

"You're special, Astrid. There's something about you. You're important to them, and to the Institute. You're the center of this mess I have found myself in." He said it without thinking through how Astrid might take it. Toro didn't feel it was her fault, yet every time he turned around there she was. Haunting him.

"What?" Her reply was short, and a hard expression overtook her face.

"I didn't mean it that way, Astrid. I'm more than happy to help you. I just … I—"Toro tried his best to back-pedal; he wanted to explain, needed to explain. But he didn't know how to. How was he supposed to explain that he was part of the reason she was there? What words could he use to apologize profusely and keep her as a friend?

"Don't bother. I didn't ask for your help, Toro. I didn't ask for this life, to be born poor, to be told I have to work three jobs just to fail. To be put in a box, drugged, and forced to forget every memory I've ever made! To be given eyes that make people uncomfortable, eyes that everybody but me can see! Still, here I am, fighting. Fighting for a better life. Fighting for my mom. Fighting for the freedom that was stripped from us." Her stance was stiff, her chest heaving with deep breaths. "You do what you want. I'm in this. I'm in this until I get her back." She turned away, leaving Toro standing by the table with a gaping mouth.

SHE'D been so happy that Toro had made it out alive.

Now here he was blaming his life problems on her. She hadn't forced him to become a security officer at the Institute; she hadn't asked him to work for that hideous doctor. She trained with him, and befriended him. She needed space to realign herself. Her goals were to survive, to rescue her mother. She needed to stay focused, and Toro seemed to blur things together.

"You all right?" Seto inquired, handing her a bottle of water.

"No." She didn't feel like talking. But she didn't want to lose Seto as well. He seemed to understand; instead of leaving to let her be, he took a seat next to her, not urging her to talk. Just sitting with her.

It wasn't long before a hissing sound presented more open doors, and other trainees fresh out of their test entered. Some filthy, wet, or close to death. Others shaking with fear and distrust, not letting anybody close. Some happy it was done while others would never be the same again. They both got up to help and explain things. Jazmin hadn't moved from her spot since Astrid arrived, and this didn't get her to move either. And nobody was talking about it. So far Astrid noted that she was the only one to share her journey and only to Seto. Nobody else was willing to share, everybody wanting to forget.

Making her way through the new entrees, she noticed Chie— weak on her feet, arms loose at her sides, her head sagging as if it were about to fall off. With a wave of notification to Seto, Astrid rushed towards her, arriving in time to catch Chie before she hit the ground.

"What happened? She okay?" Seto kneeled next to Chie, checking her pulse. They noted her breath and checked for physical signs of pain but found none. Whatever she'd gone through was mental.

What had they all been through, and why was Astrid spared?

"Everybody, listen up!" Toro's voice interrupted her thoughts, bringing with it a flush of anger to her cheeks. He stood, waiting for everybody to quiet down and give him their attention. "I'm glad everyone made it out. But these doors are only one-way. We cannot open any of them from this side. Which means, we have no way of continuing. We have no way of making sure we all complete the test. Does anybody have any ideas, information that could help?"

"Who made you queen?" Jazmin pushed her way past everybody else toward the front of the gathering, always an instigator. "This isn't your party. It's not about you. These are individual tests. Everybody has to prove themselves, not as a team."

"Wrong. They suggested we could team up. Work together."

"Man, they are playing you hard. Look around you! We're stuck here. Has anything they implied come true? Want to know why? Want to know why we are all locked in this room … each of us with a different weapon, each with a weapon that we're not good with? This is how they thin out the herd."

Slowly, murmurs grew into voices of disdain and disagreements. Other trainees wanted confirmation or something to the contrary, to disprove something, anything that Jazmin said. Everything she said rang true. Easy to believe. If this was the end why hadn't they been let out?

"She has a point," somebody agreed.

Shuffling followed his statement as everybody reached for weapons. Nobody wanted to hurt anybody else; the wide eyes and constant movement proved that. But at the same time, everybody would do what they must to survive, including Astrid. Who now remembered her knives were in her sack on the other side of the room.

Toro moved to a rock, now standing several feet above everybody else. Everyone was talking, trying to get louder than the person next to them. Trying to be heard, to come out alive.

"What about her?" someone else inquired, his dirty hand pointing straight at Astrid who was still kneeled with Chie and Seto.

"What about her?" Seto countered, standing to step between her and her accuser.

"She's a favorite, buddy-buddy with Benji. She's in on it! Aren't you? Do you know what's going on?"

"Are you delusional? She doesn't know anything." Seto responded with a bit of hostility.

"Yeah, she does. It's in her eyes. Convenient that everybody can see them but her, don't you think?"

The accusation struck Astrid hard.

"You know what she knows. She's told her story. Everybody needs to stay calm. If we turn on one another there will be a lot of unnecessary death." Seto deepened his tone, his shoulders tight, his fists hard.

"Yes, I've told mine," Astrid said. "Nobody else has told theirs. I came from the Institute. I'm here to learn how to help my mom. To break her out. I don't know why I was given the 'easy' test. It may have seemed easy to you, but it wasn't so easy to me." She stopped, watching as the faces on her fellow trainees changed—first surprise, then doubt, and back to anger. She motioned for Seto to take over supporting Chie's head. Standing to address the crowd more easily, she continued, "What about the rest of you? Where do you come from? Why are you here?"

Everybody's vocal cords came alive at once. Again everyone was talking on top of one another.

A gunshot rang, sending everybody to the ground, covering their heads. Glancing carefully over her arm, Astrid saw Toro still standing on his rock with a gun in his hand, staring at it with surprise.

"What the hell?" She stood, yelling at him, followed shortly by everybody else.

"I need you all to listen. If every single person is talking, nobody is listening. We need to work together and find a way out of here."

They were all now listening to the man with the gun. Astrid glared at him. Shooting a gun into the air solved nothing, just brought intimidation into play with a bunch of trainees armed and jumpy.

"Queenie is talking still," Jazmin stated, heading toward the food table. Nobody stopped to listen; nobody paid attention.

A massive argument continued between Toro, Jazmin, and other trainees over what to do grew. Questions bubbled from everybody. Confusion bled its way through the testers. No two tests were the same; everybody had experienced something personal, something horrific in their own way.

"Why don't we have some fun and weed out the smaller ones." Jazmin's sarcasm strung Astrid's last nerve. She immediately turned to Jazmin in time to see her palm her knives, the blades glimmering in the sunlight. "You first, freak."

"What's your problem?" Astrid blurted out, and everybody else tensed with the impending fight.

"She's the repeat, aren't you, Jazmin? This is her last chance, so she picked someone smaller to torment, to guarantee her spot this time." Toro stepped forward between Astrid and Jazmin, pushing others out of his way. Clearly he knew something that Astrid did not.

"What?" she asked, curiosity getting the best of her. She stepped back, away from Jazmin, wanting now an explanation.

"Every class gets one reject, one chance at redemption. This is Jazmin's, and if she fails again, she becomes a field hand, a farmer. Right? Her target: Astrid. She pinned you as the weak link."

"She failed, came in last?" Astrid went from confused to irritated. This was it? This was Jazmin's reasoning for always being harsh on her?

"You don't know what you're talking about." Jazmin's teeth clenched, the words being hissed instead of spoken.

"Maybe, but I know what he instructed and who Benji marked. What happened, Jazmin? Why aren't you as messed up as the rest of us? Why did you fly through your test so fast?"

Toro was touching a nerve. Jazmin was visibly uncomfortable, and anger rolled off her, her hands gripping her knives even harder.

"No, she admitted she wasn't first." Seto spoke up.

"Yes she was. I came in right after her." The admission came from another trainee, the girl with the purple pixie-cut hair.

"Shut up, you stup—"

"Time to make amends, Jazmin," Toro interrupted, moving himself to be in her direct line of sight. "We're not here to make you fail again. We can help, but you have to let us."

Jazmin didn't respond right away, her pointer fingers sliding up and down the edges of her blades, her lips worried between her teeth. "It's not real, none of the testing is real," she finally confided, her eyes darting around.

"We know that." Seto's voice harsh, impatient.

Toro shot a warning look. Astrid's curiosity peaked even more and she trailed around to see Jazmin more clearly. Not real? This did not make sense. She knew the frozen desert was real, but Ben ... maybe Jazmin was on to something.

"What do you mean?" she seized Jazmin's attention.

Jazmin fought the urge, the struggle clear, her stance unstable, her limbs fidgety. "He's right. This is my second, and final chance. They lace our breakfast with something, which is why I didn't eat this morning. To me it was just a room I stepped through. To you ... well ..." She splayed out her hands, the knives balancing on her palms.

"What happens next?"

"I don't know. I didn't make it this far last time." Jazmin's admission came as surprise to Astrid. Jazmin was strong, surrounded by walls to protect herself, but now she was shifting. Letting bits and pieces loose, showing more of herself.

Astrid didn't answer. Nodding, she moved away from Jazmin through the growing crowd to find Chie. How was she supposed to trust them to help her find her mom if she couldn't even trust her own senses? Trust always went a long way, and Astrid was now learning that maybe she couldn't trust anybody.

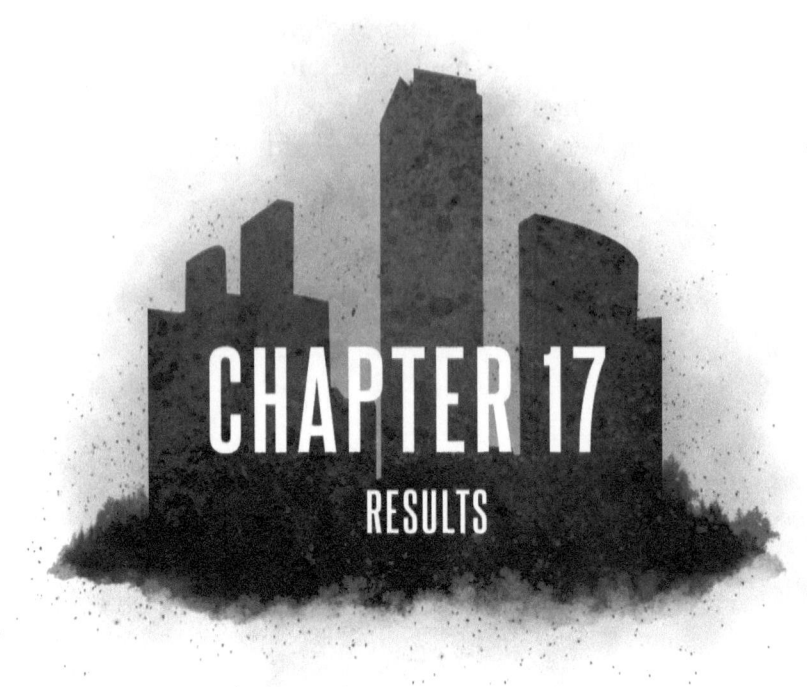

CHAPTER 17
RESULTS

NOBODY was happy to learn that the tests had been a hoax to see what they'd be willing to do. Some of the trainees' faces were ashen, grave-like as they voiced their stories of what they did to survive. Some succeeded in proving they would sacrifice their loved ones for the Reformers. The blankness coming from their eyes was disturbing.

The argument commenced without Toro's help. Instead he stood there, confusion washing through him as he tried to figure out what to take from all this.

He felt betrayed and used. *Is this what Astrid experienced? What she's still going through?* He stole glances at her as she stood back from the group listening intently to Chie.

Toro sidestepped behind Seto to talk with Astrid. "What do you make of this?" he asked under his breath, coming up next to her.

She startled at his voice, taking a deep breath, and finally shrugging her shoulders in admittance of defeat—the betrayal plain on her face as well as his. She struggled to pull away from her thoughts, taking her time to answer. Still fighting an internal battle he was unable to help with.

"It's another test," she speculated.

"What?"

"It's another test. Think about it. You said once we met up in the middle we could choose to work together or not. What if working together is the test and this constant battle for the top is keeping us here, holding us back? We know they want leaders."

It made sense. Big Jack and Benji would need to know they possessed the ability to lead and work together, know who could take orders as well as give them.

Toro jumped as a sudden fierce idea came into being. His eyes widened as he strode over to the food table. He jumped up on it, kicking everything away as he hurried toward the center, trying to get everybody's attention without becoming hostile or having to raise his voice. Astrid watched his progress with surprise and begrudging admiration. Knowing she watched him, a smile cracked across his face. It was hard not to puff out his chest and square his shoulders.

It didn't take long; soon he could see every trainees' dirty face, their dark-lidded eyes stuck on him with expectation.

"Astrid helped me realize something, and I would like to share it." He paused, waiting for permission, wanting to be accepted without it being forced. "Remember when Big Jack, Benji, and Jackson were telling us about the test? The individual parts, the center where we would meet up?" He spread his arms wide to enforce his words. "Saying that once we meet up we could choose how to finish this? That we could choose to work together or individually? What if this is a test? What if us arguing over what to do is hurting our chances of getting out of here? What if all we need to do is decide? To work together, or not?"

He waited, watching as everybody soaked in this idea, this information they all had missed.

"How do you know that? It could be another trick," a voice called from the back. A tall trainee tall, skin and bones, with blue veins popping out all over his paper-thin skin. His blond hair was dirty, matted down in his face. He stood still, a statue, his arms crossed over his chest in a protective stance.

"I'm not sure, but we need to try something. We need to work together to get out of here. Show that we can do it as equals."

The guy nodded, but other voices rose, bashing against one another in the air above their heads, each vying for their own space to be heard, to be the loudest. Everybody with their own ideas, everyone wanting to finish first.

"Oh come on," he muttered to himself, not realizing he'd spoken out loud until he heard a small laugh below him.

Astrid, stifling giggles as hard as she could, wouldn't meet his eye.

"What? It was a good plan." He sat down, swinging his feet.

"It's not that. Every person here is fighting for the first-place spot. The promise of a spot on the team that goes to L.A. Asking them to just let it go? That was funny."

"All right, jerk face, what would you suggest?"

She went deep in thought again, off on her own.

"Here, watch this." She used his shoulder, hoisting herself up on the table, kicking more food and water to the ground. "Can everyone who wants to work as a team please come over to the other side of the table?" She jumped down, moving around the table.

Toro smiled to himself. This was never going to work. It was so simple that no …

And there it was. The first person to join her was the shy, tall guy with blond hair who previously asked a question. Toro shrugged, glancing at Seto with expectancy and circling the table to join Astrid.

"Now what? The three of us will …" He let the question linger.

Astrid glared at him, suggesting he shut up. He let out a breath and shut his mouth. They didn't have to wait much longer; slowly those who wanted to get something done joined them, including Seto and Chie, who still was not meeting anybody's eyes. Astrid made a point to learn all the newcomer's names. Toro didn't care; he just wanted out. He wanted a one-on-one with Benji. He needed to know what the purpose was … know whose stupid idea this was and why they were being forced to go through it.

Gradually their numbers grew—it started out as a trickle. Slowly in groups of two and threes they joined. When it became apparent they would not gain anymore, Toro noticed every one of them waited for Astrid to give direction. Not him, the security guard with experience, but Astrid, the frail patient who was in it to free her mother. The bitterness surprised him. He should be happy. It was her original thought that led to this first meeting, and it was her announcement that brought over these trainees. He should be happy; he should be willing to help. He should *not* be jealous.

MELVINA regained consciousness, her limbs heavy from drugs, her head foggy and painful. She tried one by one to lift her arms and legs, taking inventory as she went. Her right arm wouldn't budge; it was too heavy, glued to a soft surface. She opened her eyes to the pinprick of bright lights above her, immediately closing them again to block the bright invasion. She stopped fighting, letting her body fully relax while taking a deep breath and trying again, only slower. Eyes adjusting and moving past the blurry, painful brightness surrounding her. Trying again to lift her arms, she discovered weight still there, but after taking investigating she noted she could still use her entire body; she had full control. Instead of trying to lift up, she tried to go side to side, but still nothing.

Her eyes went wide as she clenched her jaw, trying to calm the quiver in her stomach. She was strapped to an assimilation chair in an examination room. Straps over her chest, waist, ankles, wrists, and forehead there to keep her from thrashing back and forth. Panic seeped in; her eyes bulged, breath getting faster to match her heart rate. She thrashed, she fought, and she screamed. It was not supposed to be like this. They were supposed to welcome her, bring her back into their loving fold, celebrating the ingenuity of her escape and knowledge of the Reformers. Not blame her, not drug her or treat her like a prisoner.

A prisoner.

That's what they were, not patients, not citizens in need of a lesson; they were all prisoners.

Her breathing grew louder and heavy, and her chest heaved to match it. Her eyes darted around to see if anybody witnessed her slight misstep of panic, her moment of weakness. No, not that she could see. She knew that room, she knew how it worked, where one could stand without the patient … no, the prisoner—she was a prisoner now—seeing them. Again, without being able to move her head, she searched what she could see of the room. Nothing, nobody, just clean, sterile white walls with recessed lights above her.

This helped calm her down, even if it was only an illusion of being alone.

"Hello?" she called out, not quite screaming as before. "Hello?"

No answer, no swish of the door, no footsteps announcing arrival, and no movement within the room. Nothing. Now she was certain that she was alone. Utterly alone, but it wasn't so bad. It gave time to think, time to work the problem out. Being left by herself, strapped to a chair or not, there were advantages, time to regain control over her body, her emotions, her reactions.

A tear escaped, making its way down her temple into her hair. Weakness, again. This time she considered it just escaping her body. She was shedding the last of the weakness. The restraints stopped her from removing the last drop of frailty.

Melvina wasn't sure how long she lay there, unable to move. Able to wiggle enough to keep the blood flowing, keeping the tingling at bay. Her neck stiffened up, her legs and hips smarting with sharp pins and pain.

About the time the pain became unbearable, when she gritted her teeth, trying her hardest just for a moment of peace, the door opened. She couldn't see who entered, and the new distraction helped take her mind off what her body was going through. The footsteps were methodical, precise, in sync with one another. Heavy. Her eyes darted back and forth, her neck straining against the strap just to see, to know who entered her presence. Not knowing whether to be scared or not.

"Melvina, nice of you to return. I'm honored to see you again."

That voice, the long drawl of the letter and pronunciation. It struck recognition in her memory. Suddenly, there he was, standing at her side. The general, his graying hair shining bright under the lights, the silver sparkling as he moved. He stood over her, his green eyes bright with knowledge and want, his hands held together behind his back. The black suit perfectly pressed. He smelled clean, important.

"I hear we have many things to discuss. I apologize for your wait, and of course the condition in which you waited." He circled her now, his steps evenly paced.

"Where's Ben? What did you do to him?" she blurted out, every muscle tight, straining against her restraints.

"He's fine, safe, asleep." His eyebrows lifted at the last word, his head bent slightly over hers. "You gave us quite a scare when you left. We worried for your safety."

"I didn't leave. I was taken," she corrected, spittle coming out of her mouth.

"Hmmm … Three quarters of our stock was taken, or harmed. The President much displeased. She flew here specifically to see the destruction." At this he leaned even closer to her face; she could smell his breath and cologne. "Enraged, the President was." His arm moved, slightly, as not to scare her, to let his pointer finger follow a fresh red and raw scar upon his cheek. "Her punishment painful, understandably. I took it with pride and without complaint. As you will."

"I didn't do anything! I wasn't part of it!" Panic, fully arrived, took over every nerve. Her voice high and cracked, her muscles even more strained. The straps cutting off the circulation to her hands and feet. "They kidnapped me! Watch the security tapes!"

"We did!" His voice boomed with silencing command. She quickly snapped her mouth shut. "We heard a certain conversation between you and one of our security, something about discovering a secret. You failed. You didn't follow protocol." Her eyes widened at this. "Your kidnapping, to say the least, wasn't convincing, and neither was Mr. Crow's. I was surprised to hear they found you, and you came willingly. That you delivered our precious cargo. Thank you for that."

"Precious cargo? The onl—" She stopped. The only thing she brought back with her was Ben. Her breathing hitched again, her heart rate speeding up so fast she could feel it in the tips of her fingers and toes. "No. You have it all wrong. I am loyal to you, to the Institute, the government. I have not done anything wrong!"

"Wrong, you have done everything wrong. You betrayed us." He stalked in circles again, his hands calmly clasped behind his back as he paced around and around. Melvina tried to follow, but she couldn't. Her eyes lost him at certain points, behind her head and at her feet. "You committed treason. Do you know what the punishment is for treason?"

"What do you do to the patients, General?"

The abrupt change in subject caused the general to falter in his steps. He corrected, continuing, and when he came up her left side she saw his smile.

"I heard it, saw the flash of blue light. And the reports that came in after the bus attack. They told me you steal their souls." She calmed her nerves, her words precise; she was in control.

For a bit of time he just stood there, perhaps trying to decide how much he should tell her, if it was worth it. She wanted him to share, she wanted … no, she needed to know, needed to understand. Finally, after a deep breath and a stretch of his back he explained.

"It was discovered after the cleansing that we committed a grave mistake. There is an enzyme that lives in direct descendants of those who survived the cleansing. The enzyme hidden within a gene marker, something that can only be passed down the female blood line. Males can possess it but not pass it on. This enzyme is important. It can allow its host to block out any use of medical grade serums and allows alterations to the brain. The compound that you oversaw the distribution of, this gene can keep it from working and with an added sedative can help break down the compound even faster." He straightened even taller, if possible. "We also learned that this enzyme can be extracted, to make other humans—more important humans—better, make us immune, give us gifts.

"It brings out abilities which otherwise are suppressed, otherwise unreachable. We need this gene, Melvina. We have to have it. Extract it. Rip it out if we have to. The institutes were created to find and extract it, the Life Tax created to fill the institutes."

"Your ability? What is it?" Bravery took over, her anger forging the path. Benji was right. Everything she thought she knew was a lie; everything safe and correct was wrong and harmful.

He laughed, a short spurt with a smile showing all his perfectly white teeth. His hands reached his pockets this time, his stance more comfortable. He bounced back and forth from the balls of his feet to his heels.

"Was I given the serum?" She asked to see if she could get something, anything more out of him.

"Yes, but you already knew that." His grin angered her even more, raising her wrath to a level she didn't know existed in herself. "Ben, the boy you claim is your son, is not. The memories you have of giving birth and raising him are fake, implanted by a previous doctor. You are one of our clones."

"No … no, that's not right!" Her mind whirled; she replayed her memories: the birth, holding Ben for the first time, the smell of his precious head. All ten toes and fingers. Teaching him the alphabet, pushing him on a swing, waking up to find Benji gone. Those were hers; Ben was her son.

"Hmm, I see it worked well. You were one of our first successes, although it backfired when you committed treason."

The door opened, allowing another set of footfalls to enter with the sounds of a cart mixed in. Sterile tools rocked back and forth as the cart moved around her chair. The general nodded at the new arrival. "We're now going to reverse the procedure, teach you who you really are."

Melvina froze, tears trickling down into her hair, her breath and heart rate still so fast. She gripped the arms of the chair with every ounce of strength, constantly telling herself it wasn't true, that what he described wasn't real. She knew who she was. She was Doctor Melvina Heizer. She attended medical school. She was a mother! Panic reared again, and the soft rubber suction cups applied to her temples and upper chest underneath her gown made the room close in around her, made it smaller.

The first pinprick of a needle made her jump, and the effects were instantaneous. Her vision blurred; her heart rate and breathing slowed. The general came into view, leaning over her chair, that smile still on his face.

"I'll come back, to reintroduce myself. The world is not as safe as you would believe, Dr. Heizer. Do enjoy."

The only thing left was the lights, blurred by the medication and her own tears.

ASTRID reeled at being the one they turned to for directions—that was supposed to be Toro—but as she viewed the sea of dirty faces she discovered they waited patiently for her to say something.

Yes, say something, say anything.

She couldn't. She didn't know what to say. What did they want her to say? What was there to say?

Nobody interjected, so they stood there waiting. For what they were not sure, but they waited. The group on the other side of the table was now down in number, but it did not deter them from continuing their arguing. Jazmin's sarcastic remarks always heard over everybody else's statements or ideas.

"So, do we have a plan? Or ..." The same blonde again, Brax, his bright, anxious eyes speaking more than he ever could. The rest followed his lead, nodding their heads in agreement.

"No plan, just trying something different. If we're right and this is a test, we need to work together." Toro stepped forward to be right in front of Astrid as he spoke. True to his nature, taking charge. Astrid let her head fall back, having no desire to be there.

"Work together on what?" someone else asked.

Astrid had tried to meet all of them, but the task of remembering their names proved too daunting.

"On opening a door, on getting out of here."

"Well, now that we don't have any more food, that would be helpful." Jazmin joined the edge of the group, her sarcastic remark floating above their heads.

Astrid caught a smile overtaking her lips, stopping it carefully to make sure nobody noticed.

"Yeah, I didn't quite think that through. It's still good. I didn't step on any of it." Toro rushed through the bodies, picking up the scattered snacks and placing them back on the empty table. "There's still plenty of food here."

Grins spread through the crowd, and the mood lifted, anger disappearing. The pressure of the situation easing. Astrid took a deep breath, feeling herself loosen up in acceptance. The next step was to work her way through this. She moved away from the group, strolling her way around the enclosed space, brushing her fingers across the doors. Her mind whirling with different possibilities—different tests. Different outcomes.

Suddenly she felt exhausted. With no time to recover from her concussion, she had been shoved into this nightmarish situation. She stopped, leaned against the door her hand currently rested on, and followed the door with her back until she sat against it, her head resting on her knees.

It didn't take long before she was sound asleep, the voices of surrounding trainees blending together to create a white noise that whisked her off into a dreamless, restless sleep.

A tap on her shoulder popped her head up, and she came eye-to-eye with Toro, who squatted next to her with an aggravated expression on his face.

"Hey," she managed through a dry throat.

"You still feeling woozy?"

"No, just tired."

"Me too, but we need everybody's help if we're going to get through this."

"I know. I was pacing in circles, thinking. I-I'm so tired." Her eyes slowly blinked Toro in and out of sight.

"Hmmm."

"You guys come up with anything?"

"Other than we're all tired and want out?" Not getting a reaction out of her, Toro took a pausing breath. "No, all the doors are still sealed."

"I don't mean to be obvious, but has anybody tried going over the wall?" The idea was fresh and welcoming. With her head against the door, gaze facing upward, she decided it could be done. "We'd have to do it together. It's too high to get over on our own."

"Seriously? What if we get thrown back into the tests we just c—wait. That would be it though, right? Test us to the breaking point, where everybody would agree to never go back." Toro stood quickly, gazing toward the top of the wall.

Astrid dared not move. She let the knowledge fall into the deep crevices of those around her. An idea that could end this. Seto and Chie found their way over to them questioningly. Astrid confirmed that Chie was on the mend before turning back to Toro.

"Would you?" she asked him.

"Go back? If I knew it was the way to get out of here. But how do we know?"

"We don't." Astrid stood, brushing her hands off on her pants. "Give me a leg up." She steadied herself against the wall. Toro hooked his hands together, giving her a step, bracing himself.

She used Toro's hands to propel herself toward the top of the wall. Her tired, torn hands barely gripped the edge. Toro helped by pushing her feet so that she could get her head and line of sight over the wall. She giggled, pulling herself up to where she sat on the wall facing out. She motioned to Toro to get everybody's attention and share their plan.

"What do you see?" he yelled up at her.

"The end," she answered, swinging her legs over to the outside and staring. And there it was, the exit. They were stationed inside a warehouse of sorts, a big space. From this vantage point she could see the fake lights over the center of the wall, which from below had been viewed as natural sunlight. Just a few meters out next to a parked bus sat Jackson studying her from his chair, grinning widely.

"I knew it would be you," he called to her.

Astrid smiled, turning back around to see everybody bunched around right below where she perched watching in astonishment.

"You coming?" she asked, laughing.

Together they created lines and lift ups, helping each other they created a working human ladder to get up, over, and down the other side of the twelve-foot wall that had inserted so much fear in each of them.

A fight broke out with only ten trainees left on the inside of the wall. Astrid was standing on top the wall, overseeing safety and making sure nobody would fall when it drew her attention.

"Hey!" she yelled down to them, her balance wavering at the sudden burst of force. "We're almost there!"

"Who's last? The last one doesn't get a spot, right?"

She sighed; they were right. Who would be last? She turned her head, wanting insight from Jackson, a way out. He just smiled, shrugging his shoulders. Toro, who was on the wall opposite her watching the other side of the two-humans-wide ladder, had the same concern covering his face. It couldn't be her. She needed this to save her mom. Toro wouldn't stay back, either; it was in his blood to be a soldier.

"I'll be last," came a voice. Brax, the tall, lanky, blue-veined boy who constantly spoke up right when they needed him to. He was currently underneath Astrid inside the wall, peering at her. His hand held high to block the bright lights. "I'll come in last. I don't think I was made for this anyways."

"Are you sure?" she asked, comforted by his words.

"Yeah, it'll be okay. They have another place for me, I'm sure."

"Okay. It's settled. Let's continue."

It didn't take them much longer before Brax stood alone, the last one on the ground below them inside the containment. Everybody else worked their way over and watched the final three: Toro, Astrid, and soon, Brax.

Toro and Astrid lay down facing one another, putting both their hands down as far as they could reach. Brax would have to run up the wall and grab their arms in order for them to pull him up.

"Think he has it in him?" Toro asked, doubt shadowing his voice.

"Yes," she declared firmly.

Brax braced himself on the other side of the circle. Breathing heavy and swinging his arms around, he got ready to propel himself up and over. He jumped slightly, taking his stance, and with a steady start bolted toward them.

He ran, his breathing even, his steps steady. He reached them with a surge upward, his feet gripping the wall, his arms and hands stretching as far as he possibly could. Astrid strained as Brax's hand contacted hers, the sweat threatening to let his hand slip. Showing amazing momentum and control of his body, he continued propelling himself up the wall, and over the top. Astrid watched in awe as his momentum jerked his hand out of hers and tossed him over the wall into the waiting hands of the other trainees.

"*No!*" she yelled as Toro refused to let go, tumbling down after Brax. Her breath caught. She was officially the last one on the wall.

CHAPTER 18
PLANS

ASTRID stood on the wall in horror, replaying what just occurred over and over. Her head moving from one side of the wall to the other. The shadow of Brax letting go of her, pulling Toro down after him. The consequence was last place. That's what she was. Last place.

Toro picked himself up, brushed off, shoving Brax as hard as he could, sending the skinny kid flying into other trainees, profanity streaming from his mouth. Brax just shook his head, a smug smile across his face.

"Now she's not so special. Now she's just like everybody else," Brax spit out, not just to Toro, but to everybody. Nods of agreement came from others standing around him. Brax stood amid his followers with venom pouring from his eyes; he didn't seem so fragile or skinny with this newfound animosity.

"Astrid, come on." Jackson pushed his way through the crowd, motioning at her. He turned, pointing toward the bus on the other side of the warehouse. "Buses are waiting. Go load up," he commented to the rest of them.

Toro stepped to be underneath her, reaching his hands up to help her down. Astrid turned, letting herself fall against the wall, catching her weight on her hands, her feet and calves meeting Toro's strong hands. She let go, and he caught her, letting her down to the ground with ease.

There were no words. Instead, Astrid nodded her thanks and curled into herself. Her arms wrapped around her midsection, and she headed toward the buses, giving Jackson a wide berth as to make sure there was no contact.

Toro wasn't as thoughtful. Astrid heard a grunt and a hard thud behind her and spun to see Toro shoulder into Jackson with an angry, spitting force.

Still no words. What could they say?

Jackson chuckled, rubbing his shoulder and turning to follow them out.

The bus ride was silent. The stench of unwashed bodies, mixed with the never ending smell of dead fish embedded into the worn cloth of the seats, worked its way into her nose.

She sat in an inside seat with Toro next to her sitting guard, daring anybody to say something. Her head rested against the cool window, the condensation contacting her forehead, cooling her anger. Her thoughts swam together, depression making its way in between them, threatening to shut her down. Her mom was in her mind's eye, her hair flowing with the wind, sitting on an old merry-go-round on a fake horse, the colors vibrant but worn. Always so happy, carefree.

Astrid hadn't known the extent of her mother's worry until later in life, when she herself was forced to get jobs to make ends meet.

"You have to help pay now. You're an adult. I've worked hard. I've waited so you could have a childhood. Now you need to be an adult. I need you to help," she had begged Astrid, saying she knew a contact that could get her setup with a non-labor position. It would be easier on her, her mother repeated. Astrid had finally understood, understood the depth of the sacrifice her mother made.

Without asking why, without questioning her mother, she fell full thrust into her methods and took the position offered. They worked twelve to eighteen hours every day, to pay the government for their right to survive in the country they were born in. Thoughts of her mom continued to flood through her, especially her smell. Her mom was always clean—they could go days without a shower or clean water, but no matter what her mom always smelled good. She remembered that fateful day they turned themselves in, the memory bursting forth, forcing itself into her head. Their check-in point, per the notice, was located just a few blocks from their house in an old abandoned shopping center. They were in line, with only a few people who were not in a uniform. Greeters nodded their heads at the doors when they saw the note that was in her mom's hand. Her other hand tightened the grip on Astrid's; she claimed it was to stop the shaking.

"If we share the fear, Astrid, we can do this. We can bear it together, evenly," her mom told her.

Not wanting to go through with it, Astrid's panic rose to unsuspected levels as they were supposed to leave their home. She tried everything to get her mom to leave with her, to go in the opposite direction, but her mom answered always refused.

"We have to be responsible. We have to face the consequences of our actions. Regardless if we agree with them or not, we must go." After arriving at the government building she squeezed Astrid's hand, repeating, "Together, let's share the fear."

It was just enough to get Astrid to take the step she needed, to be strong and do what was needed. They turned themselves in, with heads held high and dry eyes. Fear shared between them, locked in their clasped hands.

But here, now, Astrid failed. She failed her mother. And more than anything, it caused the most pain. She kept imagining her mom in a white shirt, barely covering paper thin skin showing bone and veins. Being starved, mistreated, experimented on. Her only hope her daughter, and she'd failed.

Her heart cracked, her soul shattering again. How could one person survive this? Over and over, hurt and betrayal, failure and anger.

Hand-in-hand without laughter, without love, without family, without hope.

She was crying now, her failure plain on her face. Tears streamed down, falling from her cheeks and chin to her jacket and hands.

"You can't give up, not now. You're so close, Astrid." Toro leaned closer to her.

"Yeah, it'll be okay." Seto was sitting in front of them with Chie, and his head popped up over the back of the seat.

"What else am I supposed to do? I'm clearly out of the training program, so I won't advance to be a part of the L.A. takeover. After that is Vegas, and Vegas is where I need to be. Vegas is where she is!" Her voice rose with passion and determination to convince him. To make sure they knew.

"We'll go talk to Benji. Big Jack, Jackson, Red. All of them! You're one of the best trainees here. They can't just pull you. This is not over. And you can always go through training again."

"And what do you think the other trainees will think?"

"Who cares? They ca—"

Astrid lifted her hand, cutting him off. "I'm too tired for this. Let me rest."

"Astrid, please? I want to help. I-I want … please?"

She jerked, her eyes wide open. His tone and the look in his eyes suddenly made her see something she had missed. He liked her? He wanted something more in the middle of this hazardous fight for freedom. She did not have energy for love, or time for a relationship. Worrying about herself took up just about all her energy. What was left she used up on her mom and Ben. She could not add somebody else to this as well.

"It's all wrong!" she exclaimed, deciding to ignore his feelings. "The government, the Reformers. They're all wrong!"

He squinted as he pulled his head back, and she could see him processing the way she threw his emotions aside.

"Yes, but we have an opportunity to be on the right side of wrong." Chie, finally come out of her spook, spoke up after shifting to have a better position, to be seen. "If you have to choose a side, don't choose right or wrong; choose passion and conviction. Choose to do something that will make a change."

"Make a change," Astrid whispered, more to herself than to them. "The right side of wrong."

Was Chie right? Could she do something big enough to make a change, not just for herself, but for other people as well? Make a big enough splash to send ripples through time?

The bus came to a lurching stop. Reaching the parking tank, the fish smell grew stronger when the door opened and people filed out. Astrid wiped her face, removing her tears.

Toro waited until they were the last ones on the bus, having to wave off Seto and Chie with confirmation that he could handle it. "Don't give up," he said as he stood, leaving her to her misery.

Astrid didn't follow. Instead, she pulled her knees against the seat in front of her, folded her hands in her lap, placed her head against the window, and slept.

TORO didn't know what else to do, what else he could say to make her see that he wanted to help.

So instead, he left her. He headed to the debriefing, ready for a fight. Ready for his assignment.

They filed, sluggish, tired, and smelly, to the training hall where all this started, ages ago.

The training hall was the same as when they left—equipment pushed to the sides and back wall, the white tables set up with chairs behind them. Big Jack paced wall to wall behind the chairs. Benji sat calmly perusing reports ... reports Toro assumed contained information and results from their tests. Jackson joined Benji in a chair behind the tables, adding his own papers to the stacks. Red stood back by the door, leaning against the wall with his right knee bent, his foot against the wall, fidgeting with his knife.

Toro came up last behind the excitement of their return. He stood, feet apart, his arms crossed in front of his chest. Red closed the door, coming up behind Toro, imitating his stance.

Big Jack spoke first. Anger poured through his limbs as he stomped back and forth, his arms swinging and pointing. "A bunch of sissies! These kids, they just think they're soldiers. They tricked and wormed their way through this test! They deserve nothing! They deserve water and bread crumbs!"

Huh? Toro wasn't the only one confused. Heads shook, trainees trying to stifle questions.

"They all should walk the plank!" Big Jack now stood behind Benji with a wide grin on his face.

"Jack, thank you." Benji shuffled through papers, clearly trying to decide where to start. He was usually ready for everything; this was unlike him.

Brax took charge, jump-starting the meeting without needing any coaxing. "Was it worth it? Watching us go through that? Watching us kill our loved ones to prove to you that we can follow orders? That we can kill if ordered, or even if not?"

The kid's nerve sparked a reaction in others. Wide eyes and open mouths faced him. After hours of training with a silent kid, his harsh voice—a voice that demanded to be heard—was now breaking through unasked questions and stoic mannerisms.

"We needed to know." Like always, Benji's voice was calm and deliberate. "These enemies of ours are not just soldiers, doctors, or workers. They will be friends, family, coworkers, and loved ones. We needed to know that if it came down to you or your past, that you would choose correctly. And now, we know."

Brax didn't push the subject further. He melted away, disappearing into the crowd again.

"Most of you did really well. Most of you took what Jackson suggested to heart, using the information to further your testing. Others brushed off his advice, going headstrong into their own personal hell. Every one of you survived. This is a tremendous moment, for this has never happened before. I watched all your simulations, all of your tests personally, and drew my own conclusions." He had been shuffling through his stack of papers, emphasizing his words, but now he finally looking up and scanned the crowd. A quizzical look came over his face. "Where's Astrid?"

"She's still on the bus." Jackson answered.

"The trick Brax pulled on the wall was self-serving. A trick to better himself and harm his comrades. This we do not take lightly. A disciplinary hearing will take place to rectify this wrong. Until then, Brax, you are dismissed." He marked Brax with his last sentence, his gaze unwavering.

Toro waited for Brax to argue, fight back, something. Instead, he nodded and simply left the room.

"Now, the rest of you, good job. Take a deep breath, because you're in. Testing is over. If you haven't already shared your experience, you're allowed to at your discretion, or you can keep it to yourself. Hit the showers, eat, sleep. We meet again in three days to discuss the L.A. mission." With that Benji stacked his papers and moved around the table.

Toro pushed forward, heading him off. "Sir, can I go get Astrid and tell her?"

"She's been taken care of, but I appreciate your concern."

"My concern? You guys have destroyed her, but it's taken care of?" His anger rose; his words jumbled.

"Easy. If you want to check on her, go." Benji pushed past him.

Toro turned around and saw he was the last trainee. Red stood watching him while cleaning his nails with his pocket knife. "What?" Toro snapped at him.

Red didn't respond, just shook his head with a grin that spread across his whole face.

Toro went to the bus first, only to find Benji was correct. Astrid was not there. He checked the mess hall, where half of the now graduates celebrated with whoops and hollers. He decided next to check her room. Which also proved to be empty.

Where could she be?

He came across Seto and Chie making their way to their own rooms and asked about Astrid. He received a whispered answer that she resided in the infirmary, sedated and healing. Confirming for himself, Toro stood outside Astrid's space in the infirmary, watching as she breathed easy and slept. He'd talk to her as soon as she woke up. For now, he would take care of himself. Three whole days off, no training, no testing. He could check on Astrid later. Talk with her, apologize.

"**STOP** the buzzing! Why is there buzzing?" It wouldn't stop, the noise piercing her blissful sleep. She hated it. She rolled over, her arm aiming for an alarm clock, only to find nothing. Just air. Her fingers contacted something cool and smooth. Her arm hung over the side of her bed, her fingers searching for the button to stop the noise. Finally, with impatience bursting forth, she lifted her head to see a small white room, her bed, and a shelf coming out of the closest wall. The sound came from the surrounding walls. In shock, she jumped, standing in the center, watching in amazement as her bed disappeared into the wall. Only then did the buzzing stop.

Melvina, now known as Patient 142/357, spun in a tight circle to see the four brilliantly white walls containing her. She wore a white cotton uniform—loose and comfortable—her patient number embroidered on her left breast. She racked her brain, trying to remember ... anything. Something. Childhood memories, her parents, anything! Nothing came to her. Her name, the way her face was shaped. Her hands shot up, her fingers following every inch, her eyes, eyebrows, cheekbones, nose, lips, and her chin. Following her ears top to bottom, then her hair. Nothing familiar.

She spun, following a noise and seeing an opened space, an extension to the current room she was in. She took a step toward it, her arm reaching out in fear and expectancy. The new addition was smaller than the first room, a rectangle of sorts, with three silver knobs on the left side in a row. She reached farther into the new room, testing. A spray emitted from the knobs, misting her hand before giving her warning to move out of the way. The surprise made her jump back, squealing, holding her left arm against her chest for protection. She tried again, this time knowing what to expect. She turned her hand over and over in front of her, feeling the warm, comforting spray, trying to force the understanding.

Concluding no other option, Melvina stripped her uniform and entered the new room. The spray jolted out immediately, stinging her skin with sharp pins as the water hit her. Another yelp escaped her, her hands shooting out to protect herself. She spun, trying to escape the pressure. The cool water pounded against her with force, cooling her body temperature, forcing her teeth to chatter and goose flesh to appear. When she had enough, she exited the room, the water stopping, and warm air took its place.

The temperature change was unbearably welcoming; the ecstasy that took place overwhelming. She got closer, letting the warm air dry off the cool water droplets on her body. As soon as she was dry, it ended just as suddenly as it began. She stood, warm and naked. Finally stepping out, she saw that the unfolded, worn clothes she left on the floor were gone. On a shelf to her right a clean folded uniform waited, exactly like the last one.

After she dressed, a table, chair, and food appeared. This task easier to determine and conquer as her stomach guided her way. The soup was hot and delicious, the taste bursting across her taste buds and down her throat, healing a wound she was unaware of. The table disappeared at the same time one of the walls opened, revealing a tall, handsome man in a black suit, with graying hair and a killer smile.

"Good afternoon, Melvina, do you remember me?" he asked, his voice matching his appearance—soft and in control.

"No," she forced out, unable to move.

"Hmmm." He nodded his head in approval, his smile warming her, making her feel safe and accepted. "As you shouldn't. I am the general here. My name is Mark Thaxton. I run this institute."

"Institute? What is that?" Her voice pitched to a higher level, and her hands clasped together, resting in front of her, swaying back and forth.

"It is a place for those who can't follow rules. For those who make this world a dirtier place." His face changed as he explained, eyeing her to the point of discomfort. She dropped her gaze to the floor, wringing her hands in front of her. "A place for you."

"I don't understand," she mumbled, her eyes downcast.

"You are here because you couldn't follow the rules. Because you used the government, took advantage of them when you shouldn't have. You used them!" His voice got louder with each sentence, filled with disgust. Stepping forward he berated her, toe to toe with her now.

Melvina shook, frightened of this man she had momentarily felt safe with. Not sure what she could say to stop him. "I don't know. I don't remember anything." Her voice was quiet, quivering, and small.

"*No?* Not yet anyways." He took a deep breath and a step away, straightening his back and clasping his hands behind him. "An alarm will go off when your memories return. Try not to be frightened. They will come get you and bring you to me. We will have another discussion, about your place here, about what you've done." With that he turned on his heel and exited the room, the door closing behind him.

Her whole body shook violently. The panic from when she first woke up returned with vengeance; her knees gave way and landed her on the floor. The tears flowed freely, down her cheeks, landing on her thighs. Her torso shook with the sobs of failure and disappointment, in herself and others who counted on her. If what that man taunted was true, she deserved to be where she was.

CHAPTER 19

REVELATION

AFTER sleeping what felt like the entire three days, Toro awoke to a quiet room, stuffy from disuse with a stench of sweat and bad breath. He worked his way out of the twisted sheets, pulling on pants and a tank top, his body sluggish, full of sleeping cells. In a desperate need of nourishment, he headed off to the mess hall.

The room was full; standing room only. The air thick with excitement and voices fighting to be heard over others and noises of dishes clanking, benches scraping the floor, and laughter. The mood of the room immediately filled Toro with happiness. He was surprised to find the change in the compound residents. Sleep, food, and showers really did work well. He shimmied his way past other graduates and Reformers headed for the buffet of food. The closer he got the more the smell tormented his stomach and taste buds. His mouth watered, and his stomach rumbled. After filling a tray, he found a vacant seat by circumstance; right place, right time.

The food was amazing, the flavors meaning little as he inhaled the nourishment his body required. Three full trays later, he was feeling sated and able to think straight. He cleaned up, conversing briefly with other recent graduates, and headed out to find Astrid. The imminent apology breaking its way through the post-sleep fog that had dissipated, speeding up his heart rate and forcing sweat out of his forehead. Never one to be nervous or scared of facing anything that squared off with him, but the thought of approaching Astrid shook him to his core.

After a quick shower he put on a clean black uniform outfitted with a red band around the right upper arm, which had been delivered to his room while he was out. Then he went in search of Astrid. He checked her room first, found it made and unused, then the mess hall, and training room, all with no luck, remembering finally the infirmary.

On his way out Benji walked in, his face lit up at the sight of Toro.

"How is Astrid doing?" he asked bluntly.

"Straight to the point, I like that in you. She's in the medic bay recovering. Her concussion and the test really pulled a lot from her. Doctor says she should make a full recovery, though. You're looking sharp. Just remember, with it comes a level of respect and trust."

No concern or remorse shown for Astrid. After all that Benji put her through, Toro thought he should be a little bit more apologetic.

"Why did you force her through the test in the condition she was in?"

At this Benji stopped what he was doing and gave Toro his complete attention, concern etched on his face. Toro could see his confusion.

"Because she needed to go through it. We have already discussed this. You know why."

"No, I don't. I don't understand why she couldn't get a medical pass, or an exception." His arms flailed, trying to help his case.

"Keep in mind, she did phenomenal. She flew through this test, top of the class. Even better than you. Why are you complaining? She wasn't hurt. Her recovery will just take a little longer than normal."

"I'm complaining because she was put in a situation that could've been harmful, and it was avoidable. The risk you take with lives that aren't yours isn't right." His passion was now out in full view, his caring heart on his sleeve.

"Yes, she was, but it's over and she's safe. You're safe. Time to move on." Toro had lost Benji's full attention; he could see his eyes start to wander, his mind already on something else.

"Can I go see her?"

"Yes, you can." Benji didn't watch Toro leave the training room, offered no good-bye or 'good talk,' just moved on to other concerns.

Toro navigated the corridors with ease, his mind turning with their previous conversations. Benji had no concern, no respect for the lives of others. It made him sick, yet here he stood, his life in Benji's hands. While the man gave orders that could determine whether Toro lived or died. The dilemma was not what he wanted. The Reformers were always a best kept secret; everybody knew about them, but nobody discussed them. They hurt the government where it counted the most, and disappeared. Caused havoc only to not exist. A novelty. Everybody wanted to be a part of it, but nobody wanted to commit. Toro now understood why.

Turning the last corner to the infirmary and seeing Astrid sitting up in her bed reading a book put cheer back in his soul. As carefully and quietly as he could, he entered the room, taking a seat, trying not to disturb her tranquility. The escape was on her face; She was clearly someplace else, so he sat watching, not making a sound.

It didn't last long, their quiet interlude of peace—the doctor soon burst through with commotion and disturbance to check on his patient. Upon noticing Toro, he stopped to say his greeting. At this Astrid's head snapped up, her eyes coming back to the present to see what was happening. Seeing Toro, a small smile spread and lit up her face.

"Hi, Astrid," Toro greeted, a little more shyly than intended.

"Toro, how are you?" She put a piece of string in her book, marking her place.

"Good, rested. You?" Toro stood to get closer to her, his hands finding his pockets.

"Getting better. Lots of fluids and tests, but it seems to be working. I feel better. Headaches and pains have almost stopped completely … almost. Doctor wants to test my eyes, and he's upset I won't let him. Saw Seto and Chie. She's doing better, still won't talk about her test."

That smile again; it started his heart up, heating his face.

"Good. I'm glad you're on the mend. I haven't seen them."

They sat in an awkward silence, each waiting for the other to speak. The doctor moved around them, checking blood pressure and her saline drip, asking questions about her eyesight and pain levels. After he left, marking notes on a pad with his head down, they were finally alone.

"I came to apologize and to see how you were doing."

"Apologize? For what?" Astrid's face showed her confusion.

"For the testing, for not seeing what Brax was going to do. For everything that went wrong, for not making it easier on you, for this mess we're in and making you think that you're the cause, which you're not." He blabbered, throwing things out to make sense, not only to himself, but to her as well.

"Nothing that happened was in any way your fault, Toro. If anything, you helped me a lot. I feel I may have been a burden, and for that I should be apologizing. To you and to Seto, and I should be thanking you for helping me! You don't have anything to apologize for, I promise."

Relief flooded through him; he'd been uncertain how this would go. He pressured himself to force her to like him, to accept him, in any way she was willing.

"So, we're good?" she asked. Her fingers flipped through the pages of her book, anxious to get back to the story.

"Absolutely!" he stated, excitement pouring across his face, his smile pulling muscles in his cheeks. "Thank you."

He relaxed, a little more comfortable now. With the tension broken, they were on equal footing, and he wanted the conversation to continue. "You heard about Brax?" he asked.

"Vaguely. Benji always seems to be in a hurry when he talks with me, or he wants something. I do know I'm not excluded from the L.A. mission, which was the important part. When is the hearing?"

"Later today." He watched while she nibbled on her lip and thought, her hands still fidgeting with her book, her hair brushed but slightly messy. He was thrilled she was doing so well, excited she was back on track, and worried that she would be going to L.A. with him. She became a source of distraction for him. He knew he needed to find a way to deal with it and trust that she would be able to take care of herself. She never did seem to be a damsel in distress kind of girl. "When will you be out?"

"As soon as the final test results come back, and if they're clear. I'm ready to be able to train again. I hated it at first, but now I miss it." They laughed.

They talked a bit more, about the book Astrid currently read, the library in which it came from, and the hopes and excitement for the meeting that afternoon—which positions they would be assigned for the mission.

Toro was happy, happier now than ever before. He was doing something about the condition of their world. Helping to make it a better place. He only hoped that the world would feel the same way about his actions.

BENJI and the doctor insisted on careful treatment, rest, and tests. With Astrid's concussion not fully healed, her thought process was still slow, headaches causing pain in her temples and eyes. The blue circle encasing her vision had settled, helping her keep her secret. She reluctantly agreed, thinking a bed was a bed and if she could sleep she would agree to almost anything.

She remembered bits and pieces of Benji updating her on the testing results and Brax, even though she didn't care. She decided on the bus ride back that no matter the outcome she would continue to try and rescue her mom. The Reformers just needed to decide if they were going to help or not. Toro's visit came as no surprise, but his apology did. Regardless, she was glad he was there. If not for him she wouldn't have made the bus to complete the test. She did owe him and would have to find a way to show her appreciation. And here he was, still sitting across from her, in what seemed to be an ancient chair, creating topics to continue talking with her.

It was kind of him, but his constant advances bothered her. He took her rebuttals with grace and acceptance, never giving up, his smile always softening her to his cause. But he created confusion and disturbance to her goals.

"Your mom, do you know where she is?" The topic came out of nowhere, shocking her spine a bit straighter and her eyes open a bit more.

"According to Benji, she is in the experimental institution in Las Vegas." She receded into herself a bit; talking about her mom always made her feel vulnerable. Toro sat silently, listening intently, nodding his head as she explained the situation landing them where they were today. "I only have Benji's word on that though."

"They hope to get her out?" He sat forward, his elbows resting on his knees, a serious expression on his face.

"I'm told they hope to get everybody out. I haven't been given any reassurances that are specific to her." She changed her position, careful not to pull her IV out, playing with the tube instead of her book, giving the brittle pages a break from her nonstop fingers. Now that the conversation moved into a topic that exploited her vulnerability, she was no longer excited. She felt tired and worn out.

They sat in silence for a few minutes, and Toro stood up suddenly. "I'll let you get some rest. Hopefully I'll see you at the meeting this afternoon. If not, I'll swing by and update you … if you'd like?" His hands searched for something to do; they went from rubbing each other to his pockets and back out again.

"Thank you. That would be nice. Hopefully I'll be able to attend."

Toro nodded at her answer, stepping out.

Astrid let out a breath at his absence. After spending so much time constantly surrounded by people, she found the solitude comforting and much needed. Instead of continuing her book, she cuddled down into her bed, closing her eyes, her brain sore from too much activity.

She woke later to the doctor's rambunctious entrance and voices that she didn't recognize. Astrid peeled her eyes open, pulling at the cocooned space created by her blanket to see the disturbance in the room.

The doctor, Benji, and Jackson were all talking in a tight circle around the other bed in the corner. The bed previously empty; with everybody resting for days there was no need for it. Astrid was careful not to move too much to bring notice to her. Instead, she opened her blanket just enough for fresh air and the ability to hear better, letting it fall back over her line of sight.

"I don't know what happened. We were in the middle of his hearing, and I was suggesting things to get him to accept without much trouble when he collapsed." Benji explained the situation to the doctor.

"I knew this would get out of hand! I told you to be careful with it." Jackson this time, worry in his voice.

"How old is this kid? Have you done this before to him?"

"During the debrief, to keep him from creating a scene. He's of age."

"He doesn't look it. I thought you screened all the trainees?" the doctor remarked, getting brave.

A slight chill caressed Astrid's body, forcing her to continue listening or announce her presence. She chose to listen, silencing her inner fears.

"We did." Jackson this time, trying to talk the doctor down. "And he told us he was nineteen."

"Maybe, but I'm thinking more like sixteen. His heart rate and breathing are good. I'll keep an eye on him and see if he comes out of it. Do some tests on his brain, see what kind of damage you've caused." There were footsteps.

"What?" Benji exclaimed, his voice breathy.

"Has this ever happened before?" Jackson asked him, followed by some shuffling around.

"No. The only person I've ever met that can resist it was her, but he didn't resist, he collapsed. No push back or anything. His conscious was there, then …" A pause. "Nothing." He let out a large breath of air, frustration clear.

There was no answer from Jackson; instead more footsteps, the room going quiet again. Astrid counted to ninety before moving the blanket.

Brax, his skin gray, his body skinny and underweight, lay in an uncomfortable position in the bed, having been placed that way by somebody else. She could hear his breathing, steady, loud. In. Out. In. Out. The rhythmic sound causing Astrid's own breath to catch and speed up. She played the conversation she heard over and over in her head. As she was the only 'her' in the room she must be the only one who could resist Benji's 'suggestion,' whatever that seemed to be.

Benji could harm someone just by having a conversation?

The doctor came bustling back in with tools on a tray and a whistle on his lips. He spotted Astrid's open eyes and caught himself.

"Oh, you're awake! I hope we didn't make too much noise. New patient. Always exciting for me!" He was always so bubbly, his eyes bright with knowledge and excitement.

"No, it's fine. What happened?" she asked, sitting up so he could take her blood pressure and listen to her heart.

"Not sure. He passed out during a meeting, so I'm going to run some tests. But while you were sleeping yours came back. You're clear and good to go. Heart sounds good, your eyes are clear, you're all healed."

Astrid had enjoyed her seclusion and lack of visitors but was happy to be able to move around and be included again. To continue her training.

She thanked the doctor, grabbed all her belongings, and headed to her room. She was in desperate need of a shower, and fully planned to talk with Benji about Ben.

THE meeting started like all the rest he attended—updates on the compound, congratulations to the new inductees. Any changes in command or promotions announced, and then Benji turned to the maps and plans tacked to the wall behind the table. Jackson and Red acted as his lackeys, using a stick to point to the portion of plan or map Benji currently talked about.

Benji described L.A. as a spider web full of traps and death, mentioned numerous times that the government would expect them to return to finish what they started, that the soldiers of the Reformers needed to be at their best if they were to succeed.

"No mistakes! None of us can afford it. Our lives aren't at stake; this isn't fighting for freedom; this isn't a war for our country; this is a fight for our humanity. If we win this, we continue for our freedom and rights. They're already there. We just have to get them back." He stood, passion and conviction in every word he spoke, every lift of an eyebrow, every movement. The energy in the room built on every word, every thrust of his fist in the air. Benji continued this way for a while, explaining why they were in this situation, whose fault it was, thought it was of no consequence; they needed to find a way out regardless.

"It is not our place nor job to point fingers. We're born into this war. I don't want my children to finish the fight. I don't want my grandchildren to know the fight. *We* will finish this."

An uproar of approval followed. Everybody hoisted themselves to their feet, and thrusting fists filled the air as they yelled and hollered. Toro stood and clapped; he did not holler or yell in agreement with Benji. He wasn't sure he agreed.

The room calmed, the energy striking the air, waiting to be activated again. Toro caught Astrid's arrival. She stood near the entrance on the wall with other latecomers. He waved, motioning for her to join him. He smiled, receiving her smile in acceptance as she made her way to him, nudging others to the side.

"Thank you. I fell asleep and missed the start. Anything interesting?" she asked, sitting next to him, her thigh and hip brushing against his. His heart rate sped up, his palms sweaty. He explained in a soft whisper what she missed. She nodded her understanding, both turning their attention back to the front of the room.

Jackson pointed the stick to a blueprint of the Institute. Toro recalled it immediately. Their goal: empty the place of patients while others strategically placed bombs throughout the foundation and storage floors below ground, all timed to go off at intervals. Then the plans got interesting.

"We have an advantage they're not expecting, which will get us in. We have a guard and a previous patient in our employ." This statement caught both Toro and Astrid's immediate attention. They sat up straighter, attention fully on Benji. Astrid took a deep breath, her face flushed.

"I didn't think he'd actually do it," she revealed, more to herself than to anybody who was listening. Confused, Toro's full intention was to ask her what exactly Benji planned, but he didn't have too. Benji answered the question for her.

"Astrid, who can stumble onto their property being accepted as a lost patient returning to the only home she's known, and Toro." His eyes caught Toro's, forcing acceptance to a plan he knew nothing of. "A prisoner of war, who escaped our facilities with a patient."

"Wait!" Toro propelled himself to his feet, his emotions taking control before his mind could make sense of the information. "You plan to use her as *bait*?"

Benji did not respond immediately; instead, he stared straight at Astrid.

"Toro, sit down," she demanded, her hands on the table, her big eyes begging him to do what she asked. He caught himself, his gaze bouncing between Astrid and Benji. He didn't argue. He sat.

"Astrid ..." he began, but her sorrow-filled face stopped him. His hand finished its course and found hers.

"It's okay. I want to help. I think this is the best way. I'll be fine. Even if they try to re-assimilate me, it won't work. It's the best use for me. I want to do this." She wasn't convincing him; he shook his head as she explained. Learning this had been the plan since the inception made his reluctance to accept it even stronger.

"You done?" Benji asked, clearly wanting to get back to his presentation. The whole of the room stared in their direction, some struggling to hear the private conversation.

"If she's bait, what am I?" Toro asked, squeezing her hand, feeling her strength in return.

"You're the mole. You forge the way for the rest of us," Benji continued, not caring or wanting to know if Toro accepted it or not.

248

They went over floorplans, security measures, escape routes, and bomb placements. Assignments followed as platoons were formed, each assigned a captain and lieutenant. A few questions asked and answers given. After dismissal, plans for another meeting for the next day would consist of weapon check out, transportation assignment, and times.

Toro didn't get up, and neither did Astrid. They waited until the room emptied, the chairs and tables left in place. Red, Jackson, and Benji stayed at the front discussing further plans and details. Seto and Chie obviously wanted to hang around to hear, to know but were pushed out with the rest of the soldiers leaving the room.

"Toro, don't be upset. This is what you wanted. You wanted to be a part of the mission, this revolution."

"This is not a revolution! This is a madman's plan to take over the world. Astrid, don't you see it? You went from being used by the government to be used by the Reformers."

"Maybe. But here I have a choice, even if it's a small one, and here I'm making a difference. I was told once to make a choice, even if it's the wrong one. I've made my choice. Sounds like maybe you need to make yours." She was gone.

Toro sat alone in the training room with only his raging thoughts to keep him grounded. He didn't agree with Benji's plan. To destroy the institutes meant taking on the government one-on-one. No room for error, no room for a plea deal if something went wrong. They either succeeded, or died.

"Don't forget the bigger picture here," Red insisted, startling Toro.

"For a guy who doesn't talk much, you sure seem to talk much," he said as Red joined him, making himself comfortable with a smile and a nod of his head. "Tell me, what exactly is the big picture?"

"To be able to live our lives the way we want to. To create and contribute to society, to make it better every day. There have been sacrifices throughout history for freedom, lives upon lives ended, and for what? For the president to tell us the sacrifice wasn't enough, for our humanity to be taken, to be turned on one another for survival, for rights we should've already owned. Don't waste this opportunity to be a part of history. We can write it however we want to."

Toro shook his head, the back of his neck hot. He'd lost sight of what was at stake. He would never admit it, but he felt the only reason he was still there was for Astrid and his family. He didn't mind helping, to be a part of something that would change the world for not just himself, but everybody he knew. He could free his family. Toro always just wanted to live, to love. To stay in his own little world, without everybody else telling him how to run it.

CHAPTER 20
ACCEPTANCE

ASTRID was more than ready for anything that came her way. Ready to go back to the Institute, ready to face the doctor, to find Ben, and more than ready to find her mom. Confident that Toro would come around; the plan wouldn't work right without him. They would have to re-plan, come up with another strategy. Try again. Astrid didn't have time to try again; her mother didn't have time.

After leaving Toro in the training room, she searched for another book to pass her time. Orders were given to keep their conditioning light, their fitness intact, ready. A book would help fill the void the lack of training would leave. The room she dubbed the 'library' was her new favorite place. Turning the last corner she came upon Jackson lying in wait outside the library door.

"We only have three weeks until we're supposed to be in Vegas. You think your mom can hang on?"

"Does she have a choice?" The thought plagued Astrid, ever at the forefront of her mind.

"You don't look at all like you've been a prisoner of war these past few months. You're toned, in good condition, muscled, well fed. We must change that. Your calorie intake needs to drop drastically, and … we need to beat you up a bit."

"Beat me up?" Not only were they going to use her as bait, she needed to be feeble and gaunt as well?

"Grab some books. You're headed to the cells."

"Seriously?" She didn't argue; she'd already agreed. Even though she didn't know all the details and plans. She continued past him through the rickety door into the dark storage room serving as the library. She grabbed ten books, handing five more to Jackson, nodding her head for him to lead the way. "Do I get to say good-bye?"

"No, less emotion this way. They'll understand."

They patrolled a while, toward the north-eastern end of the compound. The rooms less kept, not taken care of. Some not even fully carved out of the dirt, the small marks of shovels left behind, the job unfinished.

"I'm assuming my limited number of calories will be delivered to me?"

"Of course, but no showers. You'll get a bucket and some interrogations. Big Jack volunteered."

"Great, the one person in this place I don't want interrogating me."

"Which is why he volunteered."

"Dehydrated, malnourished, dirt, blood and bruises. Should do the trick, huh?"

"Sorry, Astrid. If it helps, I don't agree with it."

"It doesn't."

They reached the end of the dirt hallway. The small light available illuminated twelve small jail cells, six on each side—she counted, turning around slowly and gathering her surroundings. Having not fully paid attention, she was unsure of her exact location. She wasn't scared, a little out of sorts, but not scared. "These might last me the entire time. Can you make sure I have light to read by?"

"I'll rig something up. The only lights we have down here are in the hallway. You'll have to stay close to the bars to get light until I get it done." Jackson pulled out a set of keys, opening the last door on the left, motioning for her to make herself at home. She placed her books on the ground in a neat stack, biggest to smallest, just inside the cell door, Jackson held out his stack for her. "Try to stay warm."

She listened to his footsteps recede, the lonely swinging light bulb outside her door her only source of light and life. No noise, no fellow voices or conversations around her. Laughter, the sweet sound of laughter that she now so desperately missed, gone.

Astrid decided, instead of wallowing in her situation, she'd take advantage of the silence. She re-stacked her books, this time in alphabetical order, sat in the corner away from the door, and cracked open *Affirmation* by John Cooley. The crackle of electricity pouring from the bulb above her was her only way of knowing time continued without her.

Four books, six naps, and only three bowls of watered down soup with bread and a glass of water later, Astrid was officially bored out of her mind. There had been no sign of Big Jack. Her food appeared while she slept, and she still had no sound to keep her company besides her own breathing and the sound of her fingers turning the crackling pages of the books.

"Well, what to do, what to do? I could use some more lights, Jackson!" she bellowed loudly, her head bent back, fists gripping the bars in front of her. Her cell was a square room made of dirt, carved out of the earth with a door slapped on. No cot, just the promised bucket and her books. With only one meal a day, her stomach ate at itself, and she dropped weight and muscle faster than she anticipated.

Her mind played tricks on her, but she could still determine what was real and what was not. Talking to herself was necessary; it helped her mind stay calm and clear. The books worked enough to help her escape, no matter how uncomfortable and hungry she became.

She missed Ben, and her mother. She thought of them often, sometimes having to go back to reread what she just read because her mind refused to grasp the words on the pages. Toro, Seto, and Chie often pushed their way into her dreams and thoughts. She wondered how they fared, if they still trained, or if they had received orders for the mission.

Footsteps. Footsteps. Astrid had completely lost track of time. Four ... no, five books she'd devoured. So, five days? No, six maybe. She didn't know! No way to tell. *Footsteps!* Louder and louder with each echo. Right outside the cell door, a shadow appeared: tall, another human. Her heart thundered excitedly. She tried lifting her arm in greeting, croaking out a hello, anything. She tried, and tried again. Her tongue and throat were dry, unused.

"How long?" she finally managed to croak out. She must know, needing to orient herself, since she'd lost track after the food and water ceased to appear. No answer. "Please, I need to know. Please."

A jingle as the door swung open. She poured out after it, landing in the hallway, her body weak and tired. Strong arms picked her up and heaved her over a shoulder, the strong muscles pushing into her abdomen, her head and arms swinging free. Back and forth with the rhythm of the walking, the only noise the strong footsteps, boots hitting the ground in an uneven pattern. The moving walls made her head spin. The blood poured in, filling her eyes and ears, nose plugging up. Her head heavy, a pounding pain between her eyes on her forehead making her vision blurry.

She was slammed into a hard metal chair, rather hard. Her butt throbbed from the sudden impact, her bones ringing with the residual pain coursing through her. Her head logged forward, swinging on its axis, her hair falling forward and shielding her face. Her arms were ripped back suddenly, straining her shoulders, and her wrists were bound to the chair, forcing her to stay. Hands on her ankles determined the same fate.

The first blow wasn't so bad—if anything, it helped clear her thoughts, forcing her participation. At about the sixth one she screamed, blood pouring from her eyebrows and lips, swollen tissues bruising with every second that passed.

THE newest patient settled into the schedule, now used to the hissing noise in unison to the change in her cubicle. The bed retreating, the table and chairs appearing. It was comforting, knowing what would come next. She knew the schedule, knew what was going to appear for each meal. Each day she woke up with a clean slate, no alarms, no memories, and no return visits from the man who called himself the general.

With only the different foods appearing, her only way to tell time, it became easy to forget, easy to get lost. She moved mechanically through her tasks and days, relieved when her bed appeared at the end, letting her mind slow down in blissful sleep.

The dream appeared as any other dream—first realization that it was different, a dream, not real.

Horror and terror. Melvina found herself in a tube: full of liquid, thicker than water. Her eyes shot open, and her hands reached out to feel the glass tube encasing her. Suspended in the middle, she floated with tubes and needles entering her body; a face mask covered her nose and mouth while a tube snaked down her throat, a machine doing her breathing for her.

A face appeared, and a knuckle knocked on the other side of her tube, the sound amplifying, pushing the fluid around. Melvina moved forward as best as the tubes would allow. It was not anybody she knew, or so she thought. He spoke to her. She cocked her head in confusion, trying to let the man know she couldn't understand or really hear him. He nodded his head, got closer to her tube, speaking louder.

"It's time," he vowed.

Time? Time for what? Her pulse picked up. His voice, the movements outside her tube—they concerned her. What did they plan to do? What was it time for? Stepping away, his form shifted, blurry and small.

A gurgling sound followed his departure, and fluid whirled around her. Draining, leaving her. Her cocoon of safety and warmth abandoned her to the cold glass and rubber tubes. With the loss of fluid, her body lost its weightlessness. Toes and feet contacted the bottom drain, the metal hard, uninviting. Her hands splayed out on either side of her, helping her to stand, watching with horror as the last of the warm purple fluid left her behind. Her world tilting, she lost her footing, smashing into a side of the glass tube as the outside world went on its side.

Her shoulder throbbed from the contact, the glass having no give or comfort. It spun, not slowly, but fast enough to throw her around, wrapping the tubes and wires around her body, pinning her arms and hands to her side. Her face smashed against the bottom of the tube as it finally stopped. Her head still spun, the pain of her body and muscles waking up with pins and needles. Hands covered in rubber gloves reached in, manhandling her, pulling her out, letting her head drop without support. The strain on her neck noticeable. The cold air smacking into her with hurricane force, causing her body to convulse and shake.

The hands laid her down on a soft surface that gave way beneath her weight. She felt pulling and ripping at the wires and tubes attached to her body, and the mask was pulled off as a tube previously occupying her throat was forced up and out, letting in pure, clean, medical air. Her body jerked, and she coughed as her lungs let go of fluid, her throat in searing pain from the absence of her breathing and feeding tubes.

"Easy. Try long, deep breaths," a voice cooed at her. Soft hands rubbed her back in clockwise circles. Melvina took the voice's advice, forcing her breathing to slow, the coughing stopping as she sucked in a lungful of air. "There you go."

Now that she was calm, they covered her with warm, heavy blankets. Her eyes darted, trying to see, trying to make sense of the shapes and colors surrounding her. Hands lifted her head, covering her eyes with a strap wrapped around her head. Her hands shot up to feel, to experience.

"Leave it. Your eyes need time to adjust, and this will help." She felt hands around her wrists, forcing her arms back down by her side. "We need to give you something to help you sleep. We have to run some tests. This will make it easier for you." A warm sensation ran up her arm, and by the time it reached her chest she was sound asleep.

Melvina now found herself sitting up in a bed, blankets covering her legs. An IV in her left arm. Her understanding grew day by day. The doctors told her she was one of a kind, her brain specifically designed to accept new downloads; instead of learning how to speak they just gave her the right program.

"Different programs for different motor skills—eating, speaking, walking even. So far, you're up to speed with your projected age. You can do everything anybody else your age can do. We only need to give you the history of the land, and your job skills. How do you feel?"

The doctor was thorough at explaining everything to her. Since being pulled from the glass tube she hadn't experienced fright or confusion. She did everything they told her, anxious to see and learn.

"My head hurts after each download. It dissipates after a while."

"Okay, anything else?" He typed notes into his digital pad, his face serious and firm.

"No. I do my exercises every day." The last bit she added enthusiastically, trying hard to impress him.

"Good, your muscle tone is excellent. You're eating well. We did receive your final orders, memory bank, and job title this morning. As soon as it's formatted we'll get started on that. We'll try to space it out so the pain isn't so overbearing. Try to rest, you're almost done." The doctor left her room, granting a serene peace. She never found herself alone and rested; usually it was alone and exhausted, fighting a headache.

She enjoyed it while it lasted, knowing it wouldn't be long before they returned, hooking her up to machines, making her head hurt. She lay with her eyes closed, enjoying the silence when a squeak of the cart alerted her to the presence of the doctor, his nurses, and that dreadful machine.

"So soon?" she questioned.

"Yes, your timeline has been adjusted. The general wants you out by tomorrow morning and working. Your name will be Melvina Heizer, and you'll be a doctor!" He was excited, but why? Would she be like him? She supposed she liked him, but would she like what he did? She held her reluctance back, showing him a smile. "We're going to start with your memory bank as it's less abrasive, give you a short break, and do your job training. Sound good?"

She nodded. The rubber suction cups applied, and a small needle—placed into her head just below her left ear behind her lobe—slid like magic into its receiving port. The click sounded, reverberating through her eardrum louder than those before. An oxygen mask was applied next, the heart monitor beeping steadily next to her. Having done this numerous times, she was not nervous; her heart rate was steady, right where it needed to be.

She lay back, getting comfortable, closing her eyes. The memories came in a flood. Shapes and colors rolling over her mind's eye too fast for her to grasp who she was becoming. One image constant—a boy, her boy. She watched as *she gave birth. He grew taller. He was gorgeous, and he was hers. The love cracked her heart open, tears bursting forth past her closed lids. She was a mother.*

She shot up. Her breath caught in her chest. She was back in her cubicle, an alarm in full swing, the walls and floor beeping red with the sound. She remembered what she was.

TORO watched, gagged, as Big Jack punched Astrid. When she passed out—her head flinging toward one side, the pain shutting her brain down—he relaxed a bit, stopping the fight against his bonds. They had come for him in the middle of the night. No explanation, no time to adjust. He spent weeks in dirt and darkness, a beating guaranteed every day, and only water for nourishment. He was weak, confused, and thoroughly outraged.

Big Jack turned toward Toro, wiping his fists off with a rag. He reached forward and not so gently ripped the gag from his mouth.

"What kind of man hits a girl?" Toro spat at him, his lips on fire.

"Just following orders. I'm not enjoying this! She has to look like she's a prisoner."

"I'm the prisoner. She was a patient."

"Man, again, just doing what I'm told. How's ya eye doing?" Reaching forward, Jack grabbed Toro by the chin, tilting his head back, prying at an old wound on his right eye. It had busted open a couple days' prior during one of their daily meetings.

"Why didn't they tell me the plan?"

"Don't know."

"Why didn't Benji tell me Astrid agreed to go through this?"

"Probably because of what ya would have done. He's not a stupid man, the boss." He let go, backing up.

"Another beating today?" His breath came hard through his nose as he tried to prep his face and torso for the oncoming onslaught.

"No, just hers, then ya leave us. Ya get to break out and take her with you."

"What? That doesn't fit the timeline. None of this fits. The attack should've already happened."

"No, you're right." Benji's voice let his presence be known somewhere behind Toro. He tried adjusting to see him, the bonds cutting into his wrist and ankles stopping him from twisting too far. Benji paraded around him. "We didn't tell you everything, because you have to have some sense of confusion. If they don't accept you as we think they will, you cannot have our plans to give them. When they start torturing you, you'll wish for Big Jack again."

"I have the plans. I was in the meeting looking at the blueprints for bomb placements and exit strategies," Toro pointed out.

"You have a plan, not exactly the plans," Benji countered.

"I still don't understand Astrid having to be hurt. Shouldn't you have been taking care of her? She was a patient, not an employee." He struggled with his anger, wanting to lunge at Benji and pummel him into the ground.

"She joined your way of thinking, wanting to go back, fought against our help." He spoke as if the events had truly happened. "When they ask, you exercised every day within your cell, to keep your shape and strength to fight and escape. When we found out what you were doing we withheld your food. Shortly after that appeared an opportunity to escape, and you, of course, took her with you."

Big Jack stepped behind Toro, taking his knife and releasing him from the bonds to the chair. The relief was instantaneous, the burn in his shoulders and hips releasing as he stretched and stood.

"Get me out of here."

"You have your instructions from Jackson? You're not happy? Good. Take that with you," Benji proposed, pointing at Astrid. He simply left. Toro took a step, going after him, his anger taking root and finding a target. Big Jack stepped in, placing his hand on Toro's bicep, pulling him back and forcing a halt.

"Don't do it. Get ya girl and leave. Just leave." Big Jack shook Toro a few times to get him to take a breath and clear his rage-filled head. Toro stopped—his breathing heavy, his fists tight at his sides—

sending a putrid glance at Big Jack, finally heading to free Astrid, who lay unconscious.

Astrid didn't weigh much. Her skin was ashen and sunken in, bones sticking out from lack of food. He lightly touched her face, whispering her name. Big Jack moved behind the chair, cutting her bindings. She didn't move. Blood and bodily fluids seeped from her face, her eyes, cheeks, nose, and mouth. Her whole face was so swollen he hardly recognized her. Under the conditions he was in, Toro struggled to carry her. But after two tentative steps, he found his strength and balance.

Big Jack led him up through back corridors and steps until they reached ground level. The stars were bright, the air cool. He hung a canteen full of water on Toro's shoulder and pointed in the direction he should head, shutting the door.

Toro repositioned Astrid's head so it would rest on his shoulder instead of lolling over his elbow and started walking.

He wasn't sure how long he had been on his feet. Well away from the Reformer's compound by now, along the highway, headed north. He didn't think he should have to travel far; the Institute should be watching, keeping an eye out for movement. They would come.

His arms burned, his legs seconds from giving way beneath him. But he held fast; he trudged on. *For Astrid, for her mom*, he told himself. For his own family.

Needing a rest, he found the nearest tree, laying Astrid down, sitting beside her, and placing her head in his lap. Moving her hair smoothly out of her face, he tucked it behind an ear. His skin briefly contacted her cheek, leaving marks of blood on his knuckles and fingers. He took note of her breathing, which was even, making sure she was comfortable. He tried pouring water onto her lips, and her tongue darted out to taste, to moisten her mouth.

"Astrid, we're out, we're on our way back," he confessed, unsure if she could hear him or not. She stirred, moved around, moaning with each movement. He could see the pain in the grimace on her face. Her movement slow, calculating which motions caused pain, and adjusting to accommodate.

After she made it into a sitting position, Toro gingerly handed her the canteen. She took a couple gulps and handed it back. Ripping a part of his shirt off, Toro wet it, helping her clean her face.

"Ouch! Dang, he has a mean hook," she managed. Her left cheekbone was bruised, the skin puffy and purple. Her left eye swollen shut, a cut in her eyebrow.

"He held back, just needed it to look like he taught you a lesson."

"Did it work?" she asked, gazing up at him with her good eye and a sly smile.

"Yes. How long did they imprison you?"

"I don't know, long enough to make me weak." She finally scanned Toro; he saw her eyes go over the cuts and bruises, all in different stages of healing. "They took you, too."

"Yes, in the middle of the night. I didn't know what was going on until they tied me to a chair, took my blindfold off, and made me watch as Big Jack beat you."

"They didn't tell you?" Her good eye went wide, her mouth open in shock.

"What, they told you?" He didn't mean to be judgmental—he was jealous and hurt that she knew what was happening to her, what the outcome would be. That there would be an end, and he had not.

"Yes, I walked to my cell, on my own accord. Jackson led me."

"Seriously!" Toro bolted up, pacing in front of Astrid, cursing under his breath. "I was in. I would have done anything! He could have told me! He cou—"

"It needed to be real. You had to have real anger about the situation."

"Oh, I have anger all right." Still he paced, trying to calm his breathing and heart rate. After a while he glanced over and saw Astrid curled up sleeping at the base of the tree. Why didn't this bother her? She should be just as mad! He took another deep breath. After all, there was nothing he could do about it now, and he could use the rest. Even though he didn't plan on sleeping, he knew some rest would help, so he joined her. He lay next to her, curled up with her frame pulled against his. Her heat thawing his anger, letting it seep into the ground below.

Toro's anxiety level was high, his protection instincts on alert; he wanted to protect her. But he knew what he would do next would just put her in danger, and possibly cause her to go back to hating him.

CHAPTER 21

RELUCTANCE

I'M not real?" she confirmed with the general. It wasn't long after the alarm went off when two security guards showed up to escort her to his office. He had expected her. She shot off her first question as memories buzzed through her head. The smell of the nape of Ben's neck fresh out of a bath. The feel of his hair, his tiny hands. It was too much, all of it too much. A thought plagued her, toying with her essence of who she was: Is my boy real?

"Yes, you're real. You're standing here before me, having a lucid conversation. You're able to feel, yes? You can deduct reasoning, yes? You're real. You're just programmable."

She nodded along, answering his questions and trying to follow his reasoning to her situation, her being.

"Programmable? You can turn me into anybody, anything?"

"Yes. You were our first success. You were the first integration. And you handled it flawlessly. You were perfect … that is, until you got kidnapped."

"I didn't mean to get kidnapped." She cocked her head as the memory played for her.

"Maybe not, but you let them take Ben? We underestimated how strong the mother-son bond could be. You felt that he would be better off with the Reformers than with you. Is that correct?"

She thought about it, replaying the scene in her head, feeling the relief again after seeing him step over the rubble and into freedom. Reliving it all over again, the hurt and pain of maybe not ever seeing him again. Another release, when she knew she would. When she knew for certain she would see him again.

"Freedom. He would have freedom." A tear escaped, and she quickly wiped it off.

"Freedom is just a word. Freedom is not real. It's an illusion that never existed. Is he *free*, Melvina?" His emphasis on this word shocked her. Were they not all free? If not, what was it they worked for? What was it they sacrificed for if not for freedom?

"No," she answered, her meek voice soft.

"No. You brought him right back to us, why?" This one she thought about intensely. The general patient, he sat unmoving, his eyes never leaving her. They traveled her full length, studying every inch of her. "What happened, Melvina?"

"I escaped. I felt more betrayed there, than here. I thought I would be welcomed back, protected. Safe again. Ben is ... wa—" She took a breath, unsure how to classify him. "He needed me. I needed to rescue him."

"Were they hurting hi—"

She cut him off. "He belongs to me! He is my son!" She didn't mean to say it so loudly, but as the memories grew inside of her, she knew who he was. He was hers. She was his. They belonged to one another, a bond that could not be taken away, reprogrammed, or erased.

"He belongs to me," the general corrected, his eyes sinister and firm. His face contorted with anger. "I own him. I put the work into him. Letting you borrow him to fulfill your roll, I blessed you with him. Do not ever forget that."

"Sir," she sniffled, her eyes filling to the brim with tears. Anger and frustration toiled inside of her, wanting to break free.

They sat in silence for an eternity, neither one wanting to reveal anything. Melvina's head swirling with false truths and hidden lies. She thought her life fulfilling and happy. Needed by others, she helped, was an important citizen ... or so she thought.

"How—" She stopped, not sure if she wanted the logistics of how she came to be, if she needed to know. Instead she asked, "What happens now?"

The general didn't answer right away; he watched. She could feel his eyes, examining her, trying to decide if she was worth the information. "Now, you return to your cubicle. You have more downloads and resets that must take place, more blood tests. Do you know where they took you?"

The question caught her off guard, her loyalties shifting again. Her morals in question. If she gave up the Reformers' compound, she proved she was nothing but a pawn. A robotic, engineered clone made specifically to do somebody else's bidding. If not, she stood apart. She earned meaning again, a purpose.

"South, I think. I was drugged, woke up later already there, in a room."

"Your morals are starting to show. You're lying. We extracted all your memories and have been poring over them since you got back."

Goosebumps flooded her skin, and the hairs on the back of her neck stood erect. He knew.

"If you knew, why did you ask?" She should not have spoken out, her respect lacking. She gingerly added a 'sir' just to get him to answer.

"To confirm a suspicion."

She lost his attention. He dismissed her with a wave of his hand as he tapped on his tablet, swinging his chair to the side, expressing more disdain as she exited his office.

Melvina was met by two security guards, different than the ones who escorted her there. They flanked her, marching to a different beat, their long legs forcing her to career faster in order keep them from reaching back and jerking her forward. Returning her to her cubicle, where she immediately fell onto her bed with shock and emptiness.

She regained consciousness later, having no sense of time, not realizing she'd fallen asleep. She didn't know how long she slept—her face and eyes felt swollen and sore, the sleeve of her uniform and pillow soaked with sorrow. Her mouth and throat in need of moisture, to cure the painful dryness. She sat, rubbing at her eyes and face. The instant she stood, stretching her legs and back, the bed hissed, disappearing. Water appeared; no table or chairs, just a hard-plastic cup with crystal clear, thirst-quenching water. Melvina lunged for it, wanting to get it in her hands before it was taken from her. But the drink was not enough.

She smacked her lips, her tongue darting out to make sure she absorbed every drop. She sat the cup back down, willing it to refill, but instead it also vanished. Nothing else appeared—no more water, no food, not even a pair of clean clothes for her to change into. She sat on the floor in the middle of her barren cubicle, forcing herself not to cry.

When they came for her she was ready. In full acceptance of what happened, who she was, and what was to be. She followed them, through the aisles of empty cubicles, open and wanting. Up the stairs and past offices. Soon she sat in the chair again, being strapped down, the machine rolling in, forcing her heart rate up. The connecting click signaled a new dawn, sending something ominous pouring through her.

TORO and Astrid opened their eyes to a blood red sunrise, clouds dissipating to make way for a warm, clear day. Their backs stiff and sore from sleeping on the ground after the ordeals already finished. Their joints cracking with each movement, busting away stiffness and pain. Toro stood first, stretching, placing his hand out to help Astrid. He pulled gently, making sure she was strong on her feet before forcing himself to let her go.

There was no need for words; they each knew what they were doing and why. They headed off, stepping at a slower than normal pace on the side of the highway. The pavement heated as the sun crawled higher in the sky. A brisk, warm wind came from the north, cooling the sweat beads already appearing on their temples and necks.

"We need to find fresh water," Astrid stated. "And some food."

"We won't need to. They're going to find us way before we need water and food."

"Ho—" Again, she didn't need to finish. Helicopter blades cut through the warm summer air, answering her unasked question. They had been found.

Toro instantly grabbed Astrid's wrists, pulling a zip tie out of his pocket, securing her arms behind her.

"Toro?" she screamed at him, trying without success to fight against his strength.

"Has to look real," he replied.

Stepping away from her into the middle of the road, he waved his hands and arms like a lunatic. He watched the helicopter bank a sharp turn, heading their way. He stopped waving, stepping back to Astrid with his gaze low. She glared at him, anger shooting out, willing him to drop dead. He refused.

"I'm not going to run," she clarified to him, fighting against her bond.

"No, but you didn't want to leave. I forced you."

"Where are you getting this from? We have a plan, and this is not it. I was supposed to want to come back. I was supposed to believe you. What is wrong with you?" Her voice climbed as the noise from the engine and blades got closer, the wind forcing her hair about in every direction, her clothes being pinned to her body. Her stance altered to keep her balance against the onslaught. The helicopter set down in the middle of the highway, and security guards armed with weapons dressed in white poured out, yelling instructions and asking questions.

"Toro Crow. I work for the Institute. I was kidnapped after the break-in." Toro spoke loud and firm. The guard lowered his weapon, gestured to Astrid, silently asking about her presence. "She was a patient. An opportunity appeared to take her with me, so I did."

"You escaped from the Reformers?" one of the guards asked, disbelief on his face.

"Yes. It wasn't easy." Toro pointed to his face, emphasizing the dried blood and scars.

"Okay, we'll have to radio this in. Is she secure?"

"Yeah."

"Load up," someone called from closer to their ride.

Toro reached back, grabbing Astrid by the arm and propelling her forward. Needing to be forceful, even against his own will. His treatment of Astrid would prove his allegiance. He shoved her head down, keeping his own low, and half jogged in closer, pushing Astrid head first into the waiting hull of the helicopter. Her body hit hard, her shoulders and hips taking the brunt of the hit, forcing out a "humph."

She shot daggers from her eyes, scooting closer in and away from him. One of the guards picked her up, her weight nothing to him, and set her down in a seat before strapping her in. They lifted off, someone handing him a headset so their conversation could continue.

Listening to the banter of the crew, Toro could tell they were comrades, together for a long time. The bond of brotherhood apparent in their inside jokes and laughter. Excitement flooding their words and harsh expressions at finally finding people outside of the designated zone. Toro laughed along with them, agreeing and being friendly, ignoring Astrid, wanting to keep his attention free of the hateful gaze he knew she was giving freely and with force. He could feel it on him, the sting of betrayal prickling his neck and face.

He knew he'd deviated from the plan. He would get his chance to explain things. For now, she would survive. He would ask for forgiveness later; he hoped she would grant it.

When they landed they were greeted on the side of the heli-pad by Matthew Benson—his nose high in the air, his arms behind him, puffing out his chest with importance. He wore a navy blue plaid suit accompanied by a yellow shirt and a striped tie, his fashion sense combating with his important position.

"Welcome back! We thought for sure you were lost to us!" His excitement at Toro's return caught Toro off guard. He wanted to be accepted back in, but not before a thorough debriefing session.

"Thank you, sir," he replied, first saluting then presenting Astrid. "I was able to grab a former patient of ours on my way out. She resisted a bit." He gestured to her beaten, bruised, and bloody face. Her eyes wide full of shock and hatred. She played her part well.

"Wonderful. She has interesting eyes, huh? Let's get her to the infirmary. They can clean her up and take care of her. You should take a shower and get some food, and I'll set up a debriefing session. You'll have to tell us everything. Until such time, you don't have any clearance, understood?"

"Yes, sir."

They moved forward, loading on an elevator, descending into the building. The first stop was Toro's exit; he stepped off, nodding at Matthew before heading down the hallway. The elevator doors closed behind him, taking Astrid with it.

Toro found his room as he'd left it. All employees had on-site quarters as sometimes the hours and schedules required them to stay. The comfort was minimal, the goal having been the necessities only. He stripped, showering before suiting up in a familiar white garb, loose and unencumbering. He headed to find food and water, his body now screaming at him for the misuse and neglect.

The building identical as before—the hole in the side had been patched, suggesting it never happened. The cubicles were replaced with new hardware and more secure walls. The blood, dust, and debris swept away. He could see only a quarter of the cubicles were occupied; the rest stood empty. A result from the break-in. More patients would soon arrive; the place never stayed empty for long.

"Feeling better?" Benson came up beside him, his gaze going over the railing at the floor below them.

"Much. Glad to be back."

"Good. If you'll follow me we should get the formalities out of the way."

He turned and Toro followed, having nodded in agreement. Not having to go far, Matthew pushed open doors to a conference room. The long oak table surrounded was by comfy chairs, a beverage center on one of the far walls. Windows opened to the rooftop of the floor below them, letting in natural light Toro desperately missed. He took the seat Matthew gestured at, getting comfortable.

"We reviewed the tapes, so we know what happened up until you were punched and loaded. What we don't know is what happened after that." Benson leaned forward and put a recording device in front of Toro, waiting for him to share his adventure.

He weaved his fabricated tale, adding profanities and made up details to make it more realistic, to prove his loyalties never shifted. He told the tale of a war prisoner, someone thrown into a cell and forgotten, beaten for daily sport. He made the Reformers out to be crazed animals—each fighting daily for the top position, alliances changing hourly, plans taking months if not years to agree upon and fulfill. He painted them as the government saw them. He proved their theory; he witnessed firsthand what they suspected. He gave them a reason to believe every word he divulged.

"The leader, the one who orchestrated the attack, who was he?" Benson prompted.

"Benji, Melvina's late husband. That was his idea, his plan."

Benson's eyes widened as he stood, pushing his chair into the wall behind him with too much force. The clattering rang off the walls, forcing Toro to jump as it intruded his ears.

"You did well, Crow. The general will hear your report. Until then, rest, build your strength back up. We'll get you back into rotations soon enough, after we get clearance of course." He snatched up the recording device, leaving in a hurry.

HE *knew the plan! I was supposed to be trying to get away from the Reformers, to go with him willingly. Why did he have to do this?* Astrid's limbs shook with the effort to hold back a scream, placing her options fictionally in front of her. Having no other choice, she played along. Going against him would mean certain distrust, making things even harder for them. After Toro disembarked the elevator, they continued down to the ground floor, where they led Astrid to an intro cubicle, outfitted for her every need. Too hyped up to focus on one thing, she drank water tentatively and ate little bites, pacing the small area.

A monitor came to life on one of the walls, showing the face of an older woman. Dressed smartly, which complemented her white doctor's coat.

"How are we doing in there? You haven't eaten much, sat down, or even showered." Astrid didn't answer, just paced around, trying to cool her temper. "I need to come in and do a physical exam, tend to your wounds," the voice instructed.

Again, Astrid did not communicate. She simply took her overcoat off, covering the monitor and camera, forcing a sigh out of the speaker.

"All right then, as you wish." A hiss sounded, fog shooting from underneath the jacket covered monitor, a mist thin and moist.

"Oh man" all she managed before the drugs overtook her respiratory system, entering her blood stream, forcing her to collapse, asleep.

The pain. Her head pounded, white bright stars flashing behind her lids, the blue circle pulsing with her heart. She woke to a growing pain, the light brighter. Her cheek and face were covered in gauze. The doctor got what she wanted, a physical exam and her wounds tended to. Tentatively she moved, the drugs dissipating in her system, giving way to cells waking up to do their jobs.

Astrid sat, swinging her legs off the side of the bed, touching her bare feet to the cool tile below. The shock sent sensations through her legs, forcing the rest of her body to wake. Her fingers tentatively touched the tender flesh through the gauze on her face. The dried blood no doubt gone, stitches closing her torn skin together. Her stomach grumbled, and glancing around she noticed an IV bag and followed the tube to her arm. Standing, she read the label on the bag, her name, patient ID, and in big bold letters 'Saline.'

Just saline. That's okay.

Releasing her held breath, she reached across the small enclosed space and grabbed the bowl of warm broth, bringing it to her lips. She took small sips at first, but as hunger took over she tipped the bowl, downing its contents. Her stomach flipped over, churning with something to digest and feed her body. Astrid replaced the bowl, watching it disappear only to reappear full, this time with little chunks of white meat. Somebody, somewhere was watching.

Her head moved in full range, her eyes searching the wall and ceilings for camera lenses. Finding none. *Good.* Last time she covered a camera she was put to sleep.

Reaching forward, grabbing the now refilled bowl, she slowly consumed it. No longer feeling weak and tired, she stretched, deciding a shower would help immensely. She worked out the saline bag issue, ending up hanging it from a hook above the toilet while she showered. The hot water stung her skin, cleansing away dirt, certain decisions, and loneliness.

During the shower, Ben entered her mind, his frail body shaking with uncertainty and fear. She missed him, the feeling causing her to catch her breath and fight back tears and heartache. Astrid thought a silent prayer for his protection, hoping he was calm and being taken care of. Promising herself that she would see him again soon. She would rescue Ben. He would make it out; he would be happy and safe.

It wasn't long after her shower when she rested upright on her bed that the wall opened, permitting the doctor who spoke to her earlier through the monitor. "Nice to see you up and about. How are you feeling?" Her soft voice was kind, with insufficient authority.

"Better. I would like to speak to somebody in charge, about a little boy who was taken with me. Ben Heizer?"

The doctor held a blank stare, shaking her head. "You are not permitted to see anybody else until we hear your story. What you remember, what you don't. What they did to you. We are concerned for the rest of our patients." She cocked her head to the side, speaking with a small smile on her face.

"I want to see him!" Astrid braced herself against the floor, her toes digging in.

"I'm sorry. Can you walk? Do you have enough energy?"

The change in subject was not lost on Astrid. Instead of fighting this, knowing soon enough she would have the upper hand, she swallowed her rising anger and nodded. The doctor reached forward, clutching her bag of saline to help move Astrid easier.

They left her new cell and filed down a bare hallway. She was in a part of the Institute that she could not find a memory of—whether she hadn't ever been there before or they stole the memory from her, she wasn't quite sure.

Not wanting to irritate her escort any further, Astrid kept her mouth shut, biding her time. She was supposed to get as much information as possible before they tried wiping her memory and integrating her again. Knowing it wasn't possible did not make it easier to deal with. Her real concern always Ben. She needed to get to him before the evacuation started.

Turning a corner and entering an exam room, she saw a high table covered in a white sheet placed in the center of the room, counter spaces on the walls, and a stool on wheels.

Interesting.

"This room is old. Where's all of the computerized equipment? Like the cells?"

"So you do remember your time here? We weren't sure." The doctor motioned for Astrid to take a seat on the table while she took the stool as her own, committing to her interrogation. "What is the first thing you remember?"

"Starting?"

"Before the Reformers took you," she prompted.

Astrid told her story. She watched the doctor tap her notes into her tablet, nodding along, asking questions when she needed. When she completed her tale, the doctor took her time finishing her notes, put her tablet aside, and simply asked, "Care to tell the truth this time? Keep in mind I examined Toro Crow after listening to his report, and he claimed he exercised in his cell until he was discovered, but even if that were true, he wouldn't have been able to retain that much of his muscle mass. He wasn't malnourished enough. His bruising only maybe a week old. Nothing to suggest he had been beaten for the months you guys were gone."

"What?" Astrid tried hard to be offended, aghast at what the doctor insinuated. She never thought of herself as a bad liar, yet here she was being called out. "That was the truth!" She decided to go with anger as a base reaction. Her voice heightened as she pushed her eyes big, forcing her back even straighter, gripping the edges of the padded table she sat on.

"Your body doesn't show the symptoms of the story you just told. You're malnourished, but not to a threatening state. You're dehydrated, yes, but not enough to match your story. You have no old injuries except your pinky, just new bruises and cuts, oldest a few days at most. Your story tells an entirely different tale. You wanted to stay there, didn't you?"

CHAPTER 22
PUPPET STRINGS

ASTRID breathed deeply, trying to buy time to decide what she should do. They hadn't prepared her for the possibility that her tale would not be accepted. If she decided to tell the truth, she was a traitor to the Reformers, but if she held out and stuck to her lies, she would be drugged and the truth pulled from her mind like an inch worm being yanked from the ground. That did not seem like something she wanted to go through, just to give them something they would take no matter the cost.

"Why would they take patients from us, to turn them into prisoners and abuse them?" the doctor continued.

"I wasn't a prisoner until …" Astrid feigned a struggle, what to tell, what not to tell. "Until I told them I didn't want to be there anymore. They caught me trying to escape, suggested that they would show me what you planned to do to me if I came back, and that's when they threw me in a cell. Taught me what to expect, until another prisoner escaped, broke me out. Here we are."

Did it work?

Her brain reeled against the truth of the situation. Would the doctor believe this lie over her last?

"What happened before they put you in a cell?"

"They were nice. They fed us, let us make friends, communicate with one another. Gave each of us a trade, taught us how to be a part of their community."

"Why did you want to leave?"

"To find my mother." Too much truth now, mashed up within the lies she was supposed to tell. As the doctor dug deeper, the truth started to seek light, to break free from the darkness.

"Is she here?"

"I don't know." The truth of this situation and knowledge pierced her, causing pain. The truth was as she stated. With no proof, no substance to hold onto to give her hope. She didn't know where her mother truly was.

The doctor didn't ask any further questions—she didn't reach for her tablet or a syringe full of a liquid that would make Astrid forget, to accept, spill all the truth that would show her as a lying traitor. Instead, she nodded her head, proclaiming, "Very well, you're to stay in the intro cubicle until the general reads my report and makes a decision. Please, eat and rest. You're going to need it."

What? Why would the doctor be so accepting?

Astrid spun her head to follow her as she left the room, an expression full of concern and confusion on her face. She didn't know what to do from here. They already broke protocol by breaking the plan when they first arrived, and again just now by telling the truth. But the doctor didn't record it or shake her head in disappointment. Just acceptance.

"Doctor, if I may?" she interjected, just in time to stop the doctor on the other side of the door. She hesitated, turning and reentering the room, letting the door close behind her. "Am I to be re-assimilated? Drugged again?"

"I don't know. To reciprocate your truth, this is unprecedented. Your report will be written up and reviewed. I will suggest that your sentence be marked as time served, due to us being unable to keep you safe, hopefully ending with you being sent home. I'm not able to make that decision on my own. The board of the Institute, along with the general, make those decisions. I'll let you know when I do. Get some rest, and try not to worry."

Astrid didn't stop her this time. She had baited the doctor; patients were not supposed to know they were drugged. They were not to know that it was a program of assimilated humans, being used against their will. The doctor didn't ask about Astrid's choice of words; she simply answered her question with honesty.

Benji told her most likely they would put her back into the program … drain her memories and assign her back into a cubicle. Which was trivial, as their program didn't work on her. She was an anomaly; she understood that now. No fear of the blue liquid that was previously pumped into her. She knew she could overcome it. Each time easier; each time it didn't take as long; each time she knew what happened.

Astrid waited on the exam table, sure somebody would be along to collect her and lead her back to her intro cubicle eventually. While she waited she sat quietly thinking of her mom, of what was coming. Thought of Toro and hoped his new plans hadn't taken him astray. So much hope in a world of control and darkness. Taking a new breath on a new dawn.

Everybody's lives were about to change. Everybody would soon see the face of the Reformers, would know people still existed out there who cared and fought for humanity, for the right to live. It was exhilarating; her flesh tingled as excitement flew through her veins, reaching every inch of her body. Making it hard to contain the happiness she felt, her cheeks smarting against the smile on her face. Her eyes grew moist with anticipation. She needed to check herself, regain control. Her emotional reaction to the situation would tell them an entirely different story than the one she just spun. Time was against her, and she needed to wait it out.

Another thought entered her head—she forgot to ask about Ben. Being so close to wrapping up, trying to get her part completed, she'd forgotten her own agenda, the next phase of her mission. She would ask.

They couldn't put her in a box and ignore her forever. She needed to get to him before he didn't know who she was. Astrid jumped down from the table, flying toward the door, just in time for it to swing open, putting her face to face with Toro. A cruel smile on his face, wearing a new uniform, shiny and pressed, a gun on his hip. Astrid came up short; after nearly being knocked out, she chose to take a step back, regaining control.

She reached for him, wanting some sort of contact, some sort of confirmation that he was still with her. But she stopped herself.

"I'm here to escort you back."

Toro reached in, face-planting her into the exam table, sending new waves of pain through her already wounded skin, forcing her arms into a bind behind her back. Not a word spoken. She kept her now swollen lips shut while he pushed her along the hallways and corridors, onto the patients' floor, and eventually into a cubicle. Her feet tripped over the sudden force when he shoved her, and she landed her on her right shoulder in the middle of the twelve-by-twelve white prison.

Astrid turned quickly to see the evil smile spread across Toro's face while he punched an unseen button, causing a door to slide into place between them. He didn't even bother untying her hands.

TORO did as Benson suggested—he ate, he slept, he ran, working the muscle memories of his body. He ate some more, slept again, another run. How long would it take for the general to make a ruling, to decide the beginning of the battle sitting on the horizon? It loomed over Toro; day and night, he struggled with the reality of the situation. He wished he was with the Reformers preparing instead of sitting in this snake pit waiting for the strike. Waiting for the war to begin. Waiting, always waiting.

He struggled, his thoughts running away from him, as he did push-ups in the weight room, conditioning his body to bring his cells and muscles alive. The burn of the resistance, to build muscle on muscle. He thought of Astrid often, and Ben as well. About how he betrayed Astrid when they arrived. How he strayed from the plan she thought she knew, how he followed orders, even though they differed from hers, doing what was instructed. Just following orders.

"I was just following orders. Follow the orders, Toro." He said it aloud, to the beat of his body rising and falling to what his arms and chest could push. The burn grew, until his arms gave out, his chest collapsing on the floor—his face against the mat, his sweat making his skin sticky, moist and warm. His breath heavy, his lungs expanding with every intake. Droplets of perspiration formed next to his mouth and nose. The smell of rubber and sweat stung his nostrils.

Fellow guards wanted his story, wanting to know how he escaped the Reformers, why he was allowed back to work. He told his tale numerous times in the mess hall and locker rooms to anybody who wanted to listen. For the most part, his coworkers were accepting of it—believed him a miracle, somebody who should be training the rest of them. They were friendly, wanting to be his best friend, knowing that he would have their back.

It was unnecessary, knowing their fate, knowing what came down the pipe. He tried hard not to get to know them. No personal stories, no caring about their kids, and no desire to see pictures of their wives. Wife? To have an opportunity to have a wife. Toro knew that would never be. He was on a fast track to death, and if by chance he survived this, he would not be the same person. After a wife comes children. Bringing children into this cruel world, forcing them into a life of servitude, was not fair. He would have no part of it; he would claim celibacy first, get the shot to make him sterile. Anything but watch his children work for somebody else's dream of a distorted utopia.

He awoke after a mid-afternoon nap to find a message on his assigned screen next to the entry door to his room. He hit the corresponding buttons, putting him on the right screen. New orders; he was being reinstated, and his new shift schedule was attached. He could pick up his new passcodes and get his chip reprogrammed by security at any time. Excellent news. His schedule would help him keep his mind off the inevitable ... off what he was there for.

He continued reading. The briefing stated he passed all his tests upon his return through the debriefing ceremony, and they were glad to have him back and ready to work again. Blah, blah, blah.

Toro had been reassigned to the patients' floor as head of security. No longer a floater, answering to Matthew Benson and only to Matthew Benson. The rest of the staff would be notified and updated of his return and newly acquired status immediately. He again hit the correct buttons to signal his acceptance, let the screen scan his thumbprint for verification, and closed out the message.

Time to get started. His first shift began in thirty-six hours, giving him plenty of time to do what was necessary.

He searched for Astrid, who was currently being held in an intro cubicle. Her rash reactions would start the war. She was the key. No sooner had he opened her file than he received a request for an escort to take her to a new cubicle on the patients' floor, one to give her more comfort as she awaited her judgment. Instead of delegating the assignment to another guard, Toro took it upon himself.

The happiness on her face at seeing him astounded him. He thought she would be angry; he needed her to be mad at him. He played his part, may have been a little bit more aggressive than essential, but he found it paid off—the hatred pouring out of her eyes as he left her on the floor gave him all he needed. He could now signal Benji.

A few days later, the building shook violently when the first wave of attacks hit. The outer fence and defenses falling at precisely three in the morning. Pulling the night shift on purpose, Toro disarmed the main alarms and rerouted any calls from the outer perimeter as they were slaughtered by the incoming men in black. His skin overcome by goose bumps, his heart rate high, thudding inside of him. It was finally time. They were going to fell one of the greatest institutes in the country. He finished imputing the codes, keeping the alarms from blazing and awaking reinforcements. Next he headed to the armory.

Toro set the bombs to the agreed time within the small room, laying the boxes of bullets and loaded spare magazines around the explosive for maximum effect. This one was scheduled to go off last. The devastating blast would send bullets in every direction, causing anybody in the vicinity harm … or better, death. He left the room, locking it behind him, set the security code on the room to the highest capacity, keeping everybody else out. They didn't want anybody stumbling onto the plan before it was enacted.

His next job: free Astrid, who would find Ben while Toro released patients and escorted them out of the building. Before he could do that, he waited until the Reformers' arrival at the main building where they took out night security and the doctors who might raise an alarm. Toro half jogged to the patients' floor, opening the door to Astrid's temporary cubicle. He snuck in next to her bed, placing his hands over her mouth, shaking her gently. Her eyes snapped open, her body struggling against the unknown subject holding her down, her eyes squinting with recognition against Toro, glowing slightly in the darkened room.

"Easy, it's time. You ready?" he whispered, slowly removing his hands and releasing her. She stood, straightening her shirt, her right fist springing out and catching him along the left side of his jaw.

"That's for lying to me." She raised her hand to hit him again.

Toro caught her wrist, this time jerking her body against his. "We don't have time for this. Be mad, be angry, but use it now and take it out on me later. Right now you need to get Ben."

She relaxed against him, hopefully agreeing to his logic. When he saw her nod, he released her, moving out of the way to let her pass.

"Do you know where he is? They wouldn't tell me or let me see him." They moved light on their feet as fast as they dared, stopping at every intersection of cubicles to check for security or doctors.

"Yes, they're keeping him on the top floor. Next to the general's quarters. Here." He handed her an earpiece, equipped with a microphone. "I'll talk you through it as you go. There will be security on every level, but the elevator on this level will be clear. Take it to the second to last floor. From there you'll have to take the stairs, and there's a service desk in the hallway that's manned. After you neutralize him let me know. I'll tell you where to go after that."

Stopping at the last row of cubicles, he crouched low in the dim lighting. The brightness from his data pad illuminated his face as he checked for other guards and activity around the corners.

"Are you sure about this? It's not what Jackson told me." Astrid sounded worried.

"My instructions came from Benji. I deviated a little, but we'll get the same outcome. I did it to help you. These people needed to believe me, Astrid. I was being watched. I had to treat you that way. I'm sorry if I hurt you."

She didn't answer, her eyes searching his face, for what, he did not know. She smiled. They were already so close, their knees brushing when their balance waivered, Astrid's hair and her clean skin in Toro's senses. She was almost too close.

Astrid kept her smile. "Be careful, Toro." She went left, crouched below the height of the cubicle walls, seeking out her own form of justice, leaving him slightly dazed and warm in his stance. Coming to himself again, he banked right.

He met Jackson and Red, accompanying a platoon of trained, ready and able soldiers at one of the back entrances to release the security lock and let them in.

"Ready?" Jackson, always ready and to the point. The familiarity was comforting to Toro. He let a smile spread on his face and nodded in welcome, handing off his data pad.

"Of course. Everything is right on target. I just sent Astrid up. We should be ready to go within the allotted time."

"You've been here too long. Relax, we got this." Jackson smiled at him, moving Toro aside and letting a dozen or so Reformers come in to take up their positions, spreading out in different directions. Some going upstairs, others down to sublevels, each with a mission to accomplish. Toro nodded as they passed; some he noticed from his class.

This was going to be glorious. They were covered in water, the men shaking their heads, sending cool droplets of water onto the surrounding surfaces, including Toro. The females in acceptance of being wet, wiping only their faces dry.

"There, we're all wired to your and Astrid's frequency. Let's go."

Toro did not fail to notice that Seto and Chie were not among them. He followed Jackson through the cubicles, watching as hidden forms in black took out the watch night men and any medical staff currently on duty. Once the floor was clear with confirmation on their earpieces, Toro lifted his data pad, releasing all the locks on the cubicles. Flipping the switch and turning the overhead and in-wall lights on to awaken the patients.

Instead of patients groggy and drugged emerging from their prison, the light revealed the Institute's security force, dressed in high white and heavy gear, armed with guns and pistols they pointed straight at him and Jackson.

"Toro, I thought we were good?" Jackson confirmed, crouching a bit lower and placing his right hand on his gun. Toro imitated Jackson's stance, trying to count the men surrounding them.

"We were. I-I … we were!"

He was head of security. If the Institute knew about this why would they place him at the head of security with codes and clearance? Then it hit him. Because they did know; they knew he would let the Reformers in. They let him believe he regained his clearance and authority so that he could do just what they wanted him to. Which meant there was a rat, somebody feeding the Institute the Reformer's plans. He glanced at Jackson.

"I don't know Toro." His voice small and thought provoking, trying to figure it out himself, knowing what Toro was thinking.

A blow came behind, from a guard sneaking up behind them. He used the butt of his metal gun to hit Jackson in the back of his head, sending him to the ground at Toro's feet.

"Turn over your sidearm and any other weapons you have." The guard came closer, his hands up in a calm gesture, waiting to see what Toro's reaction would be.

Toro watched the guards surrounding him; they were a sea of white straining against the stain of black at his feet. He saw several black forms at the edge of his peripheral vision, all restrained, being held at gun point. With no other choice, he complied, shaking his head, wondering now what his fate would be.

Astrid's voice came over the frequency in his earpiece, just as the guard reached out and plucked it from his ear.

CHAPTER 23
HIDDEN LIES

TORO!" Astrid tried again, and again. She made it to the final door in the stairwell and was trying to notify Toro that she had arrived so he could guide her through the offices to the correct door. Without him, she would have to guess. She took a deep breath, tried again on the coms, slightly pushing the door open, holding the click to make as little noise as possible.

Toro was correct—right in front of her about ten yards down the hallway was a manned desk. The man in question sat behind his desk watching something on a screen, chuckling along with the show. All the lights were lit; she would have to move quickly to keep him from raising an alarm.

Letting the door close, she tapped her earpiece, trying to raise Toro again. No answer.

If he sent me up here just to get caught …

Confusing thoughts had made themselves known after he'd thrown her into a patient cubicle with her arms tied behind her back and a smug grin upon his face. All sorts of distrustful and betraying thoughts plagued her. She found herself exceptionally surprised and a bit relieved to find him still on the correct side of things. But now ...

Fool. She was a fool, following him blindly without confirmation of the plan.

Shaking her head to clear her thoughts, she reminded herself why she was there. For Ben. She needed to get to him. Others had their jobs, and now she needed to accomplish hers. She palmed her pistol, counted to ten, and pushed the door open, rushing through at a sprint as quietly as possible. When she cleared the door her right arm extended, armed and aiming true, straight for the guard. He never noticed. She advanced, her feet padding softly against the tiled floor, the sound reverberating through the still, stale air and returning to her. She made it behind his desk, pushing the barrel of the gun right into his temple. He stilled, his hands moving slowly in a surrendering motion.

"Get up, slowly."

The guard complied. He pushed the chair back gently and stood. Seeing he towered at least two feet taller than her, she compensated by moving her target to his chest.

"You won't get out of here. They already have your friends." The guard spoke clearly and slightly quiet, so she stepped forward a bit to hear him.

Her eyes caught the motion on his screen. The patient floor, high in one of the corners, lit bright. She followed Toro's form, being led away by a dozen guards in white, another form in black being carried by six guards. *Jackson.*

"What? No!" She struggled to understand. Her hand shaking. If the plan failed, her cause was lost. She kept her gun trained on him. "What happened?" she demanded.

"The plan?" A new voice, but still familiar.

Astrid kept her gun and stance cemented, sending a warning to the guard with her eyes. She observed slightly the hallway past him. *The general*. Standing tall and confident, his hands in his suit pocket, an amused expression on his face.

"The plan failed. You failed. Hello, Ms. Stocklin."

She didn't reply; she didn't have to. He treaded toward her, making her jittery and nervous.

"I'll kill him! Stay back!" She startled herself with her words, but the general didn't seem bemused at all.

"Kill him. I have thousands more where he came from."

The expression on the guard's face painted a different picture. He feared for his life. His head shot back and forth between the general and Astrid, pleading.

"Where's Ben?" she asked instead of pulling the trigger.

"Safe" came his curt reply.

"I want to see him."

"No."

Astrid turned the gun on the general, stopping him in his superior strut toward her, and the guard took another step back, glad to be out of the line of fire. She was banking on his gratitude that she hadn't shot him. Hoping he would not turn against her.

"Take me to him." She tried, this time with a bit more control, to put more demand in her entire body.

The general chuckled, turning back the way he came. After a few steps he turned. "Agreed, but you'll have to follow me."

Astrid hesitated, knowing full well this could end badly. Ben's shaking body and swollen face flashed before her eyes, forcing her to step past the guard, nodding at him as she went to follow the general down the hallway.

"He's been well taken care of. He's a happy, bright young boy. We're glad to have him back."

"Shut up."

"You took care of him as well? All this death, we could have avoided it."

"Shut. Up."

"Tut-tut. Such demanding, harsh words. I could have done amazing things with you if you hadn't run off." Disappointment and hatred entered his voice. He slowed, turning, gazing at a closed door in front of him.

Astrid glanced around without turning. She could see the desk and guard at the end of the hallway. The general scanned his wrist, and the corresponding green light clicked on, signaling the door unlocked, but he didn't reach forward to open it.

Instead, he moved back, gesturing for her to go. "Ladies first."

"No." She used her gun, motioning him to open the door and enter before her. She needed to keep ahead of him, even if only by one step. The general reached forward with one of his big hands, pushing the door in. An automatic light came on as he stepped forward through the doorway. Another hallway.

"What exactly do you take me for?" Astrid protested; she hadn't followed him in yet.

"Well," he informed, shrugging his shoulders and placing his hands back into his pockets before he stepped out of the doorway, "a distraction is only best if it succeeds."

She caught on too late; she spun to see the guard right behind her. He reached forward, grabbing her from behind and knocking her gun loose. She watched it scatter across the floor, following the path it was put on by the general's foot. She fought, all her training lost in the panic that infested her current mindset. But instinct took over, and she spun hard, hitting his sternum with her elbow, following with a knee to his nose and her foot in his groin. He fell fast. It was second nature now. She made a mental note to thank Big Jack for all the hours of merciless training.

"Nice job. They did train you well. The damage has already been done though."

She stood, in a ready position to take him on, but she didn't need to. A second guard came up behind her, wrapping her in a grip she could not break. With the constriction of his arms came anger that he bested her, showing the weakness that resided inside. Fear arrived next as she watched the general smile.

"This way if you would."

The guard picked her up without letting her arms loose and, while keeping a watch out for her kicking legs, followed the general.

JACKSON, dude, wake up!" They had been dropped in a large space, with only one light on above them. Toro's restraints were removed, he hoped out of professional courtesy. Jackson dumped unceremoniously on the floor just inside the door after they shoved Toro in.

Toro currently shook his bulk, trying to elicit a response. Finally, a moan and flutter of eyelashes signaled a return to consciousness. "Jackson!"

"Not so loud. I have a jack hammer inside my head, mate." He moved slowly, his hand going to the sore spot on the back of his head. He eyed his hand, searching for blood. "What happened?"

"They knew! They knew you were coming, and they knew I'd help, and they were lying in wait. We played right into their hands!" Toro stood, pacing furiously back and forth in front of Jackson, who backed up and perched against the closest wall.

"I gathered that. Where are we?"

"In a storage room at the back of the facility." Toro's footsteps echoed off the ceramic tile, irritation and anger fueling his feet, pushing him in a faster pace. Back and forth. They stripped him of his weapons, his seniority, and importance. Jackson didn't seem to be taking it too bad. "Why aren't you mad?"

"How many of us did you let in, Crow?" His body language was carefree, his head resting on the wall, his hands on his knees.

"I-I don't know. A few dozen?" he guessed. He needed to calm down.

"And how many are in here?" Jackson's hands now splayed out, gesturing to the emptiness of the room.

"Just two." A sudden thought dawned. A new realization. "They captured them, after you were hit."

"Not everybody." Jackson knew something Toro was not privy to.

"Then where are they?" His patience running thin. He should have been told the entirety of the plan, not just his part. This was not right; they were not supposed to get caught.

"Doing their job, hopefully."

"Jackson, I set the bomb." The armory would blow. This setback would surely put them in danger.

"Good" was all Toro could coax out.

"Anything you'd like to update me on? Perhaps parts of the plan I wasn't told?" He was irritated, along with his anger and helplessness.

"No."

Just great. That helped the situation.

"Sit, save your strength." Jackson's eyes closed, no doubt fighting off his headache.

With nothing else to do; he sat a few feet from Jackson, trying to calm himself. Pacing wasn't doing any good, so might as well do as he was told. There was no sound except for their own breathing and heartbeats, and the one singular light showed no sign of giving out.

All at once all the lights in the room flicked on. The sound and brightness startling the two. Both jumped to their feet. Eyes adjusted, and seeing nobody was going to jump out and grab them, they calmed and straightened. What they thought a vast space ended up being small—three sides, walls with blackened windows, one locked door, and the fourth wall to the right of the door a mirror. Stepping up to it, Toro lifted his hand, barely touching the pads of his fingers to the surface before an electrical jolt traveled straight to his elbow. He jerked his hand back, cradling it, letting the pain fade, the sensation of power remaining.

"Charged. It's a force field, but why the mirror?" Jackson had watched him tempt fate, not saying anything to caution or stop him. They stood glancing at each other through the mirror, a battle of wills. As always, without any more words uttered, Jackson won.

His question answered quicker than Toro could come up with one. The mirror faded away, leaving the light blue shimmer of power. Behind the force field appeared Astrid, slumped on her knees, her hands bound in front of her. Benji stood behind her with his sidearm at her head. And with him, Dr. Heizer and the general.

Toro stood frozen in shock, his eyes darting from Astrid to Dr. Heizer back to Astrid, only to see Benji again. His anger flared, breathing heavy, muscles tensing up. His eyes widened, and through clenched teeth he growled, a feral animal noise shaking him to his bones.

Jackson stood, unsteady on his feet, his eyes squinting at the scene unfolding in front of him. He relaxed, placing his hands on his hips, shaking his head in disbelief and unreal understanding.

"How long?" No anger, just calculation.

"Since the beginning," Benji answered, his voice holding command.

"How many are with you?" Jackson stared, his shoulders stiffer, breath harder to obtain.

"Just me."

"So many lost. A quarter of our ranks were killed when you took over!" Now Jackson showed it. Anger, grief, and loss poured from him. Something had occurred before Toro came in, something bad. "The memory loss, the compulsion? Is that the government as well?"

Toro jerked at this, remembering the story Sibella told and his own experience with memory loss. Watching the exchange between Benji and Jackson did not calm his nerves; if anything it created more tension as secrets pulled tight, waiting to snap.

"It's a gift, from me," the general spoke up, lifting his chin with pride.

"Compulsion. If I try hard enough, yes, I can suggest memory loss." Benji was just as proud, his revelation causing more confusion.

Jackson didn't answer, but Toro could see the thoughts. Jackson was going over every bit of information, replaying memories, snippets of time coming to mean so much.

"You're an experiment," he finally clarified, or asked—no—Jackson was confirming.

"No," Toro spoke. "If he was he would have a colored ring around his iris, like Astrid and Ben."

Jackson watched him, his mind processing the information.

"That's the beauty of it," Benji interjected. "I do, but it's white, no real difference. It can only be seen on a close examination, and by someone who already knows it's there. A bit of luck for me."

"Such great talent, used with perfect execution." The general doted on Benji, like a prideful parent.

Toro had had enough. He yelled, going for the force field, demanding Benji release Astrid. His mind reeling from the betrayal and confusion. Deciding he only wanted one thing, not revenge or even justice, just her.

Jackson reached up, pulling him back this time, stopping him from jolting his entire body. "Easy, mate. There's nothing we can do except hope Red pulls through."

Toro calmed a little, trusting in Jackson. His hands fisted, primed to jump at a moment's notice. He just needed a direction.

"We ready to get on with it? Glad you followed your directions. If you hadn't, this would have been difficult to arrange," Benji said with a grin on his face; he enjoyed every minute of the betrayal and death he caused. "As you can see, Astrid is here. We wanted her to watch. She has a gift, a gift, as I'm sure you now know, given to her by the Institute and the general, a gift she is refusing to use." His other arm waved around, gesturing to Melvina standing behind him off to the side. "A clone, made specifically to guide Astrid, but she failed to produce. She even managed to pull you guys in on the delusion."

"What delusion?" Toro asked.

Jackson jumped next to him, sucking in air between his teeth as a warning.

"The delusion that you can be free, that you have a reason to fight."

"That 'delusion' was there before she came along, mate. You fed it to us long enough."

"Toro, on the other hand, was a wild card, something we didn't expect, but he added so much. You have such talent, boy. You really should be using it for the right side."

"What are you going to do to her?" Toro could see Astrid's eyes opening. She was propped up, her own body weight balanced on her spine so she would not topple over. Her head moved a bit, and she struggled against her bonds. She knew this scene and what part she was to play.

"Come on, boy! Do use your head! We have to force her to use this gift, so we know her talent works. Even after all I put her through in the training and testing, she failed." He shook his head in disappointment. "We no longer need you two though. You know too much."

"And the doctor?" This question from Jackson. He nodded toward Dr. Heizer, who hadn't moved a muscle since the exchange began.

"She's re-programmable. She's … perfect," the general answered.

Toro studied Dr. Heizer. She stood stone still, her eyes and face blank to all emotions.

Benji just shrugged. "Well, this has been fun."

He nodded to a corner above him, a device Toro couldn't see but deduced was a camera. The door opened behind them, letting in four guards dressed in white with blood splattered all over their uniforms. They marched in single file, holding their weapons at hip height, straight at Toro and Jackson.

Both men put their hands up in surrender, now facing the guards, their backs to Benji and Astrid. Guns in front and a substantial force field behind them.

"Any time now, Red," Jackson muttered under his breath.

"Seriously?" Toro asked. "You think Red can get us out of this?" His voice rose.

"Red can do anything."

ASTRID'S legs tingled, and her wrists hurt. On her knees at gunpoint, she was about to watch Jackson and Toro be gunned down in front of her. With absolutely nothing she could do. The gag in her mouth stopping her protests, her tears running free. Her head hurt from the drugs they kept giving her. If she never slept against her own will again she'd be the most grateful person.

The guns poised, the death sentence handed down, the guilty set to die. Time seemed to stretch. She watched in slow motion as the security guard on the far right, just across from Jackson, slid to the side and opened fire on his fellow guards. At the same time he tossed weapons to Jackson and Toro. Within a few seconds the three of them faced each other. The helmet was removed, and Jackson and Red embraced. Astrid let out a breath she did not know she was holding, laughter bursting past the soaked rag.

"I thought we captured them all?" The general behind her demanded, his face red with effort.

"Red wasn't scheduled to come in with us. He's supposed to be at the front gate," Benji explained, clearly scared, his voice shaky as he attempted to explain the turn of events, backing away from the division in the room. Astrid thought it odd at first, but as her mind cleared, everything made sense. Benji—an employee of the government. Trying to run from her enemy, Astrid managed to run right into their evil, clawed open arms.

"I'll handle this." The general stepped forward, his hands rising, elbows at a ninety-degree angle, his palms face up. He widened his stance, taking a breath. Pillars of blue light appeared in the adjoining room next to Toro, Red, and Jackson.

Knowing what was going to happen, Astrid lunged forward without a second thought, pushing her shoulder into the back of the general's knees and knocking him down on top of her. Her head banged against the floor. She could hear cussing being spewed out around her.

Her vision faded in and out, and she tried to concentrate on Toro. Had she managed to save them? As her vision faltered, the faint blue light came in around the edges, a circle helping pull the scene in and out of focus, in and out of light. The blue light covered everything in her vision, finally taking its opportunity to take over.

A voice inside her head called her name. A voice she didn't recognize, a voice full of love and worry. Her eyes closed again, the pull too strong to fight this time, giving in with a surprised relief.

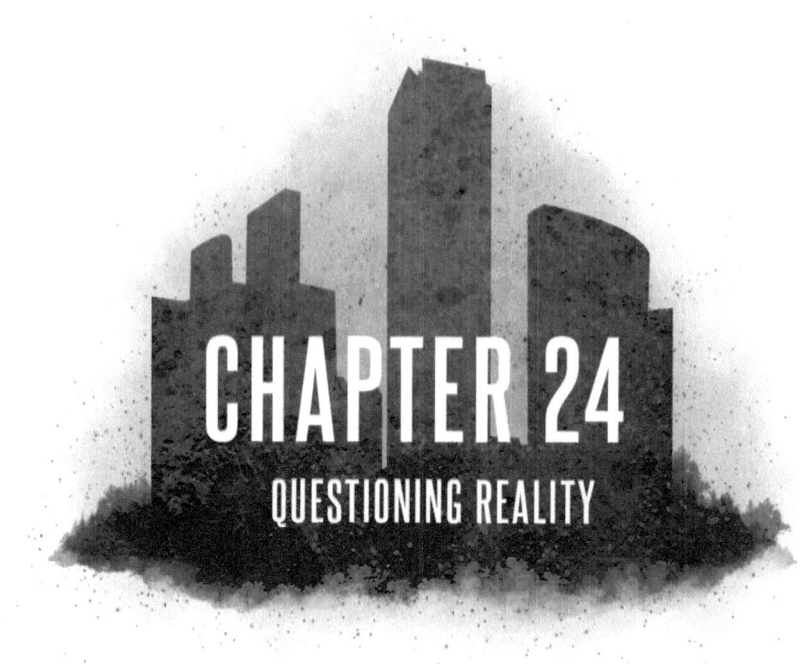

CHAPTER 24
QUESTIONING REALITY

WHEN her eyes reopened, Astrid rested in a chair under a light. A doctor and a nurse stood above her. As her vision cleared some more—the blue circle visible, right out of direct sight—the clicking sounds of instruments being placed on metal trays and footsteps let her know her hearing had returned.

"She's back, we did it!" the doctor exclaimed, the excitement clear on his face. "She has the gift of sight. Did we get the whole recording?"

"Yes," the nurse answered, her fingers tapping away on a data pad. "The general will be thrilled. This has never been done before. Now we have all of them."

"Why don't you deliver that, and I'll get her fully awake and moving around. She's going to have some questions." A wild grin was on his face.

"Where am I? What happened?" Astrid's heart leapt, nervousness settling into her chest. Her world was gone, her friends, family—all gone. What happened? She struggled against herself, her body not responding the way it should, the sluggishness of limbs too heavy for her to lift. "Was it all a dream?" she forced out.

The questions and confusion burst into the forethought of her mind, causing chaos of which she'd never known. It was all so real—the pain, the loss, the protectiveness. It must be real. And Toro ... his warmth and sense of security caused her throat to clench.

"Kind of," the doctor answered, motioning for the nurse to leave the room. He undid her restraints, helping Astrid sit up, her body stiff and sore. Tubes extended from her head, stomach, and in between her legs. "We have granted you a great gift, an opportunity to work for the government. You, my dear one, can see the future."

"And if I don't want it." She wasn't asking. She had fallen into the family fold of the Reformers. She belonged, and they extracted her against her will.

"I'm afraid you don't have much of a choice, Astrid. You belong to the Institute. You're our property. We gave you a gift, woke up what once was dormant. We made you whole, and we will use you as we see fit."

The vision came fast and hard, the blue circle forcing her sight to fail, as if an unseen outside force dropped a curtain on her eyes. Reopening on another scene—direct world domination. The government, spreading the institutes across the globe, experimenting on more humans to unlock more hidden parts of the brain. She watched as bodies stacked up and flames licked at once great wonders and structures. Humans fought again not for freedom, but for humanity, the right to exist. She forced her eyes closed against the sight, bile rising, the stench of fear filling her nose, the heat of the flames on her skin. This time when she reopened them she was perched on the chair facing the horrid doctor.

"What did you see?" he asked.

She squinted. How did he know?

"Your eyes go black, and the circle of blue light that outlines your iris expands, turning your entire eye blue when you have a vision."

"I saw the end of the world." Hot tears forged a path down her face. Anger boiled within, her body shaking.

"The powers of the mind we discovered, the sight, telekinesis, telepathy, powers of suggestion, and ... and ..." He trailed off, remembering who he spoke to; his excitement of success had taken over for a moment.

Astrid reached up, pulling suction cups off her hairless head, off her chest and shoulders. The unreachable ones she jerked by their cords, leaving the cups behind. The doctor stepping forward with a sigh and helped.

"Lie back. I'll remove all the tubes, except the IV. You need the fluids."

Astrid did as he instructed. Pulling the top of her gown down, he removed a tube connected to a port and the suction cups on her back along with the neuro lines attached to her head.

"This?" she asked, pointing to the port in her stomach.

"So we could feed you while you were under. We didn't know how long, and we needed to keep you alive."

"Why?" It was confusing.

The doctor gestured to the catheter, explaining a female nurse would attend to it. "Because you're one of us now. We're on the same side." He stood back, clasping his hands in front of him.

"Maybe." She moved fast. Picking up one of the machines, which no doubt was used to help keep her alive, throwing it as hard as she could at his head. The unsuspected motion took him by surprise. Her aim was true. He collapsed with blood pouring down the right side of his face.

She stood carefully, her legs weak, unused, having to keep her balance by holding onto everything within reach. Reaching between her legs, she grabbed the tube and gently pulled, the end coming out. Leaving only the IV tube between her and freedom. She yanked it free, leaving a trail of blood welling up on her left arm from the open wound.

Stripping the doctor of his white lab coat took more energy than she possessed. His weight was difficult to roll while working his arm out of his sleeves. Taking deep breaths, she forced herself to rest, but only for a few seconds. Pulling the coat on, a silver flash caught her eye: the name tag.

"Dr. Menestas Locati," she read. Glancing back and forth between the name tag and the form on the floor. "Where's my mother?" The words rushed out with harsh implications, her fists holding his scrubs in a balled up tight grip. What little strength she had left was refueled with anger and adrenaline coursing through her system. A scream escaped her clenched teeth. Her head dropped to his chest, still clenched by her white knuckled fists. She worked her way back to her feet, needing to get out. If what the doctor said was true, they would wipe her memory and put her in a cell; they would wait, wait to see if what she saw would all come true.

Stopping at the door, she paused, listening. When confident it was clear she stepped across the threshold, making her way down the hall, her right hand keeping balance as it followed along the wall. Astrid's legs threatened numerous times to give out, almost buckling underneath her, but they held strong. Out of determination and sheer force of will.

Knowing her mom did not reside there, she searched for Toro and Ben. Toro would be real; he would help. She stumbled along, going over memories like a waking dream, with details fading, becoming gaps in the story the longer she focused. Rounding another corner, a break became necessary. She leaned against the wall, her breath hitching, getting caught, her heart picking up speed. Glancing around, a form made itself known. Somebody stood at the end of the hall.

Her mind knew there was resemblance; she should know him. Tall and fierce, with short brown hair in a military cut. The closer he got the clearer he became. He had a scar above his right eyebrow.

I knew him, right?

Who was she looking for? What was she doing? She waited, shoulder propped against the wall, trying to force herself to remember, her hand finding and rubbing the tacky skin of her bald head, drips of blood on her arm. *How did that get there?* Confusion now fully gripped Astrid. She stood, lost and confused in an unknown building with splatters of blood on her. The hairs on the back of her neck stood erect. The guard's tall figure sauntered toward her in a hurried way, and the closer he got the more fidgety her body became.

Just before he arrived within touching distance, she pushed off the wall in fear. This man would not help her. "Come on, I'll take you back. Dr. Locati is waiting for you." His voice was soft, comforting, the sound confusing, wrong. "It's okay, we won't hurt you here. Let's just get you through your sentence."

The guard's name tag—briefly catching her eye as he turned her around—reported him as Toro Crow, security force. Toro—the name safe, strong, friendly, the exact opposite of what the guard portrayed. Gently grabbing her arm, he forced her to turn around to go back.

"No, please, I don't belong here."

He stopped suddenly at the plea, letting a tiny ray of hope enter. Maybe she was right about him; maybe he was a friend. His gaze went deep into her eyes.

Ahead of them came a voice, busting the brief connection they created. "Mr. Crow, if you would."

She pulled her glance away from the strong gaze the guard held her with. The man, holding a rag to his head, stood outside of a doorway, motioning at him. His voice of authority pushed the guard back into motion.

"Yes, Doctor." Toro ushered Astrid forward.

I don't belong here. Her body reacted the only way it knew how; it kicked, fought, tore against his grip.

"Easy, prisoner." The guard's sweet voice urged her on.

"No, I don't belong here. Something is wrong. They did something to me. Please, help me. He's already hurt me, please." She pleaded as she fought him, hoping to trigger a morsel of sympathy.

She kept fighting, but Toro guided her into the exam room, forcing her back in the chair where automatic clamps snapped, holding her in place. Her pleading and begging continued as she watched him take one last regard before leaving the room.

"PLEASE! Don't leave me! Why are you doing this?" she yelled over and over, her throat going raw.

Dr. Locati issued another IV, not addressing her behavior, his eyes focused, his motions rough. She struggled against the tears, emotions overtaking her system and forcing her to lose control. They burst forth in big droplets, skipping her face, landing in her lap.

"Astrid, I need you to breathe for me and try to calm down. This is not good for your body or mind. Breathe, Astrid." The doctor's voice was calming, a sense of love and caring, pride and accomplishment laced into his words.

"I don't want to do this. I don't belong here." Now she cried in full force, her sobs chopping her words.

"We've talked about this. You're one of us now, special, a survivor. You're strong, Astrid. You can do this."

He wasn't convincing; she couldn't remember any conversation she'd experienced with him, or speaking to him at all. She knew pain, tubes, white lights, many covered faces, and more pain.

"What's going to happen?" She managed to calm down to just tears, able to speak clearly while working on her breathing.

"Rehabilitation. The ports on your head and stomach can be removed, and you need to get your strength back, and then ..." He hesitated, standing within her eyesight, blood dried on the side of his head, wiping her tears with a soft cloth. "Then the testing begins."

"Testing?"

"You don't remember? The vision?"

"Vision?" Astrid concentrated, trying to remember. "I don't ... I know loss, love. I was scared. I belonged. I don't belong here."

"Interesting. I'll go easy on the memory serum from now on. We want you to remember some things."

More confusion; he was not making any sense.

"There's betrayal and pain. I know what I feel, but not why I feel them." She was still trying to make sense.

"Just rest. We'll start soon." Dr. Locati pushed some bluish liquid into a tube and then in her arm before excusing himself.

Astrid was alone with only her thoughts as the serum invaded her body. As it took over what little understanding she had faded into dreams. Her limbs heavy, eyes fighting to stay open. With one last ditch effort she pictured the security guard, Toro, his face holding a look of worry and concern. Her eyes rolled to the back of her head as she fell into a deep, medicated, dreamless sleep.

EPILOGUE

THE general received the recording with an exciting sense of accomplishment. Dr. Locati has finally succeeded. For years they had worked on this girl, from planning and playing out her entire childhood to her emotional surrender to the Institute. Astrid was a gem, billions of dollars turning her into an important asset and one of the most successful experiments to date.

Pressing a button, the general asked his brown-nosing, redheaded assistant to arrange a meeting with Benji, the newly appointed head of the Reformers. He needed to see this recording as well. The plan would be discussed, finalized, and put into motion.

Dr. Locati would have to be dealt with; his attachment to the experiment was a liability. General Thaxton smiled to himself. It was a good thing Dr. Locati's replacement was almost ready. Dr. Melvina Heizer—a name he picked out himself—would be flawless. It was time to put her to full use.

General Thaxton pulled up the recording on his view screen, pushing play with a wide, evil grin. President Margaret would be thrilled with the progress of her plan. Perfect, it was all just perfect.

ACKNOWLEDGEMENTS

HUGE thank you to my mom, Linda Aker, without whom I would have never picked this project back up. Also to my editor, Tiffany Dawn Munn, who questioned every reality I created. Making me ask the questions I had originally buried while writing this book. For the beautiful work done on my cover, I would like to thank Mallory Rock, who exceeded all my expectations. A great thank you to my husband, Jeremy, who gave me constant personality quarks for Red. And my children, Andrew and Sadie, who fed me daily encouragement. To Dana, Krista, and Sami whose constant questions of 'how's your book going?' and 'where's my copy?' that keep me in check, Thank you. And to the many, many, many people who posted positive thoughts on my negative posts on social media, I will always be grateful for you.